THE UNIVERSITY OF VIRGINIA EDITION OF
THE WORKS OF STEPHEN CRANE

VOLUME IV

THE O'RUDDY

Last photo taken of Stephen Crane with his dog "Spongie"—

Last picture of Stephen Crane (Cora Crane's Scrapbook, with her inscription, University of Virginia—Barrett)

STEPHEN CRANE

THE O'RUDDY

(COMPLETED BY ROBERT BARR)

EDITED BY
FREDSON BOWERS
LINDEN KENT PROFESSOR OF ENGLISH AT
THE UNIVERSITY OF VIRGINIA

WITH AN INTRODUCTION BY
J. C. LEVENSON
EDGAR ALLAN POE PROFESSOR OF ENGLISH AT
THE UNIVERSITY OF VIRGINIA

THE UNIVERSITY PRESS OF VIRGINIA
CHARLOTTESVILLE

CENTER FOR EDITIONS OF
AMERICAN AUTHORS

AN APPROVED TEXT

MODERN LANGUAGE
ASSOCIATION OF AMERICA

®

Editorial expenses for this volume have been sup-
ported by grants from the National Endowment for
the Humanities administered through the Center
for Editions of American Authors of the Modern
Language Association.

Standard Book Number: 8139-0341-6
Library of Congress Catalog Card Number: 68-8536
Printed in the United States of America

To
Clifton Waller Barrett

FOREWORD

THIS volume presents the romance *The O'Ruddy,* the last work written by Crane but left unfinished at his death and completed by Robert Barr. The basis for the present edition is a holograph manuscript, recorded only in 1969, owned by Mr. and Mrs. Donald Klopfer, of New York City, which was generously made available to the editor both in original and in photographic form. The editor is deeply indebted to Mr. and Mrs. Klopfer for permission to base his text upon the manuscript and to Alfred A. Knopf, Inc., which holds the Crane copyrights to unpublished material. The manuscript provides Crane's own system of punctuation, spelling, capitalization, paragraphing, and word-division. More important, it enables the editor to restore to the text four major cuts and numerous smaller excisions that resulted from the posthumous editorial treatment and censorship given the work for publication. In addition, it purifies the text of hundreds of unauthoritative stylistic alterations that were made in the printer's copy after his death and have no relation to Crane's characteristic method of expression or even on occasion to his intended meaning.

The editor was also fortunate in the offer by Professor Matthew J. Bruccoli, of the University of South Carolina, of an unrecorded set of early page-proofs of Robert Barr's conclusion to the romance, which proved of significance in evaluating the relative shares of Barr and of the Methuen proofreader in altering the text as it was originally set from Barr's manuscript. The typescript of part of Crane's chapter XXIV in the Special Collections of the Columbia University Libraries completes the unique material not previously utilized in the study of the text. Moreover, Professor J. C. Levenson made important use of the holograph contents list of the first four chapters and particularly of the notes that the dying Crane dictated about a late episode in the story, both in the Columbia University Libraries Special Collections.

The Introduction by Professor Levenson analyzes the sources and puts in order for the first time the convoluted history of the romance from its inception to publication, with a relation of its development to the complex of Crane's literary production in the last year of his life. The editor's "The Text: History and Analysis" details the physical forms of the texts, their authority and transmission, and examines specific problems concerned with the establishment of the text in its present critical form. The general principles on which the editing has been based are stated in "The Text of the Virginia Edition" prefixed to Volume I, BOWERY TALES (1969).

In the bibliographical descriptions the color designations conform to the recommendations of Dr. G. T. Tanselle in "A System of Color Identification for Bibliographical Description," *Studies in Bibliography* (Charlottesville, Va., 1967), xx, 203–234.

The expenses of the preparation of this volume with its introductions and apparatus have been subsidized by a grant from the National Endowment for the Humanities administered through the Modern Language Association of America and its Center for Editions of American Authors, but with generous support, as well, from the University of Virginia.

The editor is much in debt for assistance and various courtesies to Professor Robert Stallman of the University of Connecticut, Professors Matthew J. Bruccoli and Joseph Katz of the University of South Carolina, and his colleague Professor Levenson of the University of Virginia. Professor William Gibson of New York University, who examined this volume for the seal of the Center for Editions of American Authors, made several suggestions. Mr. Kenneth A. Lohf, Librarian of Rare Books and Manuscripts of the Columbia University Libraries, has been of unfailing and particular assistance. The editor is grateful to the librarians of Syracuse University, Yale University, New York Public Library, University of Virginia, Columbia University, and Dartmouth College for their courtesies in making available unpublished letters in their collections, and to the librarians of the British Museum and the London Library for the use of their

Chapter I.

My chieftain ancestors had lived at Glandore for many centuries and were very well-known. Hardly a ship could pass the Old Head of Kinsale without some boats putting off to exchange the time of day with her and our family name was on men's tongues in half the sea-ports of Europe. I dare say my ancestors lived in castles which were like churches stuck on end and they drank the best of everything amid the joyous cries of a devoted peasantry. But the good times passed away soon enough and when I had reached the age of eighteen, we had nobody on the land but a few fisher-folk and small farmers, people who were almost law-abiding. And my father came to his money from the difference when from any other cause. Before the end, he sent for me to come to his bed-side. "Tom," he said, "I brought you into existence and God help you safe out of it for you are not the kind of man to ever turn your hand to work, and there is only enough money to last a gentleman five more years. The Martha Bixby, she was, out of Bristol for the West Indies and if it hadn't been for her we would never have got along this far with plenty to eat and drink. However, I leave you, beside the money, these two swords, the grand one that King Louis, God bless him, gave me, and the plain one that will really be of use to you if you get in a disturbance. There here is the most important matter of all. Here is some papers which young Lord Strepp gave me to hold for him when we were comrades in France. I don't know what they are, having had very little time for reading during my life, but do you return them to him. Take them to him in England. He is now the great Earl of Westport and he lives in London in a grand house. I hear. In the last campaign in France I had to lend him a pair of breeches or he would have gone bare. These papers are important to him and he may reward you, but do not you depend on it for you may get the back of his hand. I have not seen him for years. I am glad I had you taught to read. They read considerably in England, I hear. There is one more cask of the best brandy remaining and I recommend you to leave for England as soon as it is finished. And now one more thing, my lad: never be civil to a King's officer. Wherever you see a red-coat defend there is a rogue between the front and the back of it. I have said everything. Push the bottle near me."

Three weeks after my father's burial, I resolved to set out, with no more words to deliver the papers to the Earl of Westport. I was resolved to be prompt in obeying my father's commands for I was extremely anxious to see the world and my feet would hardly wait for me. I put my estate into the hands of old Mickey Clancy and told him not to trouble the tenants too much over their rent or they probably would split his skull for him, and I bid Father O'Donovan look out for old Mickey that he stole from me only what was reasonable.

Page 1 (reduced) of the autograph manuscript (Mr. and Mrs. Donald S. Klopfer)

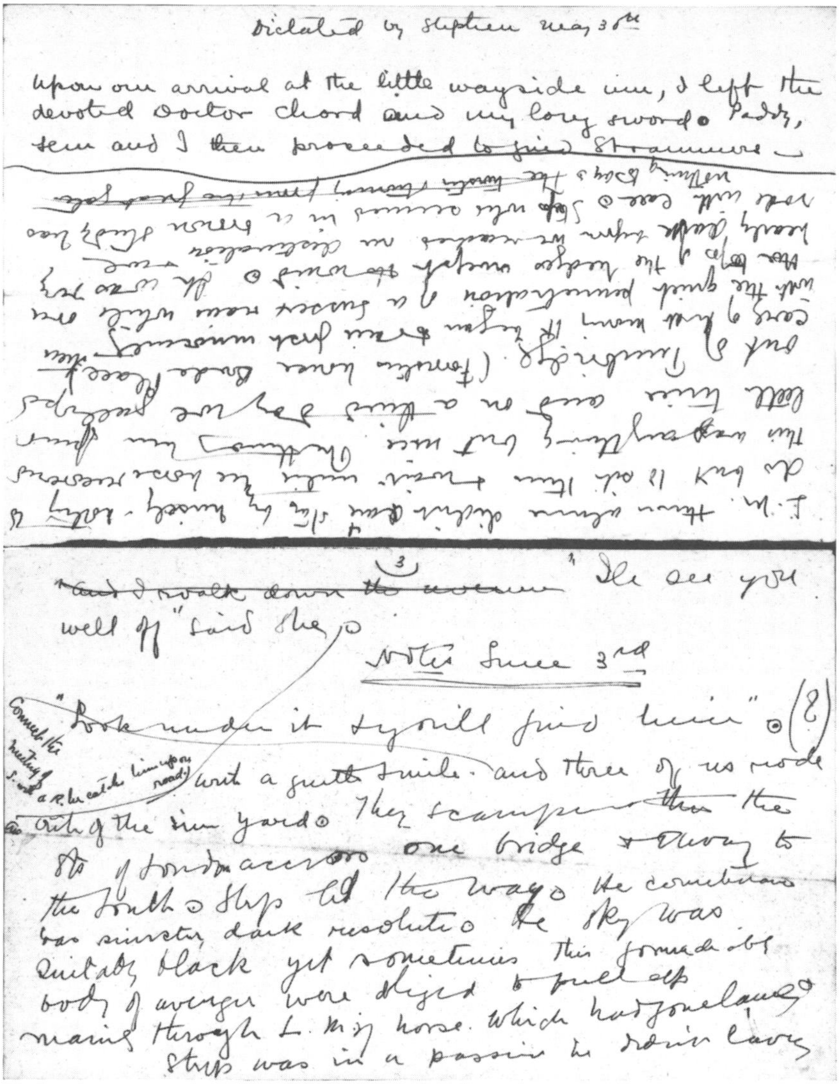

Dictated by Stephen May 30th

Upon our arrival at the little wayside inn, I left the devoted Doctor Chord and my long sword. Paddy, Sem and I then proceeded to find Strammere —

~~and I walk down the avenue~~ "I'll see you well off" said she.

Notes Since 3rd

"~~Look~~ under it & you'll find him". (2)

with a gentle smile. and three of us rode out of the inn yard. They scampered thro the Sts of London across one bridge & away to the South. Steps led the way. the countenance was sinister dark resolute. The sky was quietly black yet sometimes this formidable body of avengers were obliged to pull up [illegible] through [illegible] horse. which had gone lame. Steps was in a passion [illegible]

Preliminary page, including page 4, and page 3 (reduced) of Cora's Badenweiler Notes (Columbia)

the Armistice. "Well" he said.
Here is the company of players! Come
f –" said I "n't playing on your parts
we want those papers."

"Those papers" said f. "I haven't those
papers."

"Where are they said I – for I knew
(whole thing to play up)   the end

"I gave them to Paddy, I myself
do not care for the collection of
papers. But I like riding in the
open air on a good horse – to come
down + spend it for great water in the
red place + when I rode away
with the papers I did not go far
out of London. I saw I saw Paddy
some place etc.. + I gave him the
papers." He said this very
innocently. Sloop was very doubtful.
This is too frivolous. You must know that
after he has killed me Sloop will not
kill him – This is no nice thing

Page 8 (reduced) of Cora's Badenweiler Notes (Columbia)

Chapel End of Brede Place, April 1900, by Cora Crane (Helen Crane's Sketchbook, Columbia University)

collections. The constant assistance of the custodians of the Barrett Collection at the University of Virginia has been invaluable. The expert and scrupulous attentions of the volume's Chief Research Assistant, Miss Gillian G. M. Kyles, and her assistants Mrs. Malcolm Craig and Mr. William Holleman, have been essential and much appreciated, for in these days of relatively rapid editorial publication no single scholar can hope to assume the burden of the repeated checking for accuracy of collation, reproduction, and notation enforced by the standards for the CEAA editions. Miss Joan Crane kindly checked the bibliographical descriptions and furnished the color designations.

The editor's personal debt to Mr. Clifton Waller Barrett and his magnificent collection at the University of Virginia remains constant and can be expressed only by the dedication of this edition to him. The illustrations have been included by the permission of the University of Virginia and the Columbia University Libraries and of Mr. and Mrs. Donald Klopfer.

F. B.

Charlottesville, Virginia
January 20, 1971

CONTENTS

INTRODUCTION

WELL before he met Stephen Crane, Henry James wrote a story, half tall-tale and half parable, which provides an ironic model of his young friend's life. In "The Next Time," the writer-protagonist Ralph Limbert keeps trying to vulgarize his rare talent and win the popular success that would rescue him and his family from poverty. Time after time he tries, only to prove again and again that "you can't make a sow's ear of a silk purse." [1] With each effort to do something bad and popular, he turns out a new kind of artistic success— and the same old kind of financial failure. Though he dies young in the midst of his labors, the story testifies, in the way that fiction may, that the triumphs of art outweigh the reverses of life. Unfortunately, when Crane re-enacted the story in actuality, matters did not turn out so neatly. He had his triumphs, to be sure, but they were not consistent, inevitable, or unqualified. His talent was not incorruptible. His inventiveness was not unlimited. The pressure of creditors and, by the end of 1899, the mortal spread of tuberculosis through his system were not sublimely transcended. And yet *The O'Ruddy*, the work of his last year, which he did not give up even on his deathbed, is a fragment of such promise that it satisfies the logic of the Jamesian fable. The realist turned his hand to romance, and giving himself extravagantly to romance conventions, he discovered that the form tended to dissolve into its comic opposite, the picaresque. The exuberance of his narrative made it into something different from the expectable costume melodrama. The possibilities, only partly realized, remind us that a life as well as a book was broken off at the end of chapter xxv. The novel could be finished, in a workmanlike fashion at least,

[1] "The Next Time," 1896, in *The Novels and Tales of Henry James* (New York, 1907–9), xv, 204.

by another hand. The composite novel as it stands seems to confirm the view that Crane's brief, intense career had passed its peak and a decline had set in well before the end. But the energy and innovation in Crane's part of the story remind us that he was only twenty-eight when he died. Had he been vouchsafed a next time, anything might have happened.

Although the prehistory of *The O'Ruddy* is complicated, the question of why Crane turned to historical romance is rather simply answered. As obviously as the hero in the James story, he did so from pecuniary motives. Among Cora Crane's notes "For use in Stephens Life," a biography she vainly hoped to write, she jotted down that he was "always more or less in debt" and that he "thought O'Ruddy would free him." [2] There is no reason to doubt her judgment. If anything, she understated the debts and overstated the hopes. Once the twenty-five-year-old correspondent and his thirty-year-old comrade in arms returned from the Greek-Turkish War of 1897 and set themselves up in England as man and wife, the debts began to mount. Crane was then the author of half a dozen books, most of them well received and one—*The Red Badge of Courage*—something of a best seller. After his adventures as a correspondent in Florida and in Greece, he was ready to resume full-time his career as a writer of fiction. Cora Howorth Stewart, whose love affair with him in Florida seemed to have been sealed by the sinking of the *Commodore* and her closeness to him after his ordeal at sea, had followed him abroad and was obviously determined to stay by him forever. Joining him as a war correspondent, she discovered enough talent as a journalist that, back in England, she plausibly thought her writing could help support the household. She was mistaken. Even with the help of Stephen, she could not sustain a market for her "Letters from England" beyond that first autumn of 1897.[3]

The greater mistake was Crane's own, and it lay in his being unaware of the Jamesian proverb about silk purses. Once he

[2] MS in Columbia University Libraries.

[3] It was a costly miscalculation. She hoped for ten American papers paying four dollars a column and even began to believe in a steady $40 a week, but there is no evidence that she ever came close to that figure. The manuscript sketches with covering letters and distribution instructions are in Columbia University Libraries.

settled in Oxted, in the Surrey countryside within easy distance
of London and among new friends who valued and encouraged
his work, he began to write some of his greatest stories—"The
Monster," "The Bride Comes to Yellow Sky," "Death and the
Child," "The Blue Hotel." Characteristically, he took far more
time and care with each story than he expected, and he drew
much less reward. Before long he was in the position of having
to write a novel if he wanted money enough to work at his own
pace on stories and having to write short pieces if he wanted
money coming in to support him while he worked on a novel.
His easygoing hospitality to friends and acquaintances sup-
ported a general belief that his one famous success had made
him well off and that he drew incredible prices for his current
work. So friends and acquaintances, or at least acquaintances,
multiplied, and with them the pressure on his household budget,
his privacy, his time for composure and work.

In October, 1897, there was a hopeful spell: he made Paul
Revere Reynolds sole agent for his works in the United States
and thought that he would thus at last escape his virtual
peonage to S. S. McClure, the American publisher who had lent
him money against future work. But the mills of publication
ground slowly as well as small, and in January, 1898, he could
still bemoan the fact that he had not yet "received a cent from
America which has not been borrowed." [4] By February, when
Reynolds' negotiation with Harper's for "The Monster" resulted
in a generous contract, Crane's overdue rent and grocery bills
exceeded all possibility of being cleared by a single stroke.
About the same time, moreover, with completion of "The Blue
Hotel" the imaginative tide began to ebb. When the flow of
ideas, like the flow of money, had become negligible, Crane the
domesticated writer turned adventurer again. In April he
frenziedly raised the money that was to take him to the Spanish-
American War. The war lasted only a few months, but they
were grueling months for Crane. Remanded to the United
States because of malaria and battle fatigue, he headed back
into the war zone as soon as he could. When the war ended, he
stayed in Havana. The life of a correspondent—first in expense-

[4] Crane to Reynolds, [Oxted], Jan. 14, [1898], typed copy in Syracuse
University Library.

account luxury and then, when William Randolph Hearst had made it clear that there was no expense account to cover the luxury, in the kind of hand-to-mouth poverty he had lived with in the days before his fame—held him on and on. With Hearst holding back payment till accounts should be square, Crane fell to the task of paying off. Despite his poverty, he found that regular labor helped him organize his life. He filed his meagerly paid dispatches, worked on his serious fiction, met his newspaper friends at the cafés. His routine was sufficient unto the day, and evidently Cora and his creditors alike became remote for him. At any rate, during September and October he became remote from them: no direct word from him got back to England during that time. However much his irresponsibility comes into account for this virtual disappearance from Cora's world, his anxieties certainly included thoughts of her distressing situation. Although he was now in peonage to the "Journal people," he was "determined to make a clear slate with them—clean out all indebtedness." To do so, he was ready to go on with his Havana routine all winter. When he let Reynolds know how hard he was working and in what strapped circumstances, he was painfully aware of what difference the *Journal* people made at home: "They have come within an ace of ruining my affairs in England; indeed I am not sure they have not done so." [5] He seemed to be trapped in Havana when the war was over as he had been in England before it began. Just at this point came the break in his financial affairs that led eventually to his writing *The O'Ruddy*.

In August, 1898, the British literary agent James B. Pinker had written him to ask for a story, but it took months for the letter to get through to Crane. When the correspondence began again in mid-November, Pinker addressed his letters to Cora Crane, acting for Stephen. Ten days after he acknowledged the first stories that came to him, Cora wrote to find out whether he could do as well with a book as with magazine work. As it turned out, he could do remarkably well. By November 30 he expected to have a definite offer within a couple of days. Cora made a last-minute attempt on December 1 to fatten the pro-

[5] Crane to Reynolds, Havana, Oct. 24 and Nov. 1, [1898], typed copies in Syracuse University Library.

posed advance, but without immediate effect.[6] On December 2, he outlined the offer on which a contract would eventually be based:

I have received, today, the following offer for the book of which we spoke. Methuens are willing to advance £50, or—if absolutely necessary—£75, at once, as an instalment of an advance of £125 on a novel of not less than 70,000 words: the Ms. to be delivered in July for publication in September or October next. The advance is to be on account of the following royalties: 16⅔ per cent on the first 3000 copies, 20% on the next 3000 and 25% after, with 3½ d. per copy on the Colonial edition. The advance is, of course, not what you anticipated, but I daresay I can persuade them to increase it. But, before negotiating further, can you let me have an assurance from M[r.] Crane that he will be able to deliver the Ms. of the book by the time specified? [7]

The question of assuring delivery of a completely unspecified novel was beyond Cora's competence in several ways, but she had no reason to wish her powers greater: as matters stood, Stephen had to become more directly involved; his excessive detachment from his English affairs had to come to an end. In a flurry of cables and letters, each tried to persuade the other to join forces on his own side of the Atlantic—by the next ship. With a summons for the grocer's bill in hand and more visits from the bailiff expected, Cora could scarcely leave England. On the other hand, with the prospect of a large publisher's advance reinforcing Cora's personal powers, the attraction of England on Stephen became stronger and stronger. In the protracted contest of wills, it became more and more evident that he could not manage his affairs from a distance, though the surviving evidence is mainly in the correspondence of Cora and the agent. Pinker's letters to Cora indicate that on December 5 she had made no reply to the Methuen offer. But once enough time had gone by for her to have received instructions from across the ocean, she made up for her silence with three letters in quick

[6] Pinker to Crane, London, Aug. 22, 1898, addressed "c/o William Heinemann Esq.," ALS in Columbia University Libraries; Pinker to Cora Crane, London, Nov. 14, 25, 30, and Dec. 1, 1898, ALS in Columbia University Libraries. Cora Crane's side of the correspondence can be reconstructed from Pinker's letters.

[7] London, Dec. 2, 1898, ALS in Columbia University Libraries.

succession. By December 9, a week after he had relayed the terms Methuen proposed, Pinker acknowledged her reply on Crane's behalf and went on to ask whether she had formal power of attorney, "as you will need it, perhaps, if the publisher should ask for its production." A few days later, as he reported on his effort to raise the initial payment, he lamented that "the circumstances weaken one's hand very much, so that we cannot do so well as I think we ought."[8] When Cora could at last say that Stephen was about to arrive back in England, he took a different tone: "Directly Mr. Crane arrives, I think we shall have no difficulty in settling up for his novel on satisfactory terms." He added, however, that the Methuen firm were "naturally anxious to know what the book will be, the length, theme, and so on."[9] Grant Richards, at Methuen, must have been satisfied with what he subsequently learned, whether he heard it from Crane himself, now back in England, or from the agent. On January 24, 1899, Pinker told Crane he was about to send him a Methuen contract for his "next novel." All that was specified about the novel was that it be not less than 70,000 words and delivered in manuscript by August 1. The specifications concerning the Methuen advance were a good deal more concrete: "They agree to pay, on account of royalties, £100 on the signature of the contract, and a further £100 on publication."[10] Crane's presence thus had an almost immediate effect. Although he had been served with a writ in his first week home,[11] before the second week was out he had this promise of a big advance and a generous contract. The giddy ride from despair to hope —and back again—was to be the pattern of his economic life to the end, but at the moment, thanks to Pinker's success with Methuen, he seemed really to have a chance to get out of his money troubles. With such hopes to encourage his writing, he could put out of mind some of the motives that had prompted his departure nine months before.

Crane learned to act on his hopes with considerable steadi-

[8] Pinker to Cora Crane, London, Dec. 5, Dec. 9, and Dec. 12, 1898, ALS in **Columbia University Libraries.**

[9] London, Jan. 4, 1899, ALS in Columbia University Libraries.

[10] **ALS in Columbia University Libraries.**

[11] Crane to Reynolds, Oxted, Jan. 19, 1899, typed copy in Syracuse University **Library.**

ness, and Cora did her best to arrange circumstances toward
that end. Her acting on Stephen's behalf in the early negotiations with Pinker had been indispensable, but given her success
in that quarter, her domestic arrangements were at least as
important. She kept up associations with friends and neighbors,
including Joseph Conrad and Edward Garnett, so that Stephen
came back to a genuine social ambience such as he had not
known for a long while: it was more than two years since he
had left his newspaper and artist friends in New York City and
his fixed base at his brother's home in Hartwood, near Port
Jervis, New York. She also devised a way of getting them out of
their relatively expensive and unattractive middle-class house
in suburban Oxted and into a relatively inexpensive and very
attractive upper-class country house. Moreton Frewen, who
liked Americans and literary people, had offered them Brede
Place, a Sussex manor dating in part from the fourteenth
century and not quite reconstructed, at a mere nominal rent.
Since neither Crane calculated costs like remodeling, furniture,
or servants, they gladly accepted.[12] All Crane had to do was
assign his future income to Pinker for payment on his debts,
and his creditors' attorneys were willing to let him move. After
he settled at Brede in February, he was able to live in some
style as new debts began to mount. He responded to the apparent stability and promise of his situation rather than its
precariousness, and so having begun them at Oxted, he continued at Brede his series of Whilomville tales, stories of American childhood and tranquil domesticity. He resumed his Greek
War novel *Active Service* and industriously pushed it to completion. He rounded out his tales of the Cuban War and assembled them in a new collection, *Wounds in the Rain*. Even
before he began work on his historical novel, 1899 was obviously a most productive year.

But there were complications, too, since Crane had promised

[12] Cora Crane to Moreton Frewen, Oxted, June 10, 1898, in *Stephen Crane:
Letters*, ed. R. W. Stallman and Lillian Gilkes (New York, 1960), pp. 181–182.
Her definite acceptance, instead of being followed at once by a formal letter
of agreement, became indefinite again as economic and personal complications
intervened. When Crane on his return went down to see Brede, he immediately
joined Cora in being "mad over the place." Cora reported to Edward Garnett:
"We are going to move Heaven and Earth to get there" (Oxted, Jan. 19, 1899,
Letters, p. 206).

more than he could deliver. In signing an agreement with
Methuen, he knew full well that he first had to finish *Active
Service* for Heinemann—and for Stokes in America. Fully confident that he was "going to have two big novels this year," he
was still confident in early March that he would finish the first
of them that very month. Though he soon began to modify his
expectations, he offered typescripts of half the novel to his
London and New York agents in hopes that they would soon
sell serial rights.[13] The only concern Pinker expressed was
whether serialization of this first novel of the year might make
it cross dates with the second, the one for Methuen. He hoped
Crane had arranged with Heinemann to yield his right of
priority, but it did not occur to him to worry that the commitment to Methuen might not be met.[14] In due time Crane made
good on that agreement after a fashion, by giving *Wounds in
the Rain* to Methuen for English publication. For good economic
reasons, however, the firm was less than happy to have paid a
large advance and then to receive a book of short stories instead
of the promised novel. So a new contract was drawn up, July 12,
1899, for the work which eventually turned out to be *The
O'Ruddy*. Once more it spoke of a novel "the title of which has
not yet been fixed which shall extend to at least 70,000 words."
This time there was explicit mention of the author's other
obligations: "The Author agrees that the said novel shall be the
first new novel written by him (or published) after the novel
he has delivered (or will immediately deliver) to Mr. William

[13] Thomas Beer thought that Crane "finished 'Active Service' before starting
North [from Havana], then threw the last chapters aside and wrote them
afresh" (*Stephen Crane, A Study in American Letters* [New York, 1923],
p. 199). However, in the letter predicting "two big novels," to Reynolds, Brede,
Feb. 13, 1899, Crane also wrote: "I have got one of the big novels very nearly
finished to my satisfaction and I will send the half to you in about three
weeks if you think there is any possibility of getting any goodly sum (advance)
upon the exhibition of half of a novel for serialization." On March 2 he told
Reynolds that he expected to complete the novel by the end of the month,
and on March 16 he was making his first revised prediction, "the end of the
first week in April" (typed copies in Syracuse University Library). Actually,
he finished on May 13 (Crane to Mrs. Moreton Frewen, Brede, May 15, [1899],
ALS in University of Virginia Library).

[14] Pinker to Cora Crane, London, March 9, 1899, *Letters*, p. 217.
Pinker to Stephen Crane, London, March 20, 1899: "I am glad the novel is
going on, though I am afraid it looks as if the dates will get a little mixed"
(ALS in Columbia University Libraries).

Heinemann of Bedford Street, Covent Garden." Delivery date was set for March 31, 1900. Royalties were the same as before except—a mild sign of the firm's irritation with Crane—the rate of 16 per cent rather than 16⅔ per cent was set for the first three thousand copies. The real indication of how the firm felt was in the clause on initial payment: "The said Methuen & Co. shall pay to the said Author Two hundred pounds (£200) on account of royalties and profits mentioned in the agreement which sum shall be due on publication of the book." [15] There was to be no advance! Crane was not likely to sign on such disadvantageous terms; but since he had not even yet completed work on the short-story volume, he was in no position to bargain. Evidently he left the contract unsigned and let the matter hang fire for six months. His moral intent was clear enough, however, and so when Pinker in October received his first packet of *O'Ruddy* manuscript, he blandly inquired: "I suppose the twenty folios you sent me are the beginning of the novel which will be for Methuen here and Stokes in America. Is that so? Have you another copy for me to send to Stokes, or am I to get one made." [16] When Cora replied, she did so in the knowledge that Methuen still did not have copy for *Wounds in the Rain* and would be, if anything, testier on the subject of a new novel than they had been in July. She wrote Pinker:

The first two chapters of the New Novel Mr. Crane says for you to try to have Stokes accept. If you will refer to his contract with them you will see that it calls for "the next novel which is to be on the American Revolution." Mr. Crane says to have a copy made & send to them asking if they will take it, "Romance" on the same terms as the Rev. novel. If they won't do this, Mr. Crane will write the Rev. novel first & will sell this "Romance" to come out serially at any time & in book form *after* the Rev. novel. [17]

Only in January, 1900, when Crane was engaged in a second spell of work on *The O'Ruddy* and had a growing manuscript of

[15] MS in Yale University Library. At the head of the unsigned "Memorandum of an Agreement" is the handwritten notation "The O'Ruddy," which, though it could not have been added before the novel was named in May, 1900, rightly indicates the historic line between this proposed agreement and that under which Methuen eventually published the book.

[16] Pinker to Crane, London, Oct. 24, 1899, *Letters*, pp. 236–237.

[17] Cora Crane to Pinker, Brede, [Oct. 26, 1899], *Letters*, p. 238.

some size to show, did he reopen the question of an advance. By that time he was so desperate as to offer concessions on the no-advance offer of the previous July. Once more Cora conducted his business correspondence with Pinker:

Now, as I wrote you, Mr. Crane is in immediate need of £150— Would Methuen *advance* upon "The Irish Romance?" Of course though there is no contract Mr. Crane wants them (Methuen) to have this book. But we cannot lose sight of the fact that *if* Methuen does not care to make an immediate advance there is someone else who will. By Friday several more chapters of the story will be finished. Shall I come up on Friday morning reaching your office about 2.30 P.M. and bring what is then finished of the novel? Or can *you* see Methuen and say that now they have or can get at any time the ms. for war stories. And ask them if they will advance £100—at once on this (Irish) story? If they will do this they can send contract for Mr. Crane to sign for this book—and for the *next one* for which they are to pay £200.[18]

Pinker did his best and successfully worked out a compromise whereby Methuen would pay an advance, not on signature of the agreement nor yet on delivery of the completed manuscript, but in installments "as we deliver the MS." [19] Within a week of proposing this solution, he began delivering chapters to Methuen as they came in.[20] So the Methuen contract which had helped draw Crane home from Cuba went into its third form as an agreement for *The O'Ruddy*. The arrangement meant that Crane would really apply himself to writing the novel in the little time he had left before his physical collapse, but more crassly it meant that he must write with an eye on the day-to-day word-count on which he depended for support. When the first agree-

[18] Cora Crane to Pinker, Brede, [Jan. 9, 1900], *Letters*, p. 262. She had first raised the question more casually on Jan. 6, in an undated letter replying to Pinker's letter of the day before: "Can you get Methuen to make advance upon the next story they are to have. The Irish story" (*Letters*, p. 258).

[19] "I have seen Methuen today, and I think he will agree to make the advance as we deliver the MS. He is going to think it over and let me know tonight or tomorrow morning. Please, therefore, let me have as much of the MS. as quickly as you can" (Pinker to Crane, London, Jan. 15, 1900, ALS in Columbia University Libraries).

[20] "Thank you for your letter, and also the one from Mrs. Crane, enclosing chapters six and seven of the Romance. I will deliver them at once to Methuen" (Pinker to Crane, London, Jan. 22, 1900, TLS in Columbia University Libraries).

ment had come up, he was elated to think that a generous contract freed him to write as he would. As the matter turned out, he wrote too slowly to stay his creditors and too fast to do his best work. It is the more remarkable, then, that *The O'Ruddy* conveys a sense of freedom and elation. From the circumstances in which it was written, it is far more understandable that Crane was unable to finish for Methuen the "next novel" he had promised.

The next novels to which Crane turned his energies upon returning to England in 1899 were his sentimental melodrama with a Greek war background, *Active Service*; an abortive historical novel of the American Revolution; and his Irish romance, *The O'Ruddy*. Economic necessity had much to do with where he spent his effort, and it was no doubt proper that he should try to earn his living as best he could. Yet Crane was touchy on the subject. Once Cora sounded just the wrong note by suggesting that he "write a popular novel for money." In her words: "He turned on me & said: 'I will write for one man & banging his fist on writing table & that man shall be myself etc. etc.'"[21] To some degree his protest may be taken literally. Though sensitive to the slackening intensity of his work, he had endured such a falling off before—in the period after writing *The Red Badge of Courage*. He had then learned to put aside qualms at doing lesser work, and the qualms were less evident on this occasion. Qualms aside, he did please himself with what he wrote. He had no great prejudice against the forms of fiction in which he worked. The adventure story, the historical novel, or the swashbuckling romance might seem to Howells to be the enemies of realistic fiction, but Crane had no such theoretical views of literary form. So long as his commitment to truth-telling was not impaired, he moved from subject to subject and from genre to genre without anxiety. With a newspaperman's open-mindedness, he made no fuss at working in popular modes. After all, his adventure novel *Active Service* developed material he had gathered firsthand while covering the Greek-Turkish War. It did not occur to him that his materials could be verifi-

[21] Cora Crane's notebook "For use in Stephens Life" (MS in Columbia University Libraries).

able and his novel not be true. There was no more reason to be uneasy when he gathered his material from the past. With the Greek novel out of the way, Pinker was pressing him to take up a proposal from *Lippincott's Magazine* and do the series of articles to be called *Great Battles of the World*. Though he was slow to begin the articles themselves, he was thinking his way back in time—not always with conviction. In August he supposedly wrote "a Cromwellian tale" called "Siege" which he did not like well enough to publish or even to keep.[22] When he thought of doing a novel of New Jersey in the American Revolution, however, his enthusiasm was kindled. He sent requests for books to his brother, to the New Jersey Historical Society, and to his American publishers,[23] and he began dictating plans for the work to Cora. When the conception first took hold, he began elaborating it like a man who intended to enjoy his work. It might not have turned out to be of a rank with the great nineteenth-century historical novels, but it could have been a good deal more than costume-pageant melodramatic entertainment. The author of *The Red Badge*, even when doing minor work, could be sure of that.

Crane's enthusiasm, strong enough to persuade himself and the publisher Stokes as well, can be inferred from the plans he dictated. With the New Jersey subject, he sensed his deep implication in a continuum of past and present. His leading

[22] Ames W. Williams and Vincent Starrett, *Stephen Crane: A Bibliography* (Glendale, Calif., 1948), p. 121. They record Karl Harriman as the person who saw the manuscript. He began *Great Battles* only in October, 1899; see *The Works of Stephen Crane*, ed. Fredson Bowers (Charlottesville, 1969—), Vol. IX.

[23] Crane to the Secretary of the New Jersey Historical Society, [Brede, Aug. 26, 1899], *Letters*, pp. 224–225; William H. Crane to Mr. and Mrs. Stephen Crane, Port Jervis, N.Y., Nov. 7, 1899, *Letters*, p. 240; J. Garmeson (Lippincott's London agent) to Cora Crane, London, Jan. 2 and March 25, 1901, ALS in Columbia University Libraries. Garmeson had previously written on July 30, 1900, submitting a list of books "procured from America for Mr. Crane's use & which were to be returned when done with." "Unfortunately," he went on in his January follow-up letter, "they never were used & you said you would return them as soon as possible." The July 30 letter with its list does not survive, but the second follow-up letter of March, 1901, states that of the remainder still to come "the most important are the missing vols. of the 'Proceedings of the New Jersey Historical Society.'"

In his undated "Plans for New Novel," dictated to Cora, Crane had noted: "Ask Will and Stokes to get books on subject Rev. War" (MS in Columbia University Libraries).

characters were to be the Cranes of the Revolutionary era—old Stephen, young William and Jonathan and Howard—and he even intended to "introduce Henry Flemings grandfather as first farmer." He knew the time and the place well enough to be aware that the great obstacles to revolution were Toryism and, even more, widespread indifference. Although he meant to show the "great influence of Crane family in carrying the revolution through," he wanted also to show the social history on which his political-military events were based. To do so, he resolved to "study carefully the mood of the N.J. people," and even as he made his notes, he developed an idea of the influence of social history on military strategy. Though the best policy would have been to wage guerrilla warfare—he had in mind the Cubans against Spain and, still more recently, the Philippinos against the Americans—he saw "on second thoughts" that the better-off Americans did not want to abandon their farms and houses and so preferred pitched battles to taking to the hills. He gave thought to the problem of language, too, and was certain that he did not want to follow the superficially realistic practice of transcribing dialect: "Make no distinction of diction save a use of what might be called biblical phraseology." As for characters and events, he had a good idea of what he wanted, and he was virtually certain that he wanted the Battle of Monmouth to be the "central dramatic scene." [24] In September, 1899, while ideas for this novel began to flow and he was evidently keen on getting down to work, he secured from Stokes a contract for the projected novel and a promise to help him get the books he wanted for his research. [25] Since this contract eventually was to cover *The O'Ruddy*, the abandonment of the Revolutionary novel is linked to the Irish romance by legal as well as literary connection. But the wonder is that what seemed so sure in late September should have been so completely displaced within a month.

The trouble was that the project would demand more time and care than Crane could give it. He had originally objected to

[24] "PLANS FOR STORY," dictated to Cora Crane, MS in Columbia University Libraries. These notes are different from and far more circumstantial than the "Plans for New Novel," cited in previous footnote, which mainly projects a course of study and is described in the next paragraph.

[25] Crane to Pinker, Brede, Sept. 22, 1899, *Letters*, p. 231.

the idea of doing *Great Battles* on the ground that he was not a historian, and even when he was assured that "elaborate studies" of the battles were not wanted, he found the labor of research too much for his crowded schedule.[26] In the case of the novel, he found the prospect of research far more engaging. It must have helped him persuade Stokes to give him a contract for his "new novel" that he should ingenuously show his commitment by asking their help with books. From his brother he asked for whatever could be found in the family library and, in particular, for "an essay which Father must have written in 1874 called, I think, 'The history of an old house'." He listed other books which he had obviously read in his youth, a life of Washington and a volume of New Jersey history. Yet his idea of research was monumentally naïve, as his notes indicate:

> Write letters to all the men whom I think could help me. This list to include Henery Cabot Lodge, the librarian of Princeton Col., the president of the N.J. branch of the sons of the American rev. ect. Here in England collect the best histories of that time and also learn what British regiments served in America also what officers who served published memoirs; get books if possible. This will be difficult and it will become necessary to write to various people who might know.[27]

Though Crane wanted "the best histories of that time," he scarcely knew how to find them. He did eventually get a list of Continental Army units that saw service in New Jersey, but beyond this the direct results of his research do not survive. An indirect result was his writing about another region near the Crane family home where ancestors and relatives had taken part in Revolutionary history. On "September 31" (perhaps October 1?) he sent Pinker what he described as "the first story of a series which will deal with the struggles of the settlers in

---

[26] The reassurance from Lippincott was relayed by Pinker to Cora Crane in a letter from London, April 20, 1899, ALS in Columbia University Libraries. Eventually Crane retained Kate Lyon Frederic, who needed the work since Harold Frederic's death left her without support, to do the research for him.

[27] "Plans for New Novel," MS in Columbia University Libraries. Henry Cabot Lodge, well known to Crane as a United States Senator and presumably as the author of *A Short History of the English Colonies in America* (1881), had recently published a popular and vigorously patriotic *Story of the American Revolution* (2 vols., New York and London, 1898), after previous serialization in *Scribner's Magazine*.

the Wyoming Valley (Pennsylvania) in 1776–79 against the Tories and Indians."[28] But his possession of time and place and people was less graphic than he might have hoped. Pinker was unable to sell this or the succeeding stories during Crane's lifetime. And if he did not quite possess the subject, there were others who did. Even in his earlier notes for the novel, when ideas were running well, he had had to instruct himself to read Cooper's *The Spy* and S. Weir Mitchell's "last book," the title of which did not immediately occur to him. Mitchell's *Hugh Wynne, Free Quaker*, barely three years out, had been a best seller. Two best sellers of 1899, Winston Churchill's *Richard Carvel* and Paul Leicester Ford's *Janice Meredith*, though they may not absolutely have saturated the market for novels of the American Revolution, stood at least as warnings that anyone moving into competition with them had better be sure that he could offer as attractive a product.

The several crass reasons why Crane should have been ready to give up on the Revolutionary novel came to a head at the beginning of October, 1899. He thought that he was to get a £100 advance on the new novel as soon as he worked off his old obligations and gave Stokes the completed *Wounds in the Rain*. On September 30, and again on "September 31," he was still expressing his anxiety to Pinker lest he had missed the 80,000 words he had contracted for in the war-story volume.[29] October 1 was apparently the day when anxiety turned into explosion. On October 2, at any rate, Crane's friend Robert Barr tried to calm him by going over the facts to which he was privy:

I have read both your letter and Stokes' over three or four times to get the hang of the thing, and this is my understanding of it.
1. Crane and Stokes. (Mutually agreeing.) £100 paid on receipt of copy.
2. Crane. (Cabling.) "Book finished. Will you cable money."
3. Stokes. (Cabling.) "Yes on receipt of complete MS."
4. S Crane. (Cabling.) "I withdraw the book."
5. Stokes (Writing.) "We stand by the London Convention of 1884."
6. BLOODY WAR. . . .

[28] Brede, Sept. 31, [1899], *Letters*, pp. 232–233. For the Wyoming Valley tales, see *Works*, Vol. VIII.

[29] *Letters*, pp. 232, 232–233.

You have got things on exactly the right basis now, in leaving Pinker to deal with editors and publishers. Write, write, write, anything but business letters.[30]

It was hard to give up the wishful thought that as he finished one work, he would be paid for the next. Despite his violent response to the disappointment of his hopes, Crane could not afford open warfare with his publisher. He probably could not even afford the cables that would have provoked it. Instead, he wrote the diplomatic, if bitter, letter which left matters prudently in the hands of his agent. On October 9, Frederick A. Stokes wrote to Pinker from New York: "We have just received instructions from Stephen Crane, Esqr., that our correspondence regarding his affairs with us shall in the future be conducted with you." [31] He mentioned the long novel of the American Revolution which was contracted for and the system of advance payments that was agreed upon, and he went into specific detail in a subsequent letter. For Stokes, the £100 advance on the story volume was a separate matter. Having dealt with that, he went on: "As to the new novel on the American Revolution, we are to pay £200. in installments, as the copy is received, and on receipt of the copy another £100, the £200. being in advance of roualties on the novel alone, and the £100. being chargeable to Mr Crane's account as against royalties in general." [32] In short, at just the moment when Crane had most reason to be disenchanted with his Revolutionary War project, it became clear that the only way he could draw an advance was by actually turning in manuscript. Before Stokes' letters could have reached Pinker, he got out of his dilemma by dropping the Revolution and beginning a new novel of a very different sort.

The O'Ruddy does not betray its dismal origin, even though the want of money, time, and knowledge persisted and, having dampened and then smothered the Revolutionary novel, had

[30] Barr to Crane, Woldingham, Oct. 2, 1899, Letters, pp. 233–234.
[31] Oct. 9, 1899, TLS in New York Public Library.
[32] Stokes to Pinker, New York, n.d., TLS in New York Public Library. At least two payments were made under this scheme: on Feb. 13, 1900, Stokes sent £70 to Pinker (TLS in Dartmouth College Library) and on April 2, £40 (request for receipt, M. A. Dominick to Pinker, London, July 10, 1900, TLS in Dartmouth College Library).

their effect also on the Irish romance. The negative qualities of the new work—no attempt to capture the past or reconstruct the milieu, no search for a relation between character and action or between event and event—seemed to carry over from the abandoned project. Since research was laborious and, to Crane, deeply mysterious, the new story would take place in no very definite historical moment and no very definite landscape. If the historical work would have been more an adventure story than a book about history, why not, then, simply write an adventure story? Despite familiarity since childhood with his Revolutionary subject and pride of ancestry that made him identify with it, Crane could not write a historical novel. (Readers have instinctively classed *The Red Badge of Courage* as a war novel, not as a historical novel; and Crane himself had doubts of its being a novel in the usual sense when he spoke of it as a "mere episode.") [33] He did not sufficiently share nineteenth-century premises about character shaping events either to affirm or to doubt in any complex way that men made history. The principle that individual moral nature demonstrated itself in conduct meant little to him; his special insight was the random effect of will and circumstance on incident. While this insight made for the intensity and depth of his stories, it also made his longer works tend to be episodic. In his notes on the plot of the Revolutionary novel, for example, he indicated little more than that he wanted the narrative to get him to the Battle of Monmouth. As for the plot of *The O'Ruddy*, he made it episodic on purpose and knew little more about its outcome than that he wanted the action to get somehow to Brede Place. For the fun of it, he might have said, and that phrase would have made the crucial difference. From its very beginning, the Irish romance is manifestly written for the fun of it:

My chieftain ancestors had lived at Glandore for many centuries and were very well-known. Hardly a ship could pass the Old Head of Kinsale without some boats putting off to exchange the time of day with her and our family name was on men's tongues in half the sea-ports of Europe, I dare say. My ancestors lived in castles which were like churches stuck on end and they drank the best of

[33] Crane to an Editor of *Leslie's Weekly*, n.p., n.d. [c. Nov. 1895], *Letters*, p. 79.

everything amid the joyous cries of a devoted peasantry. But the good times passed away soon enough and when I had reached the age of eighteen, we had nobody on the land but a few fisher-folk and small farmers, people who were almost law-abiding, and my father came to die more from the disappointment than from any other cause. Before the end, he sent for me to come to his bed-side.

The old chieftain's bequest was two swords and the mission of returning a batch of papers which neither the chieftain nor his son ever read, reading was so great an effort. The papers might be worth a fortune to the young man who brought them back to the Earl of Westport in England: "They read considerably in England, I hear." What is clear from the very first page of the new work is that the exigencies of Crane's circumstances do not control it. A new surge of creative energy had intervened.

Crane moved into his new story with an exuberance that half-transformed it from romance to picaresque, from a heroic tale with conventional values to a rogue's story of outfoxing the hypocritic orders of society as he goes from one encounter to another. After a first chapter in which he established what he needed of given situations—mysterious papers, the quest for a fortune, a first fateful glimpse of the beauteous heroine, a first occasion for a duel—Crane went on as though he felt free to let adventures occur as they might. The young O'Ruddy, friendless in England and hard put to find a second for his impending duel, stumbles on a stranded countryman keening by the side of the road. On impulse he makes this bumpkin his servant and assigns him the task of playing a gentleman and learning the duties and flourishes of a second. Paddy, of course, can only make a farcical imposture of the role; first encountered in the dark as "a bedraggled vagabond with tear stains on his dirty cheeks and a vast shock of hair which I well knew would look, in day-light, like a burning hay-cock," he remains incorrigibly himself. Like Teague O'Regan in H. H. Brackenridge's *Modern Chivalry*, America's first picaresque novel, the comic servant lends a touch of quixotism to the narrative. But unlike Brackenridge's narrator a century before him, Crane's narrator will not yield the center of the stage. Crane doubled the temptation to shift interest from knight to squire—or to change the character of the hero—by having The O'Ruddy next encounter and enlist in his service a highwayman, Jem Bottles by name. Jem in his own eyes is "a true knight of the road with seven ballads written of me in Bristol and three in Bath," but he knows well enough that he "should have remained an honest sheep-stealer and never engaged in this dangerous and nefarious game of lifting purses." Once again Crane opted for farce, allowing his tale to verge on the mock-romance but never quite turning it into true picaresque. He had seriously considered the choice. In fact the idea of writing a picaresque novel came first, and he only decided in the writing to keep his wandering Irish chieftain a safe and attested romantic hero. In the only surviving evidence that he tried to plan the novel, he got so far as to write out a rationalized table of contents for four chapters:

Chapter I
In which the reader is introduced to a very wise and adventursome young man who seems almost certain to do great things before the end of the book.
Chapter II.
Valiantly assisted by a friend, our hero fights a duel.
Chapter III.
Our hero goes in search of a thief and meets only a highwayman.
Chapter IV
Finding the business of a gentleman rather arduous on an income of one guinea per the-rest-of-his-natural-life our hero turns highwayman and becomes interested.[34]

By the fourth chapter, indeed in the very first chapter, of the actual tale, The O'Ruddy would be so committed to retrieving stolen papers, avenging insults, and winning the girl that he could not plausibly switch to the easy purposeless life of a literary rogue. But the original intent of writing a picaresque tale survived in the comic tone and robust energy of the narrative.

Crane's exuberance stemmed from his naïve rediscovery of the picaresque. Either instigating the discovery or perhaps only confirming it was a new acquaintance quite different from anyone he had known before. He was Charles Whibley, a learned and lively man, one day to be memorialized by his friend T. S. Eliot

[34] MS in Columbia University Libraries.

for his unique gifts of conversation and high journalism.[35] In October, 1899, Whibley gave Crane a copy of his first full-length work, *A Book of Scoundrels,* inscribing it to the young American "with the regard of his confrère." [36] There is no record of when they met, but only of their exchange of books and of Whibley's desire to see Crane again and "renew our pleasant talk." [37] Whibley, the cultivated product of established society, was acutely sensitive—as his conversation and his writing demonstrated—to life beyond the limits of established society. Crane shared such sensitivity, but he had thought that exemption from ordinariness belonged mainly to those who lived beyond the usual boundaries of gentility—to the outcasts of the city or the waifs of the sea, to Wild West heroes who survived mainly in fiction, and to soldiers. For all of these, life was a gamble and often a desperate one, but for those with nerve enough it could be carried off with the style of a game. Whibley's idea of the distinguished scoundrel was not so different. Putting aside the question of crime and considering the scoundrel, "once justice is quit of him," the Englishman defined his subject's mastery of a way of life as nobility of style: "To the common citizen a violent death was (and is) the worst of horrors; to the ancient highwayman it was the odd trick lost in the game of life." [38] The Cambridge man's learning served as well as the small-town American's quest for experience to take him into a world where heroic action mattered more than conventional morals or ambitions. On the other hand, the Cambridge man's trained discrimination allowed him to make explicit what usually remained for Crane the implicit and ironic connections of his special world to everyday reality. Whibley's contempt for the mere brutal housebreaker as compared to the skillful cutpurse or the virtuoso highwayman and his equal contempt for the swindler, whom he regarded as the exemplary criminal of the present day, expressed social as well as esthetic attitudes. So, too, when Whibley's taste for noble scoundrels took a national-

[35] *Charles Whibley, A Memoir,* The English Association Pamphlet No. 80 (London, 1931), reprinted in *Selected Essays* (London, 1932).

[36] The flyleaf inscription by Whibley is not dated, but the date was noted by Cora Crane on the first page (Columbia University Libraries).

[37] Whibley to Crane, Haslemere, Nov. 17, [1899], ALS in Columbia University Libraries.

[38] *A Book of Scoundrels* (London, 1897), pp. 1, 12.

istic turn, it bespoke something more than nationalism: "But in Paris crime is too often *passionel,* and a *crime passionel* is a crime with a purpose, which, like the novel with a purpose, is conceived by a dullard, and carried out for the gratification of the middle-class." [39] Such arcane lore as Whibley chose to gather did not make him a mere antiquarian. Entering his special world, he did not relinquish the threads that led to the ordinary reality of everyday experience.

Crane had reason to approve Whibley's targets—moralism, utilitarianism, Philistinism—since he had encountered them all in his own experience and never benefited from the encounter. Although he may not have fully understood the elaborately built cultural stronghold from which his new friend looked down on those common faults of the age, he learned how it felt to have a stronghold from having moved to Brede Place. There he enjoyed the informal patronage of Moreton and Clara Frewen. The aristocratic British promoter, whose wit and congeniality made him a friend of the great on both sides of the Atlantic, and his charming American wife, who was one of the fabulously beautiful and rich Jerome sisters, inspired belief in such golden freedom as most people envision from storybooks. Crane had no notion that Frewen too flirted with bankruptcy and dodged writ-servers. He did not know that while Frewen chased a fortune on far continents—India, the American and Canadian West, South Africa, Australia—his wife had sometimes lived by going as self-designated guest from one great country house to another. Frewen in his large way was at least as much bemused by the scramble after money as Crane, and yet the imperialist business-man was also like the young American writer in that he came close but did not wholly yield himself to the pecuniary way of life. The house at Brede was a case in point. The Frewens rented Brede Place because they could not afford to repair or furnish or live in it themselves. Having just bought the estate from Frewen's older brother and immediately mortgaged it for more than half again as much as they paid, they had enough cash for a time so that they could do as they liked. They generously let the house and park to the Cranes for forty pounds a year—a mere

[39] P. 16.

fraction of the mortgage interest—and they were equally generous in putting up with missed payments.[40] Frewen, however
reduced he was by the incessant pressure of debt and his own
relentless effort to make a killing, retained the style of freedom.

Crane's own freedom was more than illusory. He and Cora,
as Americans with literary credentials, enjoyed the privileges of
a complex stratified society without its more obvious restrictions.
While Crane was off in Cuba, Cora had managed a swift rise in
the Society of American Women in London. It was through this
activity that she first met Clara Frewen and opened negotiation
for the house at Brede. Once settled there, she took her place
easily in country life as well. And so did Stephen. He worked
hard and regularly in his upstairs study, but there was more
than work in the routine of Brede Place. He delighted in the
hundred-acre park and liked taking his morning ride "within the
fence." [41] He wore knickers by day and dressed for dinner and
mastered local tradition well enough to suggest that Elizabethan
custom rather than poverty could account for the stone floors
of his great dining hall being covered with rushes, not rugs. Such
was the power of style that he schooled himself to write as if
economic necessity were quit of him when in fact he was writing
under severest economic pressure. But just as he felt compelled
to insist that he wrote to please himself alone, he felt the necessity of keeping the hero of his romance true to his given character. The O'Ruddy must be noble and carefree rather than
ignoble and carefree. Though the hero borrows from the highwayman, he never joins him. Though it is hard to perform the
business of a gentleman on "one guinea per the-rest-of-his-nat-

[40] The glories of Moreton Frewen are most succinctly and persuasively set
forth in Shane Leslie, *Studies in Sublime Failure* (London, 1932), pp. 249–
295. The most detailed record of his financial affairs and their corrosive effect
on his character is Allen Andrews, *The Splendid Pauper* (Philadelphia and
New York, 1968). Andrews quotes a letter from Crane to Frewen "after a
year in residence," that is, about mid-February, 1900: "You have been very
kind to me about rent. I've had a hard year of it settling my affairs, which
are nearly in shape now. I have taken advantage of your kindness to keep
you waiting until almost the last. Next month I can send you a cheque. Will
it be convenient for you to wait until then?" (p. 195). The preceding portion
of this letter, on matters at Brede and the departure of the caretaker who
had come with the place, is given in R. W. Stallman, *Stephen Crane: A
Biography* (New York, 1968), pp. 468–469.
[41] From Cora Crane's description of Stephen Crane at Brede, to Corwin
Knapp Linson, [London], Oct. 18, 1900, *Letters*, p. 320.

ural-life" or even on "only enough money to last a gentleman
five more years," the hero if he turned rogue could not turn
himself back into an eligible lover. The rogue's-eye view of society
must be dispensed with and a man play his part with carefree
spirit to the end.

Given Crane's impulse to move toward the picaresque, he was
free not to make his hero a rogue because he had made him
sufficiently an outsider in being an Irishman. When The O'Ruddy
appeared at his first duel accompanied by the uncouth flaming-
haired Paddy, he got a lesson in nationalism. At first he credited
his opponents' imperturbability to their being so considerate, as
might be expected of men who followed the code of honor anywhere. Later he decided that he gave these Englishmen "a little
more than their due," for "since Paddy was a foreigner he was
possessed of some curious license and his grotesque ways could
be explained fully in the simple phrase 'Tis a foreigner.' " Besides imperturbable courtesy, a foreigner might encounter con-
descension and ignorance in a variety of forms. Crane had been
sufficiently exasperated by both. He once declared: "The simple
rustic villagers of Port Jervis have as good manners as some of
the flower of England's literary set." [42] But what he had felt as
an American was now displaced toward a new target. He made
his villain the sort who would comment at the top of his voice,
"Why, the Irish run naked through their native forests"; and
when the boys of Bristol crowd in to see a fight and glimpse The
O'Ruddy's second, one cries, " 'Tis a great marvel to see such
hair and I doubt not he comes from Africa." Discovering a new
repertory of scurrilities in England, Crane was freeing himself
from some American attitudes which he had at least partly
shared. Brought up to a sense of the homogeneity of small-town
middle-class America, he had made the usual association of
the Irish with the urban poor, with those who were somehow
outside the real America. In *Maggie* it is not entirely clear that
Rum Alley, the heroine's home ground, is, like Devil's Row, an
Irish enclave. Bowery speech and Irish slang are indistinguish-
able in the novel. But on such slight hints as one use of the
word "micks" and one boy named "Riley," plus the general
coarse characterization of Maggie's household for its screaming,

[42] Beer, *Crane*, p. 168.

fighting, and drunkenness, readers have commonly taken her to be Irish. Not that Crane intended any special animus: he shared the national habit of identifying by caste, so that Irishmen, Italians, Swedes moved into his consciousness and his fiction as group-men. They could of course be individualized if they underwent some special experience. The innkeeper of "The Blue Hotel," who brought a little color to Fort Romper, Nebraska, and some of the brave, stoical common soldiers of the Spanish-American War, singled out in Crane's reportage, had simple Irish names as well as distinguishable identities. On the other hand, Crane did not altogether outgrow the stereotypes of middle-class culture. In his two novels with conventional, sentimental plots, *The Third Violet* (1897) and *Active Service* (1899), he paired his demure heroines with dangerous rivals whose social unacceptability seemed to be founded in their vitality. He called them Florinda O'Connor and Nora Black, as if the hint of Irish caste and sexual taboo went naturally together. The author of these novels still had to learn once and for all that the Irish do not run naked through their native forests. That he succeeded in making the intuitive leap to that knowledge he owed in some degree to the instruction of Harold Frederic.

Frederic had been one of the first people Crane met when, in the spring of 1897, he passed through England on his way to the Greek-Turkish War. The New York *Times* correspondent in London had two years before sent home the report on the English reception of *The Red Badge* and thus helped assure its American success. If there was still a note of personal sponsorship in his hearty manner, his being fifteen years older than Crane and his obviously meaning well made it possible for the younger man to swallow quite a lot without being irritated. Also, Crane liked Frederic's novels of the Mohawk Valley with their feeling for upstate New York and for American manners. Although their common New York background was a link between the men, Frederic's Utica differed from Crane's Port Jervis in something more than measurable geography. Frederic, before he ever left home, had reacted to the Methodist, temperance, small-town culture to which he was brought up and, as if to prove that he had broken free, had fallen in love with the Irish of Utica. He carried that love with him when he crossed the

Atlantic and became a devotee of Ireland, Irish causes, and Irish leaders. Also—obviously not as a matter of policy—he took a mistress of American-Irish background.[43] When Crane and Cora Stewart returned from Greece and settled in England as man and wife, Frederic helped them find a house in suburban Surrey not far from where he and Kate Lyon had established their household. A carriage accident, which occurred one day as the Cranes were driving over to call on the Frederics, threw the two couples together, and when the newcomers were sufficiently recovered, they all took off on an Irish holiday that would prolong the good fellowship. To Crane the trip disclosed a new world.

What Crane learned, in September, 1897, was first of all that Irish names and places had a reality of their own. The Old Head of Kinsale and Glandore Harbor, where he placed the O'Ruddy clan, lay west of Cobh, though they were off the railway line and the road and he may not have laid eyes on them. Farther west were Skibbereen, Ballydehob on Roaring Water Bay, and farther out on the remote western promontory, the village of Schull where the merry couples stopped. Frederic's adoption of the local scene and the local historic name of O'Mahony for his fiction (Kate Lyon Frederic was an O'Mahony, and so a private joke was involved) stood as a precedent to which Crane would return.[44] At Schull the two men settled down to write regularly as well as to enjoy the tourist pleasures. Crane's newspaper sketches show how he gradually got past a tourist notion of quaintness and acquired a feeling for the people and their language and customs. One sketch focuses on a strapping young woman named Nora, who stands in glowing contrast to her desiccated old suitor. The old man calls on her in the tavern kitchen where she works, and he eventually drops off to sleep. Her words, as she taunts the old man for trying to rule her life, have the cadence and phrasing of a deeply lived local culture: "I

[43] Stanton Garner, "Some Notes on Harold Frederic in Ireland," *American Literature*, xxxix (1967–68), 60–74. Further details on Frederic and the Irish in his earlier years may be found in Thomas F. O'Donnell and Hoyt C. Franchere, *Harold Frederic* (New York, 1961), pp. 42–49.

[44] A precedent but not, in my view, a source, despite the argument of Lillian B. Gilkes in "Stephen Crane and the Harold Frederics," *The Serif*, vi (1969), 43–45. Crane's servant and villain are closer to the general types of picaresque and melodrama than to the particular instances of Frederic's novel.

moind the toime whin yez could attind to your own affairs, ye
ould skeleton." [45] How different from the grotesque vaudeville of
Maggie: "Eh, Gawd, child, what is it dis time? Is yer fader beatin'
yer mudder, or yer mudder beatin' yer fader?" [46] Once Crane
learned the authentic accent, he could dispense with the trans-
literated dialect which was the conventional realist's claim to
authenticity. Not even the clownish Paddy, in *The O'Ruddy*, goes
in for verbal buffoonery, for Crane had caught somehow the
essential cadence and idiom which could better represent Irish
speech.

Much as Crane owed to the good offices of Harold Frederic
and the acuteness of his own ear, he came to mastery of a new
idiom by working at it. The documentary evidence of such work
is a story which neither he nor Cora after him ever sold, "Dan
Emmonds." The story bears the same title as his novel-in-prog-
ress announced by *Book News* in 1896, but instead of being
about an Irish boy in New York City, as was reported of the unfinished novel, this tale concerns a boy who leaves New York
about as fast as the hero of *The O'Ruddy* leaves Ireland. [47] Dan
Emmonds is evidently a scamp, if not a rogue, and his saloon-
keeper father, fed up with his scrapes, buys him a passage to
Melbourne—he can better stand the cost of the journey than the
cost of having the boy at home. And so the son's adventures
begin. The comic conception is little more than a fantasy of
storm, shipwreck, and survival, in which safety lies in the hero's
clinging to a hen-coop and "the dead body of a pig named
Bartholomew, who had been a great favorite with the ship's
cook." When Dan Emmonds speaks, there is no funny spelling,
no odd pronunciation, but only a little lilt and a little orotundity:

[45] "An Old Man Goes Wooing," *Westminster Gazette,* Nov. 23, 1897, pp. 1–2;
for the Irish Sketches, see *Works,* Vol. VIII.

[46] *Works,* I, 15.

[47] George Monteiro makes a convincing case that the abortive 1896 novel
Dan Emmonds and the manuscript tale of that name are not at all the same.
He quotes *Book News,* XV (Oct., 1896), 49: "Mr. Stephen Crane sails for England this month for a brief stay, returning probably a short time before the
holidays. This will interrupt his work on his new novel *Dan Emmons,* and will
probably postpone its publication until spring. . . . A few chapters of *Dan
Emmons* have been written and they give promise of something quite unlike any
of Mr. Crane's former work. Dan is an Irish boy, and the story as far as written
deals with life in New York City" ("Stephen Crane's Dan Emmonds: A Case
Reargued," *The Serif,* VI [1969], 34).

"Presently the sun broke clear and mild from the clouds with a great air of innocence as if he had never been gone when the captain wanted him, and I saw a fair blue streak on the horizon which I knew to be land. . . . I first tried pushing the coop away from the pig, and then dragging the pig up and so on, but I soon tired of this mode of travelling, for the pig lay like a block of marble in the water, and I despaired of reaching the island in less than nine years." Instead of reaching the island, he is reached by islanders who come up in a fishing smack and pull him aboard. Their further intentions are unclear: they do not relish his eloquent greeting, but they look as if they may have a taste for him in another sense. The story breaks off with his words of farewell to the pig: " 'Good fortune be with you, Bartholomew,' said I, addressing the distance. 'You are better off than I am indeed, if I am going to be killed after taking this long troublesome voyage.' " [48] Thus did Crane reduce to burlesque the stylish absurdity by which, in "The Open Boat," he had given voice to the rage of shipwrecked man against the universe: "If I am going to be drowned—if I am going to be drowned—if I am going to be drowned, why, in the name of the seven mad gods who rule the sea, was I allowed to come thus far and contemplate sand and trees?" [49] Instead of rage, he now expressed the readiness of the spirited man to face the next episode without delusion and without cowering. On such a note it seemed appropriate to break off the narrative and make a short story of a tale that might have gone on from episode to episode at length. In fact, there is a fragment of first draft narrative among Crane's papers in which a narrator, held captive, is to be taught an unnamed native language before he may go free—his teacher, an old salt who seems to have washed up in an exotic society, caught on to the language and won high office there. [50] The fragment is inane,

[48] MS in Columbia University Libraries.

[49] *Works*, v, 77. Lillian B. Gilkes notices this echo, also, as she surveys the circumstantial and sometimes speculative evidence from subject matter as well as the stylistic evidence for arguing that Crane wrote the tale after 1896 and indeed after settling in England ("Stephen Crane's 'Dan Emmonds': A Pig in a Storm," *Studies in Short Fiction*, ɪɪ [1964], 66–71).

[50] The fragment, written in Crane's hand and covering almost two pages of lined foolscap, begins, "He told me all he knew of the people of the island and their ways." If it is from the same narrative as "Dan Emmonds," there is obviously a gap in the story between the earlier part and this *Typee–Gulliver's*

and its manifest weakness explains why Crane cut back to the short-story form, if that is what he did. The story was among the first pieces that Cora sent to Pinker while Crane was still in Havana, and so the one date that can be established concerning the story—December 7, 1898, when Pinker returned the manuscript after making a typewritten copy for use in the literary market [51]—places it appropriately halfway between "The Open Boat" and *The O'Ruddy.*

"Dan Emmonds," whatever its limitations as a story, was a rewarding experiment for Crane, for he was beginning to learn the picaresque attitude and to develop his insight into a new kind of character. Instead of the Irishman as buffoon, the Irishman as comic hero was coming to the fore of his imagination. In contrast to the correspondent in "The Open Boat," who *was* Crane though he existed in the third person, this comic hero exists fictionally in his own right, and the author must make believe if he wishes to identify with him. This is what happened as Crane, for the first time in his career, told his tale in the first person. The possibilities which this experiment disclosed were challenging: to win the freedom of the comic imagination would cost nothing less than learning a new language—in that sense the story of the shipwrecked captive was emblematic of its author's fate. Instead of the characteristic Crane interplay between the diction of educated prose and the various slangs he knew, between the grandly inflated and the realistically deflated, between the brilliant, color-soaked vision and the plain, flat observation, he was now committed to hold to a single point of view and a single tone of voice. In "Dan Emmonds" the controlling imagination is still recognizably Crane's own as the narrator denounces the sun's air of innocence or the nine years' journey that the slow miles seem to take. The jaunty chagrin at the waste of "this long troublesome voyage" indicates that the author's ear was as sharp for catching his own turns of phrase as in rendering the dialogue of others. When Crane returned to the first-person narrative in his Irish romance, he was able more

---

Travels continuation. The fragment, with its covering sheet of foolscap marked "Odd Ms" in Cora's hand and in a different hand, probably hers at a later date, "To be examined someday," was brought to my attention by Fredson Bowers (MS in Columbia University Libraries).

[51] ALS in Columbia University Libraries.

consistently to take on the voice of his character. The O'Ruddy's boisterous loquacity and its underlying Irish cadence contrast with the deliberate, laconic drawl for which Crane was known. Just as he was learning the bitter lesson that pressures of circumstance and limits of physical energy affected his work and his life, he reaffirmed in the energy of this imagined voice his artistic vitality.

Crane was thoroughly taken with the narrator-hero who characterized himself by his voice and language, who acted in all things with high spirits and healthy joy, and who went his way toward danger or the unknown with constant readiness. Although his own will for extravagant adventure now had its proper vent in the work of imagination, he let his character's mood affect his own. Shortly after he had begun *The O'Ruddy,* he acted on the spur of the moment and took Cora and their house guest Edith Richie on an Irish holiday. After a three-day pause for partying in London with the Frewens and others, they made it to Cork and then westward to refresh the impressions of the earlier trip. They visited Ballydehob, Skibbereen, Schull, Bantry, and Glengariff, talking with people at inns and on trains and on the road all along the way. Edith Richie's account suggests that the trip had a literary purpose—"he wanted some local color" [52]—but he had little need for local color since The O'Ruddy departs from his homeland in the very first incident of the narrative. What the trip confirmed for Crane was that he had the idiom he wanted, that he no longer needed a guide but, having broken through his own early set of mind, had won the imaginative freedom of another country. He possessed his subject, he had fully conceived his narrator-hero, and he needed little else. When he returned from Ireland, he finished his first two chapters and sent them to Pinker.[53] Then he felt obliged to put the project aside so that he could, as Cora observed, "return to short stuff which will bring in money at once." [54] He finished his *Whilomville Stories,* started the *Great Battles* series, and occupied

[52] Edith R. Jones, "Stephen Crane at Brede," *Atlantic,* cxciv (1954), 60.
[53] Cora Crane to Pinker, Brede, [Oct. 21, 1899], *Letters,* p. 235: "I mail today the first two chapters of the book Mr. Crane told you about." The date of this "Saturday" letter may be inferred from Pinker's acknowledgment of Oct. 24, cited in note 16 above.
[54] Cora Crane to Pinker, Brede, Dec. 7, 1899, *Letters,* p. 248.

himself with other projects, including a great Christmas holiday house party at Brede Place. When the party was over, Crane collapsed with tuberculosis. That grim first hemorrhage seemed to put an end to gaiety, and with the departure of the guests, creditors and tax collectors were the next expected arrivals. When, at this point, he resumed *The O'Ruddy*, he evidently had no detailed plan to guide him other than the four-chapter outline which he quickly decided not to follow. What he did have was the storyteller as hero, and he put his faith in him as he progressed from one episode to another. In the book that came of this effort, the storytelling is more interesting than the story. Although the book is minor Crane, it is nonetheless an affirmation of life.

Crane had sent the first two chapters on October 21. Cora's covering letter predicted that the book would be "a popular success & a *good play*"—she was well aware that a success in the theater would be even more lucrative than a success with the reading public.[55] A few days later, she instructed the agent to see whether Stokes would accept this work, which still bore only the working title "Romance," in place of the novel of the American Revolution. Crane's commitment was not yet irrevocable: if Stokes should prove unwilling to make the contractual change, he would change his own plans and do the Revolutionary novel first.[56] With so little manuscript on hand, Pinker did not prematurely press the question.[57] But Crane, having told his agent to make a copy and send it out, put the matter out of mind until, at the beginning of 1900, he took the project up again. Then he raised questions about what the agent had been doing. Was Stokes "dragging things out through the mail to make better terms"? To whom had serial rights been offered?[58] Was Pinker selling both British and American serial rights? Would he telegraph the moment such a big sale was made? And, of course,

[55] *Letters*, p. 236.

[56] Cora Crane to Pinker, Brede, [Oct. 26, 1899], *Letters*, p. 238.

[57] On Dec. 5, 1899, the New York office of Frederick A. Stokes Company, preparing publicity for the volume of war stories, wrote Crane for help and incidentally revealed that the letter writer at least had no idea of proposals concerning the Irish romance: "We shall be glad to have you add any information of interest regarding your new literary work in general" (TLS in Columbia University Libraries).

[58] Cora Crane to Pinker, [Brede, Jan. 2, 1900], *Letters*, pp. 256–257, and [Jan. 4, 1900], *Letters*, p. 257.

"can you get Methuen to make advance"? [59] One hundred pounds? Or, in a moment of faltering hopes—"Will you advise if you think it would be better for Mr. Crane to drop 'The Irish Romance' and do short stories in order to raise this money." [60] But the letters relaying Crane's questions and instructions, full as they were of agonized pleas for money, could not hasten the business process enough to bring real relief. It was mid-January before Pinker had Methuen thinking over the proposition that he "make the advance as we deliver the MS." [61] He made first delivery to Methuen a week later but still had not concluded matters with Stokes. Stokes sent his first bank draft of £70 only on February 13.[62] As for the possible sale of serial rights, it was late January before Pinker was ready, after the Methuen negotiation was worked out, to ask for copy that he might show to prospective buyers. It then took more than two weeks before copy could be made at Brede (saving the expense of a London typist) and sent up to the agent.[63] But neither the Cranes' urgency nor Pinker's efforts could produce a buyer at this time.

[59] Cora Crane to Pinker, [Brede, Jan. 6, 1900], *Letters*, p. 258.

[60] Cora Crane to Pinker, [Brede, Jan. 9, 1900], *Letters*, p. 262. Even in the moment of faltering, she renewed her plea that Pinker get a £100 advance from Methuen.

[61] Pinker to Crane, London, Jan. 15, 1900, ALS in Columbia University Libraries. Except for the first delivery of manuscript on Jan. 22, there is no further mention of this negotiation, which Pinker presumably concluded as he hoped.

[62] As arranged the previous October, Stokes sent the money to Pinker rather than to Crane. The agreement to do so was obviously newly concluded. Stokes wrote Pinker: "In accordance with instructions received by cable from Mr. Dominick, we take pleasure in sending you herewith draft of Brown Bros. & Co. to your order for £70. This payment is, we understand, in advance and on account of royalty for the new, historical romance by Stephen Crane, which is to take the place of the novel of the American Revolution that he was to write for us, the latter being postponed by him. We understand that a part of the copy proportionate to the payment we are now making, is on the way to us. We will say nothing more as to other details of the matter until we hear from Mr. Dominick. We are not quite certain as to these" (TLS in Dartmouth College Library).

On Feb. 27, 1900, Pinker confirmed the arrangement in a letter to Cora Crane: "The terms of the contract with Stokes & Methuen are the terms which had been arranged for the other novel; that is to say, in Stokes' case the Irish romance takes the place of the Revolutionary novel, and in Methuen's case it takes the place of the novel the character of which was not specified" (TLS in Columbia University Libraries).

[63] Pinker to Crane, London, Jan. 22, 1900: "It would be as well to let me have the third copy, as Mrs. Crane suggests, so that I may see if we can get a serial opening for it" (TLS in Columbia University Libraries). On Feb. 8, he acknowledged receipt of the typescript in three copies of the entire novel manuscript to date. See below, p. xliv.

What made the money come in, finally, was nothing less than the actual work in progress—promises would not do. The frequent correspondence of the Cranes and Pinker, so much of which is preserved, documents the progress fairly closely, but the record of the author's promises and the agent's acknowledgment of copy received is sometimes puzzling. There is no doubt, for example, that in the first week of January, 1900, Crane took up the novel which he had set aside after writing two chapters and that he hoped to send off "two or three more chapters of the book by the end of the week." [64] Financial hysteria seems to explain the wishful slip Crane made a week later, when he had not yet sent the third chapter: "My dear Pinker: My wife's account in the bank is some pounds overdrawn already if the note for £31 had been presented. Plant is kicking for £10 and Her Majesty calls tomorrow for my income tax. Please send £20 to Brown Shipley. I am trying to get off the Chapter xii simultaneous with this interesting note." [65] Pinker finally received chapters iii and iv on January 15, and since he was then negotiating with Methuen, he added to his acknowledgment the news that Crane would do well to let him have "as much of the MS. as quickly as you can." [66] Crane must have obliged promptly with chapter v, for Pinker on January 22 was acknowledging chapters vi and vii.[67] On February 6 he acknowledged "the 11th Chapter of the Romance" and incidentally inquired as to whether the book yet had a title. On February 8 he created another puzzle by writing: "I have received Chapter x of the Romance, and also the three typewritten copies of the 26,610 words." [68] In this case the anomaly is apparently due to the typing arrangements, mentioned above: the word-count indicates that he now had typescript for the first ten chapters in enough copies to serve his several purposes; if Pinker meant to acknowledge more than that, it is easy to understand why chapter x should have been on his mind.

[64] Cora Crane to Pinker, [Brede, Jan. 2, 1900], *Letters*, p. 257.
[65] Crane to Pinker, Brede, Jan. 9, [1900], ALS in University of Virginia Library.
[66] Pinker to Crane, London, Jan. 15, 1900, ALS in Columbia University Libraries.
[67] TLS in Columbia University Libraries.
[68] TLS and ALS, respectively, in Columbia University Libraries.

The Cranes, in their haste and panic, often sent letters undated except for the day of the week, and so the schedule of
composition becomes obscure. Thus a "Tuesday" letter of Cora's
mentions sending four copies of the "Romance" typescript to
date, and since she also mentioned a total of 36,800 words, it is
clear that her "Chapter XLV" enclosed was in fact a reference to
chapter XIV. That was probably on February 20.[69] So, too, a
"Thursday" letter from Crane, probably March 8, let Pinker know
that chapter XIX was finished and waiting to be typed.[70] On the
following "Saturday" he sent the typewritten chapter, and he
hoped that chapter XX might be done in time to reach Pinker "at
the same time," even though he had not yet completed it.[71]
Pinker came through with the £100 Crane asked for, making
deposits on March 13 and 14, and so the next Crane "Sunday"
letter, thanking him and sending along chapter XXII, was written
March 18.[72] On March 24 [Crane's own dating!], while asking

[69] *Letters*, p. 241, where the conjectural dating of Nov. 7, 1899, is offered.
Aside from word-count and its relation to Crane's rate of work on *The O'Ruddy*,
the letter provides other evidence for the date of Feb. 20, 1900. In particular,
the last sentence reads: "We hope to hear that Lippincotts cheque and one
from Stokes will come soon." Stokes' first check for *The O'Ruddy* was mailed to
Pinker from New York on Feb. 13. Even if it got to the agent in exactly a
week, Cora would not yet have heard about it on the twentieth; on the other
hand, two weeks would seem rather long. The reference to Lippincott picks
up from Pinker's letter of Feb. 13, which reported that Stokes had no objection
to letting Lippincott bring out *Great Battles* in book form and asked what
terms Crane suggested for the forthcoming negotiation (TLS in Columbia University Libraries). On Feb. 14, Cora promptly responded for Crane that he
hoped to get £100 from them for the American book rights, paid at once
(*Letters*, p. 265).

[70] *Letters*, p. 264, where a conjectural date of Feb. 8 (the day Pinker acknowledged receipt of "Chapter X") is offered. Aside from Crane's progress to
chapter XIX of *The O'Ruddy*, his progress with the Great Battles series for
Lippincott's Magazine and Lippincott's provisional acceptance of Crane's price
of £100 for book rights help to establish the later date. A Great Battles article
like "Vittoria," enclosed with this letter, drew immediate payment from the
magazine's London office and so had economic priority with Crane over installments of *The O'Ruddy*, for which both Methuen and Stokes were careful not
to pay too quickly or too much. Requesting an advance from the agent himself in order to stave off an anticipated crisis on March 12, Crane promised
to have the typescript of chapter XIX in the agent's hands by that date. Moreover, if on Thursday Crane asked for a wire on Friday about funds deposited,
this must have been the Thursday before the crisis.

[71] *Letters*, p. 265, where a conjectural date of Feb. 10 is offered. Aside from
the reported progress with *The O'Ruddy*, references to the Great Battles series
and the Lippincott negotiation help to establish the later date.

[72] ALS in Dartmouth College Library. Brown, Shipley & Co. statement, account of Mrs. Cora Crane, records deposits of £50 by cash from J. B. Pinker on

for more money, Crane reported: "The XXIV Chapter of the novel is finished but not yet typed." [73] And finally, in a letter without date or day, evidently sent on March 31, Crane sent manuscript of chapters XXIV and XXV to Pinker; Cora had left for Paris where she was to meet his niece coming home from boarding school, and so the typing could not be done at Brede. In the same letter, Crane estimated that the novel was more than three-quarters complete and would "run very little beyond the 80000 words"—referring evidently to the contractual stipulation which stood between him and the last, biggest installment of his advance.[74] The next letters to Pinker were from Cora. On "Friday night" (April 6), she began: "Mr. Crane is ill. I have had a Specialist down from London & *had to give him a cheque for £50.* He was so encouraging that I am glad." The next day, "Saturday," she repeated that the doctor had given a favorable report but later became more businesslike: "Let me know if Serial is sold. If Mr. Crane should die I have notes of end of novel so it could be finished & no one will lose—if that thought should occur." [75]

The lung hemorrhages which Crane suffered at the beginning of April, 1900, began the fatal last stage of his tuberculosis. He wrote scarcely another word, but the encouragement which Cora attributed to the doctors was something which she and he pretended to believe in. Cora's letters to Pinker asked for proofs of forthcoming work, and twice she asked for the two chapters

---

March 13 and 14, 1900 (MS in Columbia University Libraries).

Coming before this March 18 letter is another undated letter from Cora Crane to Pinker: "I enclose Chapter XXI of Romance. Chapter XXII is written but not all typed" (*Letters*, p. 247, where a conjectural date of mid-November, 1899, is offered; it must in fact have been written between March 10 and March 18, 1900).

[73] *Letters*, p. 266. The same old calculations interfered with single-minded labor even when the novel progressed at a good pace. This letter includes requests to Pinker for £22, £20, and £100, spaced out by comments on his work: "The novel stands at 61000 but I am extremely doubtful about my prudence in writing it at this time. . . . I expect the 'Romance' to pull me out much more than even. I only question the wisdom of my abandoning my lucrative short story game for this long thing which doesn't pay (much) until the end."

[74] *Letters*, p. 267. Cora Crane to Pinker, [Brede, *c.* April 15, 1900], *Letters*, p. 272, provides evidence for the conjectural date.

[75] *Letters*, pp. 267, 268.

Crane had sent up for typing while she was away. Mainly she repeated her ever larger and more urgent requests for money and her anxious inquiries as to whether serial rights for *The O'Ruddy* were sold. When Pinker could not provide money, she wrote to publishers over his head.[76] But while the financial hysteria mounted, Crane did not get better. It was about two weeks before he could be brought down to sit in the April sun. At one moment he felt improved enough to start spinning plans for a trip to St. Helena—a journalistic venture to interview Boer prisoners, which some newspaper publisher would no doubt underwrite, and at the same time the kind of saving sea voyage that he needed for his health. But the lungs seemed less bad now than an agonizingly painful abscess in the bowels, and with the general debility the chills and fever of his malaria, contracted in the Spanish-American War, came back. The last desperate resort was a trip to a sanitarium in the Black Forest in May, by stretcher to Rye, by special train-carriage to Dover, then at least a week's pause to gather strength for the Channel crossing, and after that another invalid carriage for the train journey

[76] Cora's letters of [*c.* Apr. 15] and [Apr. 24, 1900], *Letters*, pp. 272, 277, call for the return of chapters xxiv and xxv, which Crane had sent to Pinker for typing while Cora was in Paris.

The first of these letters conveyed Cora's recurrent plea to Pinker: "I hope you will see your way to selling the serial rights so that no money worries need retard Mr. Crane's recovery. Please let me hear from you." In a letter of more probable dating, conjecturally April 16, she resumed the theme: "Have you gotten Tillotson's Romance rights yet? Mr. Crane says if they don't answer this week to take it away from them and try some one else. 'The New Magazine' of New York" (*Letters*, p. 273). Another "Monday" letter, presumably April 23, thanks Pinker for his letter of April 20 and goes on: "Please do your best to hurry up the sale of the Serial rights of Romance. Mr. Crane wants to know to whom you have shown it in English and who has it now" (*Letters*, p. 276). On May 2 Pinker reported: "Tillotsons declined the serial on the terms I suggested, but I hope they will make an alternative offer. In the mean time, however, I am trying *The New Magazine* so as not to lose time" (TLS in Columbia University Libraries).

Letters conjecturally dated April 7 and April 11 announced to Pinker and excused to him Cora's writing to Lippincott for money (*Letters*, pp. 268, 270). A letter from Methuen, dated April 11, advised Cora that the firm was "exceedingly sorry to hear of Mr. Crane's indisposition but we regret we are unable to make any further advance on account of the book he is writing for us. Perhaps as the negotiations were carried on through Mr. Pinker it might be worth your while to write to him on the subject" (TLS in Columbia University Libraries). Finally, Cora wrote on May 16 to Paul Reynolds in New York, too; see p. lx below.

to Badenweiler. The expense would be enormous, but the Frewens undertook to raise the money.[77] The first stage of the
journey, taking them as far as Dover, was accomplished on
May 15.

In the hotel at Dover, trying to recover his energy and waiting for a day when the Channel would be calm enough for an
easy crossing, Crane turned his mind to last things. Though
he took the manuscript of *The O'Ruddy* with him, he was ready
at last to recognize that he would not complete it himself. As his
friends called to say good-by to him, the question of who would
complete it was in his mind. He hoped that perhaps Kipling
would do it, and Moreton Frewen volunteered to raise the question with his old friend.[78] More seriously, Cora tried to get Robert
Barr to do it. On the first try, Barr's refusal was prompt and clear,
but in declining, he suggested the name of Edward Stewart
White, whom he proposed to bring with him to Dover.[79] But
when he reached Crane's hotel without having brought a substitute, he had no defense for the insistent plea. He humored
the dying man and hung upon his words. Later he described the
scene to Karl Harriman, a young American writer who was close
to the Cranes: "Even your vivid imagination could hardly conjecture anything more ghastly than the dying man, lying by an
open window overlooking the English channel, relating in a
sepulchral whisper the comic situations of his humorous hero

[77] Joseph Conrad wrote Galsworthy: "The Frewens (owners of Brede) pay
all his transit to the Black Forest,—rather more than £100" ([Stanford, near
Hythe, May 7, 1900], in G. Jean-Aubry, *Joseph Conrad: Life and Letters* [New
York, 1927], I, 294). This overestimated the Frewens' resources. Frewen did,
however, make an appeal to J. P. Morgan (*Letters*, p. 280 n.), and Clara
Frewen seems to have done her part among the Society of American Women
in London. A New York *World* story dated May 26, 1900, reported: "Owing to
continued bad health, Stephen Crane's resources have been exhausted, and
Mrs. Frewen got together a substantial sum, chiefly among Americans to give
him a chance of recovery by rest in a genial climate." The same story of a
Crane subscription fund appeared in another, unidentified paper on June 2
(clippings in Stephen Crane Scrapbook, II, 28, 42, University of Virginia Library). Frewen did send £25 of his own to Badenweiler. Contributions of £50
came from Andrew Carnegie, solicited by Walter Goode of the Associated Press,
and from Henry James, prompted by affection and solicitude for his young
friend (Stallman, *Crane*, pp. 509, 514, and note 88 below).
[78] Stallman, *Crane*, p. 512; Andrews, *Splendid Pauper*, p. 195.
[79] Barr to Cora Crane, [Woldingham], May 17, 1900, ALS in Columbia University Libraries.

so that I might take up the thread of his story." [80] The Cranes grasped an illusory hope for the novel at the same time that they came to accept the hopelessness for life. Cora wrote to Pinker:

Dear Mr. Pinker:

Mr. Crane wants this dedication put in "The O'Ruddy" book. He wants it dated from Brede Place.

I've wired you to telegraph price offered for serial. Mr. Crane wants Robert Barr to finish it & perhaps Mr. Kipling may edit (don't mention this yet). You should get big serial price. Hastily yours

Cora Crane

Then after a short postscript she put the proposed dedication:

May—1900

Brede Place

Sussex

England

To

My Wife

Stephen Crane [81]

Crane was not to have this wish; when the novel was finally published, it bore no dedication. The other hopes were equally beyond the mark. Kipling declined to mix in another man's work. [82] Worse than that, Barr had second thoughts. Less than a week after Crane's death, he wrote Harriman: "Stephen thought I was the only person who could finish it, and he was too ill for me to refuse. I don't know what to do about the matter, for I never could work up another man's ideas." [83] In one important respect, however, the instructions to Pinker were carried out.

[80] Stallman, *Crane*, p. 512; the passage is quoted without date or other citation, and it may perhaps be from the letter from Barr to Karl Harriman, Woldingham, June 8, 1900, printed with ellipses in *Letters*, pp. 286–287. The incident may be approximately dated by Cora's letter to Pinker of May 23 from Dover: "Mr. Robert Barr will call to see you and will explain our wishes about Romance" (*Letters*, p. 285).

[81] *Letters*, p. 285.

[82] " 'My own opinion is & I hold it very strongly that a man's work is personal to him, & should remain as he made it or left it. I should have been glad to have done him a kindness, but this is not a thing that a man feeling as I do, can undertake' " (quoted in Moreton Frewen to Cora Crane, London, June 16, 1900, TLS in Columbia University Libraries).

[83] Woldingham, June 8, 1900, *Letters*, p. 287.

In Cora's letter relaying his wishes, Crane for the first time gave his hero's name to the book and entitled it *The O'Ruddy.*

After a few more days at Dover, Cora was able to move her invalid. Accompanied by her niece Helen Crane and by the two nurses who attended the stretcher-patient, she reached Baden-weiler on May 27 or 28. The usual panic at being out of money with the bills mounting faster and faster was still the ground bass of her emotions, but now she began to be aware that she had traveled so far for nothing. She did not know that Crane had scarcely a week to live, but it was impossible not to see that he was dying here, among strangers and expensive consultants, painfully. Her first reaction was the familiar frenzy, and on May 29 she wrote Pinker as she returned some proofs, pressing him to sell the serial rights of the unfinished novel and to see that Barr had a typescript to work from. Her staccato incoherence expressed her frame of mind:

I enclose proof—Please let me know what has been done about serial rights? Who is your man in U.S.? Why don't you put it in Mr. Reynolds hands to sell? Have you seen Robert Barr? Now this is a matter that must be attended to. *I* can sell the American serial rights myself and I simply must have money for Mr. Crane. Please send a typed copy of the ms—to Robert Barr at once. He will explain & please let me hear from you *what* is being done. I'm sure Mr. Reynolds could sell the Wyoming stories in U.S. Do try him with them.[84]

The next day, May 30, Crane evidently rallied enough to take thought once more of his unfinished novel and to try resuming where he had left off almost two months before. He had barely sketched a single scene when he stopped, and Cora then had simply to wait. There is no record of the next day. On June 1 Cora, the daughter of an artist who had inherited a gift for drawing, made a sketch after her own fashion. What she saw at Badenweiler was a dark house, dark woods, dark hills, and over all an oppressively dark sky, with no rift anywhere in the gloom.[85]

[84] *Letters*, pp. 285–286.

[85] Helen Crane Sketch Book, Columbia University Libraries. Lillian B. Gilkes first identified the hallmark on a 1901 drawing of The Keep, Arundel Castle, as being the same as Cora's initials on some of her correspondence of this same period ("Stephen Crane and the Harold Frederics," *The Serif*, VI [1969], 39–40). The initials "C. C." are so connected as to be readable as "C.H.C.," that is, Cora Howorth Crane. The fifth sketch in the book, "Chapel End Brede

Yet another day passed, and then Crane tried again to dictate.

The notes of these two final efforts at dictation provide the clues, imperfectly reliable, of what he had in mind for the rest of the book. He had nothing to say of general plans for bringing the story to its close. He had never proceeded with analytic plans, and just as he had always gone on from scene to scene, he tried to pick up from where he had left off. He turned out fragments of scenario that indicate a thread of continuity and a readiness for slapdash melodramatic conclusions—a chase all the way from London to Brede Place, which he thought of as the villain Forrister's home. But as the notes modulate from narrative in the first person to the third person and then back again, there is a question how far the fictional persona is controlled and whether at times Crane does not naïvely identify himself with the hero. The question becomes more urgent with the second effort of June 3, for on the evening of that day Cora wrote to Frewen:

Stephen is not quite clear in his mind tonight.

I've only sad news to write you. There seems little hope of cure. The fever seems the thing that cannot be conquered. . . .

My husband's brain is never at rest. He lives over everything in dreams and talks aloud constantly. It is too awful to hear him try to change places in the "Open Boat."[86]

The mixing of imagination and reality had begun that same day while Crane struggled to set down how *The O'Ruddy* was to end. Once he got the melodramatic chase from London to Brede Place, it might have been surmised that he was safely home and had only to cap his effort with a happy ending. The O'Ruddy has already encountered Forrister triumphantly in the exhilarating moment when he kicked him downstairs and in the equally exhilarating contest of fine swordsman with fine swordsman. When the hero confronts the villain at Brede, a third such excit-

---

Place April 1900," and the seventh, "Badenweiler June 1 1900," are the only ones in the Sketch Book to bear this signature. A water color entitled "Ireland" and a sketch of Harold Frederic may also be by Cora; at any rate, Helen Crane came to Stephen and Cora in England only after the Irish trips and long after Frederic had died. There is in the Sketch Book a tipped-in drawing of a cat's head with the initials "H. C.", very squarely lettered. The Badenweiler sketch, with darkness overshadowing darkness, would be hard to identify stylistically because of its subject, but the signature leaves no doubt.

[86] Stallman, *Crane*, p. 515.

ing scene might have ensued. But Forrister confuses matters by denying that he has the missing papers, and the energy of the pursuers is arrested. Their bafflement is just suggested; the complications which smother purpose seem trivial, irritating, quite out of scale with what the mind was set for. Then there is a one-sentence synopsis of the denouement, in which things do not come out all right in the end. And a final sentence which Cora, taking the dictation, evidently took to be the character's words but must have realized, as she broke off, that they were the author's: "This is too frivolous. You must know that after he has killed me Strep will [not *deleted*] kill him. This is no nice thing"—.[87] The crossing out of that final "not" could hardly matter. After those last recorded words—"This is no nice thing"—Crane suffered about a day and a half more and died at last in the early hours of June 5, 1900.

Henry James, who had been able to conceive the case of Stephen Crane before Crane lived it, had ended his story of the writer cut off and the fragment unfinished with the proper cool note of irony. No one discerned the differences of art and life more acutely than he. On the day of Crane's death, as it happened, James wrote solicitously to Cora: "I feel that I am not taking too much for granted in believing that you may be in the midst of worrying on the money-score which will perhaps make the cheque, for Fifty Pounds, that I enclose, a convenience to you. Please view it as such & dedicate it to whatever service it may best render my stricken young friend. It merely represents my tender benediction to him." And when he got the news, he wrote again as soon as he could: "Yet I feel I can say nothing to you that you haven't been saying again & again to yourself. What a brutal, needless extinction—what an unmitigated, unredeemed catastrophe! I think of him with such a sense of possibilities & powers! Not that one would have drawn out longer these last cruel weeks—! But you have need of all your courage. I doubt not it will be all at your service." [88] So it was as she and her niece brought Crane's body back to England and then to his native New Jersey for burial. While she was receiving sympathy

---

[87] The complete text of Crane's Badenweiler dictation will be found in the Appendixes, pp. 360–362.

[88] Rye, June 5 and June 7, 1900, ALS in Columbia University Libraries.

from their English friends and then from Crane's family, whom she met for the first time, she had to turn her mind also to practical affairs. Among the most urgent was the business concerning *The O'Ruddy*.

Robert Barr had evidently been quite sincere when, in May, he had declined to take up the chance of finishing the novel. "Stephen has genius and style," he had written; "I, unfortunately, have neither, and am merely a commonplace plugger. The contrast in the work would be too horrible, and I should be hopelessly handicapped with the knowledge of my own deficiencies." [89] After the promise extracted from him at Dover, however, he did make an effort to see Pinker, pick up a typed copy of the twenty-five chapters, and study the work.[90] While Cora was back in England en route to the United States, he gave her back the original manuscript which he had taken at Dover. Meanwhile, however, Moreton Frewen had heard from Kipling and just on the eve of Cora's departure sent her word of his refusal. Cora made the mistake of letting Barr have both Frewen's letter and her own notes on the ending of the story. She thus gave him two grounds for rethinking his own commitment. On July 4, he wrote her:

I think Kipling is quite right in saying that no man should touch another man's work. I have read the story over from beginning to end once more, and have also gone over two or three times the sketch you gave me of the completion, but the latter is so vague and incomplete itself, that it gives little guidance for another to go upon.

I think you are the only person in the world who can finish the story, and thus I come back to my first idea that I telegraphed Stephen. You know better than any one else can what he had in his mind regarding the conclusion, and when the story goes forth as by Stephen Crane and Mrs. Crane, people will take that collaboration as the right and proper thing, while they will be certain to resent the intrusion of any other. . . .

I shall leave the typewritten Ms in Pinker's hands, in case any

[89] Barr to Cora Crane, [Woldingham], May 17, 1900, TLS in Columbia University Libraries.

[90] Barr to Cora Crane, Woldingham, June 3, 1900, tells of the effort to find Pinker over the Whitsun Holidays (TLS in Columbia University Libraries). On June 13 he reported that he would bring in the original manuscript to Cora, having evidently received typescript from Pinker (ALS in Columbia University Libraries).

purchaser should want to read it; so that it can be available if needed.[91]

Barr's letter missed Cora Crane at Port Jervis, and before it caught up with her in England, the rest of July had passed. Such complication and confusion were to dominate the posthumous history of *The O'Ruddy*. The most important thing was to find someone to finish the story. After Barr, others were tried who held out hope for a while and then backed out. Two and a half years went by before the task came back and settled on Barr himself, and after he finished the novel, there were to be further delays and an unhappy renegotiation of the agreement. But in 1900, the illusion that the book would soon and easily be finished encouraged Cora Crane and assorted executors and agents to try to cash in at once on serial rights in both Britain and America and on dramatic rights as well. All these efforts came to nothing, principally because no one would take an unfinished fragment. And no one could easily finish the fragment because it was not clear where Crane intended the story to go. The notes that Cora had claimed to have in April were to have told how the story ended, but only the scenario notes that he dictated on his deathbed seem to have survived. When Robert Barr came to Dover to bid Stephen farewell, he could not refuse the task of finishing the work because Stephen was too ill for that. Crane was evidently too sick, also, for Barr to press for detailed instructions. The dying man's whispered narration—"so that I might take up the thread of the story"—evidently covered what was written but stopped short of the denouement. Had Crane told Barr how he wanted the story to end, Barr would at this juncture almost certainly have shared his knowledge with Cora. Though he wished to get out of his promise, he also offered the well-meant suggestion that she finish the book herself. Yet he consulted her notes, not she his. The ending would clearly depend a good deal on whoever took up the thread of the first twenty-five chapters.

The popular novelist H. B. Marriott-Watson was Barr's first successor in the undertaking. It is a wonder he was not put off at once by the confusing of literary tasks with business compli-

---

[91] Woldingham, July 4, 1900, TLS in Columbia University Libraries.

cations: on Monday, August 13, the day he received a copy of
the unfinished novel from Cora, he got a second letter from her
asking the novel back at once. He worked late that night, getting
through more than half the manuscript, and mailed it back in
the morning. On Friday he reported that though he liked the
"agility and ingenuity" of the tale and found it "an admirable
example of the picaresque novel," he did not see himself as
adequate to finishing it. "I would have suggested Mr Barr," he
wrote. "I shall look forward to finishing my reading of the book,
as ended by someone not so hopelessly bound to his own conventions as myself." Shortly after writing thus, he got the
manuscript again, read the rest of it, and the next day reported
himself confirmed "in my belief in my unsuitability." [92] Marriott-
Watson made up his mind in less than a week. The next week,
the novel went to A. E. W. Mason, who was to hold it the better
part of two years and yet do nothing.

Mason, on August 24, 1900, acknowledged receiving the
manuscript and suggested all too fully the difficulties that were
to follow. He began by querulously noting that since Barr had
been announced for the job he had held back from volunteering
at first: "I could have done it right away then." Now he offered
November as his earliest starting time. But the real problem lay
with the kind of work involved: "I suppose you have some idea
as to how it was to end." In September he touched on the subject
again: "Stephen's notes I will certainly require." The request
became more urgent the next time: "Of course as I told you I
have work to get through before I can start upon the O'Ruddy.
But I should like very much to have Stephen's notes; as I am
very anxious to know what those papers were meant to refer
to or how far he had planned out the rest." [93] The months went
by, word leaked out (perhaps with Cora's collusion), and the
press announced that "Mr Mason is at work" on the Crane
novel. It was enough to disturb Mason's late winter travels. He

[92] Marriott-Watson to Cora Crane, Chiswick, Aug. 13, 17, 18, 1900, ALS in
Columbia University Libraries. The Aug. 13 letter, acknowledging receipt of the
tale and a letter, adds the postscript, "I have just received your letter today, &
will send back the tale in the morning." Cora had recalled the manuscript to
take it to David Belasco's London agent, from whom she hoped to get a
contract for dramatic rights; see pp. lvii–lx below.

[93] Mason to Cora Crane, Marlow, Aug. 24, Yarmouth, Sept. 26, and London,
Oct. 7 [?], 1900, ALS in Columbia University Libraries.

wrote to tell Cora of his irritation and, in doing so, made it clear that beneath his irritation was a more serious problem:

My wish was to do what I possibly could for Stephen Crane's memory, which is more important than whether a few newspaper paragraphs preceded or not the publication of the O'Ruddy. And as I do not profess to be other than a slow worker in my own case, I did not purpose to be anything else in Stephen's. The fact that the publishers press for copy is not the important thing. The important thing is that the book should be done as well as possible (even if the publishers have to wait—) or rather I should say as well as it is possible for me to do it. It is the same with Mr Belasco. Mr Belasco says "hurry". But supposing that the book CAN'T be done in a hurry, what then? I could finish it in a week if I chose, to suit Mr Belasco, and the result would be that Mr Belasco would not dramatize it because there would not be a play in it to bring out. I really do not think that you quite realize what a difficult task it is although from Mr Barr's not in the end undertaking it, I should think it easy to realize. In The O'Ruddy up to the present the crux is not reached. It works through a series of incidents up toward something but what that something was going to be, Mr. Crane has not said. You will know as well as I do that up till the present point in the book, we are in the dark We have got to guess & make A NEW STORY of which we have barely a hint.[94]

At the time Cora left England in April, 1901, he was still promising the finished novel "very soon now" even though he had apparently nothing to show for his effort.[95]

The snatching back of the manuscript from Marriott-Watson no sooner than he had received it and Mason's protest against being hurried both resulted from the same complication, namely, David Belasco's interest in mounting a theatrical version of The O'Ruddy. Dramatic rights, especially if taken up by so successful a producer, might have been worth a small fortune. Certainly the Cranes had thought from the beginning that when The O'Ruddy provided a solution to all their financial problems, one major source of income would be from the

[94] Cairo, March 29, 1901, ALS in Columbia University Libraries. Mason stuck to his guns about the difficulty involved. He wrote to Vincent Starrett from London, Oct. 4, 1945: "Stephen had left nothing whatever to guide you as to how the story was going to run. I think he was letting it go its own way" (Letters, p. 344).

[95] London, April 30, 1901, ALS in Columbia University Libraries.

theater. The idea was illusory, but since clinging to illusions was becoming a necessity of life, Cora yielded very slowly to the truth about her unhappy widowed state. After Crane's funeral, while she was visiting the William Crane family in Port Jervis, she broached the question of a dramatization with Paul Revere Reynolds. His reply of July 3, 1900, told her the simple truth: "I should not think that the new romance which you mention could be dramatized until it had been brought out as a book and had a success as a book. The rage now seems to be to take a book that has made a name for itself and then turn it into a play, the advantage being that all the preliminaries of advertising, as it were, have already been done for the play." [96]

But when she returned to England, Reynolds' discouraging advice seemed all wrong. She got a letter from the great Belasco that said everything she could wish, and only his comical misspelling "The O'Buddy" might have hinted that the prospect was too good to be true. That, or his haste; for writing on Thursday, July 26, he announced that he would be leaving on Sunday:

My dear Mrs Crane,

About a week ago I sent a letter to your Port Jervis address, but on receiving word to-day that you sailed from America on the 19th, I see at once that my communication is destined not to reach you. Allow me to send this second letter to the address you give for England, and to say that I am most anxious to see you and to take up with you the matter of "The O'Buddy". Will you kindly wire me at once on receipt of this letter, saying when I can have the pleasure of meeting you at the Garrick Theatre, on either Thursday or Friday of the present week? I am leaving for the Continent the first of next week, and in case you do not find me at the Garrick, my address will be c/o Brown, Shipley & Co, 123, Pall Mall, S.W. At all events, I hope to hear from you soon.

On Saturday, July 28, he wrote again:

Dear Mrs Crane,

To my great disappointment I missed you to-day by about five minutes. To-morrow I am leaving for Berlin, and fear I shall not be back in London for another two or three weeks. However, I can say very definitely in advance that I will undertake the dramatiza-

---

[96] TLS in Columbia University Libraries.

tion of your brilliant young husband's new story "The O'Buddy", as well as his former book, "The Red Badge of Courage". May I hear from you again soon? By the time this shall reach you, my address for the few days will be Hotel Jungfrau, Eggishorn, Switzerland. . . .

With my very best wishes, and cherishing the hope that you may find our union of interests to be of material benefit to yourself.[97]

Cora Crane's hopes, which can be inferred easily enough from Belasco's notes, account for the rapid movement of manuscript copies from hand to hand. She received Belasco's July 26 letter while she was at Brede Place, collecting the things she wanted to keep with her and arranging for the rest of her furniture to go into storage. She wrote urgently to Pinker from Brede, asking that he send a typed copy of *The O'Ruddy* to her new London flat—"Don't fail as I am seeing someone about its' being dramatized." But Pinker did not send one in time for her to take it to Belasco before his departure across the Channel. Nor did Pinker respond to her second request, from 47 Gower Street, to send a copy "*at once*," even though she made it clear that she had "only a few days to arrange the matter which may mean so much to me." Yet a third letter, announcing her intention to call at his office and insisting on a copy "by Monday, if we have to take it away from someone," finally had the effect of calling in the Marriott-Watson copy.[98] There was good reason for her importunity. Belasco had written from Lausanne on August 6 that he was "enthused" over "the 'O'Buddy,' " that he thought of announcing the arrangement to dramatize it soon in order to help book sales along, and that he was "most desirous to see the mss. of the 'O'Buddys' as soon as possible." Moreover, a half-question in one of Cora's notes to Pinker—"I hope story will be finished by Oct 1st"—helps explain Belasco's confidence that he would soon be co-ordinating his publicity with sales of the finished book. On August 9, the producer wrote again from Lausanne and the bubble expanded still more:

My dear Mrs. Crane:—

Your letter is just received, and I am glad you can so soon send me the manuscript. I am anxious to get at work at once on "The

[97] London, July 26, July 28, 1900, TLS in Columbia University Libraries.
[98] Cora Crane to Pinker, three undated letters, ALS in Dartmouth College Library.

O'Ruddy" [*sic!*], for I think I see where it can be placed for almost immediate production, as soon as it can be finished.

Would you go, at once, to the office of my London agent, Miss Marbury, 36 St. Martin's Lane, and see Miss Woolridge about the final arrangements? I have instructed her to give you the same contract I have with Egerton Castle for his "Bath Comedy."

Or would you prefer meeting me in Paris on the 16th or 17th of this month, at my expense, and fix matters there? Either way would suit me; only, I should like to see the matter settled before I sail for New York, which will be on the American Line, Aug. 18, from Cherbourg.[99]

This must have marked the moment of greatest hope, and even though no one in Elisabeth Marbury's London office would contract for an unfinished manuscript, evidently everyone was still co-operative. By September 5, Belasco wrote Cora from New York that he had received the manuscript, read the first chapter, and felt greater enthusiasm than ever: "As soon as I have progressed sufficiently in the work of making a play out of the book, I shall send you some further word." But there was no book out of which a play could be made. The following February, Belasco said at last what Reynolds had predicted he must:

My dear Mrs. Crane:—
I wrote you a long, important letter asking you when you thought the book of "The O'Ruddy" was coming out, and stating that I would then arrange for the play accordingly. I presume you never received this.

If the play were produced first it might be detrimental to the novel from which it would, necessarily, be so different. Whereas if the book appears first, it makes no difference. Moreover, there is no value in a dramatization nowadays, until the book is published. This is what gives the play its vogue. I have anxiously awaited the announcement of its publication, as I have been in touch with several Managers and Stars with respect to it.

They would not make any business contract until the book has been placed on sale—they could not afford the terms. As you know, (or, perhaps you do not know) Plays are secured on a much cheaper basis than dramatizations, so that if Managers and Stars pay the price for a dramatization they want to get the benefit from the reading public.

Kindly let me hear from you to enable me to formulate my plans.

[99] ALS in Columbia University Libraries.

One thing is certain—I can make no arrangement until the book is published.

Another six weeks went by before Cora replied, and then, in April 1901, she could only report that she was leaving England with the business unsettled.[100]

The attempt to sell serial rights of the unfinished novel led to a whole series of fiascoes. Though Pinker was still supposedly in charge of the matter, Cora had during Crane's final illness turned to Paul Reynolds in New York with an eager inquiry. Reynolds, who had been summarily dropped as Crane's agent the summer before, was forgiving enough, but he was not eager to advance money without security. And he knew that magazine publishers were much like theatrical producers:

As to a serial, I do not think it would be possible to make any arrangement about it unless I had a prospectus of it and some of the story. Any editor to whom I speak about it will be likely to say "Well, when you have anything to show we shall be glad to consider it. . . .

In your letter you simply tell me it contains 65,000 words, that it is a "romance" and splendid stuff, and that you want to sell the American serial rights for 600 pounds.[101]

Reynolds also warned that buyers often asked for book rights along with serial rights, and once again he judged the matter correctly. For in London, Pinker was dealing with R. H. Russell of *The New Magazine* (New York), and Russell, when he learned that Stokes already had book rights, offered only £250 for the American serial rights. While Pinker may not have shared Cora's inflated notion of what he might be able to get, he refused so small a sum as this.[102] Cora, on her return to England, began a campaign to get Pinker to turn over the handling of the American market to Reynolds, who was, after all, on the spot. Rather than give up his commission—and the chance to

[100] Belasco to Cora Crane, New York, Sept. 5, 1900, TLS in Columbia University Libraries. The same, Feb. 22, 1901, ALS in Columbia University Libraries. The second of these letters bears the notation in Cora's hand, "ans April 13th 1901."

[101] Reynolds, in reply to Cora Crane's letter of May 16, New York, May 28, 1900, TLS in Columbia University Libraries.

[102] Copy of Pinker to Alfred T. Plant (Crane's executor), London, June 15, 1900, MS in Columbia University Libraries.

recover some of the funds he had advanced to Crane—Pinker
pressed harder to sell the American serial rights himself. The
first person he tried was Frederick A. Stokes, who already
owned American book rights. Stokes owned *Pocket Magazine*
and, since the departure of Irving Bacheller, edited it too. As a
magazine editor he was too shrewd to consider serial publication until Barr's supposedly sure completion of the book was actually in hand. And in replying to Pinker, he added a word as a
book publisher also: "We hope that you will prevail upon Mr.
Barr not to cut the conclusion of the story too short." [103] During
the summer of 1900, of course, the arrangement with Barr fell
apart. Pinker, while providing copy for possible successors to
Barr and for Belasco as well, kept on trying to sell the American
serial rights too. He persuaded Crane's executor in England to
allow him to seek a more realistic price than Cora had named,
but even at £350 he was not able to revive the interest of
The New Magazine. He heard again from the executor, in-
quiring on behalf of the anxious widow, before the editor's refusal finally arrived.[104] Neither Alfred Plant, the executor, nor
Cora need have worried, for while Pinker was still holding matters open with *The New Magazine*, he was having the manuscript read at *McClure's*. In fact he had given Robert McClure,
in the London office of the firm, Cora's typescript of the first
eleven chapters to read until a complete typescript became
available.[105] In the meantime, he also opened negotiations with
the Northern Newspaper Syndicate, in Kendal, Westmoreland,
offering British serial rights for £200 or all serial rights for
£700.[106] Nothing came of that, and nothing was improved by the

[103] Cora Crane to Pinker, London, n.d., ALS in Columbia University Libraries;
Stokes to Pinker, New York, June 26, 1900, TLS in Dartmouth College Library.

[104] Plant to Pinker, London, Aug. 9, 1900, TLS in Dartmouth College Library;
"Editor New Magazine" to Pinker, New York, Sept. 5, 1900, TLS in University
of Virginia Library.

[105] "As I have already told you, the 'copy' of Stephen Crane's novel has gone
over to our New York office and as soon as we hear from them on the subject
we will at once communicate with you" (Shurmer Sibthorp [of McClure's] to
Pinker, London, Sept. 6, 1900, TLS in University of Virginia Library). "I am
returning to you herewith the extra 'copy' of the first eleven chapters of Mr
Stephen Crane's THE O'RUDDY; the other complete 'copy' is in the hands of my
people in New York who are now considering your offer of the story" (McClure
to Pinker, London, Sept. 25, 1900, TLS in University of Virginia Library).

[106] Having received the following inquiry from the Northern Newspaper
Syndicate, Pinker made pencil notes for an answer which included eight

nagging letters of Cora Crane echoed in politer tones by Plant. When the McClure refusal came in, Pinker let them know. The solicitor's immediate reply expressed regret and put the civil question, "Have you any other purchasers in view at the present time?" With a negative answer from Pinker and probably some advice from Cora, Plant told Pinker on October 22 to turn over to Reynolds the handling of American serial rights.[107] Pinker held out as long as he could, but if he could not sell *The O'Ruddy* serial rights, the manuscript he would not relinquish was not very good security for Crane's debts. The solicitor's letters became more and more curt, and by the end of November the agent capitulated.[108] The copy which McClure had held in

names, Stephen Crane's being last: "We beg to say that we are open to consider one or two good serial stories for 1902, if you can make us an advantageous offer of the same. We must have good names and good stories, and for length we prefer not to exceed about 60,000 words" (Kendal, Sept. 22, 1900, TLS in University of Virginia Library). On Sept. 26 came a second letter: "What would be your best terms for a 50–60,000 words serial by [W. E.] Norris, Marriot-Watson, Barry Pain, or Stephen Crane" (TLS in University of Virginia Library). Pinker's notes on this letter, under Crane, read "200 B. S. R. or 700 all S. R." The £500 difference between the prices of British and world rights would include Empire and Colonial as well as American rights.

[107] To Cora's inquiry of Oct. 3 about British serial rights (TLS in Dartmouth College Library) and to that of about Oct. 15 concerning McClure's possible purchase of American rights (ALS in Dartmouth College Library), Pinker replied on Oct. 17 (TLS in Columbia University Libraries). Meanwhile, Plant urged Pinker "to do your utmost to dispose of the serial rights of the O'Ruddy" (London, Oct. 10, 1900, ALS in University of Virginia Library). After receiving the McClure news, he inquired as to whether Pinker had other prospects and finally he instructed Pinker to communicate with Reynolds "as I understand he will probably be able to find a purchaser of the American rights" (Oct. 18 and Oct. 22, 1900, TLS in Dartmouth College Library). Robert McClure's letter relaying the cabled news of the firm's rejection incidentally promised to send along at once the manuscript, which he assumed had already been dispatched to the firm's London office (Oct. 15, 1900, TLS in University of Virginia Library).

[108] Plant's letter of Nov. 21, 1900 referred to his having on hand a Pinker letter of Oct. 25—in short, three and a half weeks had gone by before he now wrote: "I conclude you have not yet found a purchaser for the serial rights of 'the O'Ruddy' and should like to have copy of this M.S. by return. I presume you forwarded a copy to Mr Paul Reynolds as requested in my letter of the 22nd ult." On November 27 he wrote: "I cannot understand the delay in forwarding me the various manuscripts and must ask you to kindly give the matter your early attention. I understand from Mrs Crane that you informed her they had been despatched to me last week." On November 28, he finally could write: "I am in receipt of copy of Mr Crane's Romance for which I am obliged. Do I understand you have never communicated with Mr Reynolds re the American serial rights?" (TLS in Dartmouth College Library). Pinker wrote a draft of his answer on this last letter. Having capitulated, he took a high tone: "In reply to your letter of yesterday I may say that I have not communicated with Mr Reynolds regarding the American serial rights of Mr

New York was passed to Reynolds, and Pinker gave his own copy to Plant, who gave it to Cora, who gave it to George H. Perris, another literary agent. She had been dealing with Perris and his Literary Agency of London since August and in mid-November conceived the idea of inviting an optimistic letter from him concerning *The O'Ruddy*, which she could use on the executor in order then to pry the manuscript from Pinker. The tactic was successful but the optimism was not borne out.[109]

Crane's Romance. I am a little surprised you should, in the circumstances, have suggested my doing so." The circumstances were, of course, the moneys due Pinker from Crane's estate.

Pinker, at about the time he gave up to Plant the manuscript and the outstanding Crane contracts which were kept in his office, filed a formal lien on proceeds due Crane on Methuen publications which he had arranged. (*Wounds in the Rain* had come out in September.) George E. Webster of Methuen, on Dec. 13, acknowledged a second letter from Pinker's lawyer on the subject and told the agent: "I have consulted our solicitors on the subject and they advise us that in order to avoid any responsibility we had better pay the sum into court when it becomes due, unless of course you have succeeded in settling the matter with Mr. Plant in the meantime" (TLS in University of Virginia Library).

Pinker's attempt to recoup his advances to Crane got mixed up with an attempt to clear his account altogether, but Plant, acting as Crane's executor and Cora's solicitor, caught the confusion in the account. He wrote to Pinker, London, May 8, 1901 (TLS in Dartmouth College Library):

I have written to Messrs Methuen & Co. and Messrs Harper & Brothers [publishers of the London edition of *The Monster*] to let me have a Statement of Account of Royalties now due to the above Estate as I wish to know exactly how we stand.

With reference to the balance of £51:2:1 owing to you, I find that you have included in your account the sum of £12:13:4 for commission on the balance to be paid by Messrs Methuen & Co. and Messrs Stokes at some future date but you are clearly not entitled to be paid your commission in advance therefore the amount now actually due and owing to you appears to be £38:8:9.

[109] On Oct. 22, 1900, Robert McClure in London informed Pinker: "As I wrote to you on the 15th inst., my people tell me they are unable to use Mr Crane's THE O'RUDDY. In a letter received this morning they say that, thinking you might prefer to have the MS in New York, they are holding it subject to your order. Kindly let me know what disposition you wish us to make of it" (TLS in University of Virginia Library). It was Dec. 14 before Reynolds in New York acknowledged to Cora Crane that he had received the manuscript: "I judge from glancing at it that it is not finished. The last chapter of the manuscript that I have is chapter 25 and this is evidently not the end. How long is the story going to be, and when do you expect to have the balance of it?" (TLS in Columbia University Libraries). He had more to find out than he at first realized. He knew from Cora that it had been offered to McClure, the *Journal*, and Tillotson's "Newspaper Literature" agency of Bolton, Lancashire. Before sending the letter, he learned enough to warrant a postscript: "I spoke of it to Pearson's Mag⁰ and found it had been offered there so apparently Pinker or his agent has offered it widely. I would like to know so as not to make a fool of myself offering it to people who have already seen it." On Dec. 31, Cora Crane wrote to Pinker, with questions about the cumulative statement

The real issue, of course, was who would finish the novel and when would it be done. In August and September, 1900, while the flurry of attempts to sell serial and dramatic rights was at its height, this main issue was most uncertain. Cora would not naturally inform Crane's publishers of her troubles—and theirs —but word was bound to leak out. Not to everyone, of course. In September, Methuen was still asking the old question, "Will you kindly let me know the title of Crane's new story?" [110] But Stokes in New York must have heard something and gone on to make unhappy inferences. He wrote to William Crane, Stephen's brother and his executor in the United States, in language which must have been strong. William, against his natural caution, transcribed the letter and sent it to Cora: "I enclose copy of letter received from F. A. Stokes Co., in order that you may see things from their standpoint. Will you kindly give me Mr. Barr's address? Do you not think I'd better write him a letter personally entreating him to carry out Stephen's wish? I send you this copy without Stokes Co's consent, but they urge me to act quickly and I depend on you not to let it get me into any unpleasantness." [111] The threatened unpleasantness would pass as

he had now submitted and about where the American serial rights had been offered (TLS in Dartmouth College Library).

Cora Crane wrote Perris on Nov. 19, 1900: "Do you think you could place a book of short stories [the posthumous collection which eventually became *Last Words*] and the English *serial* of 'The O'Ruddy.' Please answer so that I may show letter to the executor of my late husband's estate" (ALS in Yale University Library). On Nov. 23 she had authority to put Perris in charge: "I want you to use every effort to sell the English serial rights of 'The O'Ruddy.' . . . I have given my word that you are the people who will work the hardest to place this 'O'Ruddy' serial. . . . Mr. Crane wrote 65000 words on 'The O'Ruddy' and Mr. A. E. W. Mason is finishing the story. Let me know any offers which you may recieve" (ALS in Yale University Library). On Dec. 3 she sent copy "up to where Mr. A. E. W. Mason 'finishes' it. 65000 words," and she advised Perris that "the English serial ought to bring £300— at least" (ALS in Yale University Library).

On Jan. 31, 1901, Perris reported to Cora Crane his "very disappointing," "most disappointing" luck with the serial, two books, and a number of shorter pieces. He also let her know: "The O'Ruddy is now with the Editor of The Queen" (TLS in Columbia University Libraries).

[110] A. M. S. Methuen to Pinker, Haslemere, Sept. 13, 1900, ALS in University of Virginia Library.

[111] [Port Jervis, N.Y.], Sept. 9, 1900. Doubts about Barr, whatever they may have been that they should so have stretched William Crane's discretion, were soon irrelevant, and he was quick to pass the word to Cora: "Stokes Co. has written me that Mr. Mason will complete 'The O'Ruddy'. That settles everything, of course; Please, then, keep letter in perfect confidence" (Port Jervis, Sept. 12, 1900, ALS in Columbia University Libraries).

soon as Mason undertook the job of finishing the book, but before that word was in, Cora had given the gist of the letter to Barr. He answered in a hurt tone:

Stokes & Co are quite wrong in their surmise. I couldn't finish the story because I have not the brains. I fully intended to do it, but I wanted to do it anonymously. A d—d fool in America published a private letter of mine which he had no right to do & so the news leaked out. . . .

Nevertheless, as I read the story, I saw I would make a hash of it, & in my attempt at a chapter proved I could not do it. I told Stokes so. I hear Mason is to finish the book. I hope this is true. There could not be a better man. Still, it is a task in which any one will fail. No one could finish the book but Stephen.[112]

There is no reason to doubt Robert Barr's sincerity in 1900 and his relief that Mason had undertaken the task he had set by. He appreciated, like Marriott-Watson, the difficulty of keeping up the picaresque tone, whereas Mason, less sensitive to the original conception of the novel, grasped the simple technical difficulty of resolving the melodramatic plot. Mason's complaints about publicity and scheduling covered his increasing anxiety. Whatever promise *The O'Ruddy* may have had as an episodic comic narrative ran directly counter to the skillful entertainer's aim of turning out a neat plot. The inherent contradiction is clear in the opposite ways Crane himself had imagined the novel might go. In January, 1900, when Crane was picking up his initial conception and resuming the narrative after the two first chapters had been put aside, he still thought of The O'Ruddy as a picaresque hero. The controlling condition of the narrative was The O'Ruddy's having "one guinea per the-rest-of-his-natural-life"; with the freedom of his poverty he might turn rogue and see the world. At that time Crane told a visitor at Brede Place in some detail about the novel he was starting, and the visitor, John Ford Bemis, "recollected that, toward the end of the tale, the O'Ruddy was to be entangled with a middle-aged courtesan and to be dragged into court, again, with a long passage on the character of justice." [113] Episodes from Crane's own life—gallantly taking a prostitute's side

[112] London, Sept. 22, [1900], ALS in Columbia University Libraries.
[113] Thomas Beer, "Introduction" to *The O'Ruddy, Work of Stephen Crane*, ed. Wilson Follett (New York, 1925), VII, xi.

against a harassing policeman, and having his royalties enjoined by a middle-aged actress who thought herself jilted and swindled—let him imagine how free his hero might be from conventions and institutions and how easily comedy might veer toward satire. But the writer of such a tale must know the world which he satirizes. How different the plan of June, 1900, with its chase from London to Brede and its anticipation of a final duel between The O'Ruddy and the melodramatic villain. To write that, one would have to know something of horses and of swords and of the landscape from London to Tunbridge Wells and into Sussex, but mainly the writer would have to be skilled at making missing papers, dashing lovers, and deadly enemies come together in the right way after the right number of pages.

That was the problem to which Mason addressed himself, and the more he studied the question, the better he saw how Crane had neglected it. His ominous letter on the technical difficulties of the job, coming six months after he took it on, may indicate that in March, 1901, he was setting to work. At the end of April he was willing to say that he would have the novel finished very soon. But the lapses became worse. Cora Crane, who returned to the United States in April, could no longer manage things as she once had. She wrote to Perris from New Orleans, December 2, 1901, reporting what she knew and pathetically revealing how little control of events she had:

> Your letter of Aug 3rd has just been discovered by me among some unanswered letters. I cannot now remember if I answered it or no. I have been ill. . . . I have been, and am still, much distressed over "The O'Ruddy". Mr. Mason, as I wrote you, promised to send me the Ms. by Sep 1st but he said that, altho' he finished the book he was not satisfied with the work and wanted to do it over again. I heard from Mr. Stokes, the American publisher of "The O'Ruddy", the other day and he said that they expected a deffinate answer from Mr. Mason and would let me know.[114]

By that time, Stokes had begun to press him for copy. In April, 1902, Stokes still had not been able to get it and was ready "to take this matter into our own hands." [115]

[114] ALS in Yale University Library.
[115] Stokes to Cora Crane, New York, April 29, 1902, TLS in Columbia University Libraries.

Ironically, Stokes took action by coming round again to Pinker as agent and Barr as author, only this time it was entirely a business deal and not at all a labor of love. What the publisher wanted and the contractors finally provided was not a continuation of the comic narrative so much as a conclusion to the melodrama.

In the early autumn of 1902 Pinker thought of a deal which he proposed to Barr and in which Stokes expressed a ready interest. By the end of the year Cora herself had come to terms, and Plant, the British executor, sent word to Pinker to go ahead.[116] The mutual understanding was firm enough so that Barr went to work, but final terms were reached only in June, 1903, when the job was almost done. Just what the original agreement with Barr was is uncertain, but the contract of June 13, 1903, between Stokes and William Crane on behalf of Stephen's estate indicates the basic terms. The contract referred to Stokes' having arranged with Robert Barr to finish the book and guaranteed to Crane's estate "such proportions of the royalties agreed upon for the finished book (which was fifteen per cent of the retail price of each cloth bound copy sold in the United States) as shall equal that proportion of the whole book actually written by the said STEPHEN CRANE." Stokes got power over American serial rights, and if he sold them, the same proportional arrangement was to hold. Perhaps most important, any disagreement under the contract was to be referred to arbitration.[117]

There is no word of difficulties with the American contract, but in England, where Barr and Pinker were, major disagreements arose. Though it may have been only a question of the

---

[116] Stokes to Pinker, New York, Oct. 9, 1902: "Your letter of the 29th ult. has just reached me, and I thank you very much for the information relative to 'The O'Ruddy'. I do not know definitely what the alternative plan suggested to Mr. Barr is, and I shall be glad to have details. I am writing to him in the matter, also" (TLS in Dartmouth College Library).

Plant to Cora Crane, London, Dec. 31, 1902: "I am in receipt of your letter of the 31st ult. [sic] instructing me to accept Mr Robert Barr's offer to complete the O'Ruddy, and have informed Mr Pinker that I agree to this. The reason I informed you I thought I ought to consult Mr Perris in the matter was that you had instructed him to act for you as Agent in the matter, and I was certainly under the impression that you wished me to follow his advice. I do hope the book will now be completed without further delay, although I have not yet received Agreement from Mr Pinker" (TLS in Columbia University Libraries).

[117] Memorandum of Agreement (unsigned typed copy), Columbia University Libraries.

worker's seeking just payment for his labors, it looked as if it
were the cruder question of how much he could make on the
deal. On June 2, 1903, Pinker let Plant know what his new
client wanted, and on June 8 Crane's executor answered: "I
must confess that I am utterly astonished at the suggestion
made by Mr Barr, as you will find on referring to your letter to
me of the 16th January last that you stated Mr Barr accepted
the Agreement as altered by me." [118] A month's negotiation did
no good, and so in July, Plant reported to Cora Crane: "I am
sorry to say that Mr Robert Barr now declines to hand over the
completed manuscript of 'The O'Ruddy' unless he is paid a sum
of £220. I think he is behaving abominably in the matter, as he
knows perfectly well we have no money, and the arrangement
I made with him was that he should have the serial rights for
publication in the Idler as payment for his work upon the book.
I intend to do my utmost to force him to carry out his Agreement, and will let you know the result in due course." [119] The
money, as he pointed out, was needed to pay Harrods for stor-
ing the Cranes' Brede Place furniture, but poignant need had
nothing to do with the case. Matters hung fire until September,
when Plant began to make concessions. He offered to let Barr
have, in addition to British serial rights, some thirty pounds
"but of the money to be paid by Messrs Methuen & Co. on completion of the book. . . . Of course this offer is entirely without prejudice to my strict legal rights under the Agreement."
But Barr held the trump card in that he had a separate agreement with Stokes; if the book were published in America without simultaneous publication in England, the English rights
would be lost. So Barr declined arbitration, and Plant saw he
had no choice but to give Barr what he wanted. Once more he
protested that "it must be understood, I accept Mr Barr's proposal without prejudice to my rights in the matter," [120] but it is
hard to see what difference his rights made. The struggle was
crass, and there was no doubt as to who won.

What was in it for Pinker? What was in it for Barr? Pinker,

[118] TLS in Dartmouth College Library.
[119] London, July 17, 1903, TLS in Columbia University Libraries.
[120] London, Sept. 29, 1903, and Oct. 6, 1903, TLS in Dartmouth College
Library.

who had been generous and forbearing with Crane for so long, had not been very successful at being tough in the six months following Crane's death. Holding on to an incomplete manuscript in 1900 had been no way of realizing a cash return on his advances to the writer. In 1903, with Barr as his client, matters worked out a little differently. A few days after Plant capitulated to Barr's terms, George E. Webster wrote to Pinker on behalf of Methuen. Barr had given them permission to publish the completed *O'Ruddy*, and though they would not bring out the book until the following autumn, they supposed that Pinker's arrangement with Barr was "to let him have the money now." Webster offered to send the check at once, and he courteously added an inquiry about the amount "Mr. S. Crane's estate owes you for money advanced on account of this work." Pinker's annotation on the letter records that he still had coming £11.1.7 plus £1.4.0 for typing, and before the week was out, Methuen sent a check for £12.5.7 as the "fee due to you for making an arrangement with Mr Barr re *'O'Ruddy'* by S. Crane deced."[121] So Pinker, after all that negotiation, got back his advances without interest almost three and a half years after Crane's death.

As for Barr, the question is more obscure. Apart from the *Idler* serial rights, which can be estimated at £200, he got something of Methuen's payment due on completion of the novel. The total sum, inferred from the negotiations of January, 1900, was probably £100, and Barr's share, judging from Plant's indignation, must have been considerably more than the £30 offered by the executor. How much he deserved is still harder to figure. No one can compare in measurable terms the credit one man should get for conceiving the story or the other for working out the ending. But Crane did write twenty-five of the thirty-three chapters, or just over three-quarters of the book. What Barr thought was his share reversed the proportion. In a letter of 1903, after acknowledging "his indebtedness to Crane for notes and suggestions sent from Germany," according to Beer, he went on to a curious, modest-immodest statement of his own part in the work: "I simply did what I could to get myself in Steve's place. If you were to ask me what I think of the result,

---

[121] London, Oct. 12, 1903, TLS in Dartmouth College Library: Methuen remittance form, London, Oct. 16, 1903, in Dartmouth College Library.

I would have to answer manfully that I think most of this is pretty bad. I was obliged to drop out one episode toward the end as I really did not know in what spirit the poor boy wanted it written. [The delay en route to Brede, when The O'Ruddy stays with Lady Mary?] All that I can say is that I have done what I could. Only a fourth of the book is really his, in the strict sense of the word 'his,' but I tried to carry through the spirit suggested for the whole."[122] If, out of the second hundred pounds of Crane's advance, payable on completion of the manuscript, Barr copped all but the eleven-plus pounds that were repaid to Pinker, and if he got £200 for the serialization in the *Idler*, then he did get about three quarters of what the book brought in England. And given his contract with Stokes, he might hope to do as well in the United States. For that event he had his justification well worked out. But perhaps he did not do quite so well. In March, 1905, when Plant was writing to Pinker about other business of the Crane estate, he mentioned the rights which he had never waived: "I notice in the Agreement with Messrs Methuen & Co. for the publication of 'The O'Ruddy' that the Author is entitled to six presentation copies and shall be glad if they will forward same to me." Pinker forwarded the inquiry promptly and got as prompt an answer: "The author's presentation copies of 'THE O'RUDDY' were duly sent off as follows:—Mrs. Crane three copies. Robert Barr, six copies." But perhaps the handling of presentation copies had nothing to do with the handling of money. Plant's other business also concerned Methuen: he was trying to hold them to the contractual royalty of 12½ per cent for a proposed cheap edition of *Wounds in the Rain*, and in the reply from the publisher, Webster insisted on changing the penny-halfpenny on the shilling to a penny, take it or leave it. The reflexes of business language—"Perhaps if you point out to the author that this is far better than selling copies at remainder price he will be able to assent"—did not quite express solicitude for the author's widow.[123]

Of course, a decent man like Robert Barr could not convince

[122] Barr to Willis Clarke, n.p., n.d., quoted by Beer, "Introduction," *Work*, ed. Follett, VII, x–xi.

[123] Plant to Pinker, London, March 2, 1905, TLS in Dartmouth College Library; George E. Webster to Pinker, London, March 4, 1905, TLS in University of Virginia Library.

himself that the book was three-quarters his own work if there were no shred of a reason to think so. Even in the letter claiming the largest share in the book, he was self-conscious about his attempt to preserve the spirit of Crane's work: "He would be sure to scold me for some of my work, but I am not a chameleon, like Quiller-Couch, and it was impossible for me to do as Q did with Stevenson's *St. Ives*." [124] The extent to which he caught Crane's spirit is to be measured by his interpolation of occasional Irish words into his vocabulary, for local color so to speak, and by his utter failure to catch the vernacular cadence that made Crane's Irishman-narrator sound believable. He tidied Crane's unruly plot and made everything come to a focus: the missing papers concerned the title of Brede Place rather than of estates in the north; Brede belonged to the Earl of Westport rather than to the villain Forrister, and the hero's purpose was to keep it that way; the grand ending involved a splendid siege, perhaps modeled on Crane's supposed fragment of the summer of 1899, and there was less emphasis on personal combat, which, as Crane noticed when drifting into his final delirium, might come out either way. Barr's middle-class tidiness showed in a variety of ways—in the regularized spelling of Father Donovan's name and in the deletion of all reference to The O'Ruddy's noticing that Lady Mary evidently had a fine body beneath her heavily draped attire. There was nothing coarse—or natural— in what he added to the tale, and he went back over what had been written in order to get rid of anything that could offend the public taste. What the public would have insisted on most was the happy ending, as good as one in a standard Hollywood film. But all the things that Barr did to make the book right as a literary product were not enough to make it widely read. He succeeded in imposing on it the character of ephemeral literary entertainment, but he did not succeed in making its limited life glorious even in commercial terms.

The book came out in due course. American copyright was applied for on October 27, 1903; copyright deposit made on November 2; and publication announced in *Publishers' Weekly* on December 5. In London, Methuen doctored an advance copy of the Stokes edition, imported in wrappers, and made deposit

[124] Barr to Clarke, *Work*, ed. Follett, VII, xi.

at the British Museum on November 12, 1903, in order to hold copyright. When the serial had run its course in *The Idler*, Methuen deposited a copy of its own manufacture on July 7, 1904, and announced publication in *Publishers' Circular*, July 16. In December, 1904, when Plant was writing to Cora Crane about her Kensington creditors and the mounting storage bill at Harrods, he touched on the book's publication: "I have not yet received a Statement of Account from America as to the sales of 'The O'Ruddy' but do hope it has been a great success." [125] It was a tender subject. More than six months passed before she replied. In July, 1905, as she sent Plant a check for storage costs and asked that some of her furniture be sold so that the rest could be shipped to her in America, she came back to it: "Have you recieved any money from Judge [William] Crane yet from the sale of the 'O'Ruddy'? Did you ever get the £100- from Stokes and Co- that was to be paid on delivery of the mms-of the book? Judge Crane has not acted as a gentlem[an] should in this matter to say the least. I would have Judge Parker [the probate judge] look into the matter if I were you." [126] But Plant, a lawyer himself, knew only too well what Cora's legal rights amounted to, and no more came of the matter.

The literary fortunes of *The O'Ruddy* were summed up in the response of Crane's friends. Karl Harriman, a young writer who was close to the Cranes in affection and almost a disciple of Stephen's, had looked forward to the novel. With a sense of what it had been intended to be, he responded ebulliently to the prospect of seeing the book finished. "Now, Mrs Crane," he wrote in November, 1900, "here's what I want you to do. I want you to have 'The O'Ruddy' publishers send me *proofs* of that story before publication as I can place a long article on it." [127] He went on mainly about his own work, which had gained approval from Howells and publication by Harper's, but he obviously meant not to forget his promise. Then the years passed: he labored for the cause of realism with single mind; *The O'Ruddy* itself changed from a work expressing ebullience to something less. Both the man and the situation were different in August, 1904, when he wrote to Cora Crane:

[125] London, Dec. 19, 1904, TLS in Columbia University Libraries.
[126] Copy of TLS, n.p., July 9, 1905, Columbia University Libraries.
[127] Ann Arbor, Mich., Nov. 24, 1900, ALS in Columbia University Libraries.

I am downright glad to have your note. I have wondered again and again in the past year what had become of you, where you were and what you were doing. No, I have not read The O'Ruddy. I have never liked to think of Stephen, one of the subtlest realists of our day, turning to the romantic, but one of these days I shall get into the book for auld lang syne-sake. Write me all about yourself, what you are doing and everything and be sure that when I visit New York I shall look in upon you and we'll have a talk over English days. I can never forget your kindness to me—a stranger in a strange land—when I visited you at Brede.

Harriman's words were cordial enough, even in their candor, but as the letter continued, he did seem a smaller man:

How is *The* O'Ruddy selling? Have you profitted any by it, *materially*? I *do* want to know all about your life the past three or four years. Barr has no use for me apparently. I have sent him several letters but have never received a reply—Perhaps because he loaned me £5 once and I was four months paying it back. That occurred in the grey days of long ago but I guess Barr has a fine memory!!! [128]

In contrast to Harriman's letter is the one which Clara Frewen wrote a month later from Maam Cross, County Galway:

Dearest Mrs Crane
How can I thank you for so kindly sending The O'Ruddy, your letter & the book being forwarded to me here—where we are spending a lovely month fishing in these romantic wilds.

I enjoyed reading The O'Ruddy more than I can say—I remember poor dear Mr Crane was working at it, when I came to stay with you & slept for the first time at Brede. We used to sit after dinner in his study up stairs & I remember how very great was my interest in some of the details he told me of the plot—which you were then typewriting for him—& now I think it all so beautifully told with his powerful 'way.' . . .

Well—I have been hard at work there the last 2 years & I hope you would approve of all I have done—though of course we have to go very slowly on account of the expense—& do so much that does not show—such as strengthening floors & ceilings—etc I *did* buy the oak room you took me to Rye to see—& it now lines the porch room or—Mr Crane's study—& really looks beautiful!

I have no photographs with me here, but when I go back to Innishannon I will send you some—& perhaps some day you will come

---

[128] Battle Creek, Mich., Aug. 24, 1904, ALS in Columbia University Libraries.

across the sea again—& come to us there & see it all again—for I
know how dear the old place must be to you & that your memories
dwell there much—

I was so gratified & delighted that "The O'Ruddy's last chapter
ends at Brede & congratulate you upon Mr Robert Barr's artistic &
dashing ending— You were pleased were you not?

I must end this long epistle dear Mrs Crane as otherwise I should
miss the American mail— Moreton says he is going to write to you
also—so I send no message from him but beg you to believe me

Always your very sincere friend

Clara Frewen

Best of luck to you, who are so brave in all yʳ troubles dear Mrs
Crane—[129]

Mrs. Frewen was not a very judicious critic, but she had a feeling
for life. Her letter tells much about the style to which the Cranes
aspired. In its light the splendid episode at Brede, though they
could not afford it, took on qualities as enduring as the bitter fact
of Crane's going under.

Harriman and Mrs. Frewen account for two of Cora Crane's
presentation copies of *The O'Ruddy*. The third she presumably
kept for herself.

J. C. L.

[129] Sept. 27, 1904, ALS in Columbia University Libraries.

THE O'RUDDY

PART I

CHAPTER I

MY chieftain ancestors had lived at Glandore for many centuries and were very well-known. Hardly a ship could pass the Old Head of Kinsale without some boats putting off to exchange the time of day with her and our family name was on men's tongues in half the sea-ports of Europe, I dare say. My ancestors lived in castles which were like churches stuck on end and they drank the best of everything amid the joyous cries of a devoted peasantry. But the good times passed away soon enough and when I had reached the age of eighteen, we had nobody on the land but a few fisher-folk and small farmers, people who were almost law-abiding, and my father came to die more from the disappointment than from any other cause. Before the end, he sent for me to come to his bed-side. "Tom," he said, "I brought you into existence and God help you safe out of it for you are not the kind of man to ever turn your hand to work and there is only enough money to last a gentleman five more years. The *Martha Bixby*, she was, out of Bristol for the West Indies, and if it hadn't been for her we would never have got along this far with plenty to eat and drink. However, I leave you, besides the money, the two swords, the grand one that King Louis, God bless him, gave me and the plain one that will really be of use to you if you get in a disturbance. Then here is the most important matter of all. Here is some papers which young Lord Strepp gave me to hold for him when we were comrades in France. I don't know what they are, having had very little time for reading during my life, but do you return them to him. Take them to him in England. He is now the great Earl of West-port and he lives in London in a grand house, I hear. In the last campaign in France I had to lend him a pair of breeches or he would have gone bare. These papers are important to him and he may reward you but do not you depend on it for you may get the back of his hand. I have not seen him for years. I am glad I had you taught to read. They read considerably in England, I hear. There is one more cask of the best brandy remaining and I recommend you to leave for England as soon as it is finished. And now one more thing, my lad: never be civil to a king's officer. Whenever you see a red-coat depend there is a rogue between the front and the back of it. I have said everything; push the bottle near me."

Three weeks after my father's burial, I resolved to set out, with no more words, to deliver the papers to the Earl of Westport. I was resolved to be prompt in obeying my father's command for I was extremely anxious to see the world and my feet would hardly wait for me. I put my estate into the hands of old Mickey Clancy and told him not to trouble the tenants too much over the rent or they probably would split his skull for him and I bid Father Donovan look out for old Mickey that he stole from me only what was reasonable.

I went to the Cove of Cork and took ship there for Bristol and arrived safely after a passage amid great storms which blew us so near Glandore that I feared the enterprise of my own peasantry. Bristol, I confess, frightened me greatly. I had not imagined such a huge and teeming place. All the ships in the world seemed to lie there and the quays were thick with sailormen. The streets rang with noise. I suddenly found that I was a young gentleman from the country. I followed my luggage to the best inn and it was very splendid, fit to be a bishop's palace. It was filled with handsomely dressed people who all seemed to be yelling: "Landlord! Landlord!" And there was a little fat man in a white apron who flew about as if he were being stung by bees and he was crying, "Coming, sir! Yes, madam! At once, your ludship!" They heeded me no more than if I had been an empty glass. I stood on one leg waiting until the little fat man should either wear himself out or attend all the people. But it was to no purpose. He did not wear out nor did his business finish. So finally I was obliged to plant myself in his way but my speech was decent enough as I asked him for a chamber. Would you believe it, he stopped abruptly and stared at me with sudden suspicion. My speech had been so civil that he had thought perhaps I was a rogue. I only give you this incident to show that if later I came to bellow like a bull with the best of them it was only through the necessity of proving to strangers that I was a gentleman. I soon learned to enter an inn as a drunken soldier goes through the breach into a surrendering city.

Having made myself as presentable as possible, I came down from my chamber to seek some supper. The supper room was a-blaze with light and well-filled with persons of quality, to judge from the noise they were making. My seat was next to a garrulous man in plum-colour who seemed to know the affairs of the entire world. As I dropped into my chair, he was saying: "—— the heir to the title, of course. Young Lord Strepp. That is he—the slim youth with light hair. Oh, of course, all in shipping. The Earl must own twenty sail that trade from Bristol. He is posting down from London, by the way, tonight."

You can well imagine how these words excited me. I half arose from my chair with the idea of going at once to the young man who had been indicated as Lord Strepp and inform-ing him of my errand but I had a sudden feeling of timidity, a feeling that it was necessary to be proper with these people of high degree. I kept my seat, resolving to accost him directly after supper. I studied him with interest. He was a young man of about twenty years, with fair unpowdered hair and a face ruddy from a life in the open air. He looked generous and kindly but just at the moment he was damning a waiter in language that would have set fire to a stone-bridge. Opposite him was a clear-eyed soldierly man of about forty whom I heard called "Colonel" and at the Colonel's right was a proud dark-skinned man who kept looking in all directions to make sure that people regarded him, seated thus with a lord.

They had drunk eight bottles of port and in those days eight bottles could just put three gentlemen in pleasant humour. As the ninth bottle came on the table, the Colonel cried: "Come, Strepp, tell us that story of how your father lost his papers. Gad, that's a good story."

"No, no," said the young lord. "'Tisn't a good story and be-sides my father never tells it at all. I misdoubt its truth."

The Colonel pounded the table. "'Tis true. 'Tis too good a

story to be false. You know the story, Forister?" said he, turning to the dark-skinned man. The latter shook his head.

"Well, when the Earl was a young man serving with the French he carried rather recklessly with him some valuable papers relating to some estates in the South and one day the noble Earl—or Lord Strepp he was then—found it necessary after fording a stream to hang his breeches on a bush to dry and then a certain blackguard of a wild Irishman in the corps came along and stole——"

But I had arisen and called loudly but with dignity up the long table. "That, sir, is a lie." The room came still with a bang, if I may be allowed that expression. Everyone gaped at me and the Colonel's face slowly went the colour of a tiled roof. "My father never stole his lordship's breeches for the good reason that at the time his lordship had no breeches. 'Twas the other way. My father——"

Here the two long rows of faces lining the room crackled for a moment and then every man burst into a thunderous laugh. But I had flung to the wind my timidity of a new country and I was not to be put down by these clowns. "'Tis a lie against an honourable man and my father," I shouted. "And if my father hadn't provided his lordship with breeches he would have gone bare and there's the truth. And," said I, staring at the Colonel, "I give the lie again. We are never obliged to give it twice in my country."

The Colonel had been grinning a little, no doubt thinking along with everybody else in the room that I was drunk or crazy, but this last twist took the smile off his face clean enough and he came to his feet with a bound. I awaited him. But young Lord Strepp and Forister grabbed him and began to argue. At the same time there came down upon me such a deluge of waiters and pot-boys and, maybe, hostlers that I couldn't have done anything if I had been an elephant. They were frightened out of their wits and painfully respectful but, all the same and all the time, they were bundling me toward the door. "Sir! Sir! Sir! I beg you, sir! Think o' the 'ouse, sir! Sir! Sir! Sir!" And I found myself out in the hall.

Here I addressed them calmly. "Loose me and take yourselves off quickly lest I grow angry and break some dozen of these wooden heads." They took me at my word and vanished

like ghosts. Then the landlord came bleating but I merely told
him that I was going to my chamber and if anybody enquired
for me, I wished him conducted up at once.

In my chamber, I had not long to wait. Presently there were
steps in the corridor and a knock at my door. At my bidding
the door opened and Lord Strepp entered. I arose and we
bowed. He was embarrassed and rather dubious. "Aw," he began, "I come, sir, from Colonel Royale who begs to be informed who he has had the honour of offending, sir?"

"'Tis not a question for your father's son, my lord," I answered bluntly.

He looked at me and blushed and hesitated. "You are, then
——" he asked at last. "You are, then, the son of The O'Ruddy?"

"No," said I. "I am The O'Ruddy. My father died a month
gone and more."

"Oh," said he. And I now saw why he was embarrassed. He
had feared from the beginning that I was altogether too much
in the right. "Oh," said he again. I made up my mind that he
was a good lad. "That is dif——" he began awkwardly. "I mean,
Mr. O'Ruddy——oh, damn it all, you know what I mean, Mr.
O'Ruddy."

I bowed. "Perfectly, my lord." I did not understand him, of
course.

"I shall have the honour to inform Colonel Royale that Mr.
O'Ruddy is entitled to every consideration," he said more col-
lectedly. "If Mr. O'Ruddy will have the goodness to await me
here?"

"Yes, my lord." He was going in order to tell the Colonel that
I was a gentleman. And of course he returned quickly with
the news. But he did not look as if the message was one which
he could deliver with a glib tongue. "Sir," he began and then
halted. I could but courteously wait. "Sir, Colonel Royale bids
me say that he is shocked to find that he has carelessly and
publicly inflicted an insult upon an unknown gentleman
through the memory of the gentleman's dead father. Colonel
Royale bids me to say, sir, that he is overwhelmed with regret
and that, far from taking an initial step himself, it is his duty
to express to you his feeling that his movements should coincide
with any arrangements you may choose to make."

I was obliged to be silent for a considerable period in order to gather head and tail of this marvelous sentence. At last, I caught it. "At daybreak, I shall walk abroad," I replied, "and I have no doubt that Colonel Royale will be good enough to accompany me. I know nothing of Bristol. Any cleared space will serve."

My young Lord Strepp bowed until he almost knocked his forehead on the floor. "You are most amiable, Mr. O'Ruddy. You, of course, will give me the name of some friend to whom I can refer minor matters?"

I found that I could lie in England as readily as ever I did in Ireland. "My friend will be on the ground with me, my lord, and as he also is a very amiable man it will not take two minutes to make everything clear and fair." Me, with not a friend in the world but Father Donovan and Mickey Clancy at Glandore.

Lord Strepp bowed again, the same as before. "Until the morning then, Mr. O'Ruddy," he said and left me.

I sat me down on my bed to think. In truth, I was much puzzled and amazed. These gentlemen were actually reasonable and were behaving like men of heart. Neither my books nor my father's stories—great lies, many of them—God rest him —had taught me that the duelling gentry could think at all and I was quite certain that they never tried. "You are looking at me, sir?" "Was I, 'faith? Well if I care to look at you, I shall look at you." And then away they would go at it, prodding at each other's bellies until somebody's flesh swallowed a foot of steel. "Sir, I do not like the colour of your coat!" Clash! "Sir, red hair always offends me." Clang! "Sir, your fondness for rabbit-pie is not polite." Cling!

However, the minds of young Lord Strepp and Colonel Royale seemed to be capable of a process which may be termed human reflection. It was plain that the Colonel did not like the situation at all and perhaps considered himself the victim of a peculiarly exasperating combination of circumstances. That an Irishman should turn up in Bristol and give him the lie over a French pair of breeches must have seemed astonishing to him, notably when he learned that the Irishman was quite correct, having in short a clear title to speak authoritatively upon the matter of the breeches. And when Lord Strepp learned that I was The O'Ruddy he saw clearly that the Colonel was in the wrong and that I had a perfect right to resent the insult to my father's memory. And so the Colonel probably said: "Look you, Strepp. I have no desire to kill this young gentleman because I insulted his father's name. It is out of all decency. And do you go to him this second time and see what may be done in the matter of avoidance. But, mark you, if he expresses any wishes, you of course offer immediate accommodation. I will not wrong him twice." And so up comes my Lord Strepp and hems and haws in that way which puzzled me. A pair of thoughtful honourable fellows, these, and I admired them greatly.

There was now no reason that I should keep my chamber since if I now met even the Colonel himself there would be no brawling; only bows. I was not indeed fond of these latter; replying to Lord Strepp had almost broken my back but anyhow more bows was better than more loud words and another downpour of waiters and pot-boys.

But I had reckoned without the dark-skinned man, Forister. When I arrived in the lower corridor and was passing through it on my way to take the air, I found a large group of excited people talking of the quarrel and the duel, it being known through Forister no doubt that the duel was to be fought at day-break. I thought it was a great hub-bub over a very small thing but it seems that the mainspring of the excitement was the tongue of this black Forister. "Why, the Irish run naked through their native forests," he was crying. "Their sole weapon is the great knotted club with which however they do not hesitate when in great numbers to attack lions and tigers. But how can this barbarian face the sword of an officer of His Majesty's army?"

Some in the group espied my approach and there was a nudging of elbows. There was a general display of agitation and I marvelled at the way in which many made it to appear that they had not formed part of the group at all. Only Forister was cool and insolent. He stared full at me and grinned, showing very white teeth. "Swords are very different from clubs, great knotted clubs," he said with admirable deliberation.

"Even so," rejoined I gravely. "Swords are for gentlemen

while clubs are to clout the heads of rogues——thus." I boxed his ear with my open hand so that he fell against the wall. "I will now picture also the use of boots by kicking you into the inn-yard which is adjacent." So saying I hurled him to the great front door which stood open and then taking a sort of a hop and a skip, I kicked for glory and the saints.

I do not know that I ever kicked a man with more success. He shot out as if he had been heaved by a catapult. There was a dreadful uproar behind me and I expected every moment to be stormed by the waiter-and-pot-boy regiment. However I could hear some of the gentlemen, bystanding, cry: "Well done! Well kicked! A record! A miracle!"

But my first hours on English soil contained still other festivities. Bright light streamed out from the great door and I could plainly note what I shall call the arc or arcs described by Forister. He struck the railing once but spun off it and, to my great astonishment, went headlong and slap-crash into some sort of an upper servant who had been approaching the door with both arms loaded with cloaks, cushions and rugs.

I suppose the poor man thought that black doom had fallen upon him from the sky. He gave a great howl as he, Forister, the cloaks, cushions and rugs spread out grandly in one sublime confusion.

Some ladies screamed and a bold commanding voice said: "In the devil's name, what have we here?" Behind the unhappy servant had been coming two ladies and a very tall gentleman in a black cloak that reached to his heels. "What have we here?" again cried this tall man who looked like an old eagle. He stepped up to me haughtily. I knew that I was face to face with the Earl of Westport.

But was I a man forever in the wrong that I should always be giving down and walking away with my tail between my legs? Not I; I stood bravely to the Earl. "If your lordship pleases, 'tis The O'Ruddy kicking a blackguard into the yard," I made answer, coolly.

I could see that he had been about to shout for the landlord and more waiters and pot-boys but at my naming myself, he gave a quick stare. " 'The O'Ruddy'?" he repeated. "Rubbish!" He was startled, bewildered, but I could not tell if he was glad or grieved.

" 'Tis all the name I own," I said placidly. "My father left me it clear, it being something that he could not mortgage. 'Twas on his death-bed that he told me of lending you the breeches and that is why I kicked the man into the yard and if your lordship had arrived sooner I could have avoided this duel at day-break and, anyhow, I wonder at his breeches fitting you. He was a small man."

Suddenly the Earl raised his hand. "Enough," he said sternly. "You are your father's son. Come to my chamber in the morning, O'Ruddy." There had been little chance to see what was inside the cloaks of the ladies but at the words of the Earl, there peeped from one hood a pair of bright liquid eyes— God save us all; in a flash I was no longer a free man; I was a dazed slave; the saints be good to us.

The contents of the other hood could not have been so interesting for from it came a raucous voice as of a bargeman with a cold. "Why did he kick him? Whom did he kick? Had he cheated at play? Where has he gone?"

The upper servant appeared, much battered, and holding his encrimsoned nose. "My lord——" he began. But the Earl roared at him: "Hold your tongue, rascal, and in future look where you are going and don't get in a gentleman's way."

The landlord, in a perfect anguish, was hovering with his squadrons on the flanks. They could not think of pouncing upon me if I was noticed at all by the great Earl but, somewhat as a precaution, perhaps, they remained in form for attack. I had no wish that the pair of bright eyes should see me buried under a heap of these wretches so I bowed low to the ladies and to the Earl and passed out of doors. As I left, the Earl moved his hand to signify that he was now willing to endure the attendance of the landlord and his people and in a moment the inn sang with hurried cries and rushing feet.

As I passed near the tap-room window, the light fell full upon a railing just beneath and over this railing hung two men. At first, I thought they were ill but upon passing near I learned that they were simply limp, helpless with laughter, the sound of which they contrived to keep muffled. To my surprise I recognized the persons of young Lord Strepp and Colonel Royale.

CHAPTER II

THE night was growing and as I was to fight at day-break, I needed a good rest but I could not forget that in my pride I had told Lord Strepp that I was provided with a friend to attend me at the duel. It was on my mind. I must achieve a friend or Colonel Royale might quite properly refuse to fight me on the usual grounds that if he killed me there would be present no adherent of my cause to declare that the fight was fair. And anyhow I had lied so thoroughly to Lord Strepp. I must have a friend.

But how was I to carve a friend out of this black Bristol at such short notice? My sense told me that friends could not be found in the road like pebbles but some curious feeling kept me abroad, scanning by the light of the lanterns or the torches each face that passed me. A low dull roar came from the direction of the quays and this was the noise of the sailor-men being drunk. I knew that there would be none found there to suit my purpose but my spirit led me to wander so that I could not have told why I went this way or that way.

Of a sudden, I heard from a grassy bank beside me the sound of low and strenuous sobbing. I stopped dead short to listen, moved by instinctive recognition. Aye, I was right; it was Irish keening. Some son of Erin was spelling out his sorrow to the darkness with that profound and garrulous eloquence which is in the character of my people. "Wirra, wirra! Sorrow the day I would be leaving Ireland against my own will and intention and may the rocks go out to meet the lugger that brought me here. It's beginning to rain, too. Sure, it never rains like this in Ireland and me without a brass penny to buy a bed. If the saints save me from England, 'tis all ——"

"Come out of that, now," said I.

The monologue ceased; there was a quick silence. Then

the voice much altered said: "Who calls? 'Tis maybe an Irish voice?"

"It is," said I. "I've swallowed as much peat smoke as any man of my years. Come out of that now and let me have a look at you." He came trustfully enough, knowing me to be Irish, and I examined him as well as I was able in the darkness. He was what I expected, a bedraggled vagabond with tear stains on his dirty cheeks and a vast shock of hair which I well knew would look, in day-light, like a burning hay-cock. And as I examined him he just as carefully examined me. I could see his shrewd blue eyes twinkling. "You are a red man," said I. "I know the strain; 'tis better than some. Your family must have been very inhospitable people." And then thinking that I had spent enough time, I was about to give the fellow some coins and send him away. But here a mad project came into my empty head. I have ever been the victim of my powerful impulses which surge up within me and sway me until I can only gasp at my own conduct. The sight of this red-headed scoundrel had thrust an idea into my head and I was a lost man.

"Mark you," said I to him. "You know what I am?"

" 'Tis hard to see in the dark," he answered, "but I mistrust you are a gentleman, sir. McDermott of the Three Trees had a voice and a way with him like you and Father Burke too and he was a gentleman born if he could only remain sober."

"Well, you've hit it, in the dark or whatever," said I. "I am a gentleman. Indeed, I am an O'Ruddy. Have you ever been hearing of my family?"

"Not of your honour's branch of it, sure," he made answer confidently. "But I have often been hearing of the O'Ruddys of Glandore who are well-known to be such great robbers and blaguards that their match is not to be found in all the south of Ireland. Nor in the west, either, for that matter."

"Aye," said I, "I have heard that branch of the family was much admired by the peasantry for their qualities. But let us have done with it and speak of other matters. I want a service of you."

"Yes, your honour," said he dropping his voice. "Maybe 'twill not be the first time I've been behind a ditch but the light tonight is very bad unless I am knowing him well and I would never be forgetting how Tim Malone let fly in the dark of a night like this, thinking it was a bailiff until she screamed out with the pain in her leg, the poor creature, and her beyond seventy and a good Catholic."

"Come out of it now," said I impatiently. "You will be behind no ditch." And as we walked back to the inn, I explained to my new man the part I wished him to play. He was amazed at it and I had to explain fifty times but when it once was established in his red head, Paddy was wild with enthusiasm and I had to forbid him telling me how well he would do it.

I had them give him some straw in the stable and then retired to my chamber for needed rest. Before dawn, I had them send Paddy to me and by the light of a new fire I looked at him. Ye saints! What hair! It must have been more than a foot in length and the flaming strands radiated in all directions from an isolated and central spire which shot out straight toward the sky. I knew what to do with his tatters but that crimson thatch dumbfounded me. However there was no giving back now and so I set to work upon him. Luckily my wardrobe represented three generations of O'Ruddy clothes and there was a great plenty. I put my impostor in a suit of blue velvet with a flowered waistcoat and stockings of pink. I gave him a cocked hat and a fine cloak. I worked with success up to the sword-belt and there I was checked. I had two swords but only one belt. However, I slung the sword which King Louis had given my father on a long string from Paddy's neck and sternly bid him keep his cloak tight about him. We were ready.

"Now, Paddy," said I, "do you bow in this manner." I bowed as a gentleman should. But I will not say how I strove with him. I could do little in that brief space. If he remained motionless and kept his tongue still he was somewhat near his part but the moment he moved, he was astonishing. I depended on keeping him under my eye and I told him to watch me like a cat. "Don't go thinking how grand you are, that way," I cried to him angrily. "If you make a blunder of it, the gentlemen will cudgel you, mark you that. Do you as I direct you. And the string, curse you! Mind your cloak!" The villain had bethought him of his flowered waistcoat and with a comic air flung back his coat to display it. "Take your fingers out of your mouth. Stop scratching your shin with your foot. Leave your hair alone. 'Tis as good and as bad as you can make it. Come along now and hold your tongue like a graven image if you would not be having me stop the duel to lather you."

We marched in good order out of the inn. We saw our two gentlemen awaiting us wrapped in their cloaks for the dawn was cold. They bowed politely and as I returned their salute I said in a low quick aside to Paddy: "Now, for the love of God, bow for your life!" My intense manner must have frightened the poor thing for he ducked as swiftly as if he had been at a fair in Ireland and somebody had hove a cobble at his head. "Come up," I whispered, choking with rage. "Come up. You'll be breaking your nose on the road." He straightened himself, looking somewhat bewildered. "What was it? Was I too slow? Did I do it well?"

"Oh, fine," said I, "fine. You do it as well as that once more and you will probably break your own neck and 'tis not me that will be buying masses for your soul, you thief. Now don't drop as if a game-keeper had shot at you for there is no hurry in life. Be quiet and easy."

"I mistrusted I was going too fast," said he, "but for the life of me, I couldn't pull up. If I had been the Dublin Mail and the road thick as fleas with highwaymen, I should have gone through them grand."

My Lord Strepp and Colonel Royale had not betrayed the slightest surprise at the appearance of my extraordinary companion. Their smooth regular faces remained absolutely imperturbable. This, I took to be very considerate of them but I gave them thus a little more than their due as I afterward perceived when I came to understand the English character somewhat. The great reason was that Paddy and I were foreigners. It is not to be thought that gentlemen of their position would have walked out for a duel with an Englishman in the party of so fantastic an appearance. They would have placed him at once as a person impossible and altogether out of their class. They would have told a lackey to kick this preposterous creation into the horse pond. But since Paddy was a foreigner he was possessed of some curious license and his grotesque ways could be explained fully in a simple phrase. " 'Tis a foreigner."

So then we preceded my Lord Strepp and Colonel Royale through a number of narrow streets and out into some clear country. I chose a fine open bit of green turf as a goodly place for us to meet and I warped Paddy through the gate and moved to the middle of the field. I drew my sword and saluted and then turned away. I had told Paddy everything which a Heaven-sent sense of instruction could suggest and if he failed I could do no more than kill him.

After I had kicked him sharply he went aside with Lord Strepp and they indulged in what sounded like a very animated discussion. Finally I was surprised to find Lord Strepp approaching me. "Sir," he said, "you will pardon me. It is very irregular but I seem unable to understand your friend. He has proposed to me that the man whose head is broken first—I do not perfectly understand what he could mean by that—it does not enter our anticipations that a man could possibly have his head broken—he has proposed that this man whose head may be broken first should provide 'lashings'—I feel sure that is the word—'lashings' of meat and drink at some good inn for the others. 'Lashings' is a word which I do not know. We do not know how to understand you gentlemen when you speak of 'lashings.' I am instructed to be glad to meet any terms which you may suggest but I find that I cannot make myself clear to your friend who speaks of nothing but 'lashings.' "

"Sir," said I, as I threw coat and waistcoat on the grass, "my friend refers to a custom of his own country. You will I feel sure pardon his misconception of the circumstances. Pray accept my regrets and, if you please, I am ready."

He immediately signified that his mind was now clear and that the incident of Paddy's lashings he regarded as closed. As for that flame-headed imp of crime, if I could have got my hands upon him he would have taken a short road to his fathers. Him and his lashings! As I stood there with a black glare at him, the impudent scoundrel repeatedly winked at me with the readable intimation that if I would only be patient and bide a moment, he would compass something very clever. As I faced Colonel Royale I was so wild with thinking of what

I would do to Paddy that, for all I knew, I might have been crossing swords with my mother.

And now as to the duel. I will not conceal that I was a very fine fencer in both the French and Italian manners. My father was in his day one of the best blades in Paris and had fought with some of the most skilful and impertinent gentlemen in all France. He had done his best to give me his eye and his wrist and sometimes he would say that I was qualified to meet all but the best in the world. He commonly made fun of the gentlemen of England, saying that a dragoon was their ideal of a man with a sword, and he would add that the rapier was a weapon which did not lend itself readily to the woodchopper's art. He was all for the French and Italian schools.

I had always thought that my father's judgment was very good but I could not help reflecting that if it turned out to be bad, I would have a grievance as well as a sword-thrust in the body. Colonel Royale came at me in a somewhat leisurely manner and, as I said, my mind was so full of rage at Paddy that I met the first of my opponent's thrusts through sheer force of habit. But my head was clear a moment later and I knew that I was fighting my first duel in England and for my father's honour. It was no time to think of Paddy.

And at another moment later, I knew that I was the Colonel's master. I could reach him where I chose. But he did not know it. He went on prodding away with a serious countenance, evidently under the impression that he had me hard put to it. He was grave as an owl-faced parson. And now here I did a sorry thing. I became the victim of another of my mad impulses. I was seized with an ungovernable desire to laugh. It was hideous. But laugh I did and, of necessity, square in the Colonel's face. And to this day I regret it.

Then the real duel began. At my laugh, the Colonel instantly lost his grave air and his countenance flushed with high and angry surprise. He beset me in a perfect fury, caring no more for his guard than if he had been made of iron. Never have I seen such quick and tremendous change in a man. I had laughed at him under peculiar conditions; very well, then; he was a demon. Thrice my point pricked him to keep him off and thrice my heart was in my mouth that he would come on, regardless. The blood oozed out on his white ruffled shirt; he was panting heavily and his eyes rolled. He was a terrible sight to face. At last I again touched him and this time sharply and in the sword-arm, and upon the instant, my Lord Strepp knocked our blades apart. "Enough," he cried sternly. "Back, Colonel! Back!" The Colonel flung himself sobbing into his friend's arms, choking out, "O, God, Strepp, I couldn't reach him! I couldn't reach him, Strepp! O, my God!" At the same time, I disappeared, so to speak, in the embrace of my red-headed villain who let out an Irish howl of victory that should have been heard at Glandore. "Be quiet, rascal," I cried flinging him off. But he went on with his howling until I was obliged to forcibly lead him to a corner of the field. "Oh, your honour, when I seen the other gentleman, all blazing with rage, rush at you that way and me with not so much as a tuppence for all my service to you excepting these fine clothes and the sword although I am thinking I shall have little to do with swords if this is the way they do it, I said sorrow the day England saw me."

If I had a fool for a second, Colonel Royale had a fine wise young man. Lord Strepp was dealing firmly and coolly with his maddened principal. "I can fight with my left hand," the Colonel was screaming. "I tell you, Strepp, I am resolved! Don't bar my way! I will kill him! I will kill him!"

"You are not in condition to fight," said the undisturbed young man. "You are wounded in four places already. You are in my hands. You will fight no more today."

"But, Strepp," wailed the Colonel. "O, my God, Strepp!"

"You fight no more today," said the young lord.

Then happened unexpected interruptions. Paddy told me afterward that during the duel a maid had looked over a wall and yelled and dropped a great brown bowl at sight of our occupation. She must have been the instrument that aroused the entire county for suddenly men came running from everywhere. And the little boys! There must have been little boys from all over England. "What is it? What is it? Two gentlemen have been fighting! Oh, aye, look at him with the blood on him! Well and there is young my Lord Strepp. He'd be deep in the matter,

I warrant you! Look yon, Bill! Mark the gentleman with the red hair. He's not from these parts, truly. Where, think you, he comes from? 'Tis a great marvel to see such hair and I doubt not he comes from Africa."

They did not come very near for in those days there was little the people feared but a gentleman and small wonder. However, when the little boys judged that the delay in a resumption of the fight was too prolonged, they did not hesitate to express certain unconventional opinions and commands. "Hurry up, now. Go on. You are both afeared. Begin, begin." This rabble was such as I saw afterward in the play-houses in London and the little ruffians seemed to respect nothing. "Go on. Begin, begin. Are the gentlemen in earnest? Sirs, do you mean ever to fight again? Begin, begin." But their enthusiasm waxed high after they had thoroughly comprehended Paddy and his hair. You're a-light, sir, you're a-light! Water! Water! Aye, Farmer Pelton will have the officers at you and you go near his hay. Water!"

Paddy understood that they were paying tribute to his importance and he again went suddenly out of my control. He began to strut and caper and pose with the air of knowing that he was the finest gentleman in England. "Paddy, you baboon," said I, "be quiet and don't be making yourself a laughing stock for the whole of them." But I could give small heed to him for I was greatly occupied in watching young Lord Strepp and the Colonel. The Colonel was listening now to his friend for the simple reason that the loss of blood had made him too weak to fight again. Of a sudden, he slumped gently down through Lord Strepp's arms to the ground and as the young man knelt, he cast his eyes about him until they rested upon me in what I took to be mute appeal. I ran forward and we quickly tore his fine ruffles to pieces and succeeded in quite staunching his wounds, none of which were serious. " 'Tis only a little blood-letting," said my Lord Strepp with something of a smile. " 'Twill cool him, perchance."

"None of them are deep," I cried hastily. "I——"

But Lord Strepp stopped me with a swift gesture. "Yes," he said, "I knew. I could see. But——" He looked at me with troubled eyes. "It is an extraordinary situation. You have spared him and—he will not wish to be compelled to be spared, I feel sure. Most remarkable case."

"Well, I won't kill him," said I bluntly, having tired of this rubbish. "Damme if I will."

Lord Strepp laughed out-right. "It is ridiculous," he said. "Do you return, O'Ruddy, and leave me the care of this business. And," added he, with an embarrassed manner, "this mixture is full strange—but—I feel sure—anyhow, I salute you, sir." And in his bow he paid a sensible tribute to my conduct.

Afterward there was nought to do but gather in Paddy and return to the inn. I found my countryman swaggering to and fro before the crowd. Some ignoramus, or some wit, had dubbed him the King of Ireland and he was playing to the part.

"Paddy, you red-headed scandal," said I, "come along now."

When he heard me, he came well enough but I could not help but feel from his manner that he had made a great concession. As we walked back toward the inn, I admonished him so severely that he gave over most of his high airs but not without commentary. "And so they would be taking me for the King of Ireland and, sure, 'tis an advantage to be thought a king whatever and if your honour would be easy, 'tis you and I that would sleep in the finest beds in Bristol the night and nothing to do but take the drink as it was handed and—— I'll say no more."

A rabble followed us on our way to the inn but I turned on them so fiercely from time to time that ultimately they ran off. We made direct for my chamber where I ordered food and drink immediately to be served. Once alone there with Paddy I allowed my joy to take hold upon me. "Eh, Paddy, my boy," said I, walking before him, "I have done grand. I am, indeed, one of the finest gentlemen in the world."

"Aye that's true," he answered, "but there was a man at your back throughout who——"

To his extreme astonishment, I buffeted him heavily upon the cheek. "And we'll have no more of that talk," said I.

CHAPTER III

"AYE," said Paddy holding his jowl, " 'tis what one gets for serving a gentleman. 'Tis the service of a good truthful blaguard I'd be looking for and that's true for me."

"Be quiet and mind what I tell you," I cried to him. "I'm uplifted with my success in England and I won't be hearing anything from you while I am saying that I am one of the grandest gentlemen in all the world. I came over here with papers— papers——" said I and then I bethought me that I would take the papers and wave them in my hand. I don't know why people wish to wave important documents in their hands but the impulse came to me. Above all things I wished to take these papers and wave them defiantly, exultantly, in the air. These papers were my inheritance and my land of promise; they were everything. I must wave them even to the chamber, empty save for Paddy.

When I reached for them in the proper place in my luggage they were gone. I whirled like a tiger upon Paddy. "Villain," I roared grasping him at the throat, "you have them!"

He sank in full surrender to his knees. "I have, your honour," he wailed, "but, sure, I never thought your honour would care since one of them is badly worn at the heel and the other is no better than no boot at all."

I was cooled by the incontestable verity of this man. I sat heavily down in a chair by the fire. "Aye," said I stupidly, "the boots? I did not mean the boots, although when you took them passes my sense of time. I mean some papers."

"Some papers!" cried he excitedly. "Your honour never thought it would be me that would steal papers? Nothing less than good cows would do my people and a bit of turf now and then but papers——"

"Peace," said I sombrely and began to search my luggage

thoroughly for my missing inheritance. But it was all to no purpose. The papers were not there. I could not have lost them. They had been stolen. I saw my always-flimsy inheritance melt away. I had been, I thought, on the edge of success but I now had nothing but my name, a successful duel and a few pieces of gold. I was buried in defeat.

Of a sudden, a name shot through my mind. The name of this black Forister was upon me violently and yet with perfect sureness. It was he who had stolen the papers. I knew it. I felt it in every bone. He had taken the papers.

I have been told since that it is very common for people to be moved by these feelings of omen which are invariably correct in their particulars but at the time I thought it odd that I should be so certain that Forister had my papers. However I had no time to waste in thinking. I grasped my pistols. "A black man—black as the devil," cried I to Paddy. "Help me catch a little black man."

"Sure," said Paddy, and we sallied forth. In a moment I was below and crying to the landlord in as fine a fury as any noble. "This villain Forister! And where be he?"

The landlord looked at me with bulging eyes. "Master Forister," he stammered. "Aye—aye—he's been a-gone these many hours since your lordship kicked him. He took horse, he did, for Bath, he did."

"Horses!" I roared. "Horses for two gentlemen!" And the stable yard, very respectful since my duel, began to ring with cries. The landlord pled something about his bill and in my impatience I hurled to him all of my gold save one piece. The horses came soon enough and I leaped into the saddle and was away to Bath after Forister. As I galloped out of the inn-yard I heard a tumult behind me and, looking back, I saw three hostlers lifting hard at Paddy to raise him into the saddle. He gave a despairing cry when he perceived me leaving him at such speed but my heart was hardened to my work. I must catch Forister.

It was a dark and angry morning. The rain swept across my face and the wind flourished my cloak. The road, glistening steel and brown, was no better than an Irish bog for hard riding. Once I passed a chaise with a flogging post-boy and steaming nags. Once I overtook a farmer jogging somewhere on a fat mare. Otherwise I met no travellers.

I was near to my journey's end when I came to a portion of the road which dipped down a steep hill. At the foot of this hill was an oak-tree and under this tree was a man masked and mounted and in this man's hand was a levelled pistol. "Stand," he said, "stand!" I knew his meaning.

But when a man has lost a documentary fortune and given an inn-keeper all but his last guinea, he is sure to be filled with fury at the appearance of a third and completing mis-fortune. With a loud shout, I drew my pistol and rode like a demon at the highwayman. He fired but his bullet struck noth-ing but the flying tails of my cloak. As my horse crashed into him, I struck at his pate with my pistol. An instant later we both came a mighty down-fall and when I could get my eyes free of stars, I arose and drew my sword. The highwayman sat before me on the ground ruefully handling his skull. Our two horses were scampering away into the mist.

I placed my point at the highwayman's throat. "So, my fine fellow," cried I grandly, "you rob well. You are the principal knight of the road of all England, I would dare say, by the way in which an empty pistol overcomes you."

He was still ruefully handling his skull. "Aye," he muttered sadly more to himself than to me, "a true knight of the road with seven ballads written of me in Bristol and three in Bath. Ill betide me for not minding my mother's word and staying at home this day. 'Tis all the unhappy luck of Jem Bottles. I should have remained an honest sheep-stealer and never en-gaged in this dangerous and nefarious game of lifting purses."

The man's genuine sorrow touched me. "Cheer up, Jem Bottles," said I. "All may yet be well. 'Tis not one little bang on the crown that so disturbs you?"

" 'Tis not one—no," he answered gloomily. " 'Tis two. The traveller riding to the east before you dealt me a similar blow—may hell catch the little black devil."

"Black!" cried I. "Forister, for my life!"

"He took no moment to tell me his name," responded the sullen and wounded highwayman. "He beat me out of the saddle and rode away as brisk as a bird. I know not what my mother will say. She be forever telling me of the danger in this trade and here come two gentlemen in one day and unhorse me without the profit of a sixpence to my store. When I became a highwayman I thought me I had profited me from the low estate of a sheep-stealer but now I see that happiness in this life does not altogether depend upon——"

"Enough," I shouted in my impatience. "Tell me of the black man! The black man, worm!" I pricked his throat with my sword very carefully.

"He was black and he rode like a demon and he handled his weapons finely," said Jem Bottles. "And since I have told you all I know, please, good sir, move the point from my throat. This will be ill news for my mother."

I took thought with myself. I must on to Bath but the two horses had long since scampered out of sight and my pursuit of the papers would make small way afoot. "Come, Jem Bottles," I cried, "help me to a horse in a comrade's way and for the sake of your mother. In another case, I will leave you here a bloody corse. Come; there's a good fellow."

He seemed moved to help me. "Now, if there comes a well-mounted traveller," he said brightening, "I will gain his horse for you if I die for it."

"And if there comes no well-mounted traveller?"

"I know not, sir. But—perhaps he will come."

" 'Tis a cheap rogue who has but one horse," I observed contemptuously. "You are only a foot-pad, a simple-minded marquis of the bludgeon."

Now, as I had hoped, this deeply cut his pride. "Did I not speak of the ballads, sir?" he demanded with considerable spirit. "Horses? Aye, and have I not three good nags hid behind my mother's cottage which is less than a mile from this spot?"

"Monsieur Jem Bottles," said I, not forgetting the French manners which my father had taught me, "unless you instantly show me the way to these horses, I shall cut off your hands, your feet and your head and, ripping out your bowels, shall sprinkle them on the road for the first post-horses to mash and trample. Do you understand my intention, Monsieur Jem Bottles?"

"Sir," he begged, "think of my mother!"

"I think of the horses," I answered grimly. " 'Tis for you to think of your mother. How could I think of your mother when I wouldn't know her from the Head of Kinsale if it didn't happen that I know the Head of Kinsale too well to mistake it for anybody's mother?"

"You speak like a man from foreign parts, sir," he rejoined in a meek voice, "but I am able to see that your meaning is serious."

" 'Tis so serious," said I, rapping him gently on the head with the butt of my pistol, "that if you don't instantly display a greedy activity you will display a perfect inability to move."

"The speeching is obscure," said he, "but the rap on the head is clear to me. Still, it was not kind of you to hit me on the same spot twice."

He now arose from his mournful seat on the ground and, still rubbing his pate, he asked me to follow him. We moved from the highway into a very narrow lane and for some time proceeded in silence. " 'Tis a regular dog's life," spoke Jem Bottles after a period of reflection.

By this time, I had grown a strong sympathy for my scoundrel. "Come, cheer yourself, Jem Bottles," said I. "I have known many a lesser ruffian who was hanged until he was dry whereas you march along the lane with nought to your discouragement but three cracks in your crown."

" 'Tis not the cracks in the crown," he answered moodily. " 'Tis what my mother will say."

"I had no thought that highwaymen had mothers," said I. I had resolved now to take care of his pride for I saw that he was bound to be considered a great highwayman and I did not wish to disturb his feelings until I gained possession of one of the horses.

But now he grew as indignant as he dared. "Mother? Mother, sir? Do you think me an illegitimate child? I say to you flat in your face, even if you kill me the next instant, that I have a mother. Perchance I am not of the lofty gentry who go about beating honest highwaymen to the earth but I repulse with scorn any man's suggestion that I am illegitimate. In the quarter of an hour you shall see my mother for yourself."

"Peace, Jem Bottles," said I soothingly. "I took no thought of such a thing. I would be thinking only of the ballads and how honourable it is that a gallant and dashing life should be celebrated in song. I, for certain, have never done anything to make a pot-house ring with my name and I liken you to the knights of olden days who tilted in all simple fair bravery without being able to wager a brass farthing as to who was right and who was wrong. Admirable Jem Bottles," I cried enthusiastically, "tell me, if you will, of your glories; tell me with your own tongue so that when I hear the ballads waxing furious with praise of you, I shall recall the time I marched with your historic person."

"My beginning was without pretence," said the highwayman. "Little Susan, daughter of Farmer Hants, was crossing the fields with a basket of eggs. I, a masked figure, sprang out at her from a thicket. I seized the basket. She screamed. There was a frightful tumult. But in the end I bore away this basket of eight eggs creeping stealthily through the wood. The next day, Farmer Hants met me. He had a long whip. There was a frightful tumult. But he little knew that he was laying with his whip the foundation of a career so illustrious. For a time, I stole his sheep but soon grew weary of this business. Once, after they had chased me almost to Bristol, I was so weary that I resolved to forego the thing entirely. Then I became a highwayman whom you see before you. One of the ballads begins thus:

> "What ho, the merry Jem,
> Not a pint he gives for them.
> All his——"

"Stop," said I, "we'll have it at Dame Bottles's fire-side. Hearing songs in the night air always makes me hoarse the next morning."

"As you will," he answered without heat. "We're a'most there."

Soon a lighted window of the highwayman's humble home shone out in the darkness and a moment later Jem Bottles was knocking at the door. It was immediately opened and he stalked in with his blood-marks still upon his face. There was a great out-cry in one feminine voice and a large woman rushed forward and flung her arms about the highwayman. "Oh, Jemmie,

my son, my son," she screamed, "whatever have they done to
ye this time?"

"Silence, mother dear," said Bottles. "'Tis nought but
a wind-broken bough fallen on my head. Have you no manners?
Do you not see the gentleman awaiting to enter and warm
himself?"

The woman turned upon me alarmed but fiery and defiant.
After a moment's scrutiny, she demanded: "Oh, ho, and the
gentleman had nought to do of course with my Jem's broken
head?"

"'Tis a priest but newly arrived from his native island of
Asia," said Bottles piously, "and it ill beseems you, mother dear,
to be haggling when you might be getting the holy man and I
some supper."

"True, Jemmie, my own," responded Dame Bottles. "But there
are so many rogues abroad that you must forgive your old
mother if she grow often affrighted that her good Jemmie has
been misled." She turned to me. "Pardon, my good gentleman,"
she said almost in tears. "Ye little know what it is to be the
mother of a high-spirited boy."

"I can truthfully say that I do not, Dame Bottles," said I with
one of my father's French bows. She was immensely pleased.
Any woman may fall a victim to a limber, manly and courteous
bow.

Presently we sat down to a supper of plum-stew and bread.
Bottles had washed the blood from his face and now resembled
an honest man.

"You may think it strange, sir," said Dame Bottles with some
housewifely embarrassment, "that a highwayman of such distinction that he has had written of him in Bristol six ballads——"

"Seven," said the highwayman.

"Seven in Bristol and in Bath two."

"Three," said the highwayman.

"And three in Bath," continued the old woman. "You may
think it strange, sir, that a highwayman of such distinction
that he has had written of him in Bristol seven ballads and in
Bath three, and yet is obliged to sit down to a supper of plum-
stew and bread."

"Where is the rest of that cheese I took on last Michaelmas?" demanded Bottles suddenly.

"Jemmie," answered his mother with reproach, "you know you gave the last of it to the crippled shepherd over on the big hill."

"So I did, mother dear," assented the highwayman, "and I regret now that I let no less than three cheeses pass me on the highway because I thought we had plenty at home."

"If you let anything pass on the road because you do not lack it at the moment, you will ultimately die of starvation, Jemmie dear," quoth the mother. "How often have I told you?"

"Aye," he answered somewhat irritably, "you also often have told me take snuff-boxes."

"And was I at fault," she retorted, "because the cheating avarice of the merchants led them to make sinful paltry snuff-boxes that were mere pictures of the good old gold and silver? Was it my mischief? Or was it the mischief of the plotting swineherds who now find it to their interest to deal in base and imitative metals?"

"Peace, my mother," said the highwayman. "The gentleman here has not the same interest in snuff-boxes which moves us to loud speech."

"True," said Dame Bottles, "and I readily wish that my Jemmie had no reason to care if snuff-boxes were made from cabbage-leaves."

I had been turning a scheme in my mind and here I thought I saw my opportunity to introduce it. "Dame Bottles," said I, "your words fit well with the plan which has brought me here to your house. Know you then that I am a nobleman——"

"Alack, poor Jemmie," cried the woman raising her hands.

"No," said I, "I am not a nobleman rampant. I am a nobleman in trouble and I need the services of your son for which I will reward him with such richness that he will not care if they make snuff-boxes out of water or wind. I am in pursuit of a man——"

"The little black man," cried the alert Bottles.

"And I want your son to ride with me to catch this thief. He need never pass through the shadow of the creaking clanking tree. He will be on an honest hunt to recover a great property. Give him to me. Give him fourteen guineas from his store and bid us mount his horses and away. Save your son!"

The old woman burst into tears. "Sir," she answered, "I know little of you but, as near as I can see in the light of this one candle, you are a hangel. Take my boy! Treat him as you would your own step-son and if snuff-boxes ever get better I will let you both hear of it."

Less than an hour later, Jem Bottles and I were off for Bath, riding two very good horses.

CHAPTER IV

NOW my whole mind was really bent on finding my black Forister but yet as Jem Bottles and I rode toward Bath I thought of a cloaked figure, a pair of shining eyes, and it seemed to me that I recalled the curve of sweet proud lips. I knew that I should be thinking of my papers, my future; but a quick perversity made me dwell for a long trotting time in a dream of feminine excellence, in a dream of feminine beauty which was both ascetic and deeply sensuous. I know hardly how to say that two eyes, a vision of lips, a conception of a figure, should properly move me as I bounced along the road with Jem Bottles. But it is certain that it came upon me. The eyes of the daughter of the great Earl of Westport had put in chains the redoubtable O'Ruddy. It was true. It was clear. I admitted it to myself. The admission caused a number of reflections to occur in my mind and the chief of these was that I was a misfortunate wretch.

Jem Bottles recalled me to the immediate business. "'Tis the lights of Bath, sir," he said, "and if it please you, sir, I shall await you under yonder tree since the wretched balladists have rendered me so well-known in the town that I dare not venture in it for fear of a popular welcome from the people who have no snuff-boxes whatever."

"I will go and listen to the ballads," I replied, "and in the meantime do you await me here under that tree." So saying I galloped into Bath, my soul sharp to find Forister and to take him by the neck and to strangle out of him those papers which were my sole reasons for living. But the landlord of the best inn met me with an unmistakable frankness. "Mr. Forister?" said he. "Yes, your lordship, but Mr. Forister is gone back to Bristol."

I was so pleased with his calling me "your lordship" that I

hesitated a moment. I was almost resolved to delay for a time at this charming inn. But I was recalled to sense by the thought that although Jem Bottles and I had fifteen guineas between us, he had fourteen and I had the one. Thanking the landlord I galloped out of Bath.

Bottles was awaiting me under the tree. "To Bristol," I cried. "Our chase lies toward Bristol. He has doubled back."

" 'Twas while we were at supper," said Bottles as he cantered up to my shoulder. "I might have had two trials at him if I had not had the honour of meeting your worship. I warrant you, sir, he would not have escaped me twice."

"Think of his crack in your skull and be content," I replied. "And in the meantime ride for Bristol."

Within five miles of Bristol we came upon a wayside inn in which there was progressing a great commotion. Lights flashed from window to window and we could hear women howling. To my great surprise, Bottles at once became hugely excited. "Damme, sir," he shouted, "my sweetheart is a chamber-maid here and if she be hurted, I will know it." He spurred valiantly forward and, after futilely calling to him to check his career, I followed. He leaped from his horse at the door of the inn and bounced into the place, pistol in hand. I was too confused to understand much but it seemed to my ears that his entrance was hailed with a roar of relief and joy. A stable-boy, tearfully anxious, grasped my bridle, crying: "Go in, sir, in God's name. They will be killing each other." Taking that, whatever betide, it was proper to be at the back of my friend Bottles, I too sprang from my horse and popped into the inn.

A more unexpected sight never met my experienced gaze. A fat landlady, mark you, was sobbing in the arms of my villainous friend and a pretty maid was clinging to his arm and screaming. At the same time there were about him a dozen people of both sexes who were yelling: "Oh, pray, Master Bottles! Good Master Bottles, do stop them. One is a great Afric chief, red as a fire, and the other is Satan, Satan himself! Oh, pray, good Master Bottles, stop them."

My fine highwayman was puffed out like a poisoned frog. I had had no thought that he could be so grand. "What is this disturbance?" he demanded in a bass voice.

"Oh, good Master Bottles," clamoured the people. "Satan wishes to kill the Red Giant who has Satan barred in the best room in the inn and they make frightful destruction of chairs and tables. Bid them cease, oh, good Master Bottles."

From overhead, we could hear the sound of blows upon wood mingling with threatening talk. "Stand aside," said the highwayman in a great gruff voice which made me marvel at him. He unhesitatingly dumped the swooning form of the landlady into another pair of arms, shook off the pretty maid, and moved sublimely upon the foot of the stairs amid exclamations of joy, wonder, admiration, even reverence.

But the voice of an unseen person hailed suddenly from the head of the stairs. "And if ye have not said enough masses for your heathen soul," remarked the voice, "you would be better mustering the neighbors this instant to go to church for you and bid them do the best they can in a short time. You will never be coming down stairs if you once come up."

Bottles hesitated; the company shuddered out: " 'Tis the Red Giant."

"And I would be having one more word with you," continued the unseen person. "I have him here and here I keep him. 'Tis not me that wants the little black rogue, what with his hammering on the door and his calling me out of my name. 'Tis no work that I like and I would liever go in and put my heel in his face. But I was told to catch a little black man and I have him and him I will keep. 'Tis not me that wished to come here and catch little black men for anybody but here I am in this foreign country catching little black men and I will have no interference."

But here I gave a great call of recognition. "Paddy!" I saw the whole thing. This wild-headed Paddy whom I had told to catch me a little black man had followed after me toward Bath and somehow managed to barricade in a room the very first man he saw who was small and black. At first I wished to laugh; an instant later, I was furious. "Paddy," I thundered, "come down out of that now! What would you be doing? Come down out of that now!"

The reply was sulky but unmistakably from Paddy. Most of it was mumbled. "Sure I've gone and caught as little and as black a man as is in the whole world and was keeping the scoundrel here safe and along he comes and tells me to come down out of that now with no more gratitude than if he had given me a gold goose. And yet I fought a duel for him and managed everything so finely that he came away well enough to box me on the ear which was mere hilarity and means nothing between friends."

Jem Bottles was still halted on the stair. He and all the others had listened to Paddy's speeches in a blank amazement which had much superstition in it. "Shall I go up, sir?" he asked, not eagerly.

"No," said I. "Leave me to deal with it. I fear a great mistake. Give me ten minutes and I promise to empty the inn of all uproar." A murmur of admiration arose and as the sound leaped about my ears, I moved casually and indifferently up against Paddy. It was a grand scene.

"Paddy," I whispered as soon as we were a distance on the stairs safe from the ears of the people below. "Paddy, you have made a great blunder. You have the wrong man."

" 'Tis unlikely," replied Paddy with scorn. "You wait until you see him and if he is not little and black, then——"

"Yes, yes," said I hastily, "but it was not any little black man at all which I wanted. It was a particular little black man."

"But," said the ruffian brightly, "it would be possible this one will serve your end. He's little and he's black——"

At this moment the voice of the captive came intoning through the door of a chamber. "When I am free, I will first cut out your liver and have it grilled and feed it to you as you are dying."

Paddy had stepped forward and placed his lips within about six inches of one of the panels. "Come now, be easy," he said. "You know well that if you should do as you say, I would beat your head that it would have the looks of a pudding fallen from a high window and that's the truth."

"Open the door, rascal," called the captive, "and we shall see."

"I will be opening no doors," retorted Paddy indignantly. "Remain quiet, you little black devil, or, by the mass, I'll——"

"I'll slice your heart into pieces of paper," thundered Paddy's prisoner, kicking and pounding.

By this time, I was ready to interfere. "Paddy," said I catching him by the shoulder, "you have the wrong man. Leave it to me, mind you. Leave it to me."

"He's that small and black, you'd think——" he began dejectedly but I cut him short. Jem Bottles, unable to endure the suspense, had come up from below. He was still bristling and blustering as if all the maids were remarking him. "And why does this fine gentleman kick and pound on the door?" he demanded in a gruff voice loud enough to be heard in all appreciative parts of the inn. "I'll have him out and slit his nose."

The thunder on the door ceased and the captive observed: "Ha, another scoundrel! If my ears do not play me false there are now three waiting for me to kick them to the hangman."

Restraining Paddy and Bottles who each wished to reply in heroic verse to this sally, I stepped to the door. "Sir," said I civilly, "I fear a great blunder has been done. I——"

"Why," said the captive with a sneer, " 'tis the Irishman! 'Tis the king of the Irelands. Open the door, pig."

My elation knew no bounds. "Paddy," cried I, "you have the right little black man." But there was no time for celebration. I must first answer my enemy. "You will remember that I kicked you once," said I, "and if you have a memory as long as my finger be careful I do not kick you again else even people as far away as the French will think you are a meteor. But I would not be bandying words at long range. Paddy, unbar the door."

"And if I can," muttered Paddy fumbling with a lot of machinery so ingenious that it would require a great lack of knowledge to thoroughly understand it. In the meantime we could hear Forister move away from the door and by the sound of a leisurely scrape of a chair on the floor I judged he had taken seat somewhere near the centre of the room. Bottles was handling his pistol and regarding me. "Yes," said I, "if he fires, do you pepper him fairly. Otherwise, await my orders. Paddy, you slug, unbar the door."

"If I am able," said Paddy still muttering and fumbling with his contrivances. He had no sooner mouthed the words than the door flew open as if by magic and we discovered a room bright with the light of a fire and candles. Forister was seated negligently at a table in the centre of the room. His legs were crossed but his naked sword lay on the table at his hand. He had the first word because I was amazed, almost stunned, by the precipitous opening of the door.

"Ho, ho," he observed frigidly, "'tis indeed the king of the Irelands accompanied by the red-headed duke who has entertained me for some time and a third party with a thief's face who handles a loaded pistol with such abandon as leads me to suppose that he once may have been a highwayman. A very pretty band."

"Use your tongue for a garter, Forister," said I. "I want my papers."

CHAPTER V

YOUR 'papers'?" said Forister. "Damn you and your 'papers.' What would I know of your 'papers'?"

"I mean," said I fiercely, "the papers you stole out of my chamber in the inn at Bristol."

The man actually sank back in his chair and laughed me up to the roof. "'Papers'!" he shouted. "Here's the king of the Irelands thinking that I have made off with his papers! Ha, ha, ha!"

"You choose a good time for laughing," said I with more sobriety. "In a short time, you will be laughing with the back of your head."

He sat up and looked at me with quick decision. "Now, what is all this rubbish about 'papers'?" he said sharply. "What have I to do with your filthy 'papers'? I had one intention regarding you. Of that I am certain. I was resolved to kill you on the first occasion when we could cross swords, but—'papers'—faugh! What do you mean?"

The hoarse voice of Jem Bottles broke in from somewhere behind me. "We might easily throw him to the earth and tie him, sir, and then make search of him."

"And you would know how to go about the business, I warrant me," laughed Forister. "You muzzle-faced rogue, you!"

To my astonishment, the redoubtable highwayman gave back before the easy disdain of this superior scoundrel. "My ways may not have been always straight and narrow, master," he rejoined almost in a whine, "but you have no call to name me muzzle-faced."

Forister turned from him contemptuously and fixed his regard with much enthusiasm upon Paddy. "Very red," said he. "Very red indeed. And thick as faggots, too. A very delectable head of hair, fit to be spun into a thousand blankets for the naked savages in heathen parts. The wild forests of Ireland must indeed be dark when it requires a lantern of this measure to light the lonely traveller on his way."

But Paddy was an honest man even if he did not know it and he at once walked to Forister and held against his ear a fist the size of a pig's hind-leg. "I can not throw the talk back to you," he said. "You are too fast for me but I tell you to your face that you had better change your tongue for a lock of an old witch's hair unless you intend to be battered this moment."

"Peace," said Forister calmly. "I am a man of natural wit and I would entertain myself. Now there is your excellent chieftain, the king of the Irelands. Him I regard as a very good specimen whose ancestors were not very long ago swinging by their tails from the lofty palms of Ireland and playing with cocoa-nuts to and fro." He smiled and leaned back well-satisfied with himself.

All this time, I had been silent because I had been deep in a reflection on Forister. Now I said: "Forister, you are a great rogue. I know you. One thing is certain. You have not my papers and never did you have them."

He looked upon me with some admiration. "Aye, the cannibal shows a glimmer of reason," he cried. "No, I have not your foolish papers and I only wish I had them in order to hurl the bundle at your damned stupid head."

"For a kicked man you have a gay spirit," I replied. "But at any rate I have no time for you now. I am off to Bristol after my papers and I only wish for the sake of ease that I had to go no farther than this chamber. Come, Paddy; come, Jem."

My two henchmen were manifestly disappointed; they turned reluctantly at my word. "Have I the leave of one crack at him, your honour?" whispered Paddy earnestly. "He said my head was a lantern."

"No," said I, "leave him to his meditations." As we passed down the corridor we heard him laugh loudly and he called out to me: "When I come to Bristol, I will kill you."

I had more than a mind to go back and stuff this threat into his throat but I better knew my business. My business was to recover the papers. "Come," said I and we passed down stairs.

The people of the inn made way for Paddy as if he had been a falling tree and at the same time they worshipped Jem Bottles for having performed everything. I had some wonder as to which would be able to out-strut the other. I think Jem Bottles won the match for he had the advantage of being known as one of the most dangerous men in south-western England whereas Paddy had only his own vanity to help him. " 'Tis all arranged," said Bottles, pompously. "Your devil will come forth as quiet as a rabbit."

We ordered our horses and a small crowd of obsequious stable-boys rushed to fetch them. I marvelled when I saw them lead out Paddy's horse. I had thought from what I perceived over my shoulder when I left Bristol that he would never be able to make a half-league in the saddle. Amid the flicker of lanterns, Bottles and I mounted, and then I heard Paddy calling to him all the stable-boys. "Now, when I give the word, you heave for your lives. Stand, you beast! Can not four of you hold him by the legs? I will be giving the word in a moment. Are you all ready? Well, then, now, for your lives—wait a bit. You there with the round face, will not you see that one of my feet is caught in the stirrup? Well, now, ready again—heave!" There was a short scuffle in the darkness and presently Paddy appeared above the heads of the others in the melee. "There, now," said he to them, "that was well done. One would easily be telling that I was an ex-trooper of the King." He rode out to us complacently. " 'Tis a good horse, if only he steered with a tiller instead of these straps," he remarked, "and he goes well before the wind."

"To Bristol," said I. "Paddy, you must follow as best you may. I have no time to be watching you although you are interesting."

An unhappy cry came from behind as Bottles and I spurred on but again I could not wait for my faithful fellow-countryman. My papers were still the stake for which I played. However I hoped that Paddy would now give over his ideas about catching little black men.

As we neared Bristol, Jem Bottles once more became backward. He referred to the seven ballads and feared that the unexpected presence of such a well-known character would create an excitement which would not be easy to cool. So we made a rendezvous under another tree and I rode on alone. Thus I was separated from both my good companions. However, before parting, I took occasion to borrow five guineas from Jem's store.

I was as weary as a dog although I had never been told that gentlemen riding amid such adventures were ever a-weary. At the inn in Bristol a sleepy boy took my horse and a sleepy landlord aroused himself as he recognized me. "My poor inn is at your disposal, sir," he cried as he bowed. "The Earl has enquired for you today, or yesterday, as well as young my Lord Strepp and Colonel Royale."

"Aye?" said I carelessly. "Did they so? Show me to a chamber. I am much enwearied. I would seek a good bed and a sound sleep for I have ridden far and done much since last I had repose."

"Yes, sir," said the landlord deferentially.

After a long hard sleep, I was aroused by a constant pounding on my door. At my cry, a servant entered. He was very abject. "His lordship's valet has been waiting to give you a message from his lordship, sir." I bid him let the valet enter. The man whose heroic nose had borne the brunt of Forister's swift departure from the inn when I kicked him, came into my chamber with distinguished grace and dignity and informed me that his noble master cared to see me in his chamber when it would suit my convenience.

Of course, the old Earl was after his papers. And what was I to tell him? Was I to tell him that I was all be-fooled and be-fuddled? Was I to tell him that after my father had kept these papers for so many years in faithful trust, I had lost them on the very brink of deliverance of them to their rightful owner? What was I to speak?

I did not wish to see the Earl of Westport but some sudden and curious courage forced me into my clothes and out to the corridor. The Earl's valet was waiting there. "I pray you, sir, follow me," he said. I followed him to an expensive part of the inn where he knocked on a door. It was opened by a bending serving-man. The room was a kind of parlour and in it, to my surprise, were Lord Strepp and Colonel Royale. They gazed at me with a surprise equivalent to mine own.

Young Lord Strepp was the first one to thoroughly collect himself. Then he advanced upon me with out-stretched hand.

"Mr. O'Ruddy," he cried, "believe me, we are glad to see you. We thought you had gone for all time."

Colonel Royale was only a moment behind his friend but as he extended his hand, his face flushed painfully. "Sir," he said somewhat formally, "not long ago I lost my temper, I fear. I know I have to thank you for great consideration and generosity. I—I—you——"

Whereupon we both began to stammer and grimace. All the time I was choking out: "Pray—pray, don't speak of it—a nothing—a mere nothing—in truth, you kindly exaggerate— I——"

It was young Lord Strepp who brought us out of our embarrassment. "Here are two good fellows," he cried heartily. "A glass of wine with you."

We looked gratefully at him and in the business of filling our glasses we lost our awkwardness. "To you," said Lord Strepp and as we drained our wine I knew that I had two more friends in England.

During the drinking, the Earl's valet had been hovering near my coat-tails. Afterward he took occasion to make gentle suggestion to me. "His lordship awaits your presence in his chamber, sir, when it please you."

The other gentlemen immediately deferred to my obligation and I followed the valet into a large darkened chamber. It was some moments before my eyes could discover that the Earl was a-bed. Indeed, a rasping voice from beneath the canopies called to me before I knew that anybody was in the chamber but myself and the valet.

"Come hither, O'Ruddy," called the Earl. "Tompkins, get out! Is it your duty to stand there mummified? Get out!"

The servant hastily withdrew and I walked slowly to the great man's bed-side. Two shining shrewd eyes looked at me from a mass of pillows and I had a knowledge of an aged face, half-smiling and yet satirical, even malignant. "And so this is the young fortune-hunter from Ireland," he said in a hoarse sick-man's voice. "The young fortune-hunter! Ha! With his worthless papers! Ha!"

"Worthless?" cried I, starting.

"Worthless!" cried the Earl vehemently. He tried to lift himself in his bed in order to make more emphasis. "Worthless! Nothing but straw—straw—straw!" Then he cackled out a laugh.

And this was my inheritance! I could have sobbed my grief and anger but I took firm hold on myself and resolved upon another way of dealing with the old nobleman. "My lord," said I, coldly, "my father is dead. When he was dying he gave certain papers into my hands, papers which he had guarded for many years, and bade me as his son deliver them into the hands of an old friend and comrade and I come to this old friend and comrade of my father and he lies back in his bed and cackles at me like a hen. 'Tis a small foot I would have set upon England if I had known more of you, you old skate!"

But still he laughed and cried: "Straw! Straw! Nothing but straw!"

"Well, sir," said I with icy dignity, "I may be a fool of an Irishman with no title save an older one than yours, but I would be deeply sorry if there came a day when I should throw a trust back in the teeth of a dead comrade's son."

"No," said the bright-eyed old man, comforting himself amid his pillows. "Look you, O'Ruddy! You are a rascal. You came over here in an attempt to ruin me. I know it."

I was awed by this accusation. It seemed to me to be too grand, too gorgeous for my personal consumption. I knew not what to do with this colossus. It towered above me in splendour and gilt. I had never expected to be challenged with attempting to ruin earls. My father had often ruined sea-captains but he never in his life ruined so much as a baronet. It seemed altogether too fine for my family but I could only blurt weakly: "Yessir." I was much like a lackey.

"Aye," said the old man, suddenly feeble from the excitement, "I see you admit it, you black Irish rogue." He sank back and plied a napkin to his mouth. It seemed to come away stained with blood. "You scoundrel, you," he bleated, as soon as he could speak. "You scoundrel!"

I had a strange cowardly inclination to fling myself upon this ancient survival and squeeze his throat until it closed like a purse. And my inclination was so strong that I stood like a stone.

The valet opened the door. "If it please your lordship—Lady Mary," he announced and stood aside to let a lady pass.

The Earl seemed to instantly forget my presence. He began at once to make himself uncomfortable in his bed. Then he cried fretfully: "Come, Mary, what caused you to be so long! Make me easy! Ruffle my pillows! Come, daughter."

"Yes, father," answered a soothing and sweet voice. A gracious figure passed before me and bended over the bed of the Earl. I was near blinded. It was not a natural blindness. It was an artificial blindness which came from my emotion. Was she tall? I don't know. Was she short? I don't know. But I am certain that she was of exactly the right size. She was, in all ways, perfection. She was of such glory, she was so splendid, that my heart ceased to beat. I remained standing like a stone but my sword's scabbard, reminiscent of some movement, flapped gently against my leg. I thought it was a horrible sound. I sought to stay it but it continued to tinkle and I remember that standing there in the room with the old Earl and my love-'til-death, I thought most of my scabbard and its inability to lay quiet at my thigh.

She smoothed his bed and coaxed him and comforted him. Never had I seen such tenderness. It was like a vision of a classic hereafter. In a second I would have exchanged my youth for the position of this doddering old nobleman who spat blood into a napkin.

Suddenly the Earl wheeled his eyes and saw me. "Ha, Mary," he cried feebly, "I wish to point out a rogue. There he stands. The O'Ruddy. An Irishman and a fine robber. Mark him well and keep stern watch of your jewels."

The beautiful young lady turned upon me an affrighted glance. And I stood like a stone.

"Aye," sang the old wretch, "keep stern watch of your jewels. He is a very demon for skill. He could take a ring from your finger while you were thinking he was fluttering his hands in the air."

I bowed gallantly to the young lady. "Your rings are safe, my lady. I would ill requite the kindness shown by your father to the son of an old friend if I deprived your white fingers of a single ornament."

"Clever as ever, clever as ever," chuckled the wicked old man.

The young lady flushed and looked first at me and then at her father. I thought her eye as it rested upon me was not without some sympathetic feeling. I adored her. All the same I wished to kill her father. It is very curious when one wishes to kill the father of the woman that one adores. But I suppose the situation was made more possible for me by the fact that it would have been extremely inexpedient to have killed the Earl in his sick-bed. I even grinned at him. "If you remember my father, your lordship," said I amiably, "despite your trying hard to forget him, you will remember that he had a certain native wit which on occasion led him to be able to frustrate his enemies. It must have been a family trait for I seem to have it. You are an evil old man! You yourself stole my papers!"

CHAPTER VI

AT first I thought that my speech had given the aged Earl a stroke. He wrestled on his bed and something appeared at his lips which was like froth. His lovely daughter sprang to him with a cry of fear and woe. But he was not dying; he was only mad with rage. "How dare you? How dare you?" he gasped. "You whelp of Satan!"

" 'Tis me that would not be fearing to dare anything," I rejoined calmly. "I would not so. I came here with a mind for fair words but you have met me with insult and something worse. We cannot talk the thing. We must act it. The papers are yours but you took them from me unfairly. You may destroy them. Otherwise I will have them back and discover what turned you into a great rogue near the end of your days."

"Hearken!" screamed the Earl. "Hearken! He threatens." The door into the parlour flew open and Lord Strepp and Colonel Royale appeared on the threshold, their faces blank with wonder. "Father," cried the young lord, stepping hastily forward. "Whatever is wrong?"

"That!" cried the Earl, pointing a palsied finger at me. "That! He comes here and threatens—threatens—he threatens me, a peer of England."

The Lady Mary spoke swiftly to her brother and the Colonel. " 'Tis a sick man's fancy," she said. "There have been no threats. Father has had a bad day. He is not himself. He talks wildly. He——"

"Mary!" yelled the Earl as well as he was able. "Do you betray me? Do you betray your own father? Oh, a woman Judas and my daughter!"

Lord Strepp and Colonel Royale looked as if their minds were coming apart. They stared at Lady Mary, at the Earl, at me. For my part I remained silent and stiff in a corner, keeping my eye upon the swords of the other gentlemen. I had no doubt but that presently I would be engaged in a desperate attempt to preserve my life. Lady Mary was weeping. She had never once glanced in my direction. But I was thrilling with happiness. She had flung me her feeble intercession even as a lady may fling a bun to a bear in a pit but I had the remembrance to prize, to treasure, and if both gentlemen had set upon me and the sick Earl had advanced with the warming pan I believe my new strength would have been able to beat them off.

In the meantime, the Earl was screeching meaningless rubbish in which my name, with epithets, occurred constantly. Lady Mary, still weeping, was trying to calm him.

Young Lord Strepp at last seemed to make up his mind. He approached me and politely remarked: "An inexplicable situation, Mr. O'Ruddy."

"More to me than to you," I replied suavely.

"How?" he asked, with less consideration in his manner. "I know nought of this mummery."

"At least I know no more," I replied, still suave.

"How, Mr. O'Ruddy?" he asked frowning. "I enter and find you wrangling with my father in his sick chamber. Is there to be no word for this?"

"I dare say you will get forty from your father; a hundred, it may be," said I, always pleasant. "But from me you will get none."

He reflected for a moment. "I dare say you understand I will brook no high-handed silence in a matter of this kind? I am accustomed to ask for the reasons for certain kinds of conduct and of course I am somewhat prepared to see that the reasons are forthcoming."

"Well, in this case, my lord," said I with a smile, "you can accustom yourself to not getting a reason for a certain kind of conduct because I do not intend to explain myself."

But at this instant our agreeable discussion was interrupted by the old Earl who began to bay at his son. "Arthur, Arthur, fling the rascal out, fling the rascal out! He is an impostor, a thief!" He began to fume and sputter; he threw his arms wildly; he was in some kind of a convulsion; his pillows tossed; suddenly a packet fell from under them to the floor. As all eyes

wheeled toward it, I stooped swiftly and picked up this packet.
"My papers," said I.

On their part there was a breathless moment of indecision.
Then the swords of Lord Strepp and the Colonel came wildly
from their scabbards. Mine was whipped out no less speedily
but I took it and flung it on the floor at their feet, the hilt
toward them. "No," said I, my hands empty save for the papers,
" 'tis only that I would be making a present to the fair Lady
Mary which I pray her to receive." With my best Irish bow I
extended to the young lady the papers, my inheritance, which
had caused her father so much foaming at the mouth.

She looked at me scornfully, she looked at her father, she
looked at me pathetically, she looked at her father, she looked
at me piteously; she took the papers.

I walked to the lowering and abashed points of the other
men's swords and picked my blade from the floor. I paid no
heed to the glittering points which flashed near my eyes. I
strode to the door; I turned and bowed; as I did so, I believed
that I saw something in Lady Mary's eyes which I wished to see
there. I closed the door behind me.

But immediately there was a great clamour in the room I
had left and the door was thrown violently open again. Colonel
Royale appeared in a high passion. "No, no, O'Ruddy," he
shouted, "you are a gallant gentleman. I would stake my life you
are in the right. Say the word and I will back you to the end
against ten million fiends."

And after him came tempestuously young Lord Strepp white
on the lips with pure rage. But he spoke with a sudden steadi-
ness. "Colonel Royale, it appears," he said, "thinks he has to
protect my friend The O'Ruddy from some wrong of my family
or of mine?"

The Colonel drew in his breath for a dangerous reply but
I quickly broke in. "Come, come, gentlemen," said I sharply.
"Are swords to flash between friends while there are so many
damned scoundrels in the world to parry and pink? 'Tis wrong;
'tis very wrong. Now, mark you, let us be men of peace at least
until tomorrow morning when by the way I have to fight your
friend Forister."

"Forister," they cried together. Their jaws fell; their eyes bulged; they forgot everything; there was a silence.

"Well," said I, wishing to re-assure them, "it may not be tomorrow morning. He only told me that he would kill me as soon as he came to Bristol and I expected him tonight or in the morning. I would of course be expecting him to show here as quickly as possible after his grand speech but he would not be entirely unwelcome, I am thinking, for I have a mind to see if the sword of an honest man, but no fighter, would be able to put this rogue to shame and him with all his high talk about killing people who have never done a thing in life to him but kick him some number of feet out into the inn-yard and this need never to have happened if he had known enough to have kept his sense of humour to himself which often happens in this world."

Reflectively, Colonel Royale murmured: "One of the finest swordsmen in England."

For this I cared nothing.

Reflectively, Lord Strepp murmured: "My father's partner in the shipping trade."

This last made me open my eyes. "Your father's partner in the shipping trade, Lord Strepp? That little black rascal?"

The young nobleman looked sheepish. "Aye, I doubt not he may well be called a little black rascal, O'Ruddy," he answered, "but, in fact, he is my father's partner in certain large—fairly large, you know—shipping interests. Of course, that is a matter of no consequence to me personally—but—I believe my father likes him and my mother and my sister are quite fond of him I think. I, myself, have never been able to quite—quite understand him in certain ways. He seems a trifle odd at moments. But he certainly is a friend of the family."

"Then," said I, "you will not be able to have the felicity of seeing him kill me, Lord Strepp."

"On the contrary," he rejoined considerately, "I would regard it as usual if he asked me to accompany him to the scene of the fight."

His remark, incidentally, that his sister was fond of Forister filled me with a sudden insolent madness. "I would hesitate to disturb any shipping trade," I said with dignity. "It is far from me to wish that the commerce of Great Britain should be hampered by sword-thrust of mine. If it would please young Lord Strepp I could hand my apologies to Forister, all tied up in blue silk ribbon."

But the youthful nobleman only looked at me long with a sad and reproachful gaze. "O'Ruddy," he said mournfully, "I have seen you do two fine things. You have never seen me do anything. But, know you now, once and for all, that you may not quarrel with me."

This was too much for an Irish heart. I was moved to throw myself on this lad's neck. I wished to swear to him that I was a brother in blood, I wished to cut a vein to give him everlasting strength—but perhaps his sister Mary had something to do with this feeling.

Colonel Royale had been fidgeting. Now he said suddenly: "Strepp, I wronged you! Your pardon, Mr. O'Ruddy, but, damme, Strepp, if I didn't think you had gone wrong for the moment."

Lord Strepp took the offered hand. "You are a stupid old fire-brain," he said affectionately to the Colonel.

"Well," said the Colonel jubilantly, "now everything is clear. If Mr. O'Ruddy will have me I will go with him to meet this Forister and you, Strepp, will accompany Forister and we all will meet in a friendly way—ahem."

"The situation is intimately involved," said Lord Strepp dejectedly. "It will be a ridiculous business of watching each blade lunge toward the breast of a friend. I don't know it is proper. Royale, let us set ourselves to part these duellists. It is indecent."

"Did you note the manner in which he kicked him out of the inn?" asked the Colonel. "Do you think a few soothing words would calm the mind of one of the finest swordsmen in England?"

I began to do some profound thinking. "Look you, Colonel," said I. "Do you mean to say this wretched little liar and coward is a fine swordsman?"

"I haven't heard what you called him," said the Colonel, "but his sword-play is regular fire-light on the wall. However," he added hopefully, "we may find some way to keep him from killing you. I have seen some of the greatest swordsmen lose by chance to a novice. It is sometimes like cards. And yet you are not an ignorant player. That, I, Clarence Royale, know full well. Let us try to beat him."

I remembered Forister's parting sentence. Could it be true that a man I had kicked with such enthusiasm and success was now about to take revenge by killing me? I was really disturbed. I was a very brave youth but I had the most advanced ideas about being killed. On occasion of great danger I could easily and tranquilly develope a philosophy of avoidance and retirement. I had no antiquated notions about going out and getting myself killed through sheer bull-headed scorn of the other fellow's hurting me. My father had taught me this discretion. As a soldier he claimed that he had run away from nine battles and he would have run away from more, he said, only that all the others had turned out to be victories for his side. He was admittedly a brave man but, more than this, he had a great deal of sense. I was the child of my father. It did not seem to me profitable to be killed for the sake of a sentiment which seemed weak and dispensable. This little villain! Should I allow him to gratify a furious revenge because I was afraid to take to my heels? I resolved to have the courage of my emotions. I would run away.

But of all this I said nothing. It passed through my mind like light and left me still smiling gayly at Colonel Royale's observations upon the situation. "Wounds in the body from Forister," quoth he academically, "are almost certain to be fatal for his wrist has a magnificent twirl which reminds one of a top. I do not know where he learned this wrist movement but almost invariably it leads him to kill his man. Last year, I saw him—— However I digress. I must look to it that O'Ruddy has quiet, rest and peace of mind until the morning."

Yes; I would have great peace of mind until the morning! I saw that clearly. "Well," said I, "at any rate, we will know more tomorrow. A good day to you, Lord Strepp and I hope your principal has no more harm come to him than I care to have come to me which is precious little and in which case the two of us will be little hurted."

"Good-bye, O'Ruddy," said the young man.

In the corridor, the Colonel slapped my shoulder in a sudden exuberant out-burst. "O'Ruddy," he cried, "the chance of your life! Probably the best-known swordsman in all England! 'Pon my word, if you should even graze him, they would almost make you a peer. If you truly pinked him you could marry a duchess. My eye, what an opportunity for a young and ambitious man."

"And what right has he to be such a fine swordsman?" I demanded fretfully. "Damn him! 'Tis no right of a little tadpole like him to be a great cut-throat. One could never have told from the look of him and yet it simply teaches one to be always cautious with men."

The Colonel was simply bubbling over with good-nature, his mind full of the prospective event. "I saw Ponsonby kill Stewart in their great fight several years agone," he cried rubbing his hands, "but Ponsonby was no such swordsman as Forister and I misdoubt me that Stewart was much better than you yourself."

Here was a cheerful butcher. I eyed him coldly. "And out of this," said I slowly, "comes a vast deal of entertainment for you and a hole between two ribs for me. I think I need a drink."

"By all means, my boy," he answered, heartily. "Come to my chamber. A quart of port under your waistcoat will cure a certain bilious desire in you to see the worst of things which I have detected lately in your manner. With grand sport before us, how could you be otherwise than jolly? Ha, ha!" So saying he affectionately took my arm and led me along the corridor.

CHAPTER VII

WHEN I reached my own chamber, I sank heavily into a chair. My brain was in a tumult. I had fallen in love and arranged to be killed, in one short day's work. I stared at my image in a mirror. Could I be The O'Ruddy? Perhaps my name was Paddy or Jem Bottles? Could I pick myself out in a crowd? Could I establish an identification? I little knew.

At first I thought of my calm friend who apparently drank blood for his breakfast. Colonel Royale to me was somewhat of a stranger but his charming willingness to grind the bones of his friends in his teeth was now quite clear. I fight the best swordsman in England? As an amusement, a show? I began to see reasons for returning to Ireland. It was doubtful if old Mickey Clancy would be able to take full care of my estate even with the assistance and prevention of Father Donovan. All properties looked better while the real owner had his eye on them. It would be a shame to waste the place at Glandore all for a bit of pride of staying in England. Never a man neglected his patrimony but what it didn't melt down to a kick in the breeches and much trouble in the courts. I perceived, in short, that my Irish lands were in danger. What could endanger them was not quite clear to my eye but, at any rate, they must be saved. Moreover, it was necessary to take quick measures. I started up from my chair, hastily re-counting Jem Bottles' five guineas.

But I bethought me of Lady Mary. She could hardly be my good fairy. She was rather too plump to be a fairy. She was not extremely plump but when she walked, something moved within her skirts. For my part, I think little of fairies, who remind me of roasted fowl's wing. Give me the less brittle beauty which is not likely to break in a man's arms.

After all, I reflected, Mickey Clancy could take care quite well of that estate at Glandore and, if he didn't, Father Donovan would soon bring him to trouble and, if Father Donovan couldn't, why, the place was worth very little anyhow. Besides, 'tis a very weak man who cannot throw an estate into the air for a pair of bright eyes—I mean, eyes like Lady Mary's eyes.

Aye, and Lady Mary's bright eyes. That was one matter. And then there was Forister's bright sword. That was another matter. But to my descendants I declare that my hesitation did not endure an instant. Forister might have an arm so supple and a sword so long that he might be able to touch the nape of his neck with his own point but I was firm on English soil. I would meet him even if he were a chevaux de frise. Little it mattered to me. He might swing the ten arms of an Indian god; he might yell like a gale at sea; he might be more terrible in appearance than a volcano in its passions; still I would meet him.

There was a knock and, at my bidding, a servant appeared. "A gentleman, Mr. Forister, wishes to see you, sir," said the servant.

For a moment I was privately in a panic. Should I say that I was ill and then send for a doctor in order to prove that I was not ill? Should I run straightway and hide under the bed? No.

"Bid the gentleman enter," said I to the servant.

Forister came in smiling, cool and deadly. "Good-day to you, Mr. O'Ruddy," he said showing me his little teeth. "I am glad to see that you are not consorting for the moment with high-waymen and other abandoned characters who might succeed in corrupting your morals, Mr. O'Ruddy. My business with you may be made very abrupt, Mr. O'Ruddy. I have decided to kill you, Mr. O'Ruddy. You may have heard that I am the finest swordsman in England, Mr. O'Ruddy?"

I replied calmly: "I have heard that you are the finest swordsman in England, Mr. Forister, whenever better swordsmen have been travelling in foreign parts, Mr. Forister, and when no visitors of fencing distinction have taken occasion to journey here, Mr. Forister."

This talk did not give him pleasure, evidently. He had entered with brave composure but now he bit his lip and shot me a glance of hatred. "I only wished to announce," he said savagely, "that I would prefer to kill you in the morning as early as possible."

"And how may I render my small assistance to you, Mr. Forister? Have you come to request me to arise at an untimely hour?" I was very placid but it was not for him to be coming to my chamber with talk of killing me. Still, I thought that, inasmuch as he was there, I might do some good to myself by irritating him slightly. "I today informed my friends——"

"Your friends?" said he.

"My friends," said I. "Colonel Royale acts for me in this matter."

"Colonel Royale?" said he.

"Colonel Royale," said I. "And if you are bound to talk more you had best thrust your head from the window and talk to those chimneys there which will take far more interest in your speech than I can work up. I was telling you that today I informed my friends—then you interrupted me. Well, I informed them. But what the devil I informed them of, you will not know very soon. I can promise you, however, it was not a thing you would care to hear with your hands tied behind you."

"Here's a cold man with a belly full of ice," said he musingly. "I have wronged him. He has a tongue on him, he has that. And here I have been judging from his appearance that he was a mere common dolt. And, what, Mr. O'Ruddy," he added, "were you pleased to say to the gentlemen which I would not care to hear with my hands tied behind me?"

"I told them why you took that sudden trip to Bath," I answered softly.

He fairly leaped in a sudden wild rage. "You—told them?" he stuttered. "You poltroon! 'Twas a coward's work!"

"Be easy," said I, to soothe him. " 'Tis no more cowardly than it is for the best swordsman in England to be fighting the worst swordsman in Ireland over a matter in which he is entirely in the wrong although 'tis not me that cares one way or another way. Indeed I prefer you to be in the wrong, you little black pig."

"Stop," said he with a face as white as milk. "You told them—you told them about—about the girl at Bath?"

"What girl at Bath?" said I innocently. " 'Tis not me what be knowing your wenches in Bath or otherwheres."

A red flush came into the side of his neck and swelled slowly across his cheeks. "If you've told them about Nell!" he stammered beside himself. "If you've told them about Nell!"

"Nell?" said I. "Nell? Yes, that's the name. Nell. Yes, Nell. And if I told them about Nell?"

"Then," he rejoined solemnly, "I shall kill you ten times if I lose my soul in everlasting hell for it."

"But after I've killed you eleven times I shall go to Bath and have some sweet interviews with fair Nell," said I. This sting I expected to call forth a terrific out-burst but he remained scowling in dark thought. Then I saw where I had been wrong. This Nell was now more a shame than a sweetheart and he was afraid that word had been passed by me to the brother of——

Here was a chance to disturb him. "When I was making my little joke of you and your flame at Bath," said I thoughtfully, "I believe there were no ladies present. I don't remember, quite. Anyhow, we will let that pass. 'Tis of no consequence."

And here I got him in full cry. *"God rot you!"* he shrieked. His sword sprang and whistled in the air.

"Hold," said I as a man of peace. " 'Twould be murder. My weapon is on the bed and I am too lazy to go and fetch it. And in the meantime, let me assure you that no word has crossed my lips in regard to Nell, your Bath sweetheart, for the very excellent reason that I never knew of her existence until you yourself told me some minutes ago."

Never before had he met a man like me. I thought his under-jaw would drop on the floor.

"Up to a short time ago," said I candidly, "your indecent amours were safe from my knowledge. Now, since you have been so good as to give me your confidence, your indecent amours are safe from other people's knowledge. I can be in the way of putting myself as silent as a turtle when it comes to protecting a man from his folly with a woman. In fact, I am a gentleman. But," I added sternly, "what of the child?"

"The child!" he cried jumping. "May hell swallow you! And what may you know of the child?"

I waved my hand in gentle deprecation of his excitement.

"Peace, Forister; I knew nothing of any child. It was only an observation by a man of natural wit who desired to entertain himself. And pray, how old is the infant?"

He breathed heavily. "You are a fiend," he answered. Keeping his eyes on the floor, he deliberated upon his choice of conduct. Presently he sheathed his sword and turned with some of his old jauntiness toward the door. "Very good," said he. "Tomorrow we shall know more of our own affairs."

"True," I replied.

"We shall learn if slyness and treachery are to be defeated by fair-going and honour."

"True," said I.

"We shall learn if a snake in the grass can with freedom bite the foot of a lion."

"True," said I.

There was a loud jovial clamour at the door, and, at my cry, it flew open. Colonel Royale entered precipitately, beaming with good humour. "O'Ruddy, you rascal," he shouted, "I commanded you to take much rest and here I find——" He halted abruptly as he perceived my other visitor. "And here I find," he repeated coldly. "Here I find Mr. Forister."

Forister saluted with finished politeness. "My friend and I," said he, "were discussing the probabilities of my killing him in the morning. He seems to think he has some small chance for his life but I have assured him that any really betting man would not wager a grain of sand that he would see the sun go down tomorrow."

"Even so," rejoined the Colonel imperturbably.

"And I also suggested to my friend," pursued Forister, "that tomorrow I would sacrifice my ruffles for him although I always abominate having a man's life-blood about my wrists."

"Even so," quoth the undisturbed Colonel.

"And further I suggested to my friend that if he came to the ground with a coffin on his back, it might promote expedition after the affair was over."

Colonel Royale turned away with a gesture of disgust. I thought it was high time to play an ace at Forister and stop his babble so I said: "And when Mr. Forister had finished his graceful remarks, we had some talk regarding Mr. Forister's affairs in Bath and I confess I was much interested in hearing about the little——"

Here I stopped abruptly as if I had been interrupted by Forister but he had given no sign but the sign of a sickly grin.

"Eh, Forister?" said I. "What's that?"

"I was remarking that I had nothing further to say for the present," he replied with superb insolence. "For the time I am quite willing to be silent. I bid you a good day, sirs."

CHAPTER VIII

AS the door closed upon Forister, Colonel Royale beat his hand passionately against the wall. "O'Ruddy," he cried, "if you could severely maim that cold-blooded bully, I would be willing to adopt you as my legitimate grandfather. I would indeed."

"Never fear me," said I. "I shall pink him well."

"Aye," said my friend, looking at me mournfully, "I ever feared your Irish light-heartedness. 'Twill not do to be confident. He is an evil man but a great swordsman. Now I never liked Ponsonby and Stewart was the most lovable of men but in the great duel, Ponsonby killed——"

"No," I interrupted, "damn the duel between Ponsonby and Stewart. I'm sick of it. This is to be the duel between The O'Ruddy and Forister and it won't be like the others."

"Eh, well," said the Colonel good-naturedly, "make your mind easy. But I hope to God you lay him flat."

"After I have finished with him," said I in measured tones, "he will be willing to sell himself as a sailor to go to the Indies, only, poor devil, he won't be able to walk, which is always a draw-back after a hard fight since it always leaves one man incapable on the ground and thus discloses strong evidences of a struggle."

I could see that Colonel Royale had no admiration for my bragging air but how otherwise was I to keep up my spirits? With all my discouragements, it seemed to me that I was privileged to do a little fine lying. Had my father been in my place he would have lied Forister into such a corner that the man would be thinking he had the devil for an opponent. My father knew more about these matters.

Still I could not help but be thinking how misfortunate it was that I had kicked a great swordsman out of this inn at Bristol when he might have been a harmless shoe-maker if I only had decent luck. I must make the best of it and for this, my only method was to talk loudly—to myself, if need be; to others if I could. I was not the kind which is quite unable to say a good word for itself even if I was not able to lie as well as my father in his prime. In his day, he could lie the coat off a man's back, lie the patches off a lady's cheek, lie a good dog into howling ominously. Still it was my duty to lie as well as I was able.

After a time, Lord Strepp was announced and entered. Both he and Colonel Royale immediately stiffened and decided not to perceive each other. "Sir," said Lord Strepp to me, "I have the honour to present my compliments to you and to request that you join a friend of mine, Mr. Forister, at dawn tomorrow in the settlement of a certain small misunderstanding."

"Sir," said I, in the same manner, "I am only too happy to have this little matter adjusted."

"And of course the arrangements, sir?"

"For them, I may refer you to my friend Colonel Royale."

"Ah," said the young Lord as if he had never before seen the Colonel.

"I am at your service, sir," said Royale as if he never in his whole life had heard of Lord Strepp.

Then these two began to salaam one to another and mouth out fool-phrases and cavort and prance and caracole until I thought them mad. When they departed there was a dreadful scene. Each refused to go through the door before the other. There was a frightful dead-lock. They each bowed and scraped and waved their hands and surrendered the door-way back and forth until I thought they were to be in my chamber eternally. Lord Strepp gorgeously presented the right of way to the Colonel. The Colonel splendidly refused the courtesy and on his part made a magnificent tendering of the right of way to Lord Strepp. All this time they were bending their backs at each other.

Finally I could stand it no longer. "In God's name," I shouted, "the door is wide enough for the two of you. Take it together. You will go through like grease. Never fear the door. 'Tis a good wide door."

To my surprise, they turned to glance at me and burst into

great laughter. Then they passed out amiably enough together. I was alone.

Well, the first thing I did was to think. I thought with all my force. I fancied the top of my skull was coming off. I thought myself into ten thousand intricacies. I thought myself into doom and out of it and behind it and below it but I could not think of anything which was of service to me. It seemed that I had come among a lot of mummers and one of these mummers was resolved to kill me although I never had even so much as broken his leg. But I remembered my father's word who had told me that gentlemen should properly kill each other over a matter of one liking oranges and another not liking oranges. It was the custom among men of position, he had said, and of course a way was not clear to changing this custom at the time. However, I determined that if I lived I would insist upon all these customs being moderated and re-directed. For my part I was willing that any man should like oranges.

I decided that I must go for a walk. To sit and gloom in my room until the time of the great affair would do me no good in any case. In fact it was likely to do me much harm. I went forth to the garden in the rear of the inn. Here spread a lawn more level than a ball-room floor. There was a summer-house and many beds of flowers. On this day there was nobody abroad in the garden but an atrocious parrot which, balancing on its stick, called out continually raucous cries in a foreign tongue.

I paced the lawn for a time, and then took seat in the summer-house. I had been there but a moment when I perceived Lady Mary and the Countess come into the garden. Through the leafy walls of the summer-house, I watched them as they walked slowly to and fro on the grass. The mother had evidently a great deal to say to the daughter. She waved her arms and spoke with a keen excitement.

But did I over-hear anything? I over-heard nothing. From what I knew of the proper conduct of the really thrilling episodes of life, I judged that I should have been able to over-hear almost every word of this conversation. Instead, I could only see the Countess making irritated speech to Lady Mary.

Moreover, it was legitimate that I should have been un-detected in the summer-house. On the contrary, they were perfectly aware that there was somebody in the summer-house and so in their promenade they presented it with a distinguished isolation.

No old maid ever held her ears so wide open. But I could hear nothing but a murmur of angry argument from the Countess and a murmur of gentle objection from Lady Mary. I was in possession of an ideal place from which to over-hear conversation. Almost every important conversation ever held had been over-heard from a position of this kind. It seemed unfair that I of all men in literature should be denied this casual and usual privilege.

The Countess harangued in a low voice at great length; Lady Mary answered from time to time, admitting this, admitting that, protesting against the other. It seemed certain to me that the talk related to Forister although I had no real reason for thinking it. And I was extremely angry that the Countess of Westport and her daughter, Lady Mary Strepp, should talk of Forister.

Upon my indignant meditations the parrot interpolated. "Ho, ho," it cried hoarsely. "A pretty lady! A pretty lady! A pretty lady! A pretty lady——"

Lady Mary smiled at this vacuous repetition but her mother went into a great rage, opening her old jaws like a maddened horse. "Here, landlord! Here, waiter! Here, anybody!"

Some people came running from the inn and at their head was, truly enough, the landlord. "My lady?" he cried panting.

She pointed an angry and terrible finger at the parrot. "When I walk in this garden, am I to be troubled with this wretched bird?"

The landlord almost bit the turf while the servants from the inn grovelled near him. "My lady," he cried, "the bird shall be removed at once." He ran forward. The parrot was chained by its leg to a tall perch. And as the inn-keeper came away with the entire business, the parrot began to shout: "Old harridan! Old harridan! Old harridan!" The inn-keeper seemed to me to be about to die of wild terror. It was a dreadful moment. One could not help but feel sorry for this poor wretch whose sole offense was that he kept an inn and also chose to keep a parrot in his garden.

The Countess sailed grandly toward the door of the hotel. To the solemn prostrations of six or seven servants she paid no heed. At the door she paused and turned for the ultimate remark. "I cannot endure parrots," she said impressively. To this dictum the menials crouched.

The servants departed; the garden was now empty save for Lady Mary and me. She continued a pensive strolling. Now, I could see plainly that here fate had arranged for some kind of interview. The whole thing was set like a scene in the theatre. I was undoubtedly to emerge suddenly from the summer-house; the lovely maid would startle, blush, cast down her eyes, turn away. Then when it came my turn I would doff my hat to the earth and beg pardon for continuing a comparatively futile existence. Then she would shyly murmur a disclaimer of any ability to criticise my continuation of a comparatively futile existence, adding that she was but an inexperienced girl. The ice thus being broken, we would travel by easy stages into more intimate talk.

I looked down carefully at my apparel and flicked a handkerchief over it. I tilted my hat; I set my hip against my harbour. A moment of indecision, of weakness, and I was out of the summer-house. God knows how I hoped that Lady Mary would not run away.

But the moment she saw me, she came swiftly to me. I almost lost my wits. " 'Tis the very gentleman I wished to see," she cried. She was blushing, it is true, but it was evident she intended to say nothing about inexperience or mere weak girls. "I wished to see you because——" She hesitated and then rapidly said: "It was about the papers. I wanted to thank you—I—you have no notion how happy the possession of the papers has made my father. It seems to have given him new life. I—I saw you throw your sword on the floor with the hilt away from you. And—and then you gave me the papers. I knew you were a gallant gentleman. I wanted to say that you were a gallant gentleman."

All this time, I, in my confusion, was bobbing and murmuring pledges of service. But if I was confused, Lady Mary was cool soon enough in the presence of a simple bog-trotter like me. Her beautiful eyes looked at me reflectively. "There is only one service I can render you, sir," she said softly. " 'Tis advice which would have been useful in saving some men's lives if only they had received it. I mean—don't fight with Forister in the morning. 'Tis certain death."

It was now my turn once more. I drew myself up and for the first time I looked squarely into her bright eyes. "My lady," said I with mournful dignity, "I was filled with pride when you said the good word to me. But what am I to think now? Am I, after all, such a poor stick that, to your mind, I could be advised to sell my honour for a mere fear of being killed?"

Even then I remembered my one-time decision to run away from the duel with Forister but we will not be thinking of that now.

Tears came into Lady Mary's eyes. "Ah, now, I have blundered," she said. " 'Tis what you would say, sir. 'Tis what you would do. I have only made matters worse. A woman's meddling often results in the destruction of those she—those she don't care to have killed."

One would think from the look of this last sentence that, with certain reason, I could have felt somewhat elate without being altogether a fool. Lady Mary meant nothing of importance by her speech but it was a little bit for a man who was hungry to have her think of him. But here I was assailed by a very demon of jealousy and distrust. This beautiful witch had some plan in her head which did not concern my welfare at all. Why should she, a great lady, take any trouble for a poor devil who was living at an inn on money borrowed from a highwayman. I had been highly honoured by an indifferent consideration born of a wish to be polite to a man who had eased the mind of her ailing father. No; I would not deceive myself.

But her tears! Were they marking indifferent consideration? For a second I lost myself in a roseate impossible dream. I dreamed that she had spoken to me because she——

Oh, what folly! Even as I dreamed, she turned, with splendid carriage, to me and remarked coldly: "I did not wish you to suppose that I ever failed to pay a debt. I have paid this one. Proceed now, sir, in your glowing stupidity. I have done."

When I recovered myself she placidly was moving away from me toward the door of the inn.

CHAPTER IX

I HAD better be getting to the story of the duel. I have been hanging back with it long enough and I shall tell it at once. I remember my father saying that the most aggravating creature in life was one who would be keeping back the best part of a story through mere reasons of trickery although I have seen himself dawdle over a tale until his friends wished to hurl the decanters at him. However there can be no doubting of the wisdom of my father's remark. Indeed there can be little doubting of the wisdom of anything that my father said in life for he was a very learned man. The fact that my father did not invariably defer to his own opinions does not alter the truth of those opinions, in my judgment, since even the greatest of philosophers is more likely to be living a life based on the temper of his wife and the advice of his physician than on the rules laid down in his books. Nor am I certain that my father was in a regular habit of delaying the point of a story. I only remember this one incident, wherein he was recounting a stirring tale of a fight with a lancer and just as the lance struck the paternal breast, my father was reminded by a sight of the walnuts that Mickey Clancy was not serving the port with his usual rapidity and so he addressed him. I remember the words well. "Mickey, you spalpeen," said my father, "would you be leaving the gentlemen as dry as the bottom of Moses' feet when he crossed the Red Sea? Look at O'Mahoney there! He is as thirsty as a fish in the top of a tree. And Father Donovan has had but two small quarts and he never takes less than five. Bad luck to you, Mickey, if it was a drink for your own stomach, you would be moving faster. Are you wishing to ruin my reputation for hospitality, you rogue you." And my father was going on with Mickey only that he looked about him at this time and discovered his guests all upon their

feet, one with the tongs, one with the poker, others with decanters ready to throw. "What's this?" said he. "The lance," said
they. "Eh?" said my father. "What lance?" "The lance of the
lancer," said they. "And why shouldn't he have a lance?" said
my father. " 'Faith, 'twould be an odd lancer without a lance."
By this time, they were so angry that Mickey, seeing how things
were going, and I being a mere lad, took me from the room. I
never heard precisely what happened to the lancer but he
must have had the worst of it for wasn't my father, seated
there at the table, telling the story long years after?

Well, as to my duel with Forister: Colonel Royale was an
extremely busy man and almost tired my life out with a quantity
of needless attentions. For my part, I thought more of Lady
Mary and the fact that she considered me no more than if I
had been a potato. Colonel Royale fluttered about me. I would
have gruffly sent him away if it were not that everything he did
was meant in kindliness and generous feeling. I was already
believing that he did not have more than one brain in his head
but I could not be ungrateful for his interest and enthusiasm in
getting me out to be hurt correctly. I understood long years
afterward that he and Lord Strepp were each so particular in
the negotiations that no less than eighteen bottles of wine
were consumed.

The morning for the duel dawned softly warm, softly wet,
softly foggy. The Colonel popped into my room the moment I
was dressed. To my surprise, he was now quite mournful. It
was I now who had to do the cheering.

"Your spirits are low, Colonel?" said I banteringly.

"Aye, O'Ruddy," he answered with an effort, "I had a bad
night with the gout. Heaven keep this devil from getting his
sword in your bowels."

He had made the appointment with Strepp, of course, and
as we walked toward the ground, he looked at me very curiously
out of the ends of his eyes. "You know—ah, you have the
honour of the acquaintance of Lady Mary Strepp, O'Ruddy?" said
he suddenly and nervously.

"I have," I answered stiffening. Then I said: "And you?"

"Her father and I were friends before either she or you was

born," he said simply. "I was a cornet in his old regiment. Little Lady Mary played at the knee of the poor young subaltern."

"Oh," said I meanly, "you are, then, a kind of uncle."

"Aye," said he, "a kind of uncle. So much of an uncle," he added with more energy, "that when she gave me this note, I thought much of acting like a real uncle. From what I have unfortunately over-heard, I suspect that the Earl—aw—disagrees with you on certain points."

He averted his face as he handed me the note and eagerly I tore it open. It was unsigned. It contained but three words: "God spare you." And so I marched in a tumult of joy to a duel wherein I was expected to be killed.

I glanced at the Colonel. His countenance was deeply mournful. " 'Tis for few girls I would become a dove to carry notes between lovers," he said gloomily. "Damn you for it, O'Ruddy."

"Nay, Colonel," said I. " 'Tis no missive of love. Look you."

But he still kept his eyes averted. "I judge it was not meant for my eyes," he said, still very gloomy.

But here I flamed up in wrath. "And would the eye of an angel be allowed to rest upon this paper if it were not fit that it should be so?" I demanded in my anger. "Colonel, am I to hear you bleat about doves and lovers when a glance of your eye will disabuse you? Read."

He read. " 'God spare you'," he repeated tenderly. Then he addressed me with fine candour. "Aye, I have watched her these many years, O'Ruddy. When she was a babe, I have seen her in her little bath. When she was a small girl I have seen her asleep with some trinket clasped in her rosy hand on the coverlet. Since she has been a beautiful young lady I have— but no matter. You come along, named nobody, hailing from nowhere, and she—she sends me out to deliver her prayer that God may spare you!"

I was awed by this middle-aged sorrow. But, curse him, when she was a babe he had seen her in her little bath, had he? Damn his eyes. He had seen the baby naked in her tiny tub. Damn his eyes again. I was in such fury that I longed to fight Royale on the spot and kill him, running my sword through his memory so that it would be blotted out forever and never, never, never again, even in Paradise, could he recall the image in the little tub.

But the Colonel's next words took the rage out of me. "Go in, O'Ruddy," he cried heartily. "There is no truer man could win her. As my lady says, 'God spare you'."

"And if Forister's blade be not too brisk, I will manage to be spared," I rejoined.

"Oh, there is another thing touching the matter," said the Colonel suddenly. "Forister is your chief rival although I little know what has passed between them. Nothing important, I think, although I am sure Forister is resolved to have her for a bride. Of that I am certain. He is resolved."

"Is he so?" said I.

I was numb and cold for a moment. Then I slowly began to boil like a kettle freshly placed on the fire. So I was facing a rival? Well and he would get such a facing as few men had received. And he was my rival and in the breast of my coat I wore a note—"God spare you." Ha, ha! He little knew the disadvantage under which he was to play. Could I lose with "God spare you" against my heart? Not against three Foristers.

But hold! Might it not be that the gentle Lady Mary, deprecating this duel and filled with feelings of humanity, had sent us each a note with this fervid cry for God to spare us? I was forced to concede it possible. After all, I perfectly well knew that to Lady Mary I was a mere nothing. Royale's words had been so many plumes in my life's helmet but at bottom I knew better than to set great store by them. The whole thing now was to hurry to the duelling ground and see if I could discover from this black Forister's face if he had received a "God spare you." I took the Colonel's arm and fairly dragged him. "Damme, O'Ruddy," said he, puffing, "this can be nought but genuine eagerness."

When we came to the duelling-place, we found Lord Strepp and Forister pacing to and fro while the top of a near-by wall was crowded with pleasant-minded spectators. "Aye, you've come, have ye, sirs?" called the rabble. Lord Strepp seemed rather annoyed and Colonel Royale grew red and stepped peremptorily toward the wall, but Forister and I had eyes only for each other. His eye for me was a glad cruel eye. I have a dim remembrance of seeing the Colonel take his scabbard and incontinently beat many worthy citizens of Bristol; indeed, he seemed to beat every worthy citizen of Bristol who had not legs enough to get away. I could hear them squeaking out protests while I keenly studied the jubilant Forister.

Aye, it was true. He too had a "God spare you." I felt my blood begin to run hot. My eyes suddenly cleared as if I had been empowered with miraculous vision. My arm became supple as a whip. I decided upon one thing. I would kill Forister.

I thought the Colonel never would give over chasing citizens but at last he returned breathless, having scattered the populace over a wide stretch of country. The preliminaries were very simple. In a half-minute, Forister and I, in our shirts, faced each other.

And now I passed into such a state of fury that I cannot find words to describe it, but, as I have said, I was possessed of a remarkable clearness of vision and strength of arm. These phenomena amaze me even at this day. I was so airy upon my feet that I might have been a spirit. I think great rages work thus upon certain natures. Their competence is suddenly made manifold. They live, for a brief space, the life of giants. Rage is destruction active. Whenever anything in this world needs to be destroyed, nature makes somebody wrathful. Another thing I recall is that I had not the slightest doubt of my ability to kill Forister. There were no more misgivings; no quakings. I thought of the impending duel with delight.

In all my mid-night meditations upon the fight I had pictured myself as lying strictly upon the defensive and seeking a chance opportunity to damage my redoubtable opponent. But the moment after our swords had crossed, I was an absolute demon of attack. My very first lunge made him give back a long pace. I saw his confident face change to a look of fierce excitement.

There is little to say of the flying spinning blades. It is only necessary to remark that Forister dropped almost immediately to defensive tactics before an assault which was not only impetuous but exceedingly brilliant, if I may be allowed to say so. And I knew that on my left a certain Colonel Royale was steadily growing happier.

The end came with an almost ridiculous swiftness. The feeling of an ugly quivering wrench communicated itself from the point of my sword to my mind; I heard Strepp and Royale cry "Hold"; I saw Forister fall; I lowered my point and stood dizzily thinking. My sight was now blurred; my arm was weak.

My sword had gone deep into Forister's left shoulder and the bones there had given that hideous feeling of a quivering wrench. He was not injured beyond repair but he was in exquisite agony. Before they could reach him he turned over on his elbows and managed in some way to fling his sword at me. "Damn your soul," he cried and he gave a sort of a howl as Lord Strepp, grim and unceremonious, bounced him over again upon his back. In the meantime, Colonel Royale was helping me on with my coat and waistcoat although I hardly knew that either he or the coat and waistcoat were in existence.

I had my usual inclination to go forward and explain to everybody how it all had happened. But Royale took me forcibly by the arm and we turned our backs on Strepp and Forister and walked toward the inn.

As soon as we were out of their sight, Colonel Royale clasped my hands with rapture. "My boy," he cried. "You are great! You are renowned! You are illustrious! What a game you could give Ponsonby! You would give him such a stir!"

"Never doubt me," said I. "But I am now your legitimate grandfather and I should be treated with great respect."

When we came near the inn, I began to glance up at the windows. I surely expected to see a face at one of them. Certainly she would care to know who was slain or who was hurt. She would be watching, I fondly hoped, to see who returned on his legs. But the front of the inn stared at us, chilly and vacant, like a prison wall.

When we entered, the Colonel bawled lustily for an immediate bottle of wine and I joined him in its drinking for I knew that it would be a bellows to my flagging spirits. I had set my heart upon seeing a face at the window of the inn.

CHAPTER X

AND now I found out what it was to be a famous swordsman. All that day, the inn seemed to hum with my name. I could not step down a corridor without seeing flocks of servants taking wing. They fled tumultuously. A silly maid, coming from a chamber with a bucket, saw me and shrieked. She dropped her bucket and fled back into the chamber. A man-servant saw me, gave a low moan of terror and leaped down a convenient stair-way. All attendants scuttled aside.

What was the matter with me? Had I grown in stature or developed a ferocious ugliness? No; I now was a famous swordsman. That was all. I now was expected to try to grab the maids and kiss them wantonly. I now was expected to clout the grooms on their ears if they so much as showed themselves in my sight. In fact I was now a great blustering over-powering preposterous ass.

There was a crowd of people in the coffee-room but the buzz of talk suddenly ceased as I entered. "Is this your chair, sir?" said I civilly to a gentleman. He stepped away from the chair as if it had tried to bite him. " 'Tis at your service, sir," he cried hastily.

"No," said I, "I would not be taking it if it is yours for there are just as good chairs in the sea as ever were caught and it would ill become me to deprive a gentleman of his chair when by exercising a little energy, I can gain one for myself although I am willing to admit that I have a slight hunger upon me. 'Tis a fine morning, sir."

He had turned pale and was edging toward the door. " 'Tis at your service, sir," he repeated in a low and frightened voice. All the people were staring at us.

"No, good sir," I remonstrated stepping forward to explain.

"I would not be having you think that I am unable to get a chair for myself since I am above everything able and swift with my hands and it is a small thing to get a chair for oneself and not deprive a worthy gentleman of his own."

"I did not think to deprive you, sir," he ejaculated desperately. "The chair is at your service, sir."

"Plague the man!" I cried stamping my foot impatiently and at the stamping of my foot, a waiter let fall a dish, some women screamed, three or four people disappeared through the door and a venerable gentleman arose from his seat in a corner and in a tremulous voice said: "Sir, let us pray you that there be no blood-shed."

"You are an old fool," said I to him. "How could there be blood-shed with me here merely despising you all for not knowing what I mean when I say it."

"We know you mean what you say, sir," responded the old gentleman. "Pray God you mean peaceably!"

"Hoity-toity," shouted a loud voice and I saw a great tall ugly woman bearing down upon me from the door-way. "Out of my way," she thundered at a waiter. The man gasped out: "Yes, your ladyship." I was face to face with the mother of my lovely Mary.

"Hoity-toity," she shouted at me again. "A brawler, eh? A lively swordster, hey? A real damn-my-eyes swaggering bully."

Then she charged upon me. "How dare you brawl with these inoffensive people under the same roof which shelters me, fellow? By my word, I would have pleasure to give you a box on the ear."

"Madam," I protested hurriedly. But I saw the futility of it. Without devoting further time to an appeal, I turned and fled. I dodged behind three chairs and moved them hastily into a rampart.

"Madam," I cried, feeling that I could parley from my new position, "you labour under a misapprehension."

"Misapprehend me no misapprehensions," she retorted hotly. "How dare you say that I can misapprehend anything, wretch."

She attacked each flank in turn but so agile was I that I escaped capture although my position in regard to the chairs was twice reversed. Afterward we performed another series of nimble manoeuvres which were characterized on my part by a high degree of strategy. But I found the rampart of chairs an untenable place. I was again obliged to hurriedly retreat, this time taking up a position behind a large table.

"Madam," I said desperately, "believe me, you are suffering under a grave misapprehension."

"Again he talks of misapprehension!" We revolved once swiftly around the table. She stopped, panting. "And this is the blusterer! And why do you not stand your ground, coward?"

"Madam," said I with more coolness now that I saw that she soon would be losing her wind, "I would esteem it very ungallant behaviour if I endured your attack for even a brief moment. My forefathers form a brave race which always runs away from ladies."

After this speech, we revolved twice around the table. I must in all candour say that the Countess used language which would not at all suit the pages of my true and virtuous chronicle but indeed it was no worse than I often heard afterward from the great ladies of the time. However the talk was not always addressed at me, thank the saints.

After we had made the two revolutions, I spoke reasonably. "Madam," said I, "if we go spinning about the table in this fashion for any length of time, these gawking spectators will think we are a pair of wheels."

"Spectators!" she cried, lifting her old head high. She beheld about seventy-five interested people. She called out loudly to them. "And is there no gentleman among you all to draw his sword and beat me this rascal from the inn?"

Nobody moved. "Madam," said I, still reasonable, "would it not be better to avoid a possible scandal by discontinuing these movements as the tongues of men are not always fair and it might be said by some——"

Whereupon we revolved twice more around the table.

When the pelican stopped she had only enough breath left to impartially abuse all the sight-seers. As her eye fixed upon them, The O'Ruddy, illustrious fighting man, saw his chance and bolted like a hare. The escape must have formed a great spectacle but I had no time for appearances. As I was passing out of the door, the Countess in her disappointed rage threw a heavy ivory fan after me which struck an innocent bystander in the eye for which he apologised.

CHAPTER XI

I WASTED no time in the vicinity of the inn. I decided that an interval spent in some remote place would be consistent with the behaviour of a gentleman.

But the agitations of the day were not yet closed for me. Suddenly I came upon a small slow-moving and solemn company of men who carried among them some kind of a pallet and on this pallet was the body of Forister. I gazed upon his ghastly face; I saw the large blood blotches on his shirt; as they drew nearer, I saw him roll his eyes and heard him groan. Some of the men recognized me and I saw black looks and straight pointing fingers. At the rear, walked Lord Strepp with Forister's sword under his arm. I turned away with a new impression of the pastime of duelling. Forister's pallor, the show of bloody cloth, his groan, the dark stares of the men made me see my victory in a different way and I even wondered if it had been absolutely necessary to work this mischief upon a fellow-being.

I spent most of the day down among the low taverns of the sailors striving to interest myself in a thousand new sights brought by the ships from foreign parts.

But ever my mind returned to Lady Mary and my misfortune in being pursued around chairs and tables by my angel's mother. I had also managed to have a bitter quarrel with the noble father of this lovely creature. It was hardly possible that I could be joyous over my prospects.

At noon I returned to the inn approaching with some display of caution. As I neared it, a carriage followed by some horsemen whirled speedily away from the door. I knew at once that Lady Mary had been taken from me. She was gone with her father and mother back to London. I recognized Lord Strepp and Colonel Royale among the horsemen.

I walked through the inn to the garden and looked at the parrot. I don't know why I went to look at the parrot. My senses were all numb. I stared at the bird; it rolled its wicked eye at me. "Pretty lady! Pretty lady!" it called in hoarse mockery. Plague the bird! I turned upon my heel and entered the inn. "My bill," said I. "A horse for Bath," said I. Again I rode forth on a quest. The first had been after my papers. The second was after my love. The second was the hopeless one and overcome by melancholy I did not even spur my horse swiftly on my mission. There was upon me the deep-rooted sadness which balances the mirth of my people, the Celtic aptitude for discouragement, and even the keening of old women in the red glow of the peat-fire could never have deepened my mood.

And if I should succeed in reaching London, what then? Would the wild savage from the rocky shore of Ireland be a pleasing sight to my Lady Mary, once more amid the glamour and whirl of the fashionable town? Besides I could no longer travel on the guineas of Jem Bottles. He had engaged himself and his purse in my service because I had told him of a fortune involved in the re-gaining of certain papers. I had re-gained those papers and then coolly placed them as a gift in a certain lovely white hand. I had had no more thought of Jem Bottles and his five guineas than if I had never seen them. But this was no excuse for a gentleman. When I arrived at the rendezvous I must immediately confess to Jem Bottles, the highwayman, that I had wronged him. I did not expect him to demand satisfaction but I thought he might shoot me in the back as I was riding away.

But Jem was not at the appointed place under the tree. Not puzzled at this behaviour, I rode on. I saw I could not expect the man to stay forever under a tree while I was away in Bristol fighting a duel and making eyes at a lady. Still, I had heard that it was always done.

At the inn where Paddy holed Forister, I did not dismount although a hostler ran out busily. "No," said I. "I ride on." I looked at the man. Small, sharp-eyed, weazened, he was as likely a rascal of a hostler as ever helped a highwayman to know a filled purse from a man who was riding to make arrangements with his creditors.

"Do you remember me?" said I.

"No, sir," he said with great promptitude.

"Very good," said I. "I knew you did. Now I want to know if Master Jem Bottles has passed this way today. A shilling for the truth and a thrashing for a lie."

The man came close to my stirrup. "Master," he said, "I know you be a friend of him. Well, in day-time, he don't ride past our door. There be lanes. And so he ain't passed here and that's the truth."

I flung him a shilling. "Now," I said, "what of the red giant?"

The man opened his little eyes in surprise. "He took horse with you gentlemen and rode on to Bristol or I don't know."

"Very good; now I see two very fine horses champing in the yard. And who owns them?"

If I had expected to catch him in treachery I was wrong. "Them?" said he jerking his thumb. He still kept his voice lowered. "They belong to two gentlemen who rode out some hours agone along with some great man's carriage. The officer said that some pin-pricks he had gotten in a duel had stiffened and made the saddle ill of ease with him and the young lord said he would stay behind as a companion. They be up in the Colonel's chamber drinking vastly. But, mind your life, sir, if you would halt them on the road. They be men of great spirit. This inn seldom sees such drinkers."

And so Lord Strepp and Colonel Royale were resting at this inn while the carriage of the Earl had gone on toward Bath? I had a mind to dismount and join the two in their roystering but my eyes turned wistfully toward Bath. No; a man may not halt at many inns for the sake of drunkenness and at the same time be successful in the pursuit of his love. I would gallop on to Bath.

As I rode away, I began to wonder what had become of Jem Bottles and Paddy. Here was a fine pair to be abroad in the land. Here were two jewels to be rampaging across the country. Separately, they were villains enough but together they would over-turn England and get themselves hung for it on twin gibbets. I tried to imagine the particular roguery to which they would first give their attention.

But then all thought of the rascals faded from me as my

mind received a vision of Lady Mary's fair face, her figure, her foot. It would not be me to be thinking of two such thieves when I could be dreaming of Lady Mary with her soft voice and the clear depths of her eyes. My horse seemed to have a sympathy with my feeling and he leaped bravely along the road to Bath. The Celtic melancholy of the first part of the journey had blown away like a sea-mist. I sped on gallantly toward Bath and Lady Mary.

But almost at the end of the day, when I was within a few miles of Bath, my horse suddenly pitched forward onto his knees and nose. There was a flying spray of muddy water. I was flung out of the saddle but I fell without any serious hurt whatever. We had been ambushed by some kind of a deep-sided puddle. My poor horse scrambled out and stood with lowered head, heaving and trembling. His soft nose had been cut between his teeth and the far edge of the puddle. I led him forward, watching his legs. He was lamed. I looked in wrath and despair back at the puddle which was as plain as a golden guinea on a platter. I do not see how I could have blundered into it for the day light was still clear and strong. I had been like a fool gazing in the direction of Bath. And my Celtic melancholy swept down upon me again and even my father's bier appeared before me with the pale candle-flames swaying in the gusty room and now indeed mine ears heard the loud wailing keen of the old women.

"Rubbish," said I suddenly and aloud, "and is it one of the best swordsmen in England that is to be beaten by a lame horse?" My spirits revived. I resolved to leave my horse in the care of the people of the nearest house and proceed at once on foot to Bath. The people of the inn could be sent out after the poor animal. Wheeling my eyes, I saw a house not more than two fields away with honest hospitable smoke curling from the chimneys. I led my beast through a hole in the hedge and I slowly made my way toward it.

Now it happened that my way led me near a hay-cock and as I neared this hay-cock I heard voices from the other side of it. I hastened forward, dragging the poor horse and thinking to find some yokels. But as I drew very close, I suddenly halted and silently listened to the voices on the other side.

"Sure, I can read," Paddy was saying. "And why wouldn't I be able? If we couldn't read in Ireland, we would be after being cheated in our rents but we never pay them anyhow so that's no matter. I would be having you to know we are a highly educated people. And perhaps you would be reading it yourself, my man?"

"No," said Jem Bottles, "I be not a great scholar and it has a look of amazing hardness. And I misdoubt me," he added in a morose and envious voice, "that your head be too full of learning."

"Learning!" cried Paddy. "Why wouldn't I be learned since my uncle was a sexton and had to know one grave from another by looking at the stones so as to never mix up the people? Learning, says you? And wasn't there a convent at Ballygowagglycuddi and wasn't Ballygowagglycuddi only ten miles from my father's house and haven't I seen it many a time?"

"Aye, well, good Master Paddy," replied Jem Bottles, oppressed and sullen but still in a voice ironic from suspicion, "I never doubt me but what you are a regular clerk for deep learning but you have not yet read a line from the paper and I have been waiting this half hour."

"And how could I be reading?" cried Paddy in tones of great indignation. "How could I be reading with you there croaking of this and that and speaking hard of my learning? Bad cess to the paper, I will be after reading it to myself if you are never to stop your clatter Jem Bottles."

"I be still as a dead rat," exclaimed the astonished highwayman.

"Well, then," said Paddy. "Listen hard and you will hear such learning as would be making your eyes jump from your head. And 'tis not me either that cares to show my learning before people who are unable to tell a mile-post from a church-tower."

"I be a-waiting," said Jem Bottles with a new meekness apparently born of respect for Paddy's eloquence.

"Well, then," said Paddy, pained at these interruptions. "Listen well and maybe you will gain some learning which may serve you all your life in reading chalk-marks in tap-rooms for I see that they have that custom in this country and 'tis very bad for hard-drinking men who have no learning."

"If you would read from the paper——" began Jem Bottles.

"Now, will you be still?" cried Paddy in vast exasperation.

But here Jem Bottles spoke with angry resolution. "Come, now! Read! 'Tis not me that talks too much and the day wanes."

"Well, well, I would not be hurried and that's the truth," said Paddy soothingly. "Listen now." I heard a rustling of paper. "Ahum," said Paddy, "Ahum. Are ye listening, Jem Bottles?"

"I be," replied the highwayman.

"Then here's for it," said Paddy in a formidable voice. There was another rustling of paper. Then to my surprise I heard Paddy intone without punctuation the following words: "Dear sister Mary I am asking the good father to write this because my hand is lame from milking the cows although we only have one and we sold her in the autumn the four shillings you owe on the pig we would like if convenient to pay now owing to the landlord may the plague take him how did your Mickey find the fishing when you see Peggy tell her——"

Here Jem Bottles' voice arose in tones of incredulity. "And these be the papers of the great Earl!" he cried.

Then the truth flashed across my vision like the lightning. My two madmen had robbed the carriage of the Earl of West-port and taken among other things the Earl's papers—my papers—Lady Mary's papers. I strode around the hay-cock. "Wretches," I shouted. "Miserable wretches!"

For a time they were speechless. Paddy found his tongue first. "Aye, 'tis him! 'Tis nothing but little black men and papers with him and when we get them for him, he calls us out of our names in a foreign tongue. 'Tis no service for a bright man," he concluded mournfully.

"Give me the papers," said I. Paddy obediently handed them. I knew them. They were my papers—Lady Mary's papers. "And now," said I, eyeing them, "what mischief have you two been compassing?"

Paddy only mumbled sulkily. It was something on the difficulties of satisfying me on the subjects of little black men and papers. Jem Bottles was also sulky but he grumbled out the beginning of an explanation. "Well, master, I bided under the tree till him here came and then we together bided. And at last we thought with the time so heavy we might better work to handle a purse or two. Thinking," he said delicately, "our gentleman might have need of a little gold. Well and as we were riding, a good lad from the—your worship knows where— tells us the Earl's carriage is halting there for a time but will go on later without its escort of two gentlemen but only with servants. And thinking to do our gentleman a good deed, I brought them to stand on the highway and then he——"

"And then I," broke in Paddy proudly, "walks up to the carriage door looking like a king's cruiser and says I, 'Pray excuse the manners of a self-opinionated man but I consider your purses would look better in my pocket.' And then there was a great trouble. An old owl of a woman screeched and was for killing me with a bottle which she had been holding against her nose. But she never dared. And, with that, an old sick man lifted himself from hundreds of cushions and says he, 'What do you want? You can't have them,' says he and he keeps clasping his breast. 'First of all,' says I, 'I want what you have there. What I want else I'll tell you at my leisure.' And he was all for mouthing and fuming but he was that scared he gave me those papers—bad luck to them." Paddy cast an evil eye upon the papers in my hand.

"And then?" said I.

"The driver he tried for to whip up," interpolated Jem Bottles. "He was a game one but the others were like wet cats."

"And says I," continued Paddy, " 'now we will have the gold, if it please you.' And out it came. 'I bid ye a good journey,' says I and I thought it was over and how easy was highwaying and I liked it well until the lady on the front seat opens her hood and shows me a prettier face than we have in all Ireland. She clasps two white hands. 'Oh, please Mister Highwayman, my father's papers—' And with that I backs away. 'Let them go,' says I to Jem Bottles and sick I was of it and I would be buying masses tonight if I might find a Christian church. The poor lady."

I was no longer angry with Paddy.

"Aye," said Jem Bottles, "the poor lady was that forlorn!"

I was no longer angry with Jem Bottles.

But I now had to do a deal of thinking. It was plain that the papers were of supreme importance to the Earl. Although I had given them to Lady Mary, they had returned to me as if they were deeply involved in my destiny. It had been no fault of mine that they had returned to me. It was fate. My father had taught me to respect these papers but I now saw them as a sign in the sky.

However, it was hard to decide what to do. I had given the papers to Lady Mary and they had fled back to me swifter than cormorants. Perhaps it was willed that I should keep them. And then there would be tears in the eyes of Lady Mary who suffered through the suffering of her father. No; come good, come bad for me, for Jem Bottles, for Paddy, I would stake our fortunes on the act of returning the papers to Lady Mary.

It is the way of Irishmen. We are all of us true philanthropists. That is why we have nothing, although in other countries I have seen philanthropists who had a great deal. My own interest in the papers I staked, mentally, with a glad mind; the minor interests of Jem Bottles and Paddy I staked, mentally, without thinking of them at all. But, surely, it would be a tribute to fate to give anything to Lady Mary. I resolved on a course of action.

When I aroused to look at my companions I found them seated face to face on the ground like players of draughts. Between them was spread a handkerchief and on the handkerchief was a heap of guineas. Jem Bottles was saying, "Here be my fingers five times over." He separated a smaller heap. "Here be my fingers five times over again." He separated another little stack. "And here be my fingers five times over again. And two more yet. Now, can ye understand?"

"By dad," said Paddy admiringly, "you have the learning this time, Master Bottles. My uncle, the sexton, could not have done it better."

"What is all this?" said I.

They both looked at me deprecatingly. " 'Tis, your honour ——" began Paddy. " 'Tis only some little small sum—nothing to be talked of—belonging to the old sick man in the carriage."

"Paddy and Jem Bottles," said I, "I forgive you the taking of the papers. Ye are good men and true. Now we will do great deeds."

CHAPTER XII

MY plans were formed quickly. "We now have a treasure chest of no small dimensions," said I, very complacent, naturally. "We can conquer London with this. Everything is before us. I have already established myself as the grandest swordsman in the whole continent of England. Lately, we have gained much treasure. And also I have the papers. Paddy, do you take care of this poor horse. Then follow me into Bath. Jem Bottles, do you mount and ride around the town, for I fear your balladists. Meet me on the London road. Ride slowly on the highway to London and in due time I will over-take you. I shall pocket a few of those guineas but you yourself shall be the main treasury. Hold; what of Paddy's hair? Did he rob the Earl with that great flame showing? He dare not appear in Bath."

" 'Tis small tribute to my wit, sir," answered Jem Bottles. "I would as soon go poaching in company with a light-house as to call a stand on the road with him uncovered. I tied him in cloths until he looked no more like himself than he now does look like a parson."

"Aye," said Paddy in some bad humour, "my head was tied in a bag. My mother would not have known me from a pig going to market. And I would not be for liking it every day. My hair is what the blessed saints sent me and I see no such fine hair around me that people are free to throw the laugh at me."

"Peace," said I. Their horses were tied in an adjacent thicket. I sent Paddy off with my lame mount, giving him full instructions as to his lies. I and Jem Bottles took the other horses and rode toward Bath.

My head was full of my recovery of the papers but a sudden thought of a little issue came to me. "Jem Bottles," said I, "do you know a girl named Nell in Bath who perchance is a trifle easy in her ways?"

"Aye, that I do, master," he answered promptly.

"And what manner of creature?" said I.

Here he looked a trifle puzzled. " 'A girl named Nell in Bath a trifle good-natured'? Aye, 'tis hard to say which wench your worship may mean."

"I mean," said I, "a girl named Nell who has lately had a child by a gentleman."

He looked blank. " 'A child by a gentleman'! 'Tis very unusual. The gentlemen pay the gold but god-forgotten rascals pay the simple debt of fatherhood. What with being drunk always and kicking the wenches, these swine come to be greatly beloved."

"I misdoubt me that my question roots down into all this mud," said I. "I am thinking of a fine woman. Something which has not reached the bottom."

"And her name is Nell?" cried Bottles. "I have her. Nell Flid. She bore a child and at the time her principal lover resembled greatly this little black man, he whom the people called Satan."

" 'Tis the same," said I. "And now what of her? Once," I added sympathetically, "she was a virtuous girl."

"Aye, she was," he replied in slow tones mournful with memories. "The recollection carries me back full fifteen years."

"Fifteen?" I cried. "This is never the little black man's sweetheart. This is a beldam."

"She be no beldam. She be a beautiful woman. Master," said Jem Bottles with profound philosophy, "fifteen years be no more to some of them than a fly on your rose."

"Silence," said I. "I have learned what I wished to learn. I fear the rest of your talk relates to nothing but the ways of sinful people. I would have you to know that we do not converse upon such matters in Ireland."

"Even so," he answered agreeably, "and thus I was surprised to hear you introduce the subject."

"In my country," I exclaimed sternly, "we never allow anything to happen unless we are able to keep quiet about it afterward."

"I am not making any noise, master," said the highwayman.

"However," said I, "I would know all that you know about this Nell who has borne a child generously to her principal lover."

"She be the daughter of a draper, folk who held themselves very high. She was free and airy and, one day, her father, a hard man then, kicked her from the door. Afterward——— Then finally the father lost every penny and became a beggar and, certain, I have seen him come for bread and beer to his daughter's window."

"And did he get it?" said I.

"And more," Jem Bottles answered impressively. "Even meat and sometimes wine. 'Tis no small advantage to be the father of a popular wench."

"In God's name, hold," I cried. "I have enough and I doubt me if this monstrous evil could be matched in all France. Let us ride on hurriedly."

At where a certain lane turned off from the highway, I parted with Jem Bottles and he rode away between the hedges. I cantered into Bath.

The best-known inn was a-blaze with fleeting lights and people were shouting within. It was some time before I could gain a man to look after my horse. Of him I demanded the reason of the disturbance. "The Earl of Westport's carriage has been robbed on the Bristol road, sir," he cried excitedly. "There be parties starting out. I pray they catch him."

"And whom would they be catching, my lad," said I.

"Jem Bottles, damn him, sir," answered the man. 'But 'tis a fierce time they will have, for he stands no less than eight feet in his boots and his eyes are no human eyes but burn blood-red always. His hands are a-drip with blood and 'tis said that he eats human flesh, sir. He surely is a devil, sir."

"From the description I would be willing to believe it," said I. "However, he will be easy to mark. Such a monster can hardly be mistaken for an honest man."

I entered the inn while a boy staggered under my valises. I had difficulty in finding the landlord. But in the corridor were a number of travellers and, evidently, one had come that day from Bristol for he suddenly nudged another and hurriedly whispered: " 'Tis him! The great Irish swordsman!" And then the news spread like the wind, apparently, that the man who had beaten the great Forister was arrived in good health at the inn. There were murmurs and a great deal of attention and many eyes. I suddenly caught myself swaggering somewhat. It is hard to be a famous person and not show a great swollen chicken-breast to the people. They are disappointed if you do not strut and step high. "Show me to a chamber," said I splendidly. The servants bowed their fore-heads to the floor.

But the great hub-bub over the Earl's loss continued without abatement. Gentlemen clanked down in their spurs; there was much talk of dragoons; the tumult was extraordinary. Up-stairs the landlord led me past the door of a kind of drawing-room. I glanced within and saw the Earl of Westport gesturing and declaiming to a company of gentlemen. He was propped with his cushions in a great arm-chair. "And why would he be waving his hands that way?" said I to two servants who stood without. "His lordship has lost many valuable papers at the hands of a miscreant, sir," answered one.

"Is it so?" said I. "Well, then, I would see his lordship."

But here this valet stiffened. "No doubt but what his lordship would be happy to see you, sir," he answered slowly. "Unfortunately, however, he has forbidden me to present strangers to his presence."

"I have very important news. Do not be an idiot," said I. "Announce me. The O'Ruddy."

"The O'Ruggy?" said he.

"The O'Ruddy," said I.

"The O'Rudgy?" said he.

"No," said I and I told him again. Finally he took two paces within the room and sung out in a loud voice: "The O'Rubby."

I heard the voice of the sick old Earl calling from a great chair. "Why, 'tis the Irishman. Bid him enter. I am glad—I am always very glad—ahem——"

As I strode into the room, I was aware of another buzz of talk. Apparently here too were plenty of people who knew me as the famous swordsman. The Earl moved his jaw and mumbled. "Aye," said he at last, "here is The O'Ruddy. And, do you know, Mr. O'Ruddy, I have been foully robbed and, among other things, have lost your worthless papers?"

"I heard you had lost them," I answered composedly. "But I refuse to take your word that they are worthless."

Many people stared and the Earl gave me a fine scowl. But, after consideration, he spoke as if he thought it well to dissemble a great dislike of me. The many candles burned very brightly and we could all see each other. I thought it better to back casually toward the wall.

"You never accomplish anything," coughed the sick Earl. "Yet you are forever prating of yourself. I wish my son were here. My papers are gone. I shall never recover them."

"The papers are in the breast of my coat at this moment," said I coolly. There was a great tumult. The Earl lost his head and cried "Seize him!" Two or three young men took steps toward me. I was back to the wall and in a leisurely and contemptuous way, I drew my sword. "The first gentleman who advances is a dead man," said I pleasantly.

Some drew away quickly; some hesitated and then withdrew subtlely. In the meantime, the screeches of the Earl mocked them all. "Aye, the wild Irishman brings you up to a stand, he does! Now who will have at him? In all Bath have I no friend with a stout heart?"

After looking them over, I said: "No, my lord, you have none."

At this insult, the aged peer arose from his chair. "Bring me my sword," he cried to his valet. A hush fell upon us all. We were rendered immovable by the solemn dignity of this proceeding.

It was some time before I could find my tongue. "And if you design to cross blades with me, you will find me a sad renegade," said I. "I am holding the papers for the hands of their true owner."

"And their true owner?" he demanded.

"Lady Mary Strepp," said I.

He sank back into his seat. "This Irishman's impudence is beyond measuring," he exclaimed. The hurrying valet arrived at that moment with a sword. "Take it away! Take it away!" he cried. "Do I wish valets to be handing swords to me at any time of the day or night?"

Here a belligerent red-faced man disengaged himself abruptly from the group of gentlemen and addressed the Earl. "Westport," said he flatly, "I can ill bear your taunt concerning your Bath friends and this is not to speak of the insolence of the person yonder."

"Oh, ho," said I. "Well, and the person yonder remains serene in his insolence."

The Earl, smiling slightly, regarded the new speaker. "Sir Edmund Flixton was ever a dainty swordsman, picking and choosing like a lady in a flower-bed. Perchance he is anxious to fight the gentleman who has just given Reginald Forister something he will not forget?"

At this, Flixton actually turned pale and drew back. Evidently he had not yet heard the news. And, mind you, I could see that he would fight me the next moment. He would come up and be killed like a gentleman. But the name of a great conqueror had simply smitten him back amazed and appalled.

The Earl was gazing at me with an entirely new expression. He had cleverly eliminated all dislike from his eyes. He covered me with a friendly regard. "O'Ruddy," he said softly, "I would have some private speech with you. Come into my chamber."

The Earl leaned on the shoulders of his valet and a little fat doctor and walked painfully into another room. I followed, knowing that I was now to withstand a subtle wheedling gentle attempt to gain the papers without the name of Lady Mary being mentioned.

The Earl was slowly lowered into a great chair. After a gasp of relief, he devoted a brightening attention to me. "You are not a bad fellow, O'Ruddy," he observed. "You remind me greatly of your father. Aye, he was a rare dog, a rare dog."

"I've heard him say so, many is the day, sir," I answered.

"Aye, a rare dog," chuckled the old man. "I have in my memory some brisk pictures of your father with his ready tongue, his what-the-devil-does-it-matter air and that extraordinary swordsmanship which you seem to have inherited."

"My father told me you were great friends in France," I answered civilly, "but from some words you let drop in Bristol I judged that he was mistaken."

"Tut," said the Earl. "You are not out of temper with me, are you, O'Ruddy?"

"With me happily in possession of the papers," I rejoined, "I am in good temper with everybody. 'Tis not for me to lose my good-nature when I hold all the cards."

The Earl's mouth quickly dropped to a sour expression but, almost as quickly, he put on a pleasant smile. "Aye," he said nodding his sick head. "Always jovial, always jovial. Precisely like his father. In fact, it brings back an old affection."

"If the old affection had been brought back a little bit earlier, sir," said I, "we all would have had less bother. 'Twas you who in the beginning drew a long face and set a square chin over the business. I am now in the mood to be rather airy."

Our glances blazed across each other.

"But," said the Earl in the gentlest of voices, "you have my papers, O'Ruddy, papers intrusted to you by your dying father to give into the hands of his old comrade. Would you betray such a sacred trust? Would you wanton yourself to the base practises of mere thievery?"

" 'Tis not I who has betrayed any trust," I cried boldly. "I brought the papers and wished to offer them. They arrived in your possession and you cried 'Straw, straw, straw!' Did you not?"

" 'Twas an expedient, O'Ruddy," said the Earl.

"There is more than one expedient in the world," said I. "I am now using the expedient of keeping the papers."

And in the glance which he gave me I saw that I had been admitted behind a certain barrier. He was angry but he would never more attempt to over-bear me with grand threats. And he would never more attempt to undermine me with cheap flattery. We had measured, one against the other, and he had not come away thinking out of his proportion. After a time, he said: "What do you propose, Mr. O'Ruddy?"

I could not help but grin at him. "I propose nothing," said I. "I am not a man for meaning two things when I say one."

"You've said one thing, I suppose?" he said slowly.

"I have," said I.

"And the one thing?" said he.

"Your memory is as good as mine," said I.

He mused deeply and at great length. "You have the papers?" he asked finally.

"I still have them," said I.

"Then," he cried with sudden vehemence, "why didn't you read the papers and find out the truth?"

I almost ran away. "Your—your lordship," I stammered, "I thought perhaps in London—in London perhaps—I might get a—I would try to get a tutor——"

CHAPTER XIII

SO that is the way of it, is it?" said the Earl grinning. "And why did you not take it to some clerk."

"My lord," said I with dignity, "the papers were with me in trust for you. A man may be a gentleman and yet not know to read and write."

" 'Tis quite true," answered he.

"And when I spoke of the tutor in London I did not mean to say that I would use what knowledge he imparted to read your papers. I was merely blushing for the defects in my education although Father Donovan often said that I knew half as much as he did, poor man, and him a holy father. If you care to so direct me I can go even now to my chamber and make shift to read the papers."

"The Irish possess a keen sense of honour," said he admiringly.

"We do," said I. "We possess more integrity and perfect sense of honour than any other country in the world although they all say the same of themselves and it was my own father who often said that he would trust an Irishman as far as he could see him and no more but for a foreigner he only had the length of an eye-lash."

"And what do you intend with the papers now, O'Ruddy?" said he.

"I intend as I intended," I replied. "There is no change in me."

"And your intentions?" said he.

"To give them into the hands of Lady Mary Strepp and no other," said I boldly. I looked at him. He looked at me. "Lady Mary Strepp, my daughter," he said in ironic musing. "Would her mother not do, O'Ruddy?" he asked softly.

I gave a start. "She is not near?" I demanded looking from here to there.

He laughed. "Aye, she is. I can have her here to take the papers in one short moment."

I held up my hands. "No—no——"

"Peace," said he with a satanic chuckle. "I was only testing your courage."

"My lord," said I gravely, "seeing a bare blade come at your breast is one thing and running around a table is another and besides you have no suitable table in this chamber."

The old villain laughed again. "O'Ruddy," he cried, "I would be a well man if you were always near me. Will I have a table fetched up from below? 'Twould be easy."

Here I stiffened. "My lord, this is frivolity," I declared. "I came here to give the papers. If you do not care to take them in the only way in which I will give them, let us have it said quickly."

"They seem to be safe in your hands at present," he remarked. "Of course, after you go to London and get a tutor—ahem."

"I will be starting at once," said I. "Although Father Donovan always told me that he was a good tutor as tutors went at the time in Ireland. And I want to be saying now, my lord, that I cannot understand you. At one moment you are crying one thing of the papers; at the next moment you are crying another. At this time you are having a laugh with me over them. What do you mean? I'll not stand this shiver-shavering any longer, I'll have you to know. What do you mean?"

He raised himself among his cushions and fixed me with a bony finger. "What do I mean? I'll tell you, O'Ruddy," said he while his eyes shone brightly. "I mean that I can be contemptuous of your plot. You will not show these papers to any breathing creature because you are in love with my daughter. Fool, to match your lies against an ex-minister of the King!"

My eyes must have almost dropped from my head but as soon as I recovered from my dumbfounderment, I grew amazed at the great intellect of this man. I had told nobody and yet he knew all about it. Yes, I was in love with Lady Mary and he was as well informed of it as if he had had spies to watch my dreams. And I saw that in many cases a lover was a kind of an ostrich, the bird which buries its head in the sands and thinks it is secure from detection. I wished that my father had told me more about love, for I have no doubt he knew everything of it, he had lived so many years in Paris. Father Donovan, of course, could not have helped me in such instruction. I resolved, anyhow, to be more cautious in the future although I did not exactly see how I could improve myself. The Earl's insight was pure mystery to me. I would not be for saying that he practised black magic but anyhow if he had been at Glandore I would have had him chased through three parishes.

However, the Earl was grinning victoriously and I saw that I must harden my face to a brave exterior. "And is it so?" said I. "Is it so?"

"Yes," said he with his grin.

"And what then?" said I bluntly.

In his enjoyment he had been back again among his cushions. "'What then? What then?'" he snarled rearing up swiftly. "Why then you are an insolent fool! Begone from me—begone—be——" Here some spasm over-took him, a spasm more from rage than from the sickness. He fell back breathless although his eyes continued to burn at me.

"My lord," said I bowing, "I will go no poorer than when I came save that I have lost part of the respect I once had for you." I turned and left his chamber. Some few gentlemen yet remained in the drawing room as I passed out into the public part of the inn. I went quietly to a chamber and sat down to think. I was forever going to chambers and sitting down to think after these talks with the Earl during which he was forever rearing up in his chair and then falling back among the cushions.

But here was another tumble over the cliffs, if you like! Here was genuine disaster. I laid my head in my hands and mused before my lonely fire, drinking much and visioning my ruin. What the Earl said was true. There was trouble in the papers for the old nobleman. That he knew. That I knew. And he knew with his devilish wisdom that I would lose my head rather than see her in sorrow. Well I could bide a time. I would go to London in company with Paddy and Jem Bottles, since they owned all the money, and if three such rogues could not devise something, then I would go away and bury myself in a war in foreign parts, occupying myself in scaling fortresses and capturing guns. These things I know I could have performed magnificently but from the Earl I had learned that I was an ill man to conduct an affair of the heart.

I do not know how long I meditated but suddenly there was a great tumult on the stairs near my door. There were the shouts and heavy breathings of men, struggling, and over all rang a screech as from some wild bird. I ran to the door and poked my head discreetly out for my coat and waistcoat were off as well as my sword and I wished to see the manner of tumult at a distance before I saw it close. As I thrust forth my head I heard a familiar voice.

"And if ye come closer, ye old hell-cat, 'tis me will be forgetting respect to my four great-grandmothers, and braining you. Keep off! Am I not giving ye the word? Keep off!"

Then another familiar voice answered him in a fine high fury. "And you gallows-bird, you gallows-bird, you gallows-bird! You answer me, do you! They're coming, all, even to the hangman! You'll soon know how to dance without a fiddler! Ah, would you? Would you?"

If I had been afflicted with that strange malady of the body which sometimes causes men to fall to the ground and die in a moment without a word, my doom would have been sealed. It was Paddy and Hoity-Toity engaged in animated discussion.

"And if ye don't mind your eye, ye old cormorant——" began Paddy.

"And you would be a highwayman, would you, gallows-bird ——" began the Contess.

"Cow——" began Paddy.

Here I thought it for many reasons time to interfere. "Paddy!" I cried. He gave a quick glance at my door, recognized my face, and turning quickly ran through into my chamber. I barred the door quickly even as Hoity-Toity's fists thundered on the oak.

"It's a she-wolf," gasped Paddy, his chest pressing in and out.

"And what did you do to her?" I demanded.

"Nothing but try to run away, sure," said Paddy.

"And why would she be scratching you?"

"She saw me for one of the highwaymen robbing the coach and there was I, devil knowing what to do, and all the people of the inn trying to put peace upon her and me dodging and then——"

"Man," said I grabbing his arm, " 'tis a game that ends on the——"

"Never a bit," he interrupted composedly. "Wasn't the old witch drunk, claws and all, and didn't even the great English lord, or whatever, send his servants to bring her in and didn't he, the big man, stand in the door and spit on the floor and go in, when he saw she was for battering all the servants and using worse talk than the sailors I heard in Bristol? It would not be me they were after, those men running. It would be her. And, small power to them, but they were no good at it. I am for taking a stool in my hand——"

"Whist," said I. "In England they would not be hitting great ladies with stools. Let us heark to the brawl. She is fighting them finely."

For I had seen that Paddy spoke truth. The noble lady was engaged in battling with servants who had been in pursuit of her when she was in pursuit of Paddy. Never had I seen even my own father so drunk as she was then. But the heart-rending thing was the humble protests of the servants. "Your ladyship! Oh, your ladyship"—as they came up one by one, or two by two, obeying orders of the Earl, to be incontinently boxed on the ears by a member of a profligate aristocracy. Probably any one of them was strong enough to throw the beldame out at a window. But such was not the manner of the time. One would think they would all retreat upon the Earl and ask to be dismissed from his service. But this also was not the manner of the time. No; they marched up heroically and took their cuffs on the head and cried: "Oh, your ladyship! Please, your ladyship!" They were only pretenders in their attacks; all they could do was to wait until she was tired and then humbly escort her, to where she belonged, meanwhile pulling gently at her arms.

"She was after recognizing you then?" said I to Paddy.

"Indeed and she was," said he. He had dropped into a chair and was looking as if he needed a doctor to cure him from exhaustion. "She would be after having eyes like a sea-gull. And

Jem Bottles he was all for declaring that my disguise was complete, bad luck to the little man."

"Your disguise complete?" said I. "You couldn't disguise yourself unless you stood your head in a barrel. What talk is this?"

"Sure and I looked no more like myself than I looked like a wild man with eight rows of teeth in his head," said Paddy mournfully. "My own mother would have been after taking me for a horse. 'Tis that old creature with her evil eye who would be seeing me when all the others were blind as bats. I could have walked down the big street in Cork without a man knowing me."

"That you could at any time," said I. The Countess had for some moments ceased to hammer on my door. "Hearken! I think they are managing her."

Either Hoity-Toity had lost heart or the servants had gained some courage for we heard them dragging her delicately down the stair-case. Presently there was a silence.

After I had waited until this silence grew into the higher silence which seems like perfect safety, I rang the bell and ordered food and drink. Paddy had a royal meal sitting on the floor by the fire-place holding a platter on his knee. From time to time, I tossed him something for which I did not care. He was very grateful for my generosity. He ate in a barbaric fashion crunching bones of fowls between his great white teeth and swallowing everything.

I had a mind to discourse upon manners in order that Paddy might not shame me when we came to London for a gentleman is known by the ways of his servants. If people of quality should see me attended by such a savage they would put me down small. "Paddy," said I, "mend your ways of eating."

" 'My ways of eating,' your honour?" said he. "And am I not eating all that I can hold? I was known to be a good man at the platter always. Sure, I've seen no man in England eat more than me. But thank you kindly, sir."

"You misunderstand me," said I. "I wish to improve your manner of eating. It would not be fine enough for the sight of great people. You eat, without taking breath, pieces as big as a block of turf."

" 'Tis the custom in my part of Ireland," answered Paddy.

"I understand," said I. "But over here, 'tis only very low people who fall upon their meat from a window above."

"I am not in the way of understanding your honour," said he. "But anyhow a man may be respectable and yet have a good hunger on him."

CHAPTER XIV

IT had been said that the unexpected often happens although I do not know what learned man of the time succeeded in thus succinctly expressing a great law and anyhow it matters little for I have since discovered that these learned men make one headful of brains go a long way by dint of poaching on each other's knowledge. But the unexpected happened in this case all true enough whatever.

I was giving my man a bit of a warning. "Paddy," said I, "you are big and you are red and you are Irish but by the same token you are not the great Fingal, son of lightning. I would strongly give you the word. When you see that old woman, you start for the open moors."

"Devil fear me, sir," answered Paddy promptly. "I'll not be stopping. I would be swimming to Ireland before she lays a claw on me."

"And mind you exchange no words with her," said I, "for 'tis that which seems to work most wrongfully upon her."

"Never a word out of me," said he. "I'll be that busy getting up the road."

There was another tumult in the corridor with the same screeches by one and the same humble protests by a multitude. The disturbance neared us with surprising speed. Suddenly I recalled that when the servant had retired after bringing food and drink, I had neglected to again bar the door. I rushed for it but I was all too late. I saw the latch raise. "Paddy!" I shouted wildly. "Mind yourself!" And with that I dropped to the floor and slid under the bed.

Paddy howled and I lifted a corner of the valance to see what was transpiring. The door had been opened and the Countess stood looking into the room. She was no longer in a fiery rage; she was cool, deadly determined, her glittering eye fixed on Paddy. She took a step forward.

Paddy, in his anguish, chanted to himself an Irish wail in which he described his unhappiness. "Oh, mother of me, and here I am caught again by the old hell-cat and sure the way she creeps toward me is enough to put the fear of God in the heart of a hedge-robber, the murdering old witch. And it was me was living so fine and grand in England and greatly pleased with myself. Sorrow the day I left Ireland; it is, indeed."

She now was close to him, and she seemed to be preparing for one stupendous pounce which would mean annihilation to Paddy. Her lean hands were thrust out with the fingers crooked and it seemed to me that her fingers were very long. In despair, Paddy changed his tune and addressed her. "Ah, now, alanna! Sure, the kind lady would be for doing no harm? Be easy, now, acushla."

But these tender appeals had no effect. Suddenly she pounced. Paddy roared and sprang backwards with splendid agility. He seized a chair.

Now I am quite sure that before he came to England Paddy had never seen a chair although it is true that at some time in his life, he may have had a peep through a window into an Irish gentleman's house where there might be a chair if the King's officers in the neighborhood were not very ambitious and powerful. But Paddy handled this chair as if he had seen many of them. He grasped it by the back and thrust it out, aiming all four legs at the Countess. It was a fine move. I have seen a moderately good swordsman fairly put to it by a pack of scoundrelly drawers who assailed him at all points in this manner.

"And you come on too fast," quavered Paddy, "ye can grab two legs but there will be one left for your eye and another for your brisket."

However she came on, sure enough, and there was a moment of scuffling near the end of the bed out of my sight. I wriggled down to gain another view and when I lifted cautiously an edge of the valance, my eyes met the strangest sight ever seen in all England. Paddy, much dishevelled and panting like a hunt-dog, had wedged the Countess against the wall. She was pinioned by the four legs of the chair and Paddy by dint of sturdily pushing at the chair-back was keeping her in a fixed position.

In a flash my mind was made up. Here was the time to escape. I scrambled quickly from under the bed. "Bravo, Paddy," I cried dashing about the room after my sword, coat, waistcoat and hat. "Devil a fear but you'll hold her, my bucko. Push hard, my brave lad, and mind your feet don't slip."

"If your honour pleases," said Paddy without turning his eyes from his conquest, " 'tis a little help I would be wishing here. She would be as strong in the shoulder as a good plough-horse and I am not for staying here forever."

"Bravo, my grand lad," I cried, at last finding my hat, which had somehow gotten into a corner. From the door, I again addressed Paddy in encouraging speech. "There's a stout-hearted boy for you! Hold hard and mind your feet don't slip."

He cast a quick agonized look in my direction and seeing that I was about to basely desert him, he gave a cry, dropped the chair and bolted after me. As we ran down the corridor, I kept well in advance thinking it the best place in case the pursuit should be energetic. But there was no pursuit. When Paddy was holding the Countess prisoner, she could only choke and stammer and I had no doubt that she now was well mastered by exhaustion.

Curiously, there was little hub-bub in the inn. The fact that the Countess was the rioter had worked in a way to cause people to seek secluded and darkened nooks. However the landlord raised his bleat at me. "Oh, sir, such a misfortune to befall my house just when so many grand ladies and gentlemen are here."

I took him quietly by the throat and beat his head against the wall, once, twice, thrice. "And you allow mad ladies to molest your guests, do you?" said I.

"Sir," he stuttered, "could I have caused her to cease?"

"True," said I releasing him. "But now do as I bid you and quickly. I am away to London. I have had my plenty of you and your mad ladies."

We started bravely to London but we only went to another and quieter inn, seeking peace and the absence of fear. I may say we found it and, in a chair before a good fire, I again took my comfort. Paddy sat on the floor toasting his shins. The warmth passed him into a reflective mood.

"And I know all I need of grand ladies," he muttered staring into the fire. "I thought they were all for riding in gold coaches and smelling of beautiful flowers and here they are mad to be chasing Irishmen in inns. I remember old Mag Cooligan fought with a whole regiment of king's troops in Bantry and even the drums stopped beating, the soldiers were that much interested. But, sure, everybody would be knowing that Mag was no grand lady although Pat Cooligan, her brother, was pig-killer to half the country side. I am thinking we were knowing little about grand ladies. One of the soldiers had his head broke by a musket because the others were so ambitious to destroy the old woman and she scratching them all. 'Twas long remembered in Bantry."

"Hold your tongue about your betters," said I sharply. "Don't be comparing this Mag Cooligan with a real countess."

"There would be a strange similarity anyhow," said he. "But, sure, Mag never fought in inns for the reason that they would not be letting her inside."

"Remember how little you are knowing of them, Paddy," said I. " 'Tis not for you to be talking of the grand ladies when you have only seen one and you would not be knowing another from a fish. Grand ladies are eccentric, I would have you to know. They have their ways with them which are not for omadhauns like you to understand."

"Eccentric, is it?" said he. "I thought it would be some such devilment."

"And I am knowing," said I with dignity, "of one lady so fine that if you don't stop talking that way of ladies, I will break your thick skull for you and it would matter to nobody."

" 'Tis an ill subject for discussion, I am seeing that," said Paddy. "But, 'faith, I could free Ireland with an army of ladies like one I've seen."

"Will you be holding your tongue?" I cried wrathfully.

Paddy began to mumble to himself. "Bedad, he was under the bed fast enough without offering her a stool by the fire and a small drop of drink which would be no more than decent with him so fond of her. I am not knowing the ways of these people."

In despair at his long tongue, I made try to change the talking. "We are off for London, Paddy. How are you for it?"

"London, is it?" said he warily. "I was hearing there are many fine ladies there."

For the second time in his life I cuffed him soundly on the ear. "Now," said I, "be ringing the bell. I am for buying you a bit of drink but if you mention the gentry to me once more in that blackguard way, I'll lather you into a resemblance to your grandfather's bones."

After a pleasant evening I retired to bed leaving Paddy snug asleep by the fire. I thought much of my Lady Mary but with her mother stalking the corridors and her knowing father with his eye wide open, I knew there was no purpose in hanging about a Bath inn. I would go to London where there were gardens and walks in the park and parties and other useful customs. There I would win my love.

The following morning, I started with Paddy to meet Jem Bottles and travel to London. Many surprising adventures were in store for us but an account of these I shall leave until a later time since one would not be worrying people with too many words which is a great fault in a man who is recounting his own affairs.

END OF PART FIRST

PART II

CHAPTER XV

A S we ambled our way agreeably out of Bath, Paddy and I employed ourselves in worthy speech. He was not yet a notable horseman but his Irish adaptability was so great that he was already able to think he would not fall off so long as the horse was old and tired.

"Paddy," said I, "how would you like to be an Englishman? Look at their cities. Sure, Skibbereen is a mud pond to them. It might be fine to be an Englishman."

"I would not, your honour," said Paddy. "I would not be an Englishman while these grand—— But never mind; 'tis many proud things I will say about the English considering they are our neighbors in one way; I mean they are near enough to come over and harm us when they wish. But anyhow they are a remarkable hard-headed lot and in time they may come to something good."

"And is a hard head such a qualification?" said I.

Paddy became academic. "I have been knowing two kinds of hard heads," he said. "Mickey McGovern had such a hard skull on him no stick in the south of Ireland could crack it, 'though many were tried. And what happened to him? He died poor as a rat. 'Tis not the kind of hard head I am meaning. I am meaning the kind of hard head which believes that it contains all the wisdom and honour in the world. 'Tis what I mean. If you have a head like that you can go along blundering into ditches and tumbling over your own shins and still hold confidence in yourself. 'Tis not very handsome for other men to see but devil a bit care you for you are warm inside with complacence."

"Here is a philosopher, in God's truth," I cried. "And where were you learning all this? In Ireland?"

"Your honour," said Paddy firmly, "you yourself are an

Irishman. You are not for saying there is no education in Ireland for it educates a man to see burning thatches and such
like. One of them was my aunt's, heaven rest her."

"Your aunt?" said I. "And what of your aunt? What have the
English to do with your aunt?"

"That was what she was asking them," said Paddy, "but they
burned her house down over a little matter of seventeen years'
rent she owed to a full-blooded Irishman, may the devil find
him."

"But I am for going on without an account of your burnt-
thatch education," said I. "You are having more than two opinions about the English and I would be hearing them. Seldom
have I seen a man who could gain so much knowledge in so
short a space. You are interesting me."

Paddy seemed pleased. "Well, your honour," said he confidentially, " 'tis true for you. I am knowing the English down to
their toes."

"And if you were an Englishman, what kind of an Englishman
would you like to be?" said I.

"A gentleman," he answered swiftly. "A big gentleman!"
Then he began to mimic and make gestures in a way that told
me that he had made good use of his eyes and of the society of
underlings in the various inns. " 'Where's me man? Send me
man! Oh here you are! And why didn't you know I wanted you?
What right have you to think I don't want you? What? A
servant dead? Pah! Send it down the back stair-case at once
and get rid of it.' Bedad," said Paddy enthusiastically, "I could do
that fine." And to prove what he said was true, he cried "Pah,"
several times in a lusty voice.

"I see you have quickly understood many customs of the
time," said I. "But 'tis not all of it. There are many quiet decent
people alive now."

" 'Tis strange we have never heard tell of them," said Paddy
musingly. "I have only heard of great fighters, blaguards, and
beautiful ladies but, sure, as your honour says, there must be
plenty of quiet decent people somewhere."

"There is," said I. "I am feeling certain of it although I am
not knowing exactly where to lay my hand upon them."

"Perhaps they would be always at mass," said Paddy, "and in
that case your honour would be likely not to see them."

"Mass!" said I. "There are more masses said in Ireland in one hour than here in two years."

"The people would be heathens, then?" cried Paddy aghast.

"Not precisely," said I. "But they have reformed themselves several times and a number of adequate reformations is a fine thing to confuse the Church. In Ireland we are all for being true to the ancient faith; here they are always for improving matters and their learned men study the Sacred Book solely with a view to making needed changes."

" 'Tis heathen they are," said Paddy with conviction. "I was knowing it. Sure, I will be telling Father Corrigan the minute I put a foot on Ireland for nothing pleases him so much as a good obstinate heathen and he very near discourses the hair off their heads."

"I would not be talking about such matters," said I. "'It merely makes my head grow an ache. My father was knowing all about it but he was always claiming that if a heathen did his duty by the poor, he was as good as anybody and that view I could never understand."

"Sure, if a heathen gives to the poor, 'tis poison to them," said Paddy. "If it is food and they eat it, they turn black all over and die the day after. If it is money, it turns red-hot and burns a hole in their hand and the devil puts a chain through it and drags them down to hell, screeching."

"Say no more," said I. "I am seeing you are a true theologian of the time. I would be talking on some more agreeable topic, something about which you know less."

"I can talk of fishing," he answered diffidently. "For I am a great fisherman, sure. And then there would be turf-cutting and the deadly stings given to men by eels. All these things I am knowing well."

" 'Tis a grand lot to know," said I, "but let us be talking of London. Have you been hearing of London?"

"I have been hearing much about the town," said Paddy. "Father Corrigan was often talking of it. He was claiming it to be full of loose women and sin and fighting in the streets during mass."

"I am understanding something of the same," I replied. "It must be an evil city. I am fearing something may happen to you, Paddy, you with your red head as conspicuous as a clock in a tower. The gay people will be setting upon you and carrying you off. Sure, there has never been anything like you in London."

"I am knowing how to be dealing with them," he replied confidently. "I am knowing how to be dealing with them. It will be all a matter of religious up-bringing, as Father Corrigan was saying. I have but to go to my devotions and the devil will fly away with them."

"And supposing they have your purse?" said I. "The devil might then fly away with them to an ill tune for you."

"When they are flying away with my purse," he replied suggestively, "they will be flying away with little of what could be called my ancestral wealth."

"You are natural rogues," said I, "you and Jem Bottles. And you had best not be talking of religion."

"Sure, a man may take the purse of an ugly old sick monkey like him and still go with an open face to confession," rejoined Paddy, "and I would not be backward if Father Corrigan's church was a mile beyond."

"And are you meaning that Father Corrigan would approve you in this robbery?" I cried.

"Devil a bit he would, your honour," answered Paddy indignantly. "He would be saying to me: 'Paddy, you limb of Satan, and how much did you get?' I would be telling him. 'Give fifteen guineas to the Church, you mortal sinner, and I will be trying my best for you,' he would be saying. And I would be giving them."

"You are saved fifteen guineas by being in England, then," said I, "for they don't do that here. And I am thinking you are traducing your clergy, you vagabond."

" 'Traducing'?" said he. "That would mean giving them money. Aye, I was doing it often. One year I give three silver shillings."

"You're wrong," said I. "By 'traducing' I mean speaking ill of your priest."

" 'Speaking ill of my priest'?" cried Paddy gasping with amazement. "Sure, my own mother never heard a word out of me!"

"However," said I, "we will be talking of other things. The English land seems good."

Paddy cast his eye over the rainy landscape. "I am seeing no turf for cutting," he remarked disapprovingly, "and potatoes would not be growing well here. 'Tis a barren country."

At nightfall, we came to a little inn which was a-blaze with light and ringing with exuberant cries. We gave up our horses and entered. To the left was the closed door of the tap-room which now seemed to furnish all the noise. I asked the landlord to tell me the cause of the excitement.

"Sir," he answered, "I am greatly honoured tonight. Mr. O'Ruddy, the celebrated Irish swordsman, is within recounting a history of his marvellous exploits."

"Indeed?" said I.

"Bedad," said Paddy.

CHAPTER XVI

P ADDY was for opening his mouth wide immediately but I checked him. "I would see this great man," said I to the landlord, "but I am so timid by nature I fear to meet his eagle eye. Is there no way by which we could observe him in secret at our leisure?"

"There be one way," remarked the landlord after deliberation. I had passed him a silver coin. He led us to a little parlour back of the tap-room. Here a door opened into the tap itself and in this door was cut a large square window so that the good man of the inn could sometimes sit at his ease in his great chair in the snug parlour and observe that his customers had only that for which they were paying. It is a very good plan for I have seen many a worthy man become a rogue merely because nobody was watching him. My father often was saying that if he had not been narrowly eyed all his younger life, first by his mother and then by his wife, he had little doubt but what he might have engaged in dishonest practises sooner or later.

A confident voice was doing some high talking in the tap-room. I peered through the window but at first I saw only a collection of gaping yokels, poor bent men with faces framed in straggly whiskers. Each had a pint pot clutched with a certain air of determination in his right hand.

Suddenly upon our line of vision strode the superb form of Jem Bottles. A short pipe was in his mouth and he gestured splendidly with a pint pot. "More of the beer, my dear," said he to a buxom maid. "We be all rich in Ireland. And four of them set upon me," he cried again to the yokels. "All noblemen, in fine clothes and with sword hilts so flaming with jewels an ordinary man might have been blinded. 'Stop!' said I. 'There be more of your friends somewhere. Call them.' And with that——"

" 'And with that'?" said I myself opening the door and stepping in upon him. " 'And with that'?" said I again. Whereupon I smote him a blow which staggered him against the wall, holding his crown with both hands while his broken beer pot rolled on the floor. Paddy was dancing wih delight at seeing some other man cuffed but the landlord and the yokels were nearly dead of terror. But they made no sound; only the buxom girl whimpered.

"There is no cause for alarm," said I amiably. "I was only greeting an old friend. 'Tis a way I have. And how wags the world with you, O'Ruddy?"

"I am not sure for the moment," replied Jem Bottles ruefully. "I must bide till it stop spinning."

"Truth," cried I. "That would be a light blow to trouble the great O'Ruddy. Come now; let us have the pots filled again and O'Ruddy shall tell us more of his adventures. What say you, lads?"

The yokels had now recovered some of their senses and they greeted my plan with a hoarse muttering of hasty and submissive assent. "Begin," said I sternly to the highwayman. He stood miserably on one foot. He looked at the floor; he looked at the wall; from time to time he gave me a sheep's glance. "Begin," said I again. Paddy was wild with glee. "Begin," said I for the third time and very harshly.

"I——" gulped out the wretched man, but he could get no further.

"I am sceing I must help you," said I. "Come now; when did you learn the art of stickadoro proderodo sliceriscum fencing?"

Bottles rolled the eyes of despair at me but I took him angrily by the shoulder. "Come now; when did you learn the art of stickadoro proderodo sliceriscum fencing?"

Jem Bottles staggered but at last he choked out: "My mother taught me." Here Paddy retired from the room doubled in a strong but soundless convulsion.

"Good," said I. "Your mother taught you. We are making progress anyhow. Your mother taught you. And now tell me this: When you slew Cormac of the Cliffs what passado did you use? Don't be stuttering. Come now; quick with you; what passado did you use? What passado?"

With a heroism born of a conviction that in any event he was a lost man Jem Bottles answered: "A blue one."

"Good," I cried cheerfully. "'A blue one'! We are coming on fine. He killed Cormac with a blue passado. And now I would be asking you——"

"Master," interrupted the highwayman with sudden resolution, "I will say no more. I have done. You may kill me and it please you."

Now I saw that enough was enough. I burst into laughter and clapped him merrily on the shoulder. "Be cheery, O'Ruddy," I cried. "Sure, an Irishman like you ought to be able to look a joke in the face." He gave over his sulks directly and I made him buy another pint each for the yokels. "'Twas dry work listening to you and your exploits, O'Ruddy," said I.

Later I went to my chamber attended by my followers and having ordered roast fowls and wine to be served as soon as possible. Paddy and Jem Bottles sat on stools one at each side of the fire-place and I occupied a chair between them.

Looking at my two faithful henchmen, I was suddenly struck by the thought that they were not very brisk servants for a gentleman to take to fashionable London. I had taken Paddy out of his finery and dressed him in a suit of decent brown but his hair was still unbarbered and I saw that unless I had a care his appearance would greatly surprise and please London. I resolved to have him shorn at the first large town.

As for Jem Bottles, his clothes were well enough and indeed he was passable in most ways unless it was his habit, when hearing a sudden noise, to take a swift dark look to the right and to the left. Then, further, people might shrewdly note his way of always sitting with his back to the wall and his face to the door. However I had no doubt of my ability to cure him of these tricks as soon as he was far enough journeyed from the scenes of his earlier activity.

But the idea I entertained at this moment was more to train them to be fine grand servants such as I had seen waiting on big people in Bath. They were both willing enough but they had no style to them. I decided to begin at once and see what I could teach them. "Paddy," said I taking off my sword and holding it out to him. "My sword!"

Paddy looked at it. "It is, sir," he answered respectfully.

"Bad scran to you, Paddy," I cried angrily. "I am teaching you your duties. Take the sword! In both hands, mind you. Now march over and lay it very tenderly on the stand at the head of the bed. There now!"

I now turned my attention to Jem Bottles. "Bottles," said I peremptorily, "my coat and waistcoat."

"Yes, sir," replied Bottles quickly, profiting by Paddy's lesson.

"There now," said I as Bottles laid the coat and waistcoat on a dresser. " 'Tis a good beginning. When supper comes I shall teach you other duties." The supper came in due course and after the inn's man had gone I bid Jem and Paddy stand one on either side of my chair and a little way back. "Now," said I, "stand square on your feet and hold your heads away high and stick your elbows out a little and try to look as if you don't know enough to tell fire from water. Jem Bottles has it. That's it. Bedad, look at the ignorance on him. He's the man for you, Paddy. Wake up now and look stupid. Am I not telling you?"

"Begor," said Paddy dejectedly, "I feel like the greatest omadhaun in all the west country and if that is not being stupid enough for your honour, I can do no better."

"Shame to you, Paddy, to let an Englishman beat you so easily," said I. "Take that grin off your face, you scoundrel! Now," I added, "we are ready to begin. Wait, now. You must each have something to hold in your fist. Let me be thinking. There's only one plate and little of anything else. Ah, I have it. A bottle! Paddy, you shall hold one of the bottles. Put your right hand underneath it and with your left hand hold it by the neck. But keep your elbows out. Jem, what the devil am I to give you to hold? Ah, I have it! Another bottle! Hold it the same as Paddy. Now! Stand square on your feet and hold your heads away high and stick your elbows out a little and look stupid. I am going to eat my supper."

I finished my first and second bottles with the silence only broken by the sound of my knife play and an occasional restless creaking of boots as one of my men slyly shifted his position. Wishing to call for my third bottle, I turned and caught them exchanging a glance of sympathetic bewilderment. As my eye flashed upon them, they stiffened up like grenadier recruits.

But I was not for being too hard on them at first. " 'Tis enough for one lesson," said I. "Put the bottles by me and take your ease."

With evident feelings of relief, they slunk back to the stools by the fire where they sat recovering their spirits.

After my supper, I sat in the chair toasting my shins and lazily listening to my lads finishing the fowls. They seemed much more like themselves, sitting there grinding away at the bones and puffing with joy. It was in the red fire-light such a scene of happiness that I misdoubted for a moment the wisdom of my plan to make them into fine grand numskulls.

I could see that all men were not fitted for the work. It needed a beefy person with fat legs and a large amount of inexplicable dignity, a regular God-knows-why loftiness. Truth, in those days, real talent was usually engaged in some form of rascality, barring the making of books and sermons. When one remembers the impenetrable dullness of the great mass of the people, the frivolity of the gentry, the arrogance and wickedness of the court, one ceases to wonder that many men of taste took to the highway as a means of recreation and livelihood. And here I had been attempting to turn my two frank rascals into the kind of sheep-headed rubbish whom you could kick down a great stair-case and, for a guinea, they would say no more. Unless I was the kicker, I think Paddy would have returned up the stair-case after his assailant. Jem Bottles probably would have gone away nursing his wrath and his injury and planning to way-lay the kicker on a convenient night. But neither would have taken a guinea and said no more. Each of these simple-hearted reprobates was too spirited to take a guinea for a kick down a stair-case.

Anyhow I had a mind that I could be a gentleman true enough without the help of Jem and Paddy making fools of themselves. I would worry them no more.

As I was musing thus, my eyes closed from a sense of contented weariness but I was aroused a moment later by hearing Paddy address Bottles in a low voice. " 'Tis you who are the cool one, Jem," said he with admiration, "trying to make them think you were *him*!" Here I was evidently indicated by a side-ways bob of the head. "Have you not been seeing the fine ways of him?

Sure, be looking at his stride and his habit of slatting people over the head and his grand manners with his food. You are looking more like a candle-stick than you are looking like *him*. I wonder at you."

"But I befooled them," said Bottles proudly. "I befooled them well. It was Mr. O'Ruddy here and Mr. O'Ruddy there and the handsome wench she gave me many a glance of her eye, she did."

"Sorrow the day for her then," responded Paddy, "and if you would be cozening the girls in the name of *him* there, he will be cozening you and I never doubt it."

" 'Twas only a trick to make the time go easy, it was," said Bottles gloomily. "If you remember, Master Paddy, I have spent the most of my new service waiting under oak-trees and I will not be saying it rained always but oft times it did rain most accursedly."

CHAPTER XVII

WE rode on at day-break. At the first large village, I bid a little man cut Paddy's hair and although Paddy was all for killing the little man and the little man twice ran away, the work was eventually done for I stood over Paddy and threatened him. Afterward the little boys were not so anxious to hoot us through the streets, calling us Africans. For it must be recalled that at this time there was great curiosity in the provinces over the Africans because it was known that in London people of fashion often had African servants and although London cared nothing for the provinces and the provinces cared nothing for London, still the rumour of the strange man interested the country clod-hopper so greatly that he called Paddy an African on principle in order that he might blow to his neighbors that he had seen this fascinating biped. There was no general understanding that the African was a man of black skin; it was only understood that he was a great marvel. Hence the urchins in these faraway villages often ran at the heels of Paddy's horse, yelling.

In time, the traffic on the highway became greatly thickened and several times we thought we were entering London because of the large size and splendour of the towns to which we came. Paddy began to fear the people had been deceiving us as to the road and that we had missed London entirely. But finally we came to a river with hundreds of boats upon it and there was a magnificent bridge and on the other bank was a roaring city and through the fog the rain came down thick as the tears of the angels. "That's London," said I.

We rode out upon the bridge, all much interested but somewhat fearful for the noise of the city was terrible. But if it was terrible as we approached it, I hesitate to say what it was to us when we were once fairly in it. "Keep close to me," I yelled to

Paddy and Jem and they were not unwilling. And so we rode into this pandemonium, not having the least idea of where we were going.

As we progressed, I soon saw what occasioned the major part of the noise. Many heavy carts thundered slowly through the narrow echoing streets, bumping their way uproariously over a miserable pavement. Added to this, of course, was the shrill or hoarse shouts of the street vendors and apprentices at the shop-doors. To the sky arose an odour almost insupportable, for it was new to us all.

The eaves of the houses streamed with so much water that the side-walks were practically untenable although here and there a hardy way-farer strode on regardless of a drenched cloak, probably being too proud to take to the street. Once our travel was entirely blocked by a fight. A butcher in a bloody apron had dashed out of his shop and attacked the driver of a brewer's sledge. A crowd gathered miraculously and cheered on this spectacle; women appeared at all the windows; urchins hooted; mongrel dogs barked. When the butcher had been worsted and chased back into his shop by the maddened brewer, we were allowed to pursue our journey.

I must remark that neither of these men used ought but his hands. Mostly their fists were doubled and they dealt each other sound swinging blows but there was some hair pulling and when the brewer had the butcher down, I believe the butcher tried to bite his opponent's ear. However they were rather high-class for their condition. I found out later that at this time in the darker parts of London the knife was a favourite weapon of the English and was as rampant as ever it is in the black alleys of an Italian city. It was no good news for me for the Irish had long been devoted to the cudgel.

When I wish for information, I always prefer making the request to a gentleman. To have speech of a boor is well enough if he would not first study you over to find, if he can, why you want the information and after a prolonged pause, tell you wrong entirely. I perceived a young gentleman standing in under a porch and ogling a window on the opposite side of the way. "Sir," said I halting my horse close to him, "would you be so kind as to point to a stranger the way to a good inn?" He looked me full in the face, spat meaningly in the gutter and, turning on his heel, walked away. And I will give oath that he was not more than sixteen years old.

I sat stiff in the saddle; I felt my face going hot and cold. This new-feathered bird with a toy sword! But to save me, as it happened, from a preposterous quarrel with this infant, another man came along the side-walk. He was an older man with a grave mouth and a clean-cut jowl. I resolved to hail him. "And now my man," said I under my breath, "if you are as bad as the other, by the mass, I'll have a turn-over here with you, London or no London."

Then I addressed him. "Sir——" I began. But here a cart roared on my other side and I sat with my mouth open looking at him. He smiled a little but waited courteously for the hideous din to cease. "Sir," I was enabled to say at last, "would you be so kind as to point to a stranger the way to a good inn?" He scanned me quietly in order no doubt to gain an idea of what kind of an inn would suit my condition. "Sir," he answered, coming into the gutter and pointing, " 'tis this way to Bishopsgate Street and there you will see the sign of the Pig and Turnip where there is most pleasurable accommodation for man and beast, and an agreeable host." He was a shop-keeper of the city of London, of the calm steady breed that has made successive kings either love them or fearingly hate them, the bone and the sinew of the great town.

I thanked him heartily and we went on to the Pig and Turnip. As we clattered into the inn-yard it was full of people mounting and dismounting but there seemed a thousand stable-boys. A dozen flung themselves at my horse's head. They quite lifted me out of the saddle in their great care that I should be put to no trouble. At the door of the inn a smirking landlord met me bowing his forehead on the floor at every backward pace and humbly beseeching me to tell how he could best serve me. I told him and at once there was a most pretentious hub-bub. Six or eight servants began to run hither and yon. I was delighted with my reception but, several days later, I discovered they had mistaken me for a nobleman of Italy or France and I was expected to pay extravagantly for graceful empty attentions rather than for sound food and warm beds.

This inn was so grand that I saw it would no longer do for Paddy and Jem to be sleeping in front of my fire like big dogs so I nodded assent when the landlord asked if he should provide lodgings for my two servants. He packed them off somewhere and I was left lonely in a great chamber. I had some fears in leaving Paddy long out of my sight but I assured myself that London had such terrors for him he would not dare any Irish mischief. I could trust Jem Bottles to be discreet for he had learned discretion in a notable school.

Toward the close of the afternoon, the rain ceased and, attiring myself for the street and going to the landlord, I desired him to tell me what interesting or amusing walk could now conveniently be taken by a gentleman who was a stranger to the sights of London. The man wagged his head in disapproval. " 'Twill be dark presently, sir," he answered, "and I would be an ill host if I did not dissuade a perfect stranger from venturing abroad in the streets o' London of a night-time."

"And is it as bad as that?" I cried surprised.

"For strangers, yes," said he. "For they be forever wandering and will not keep to the three or four streets which be as safe as the King's palace. But if you wish, sir, I will provide one man with a lantern and staff to go before you and another man with a lantern and staff to follow. Then with two more stout lads and your own servants, I would venture——"

"No, no," I cried, "I will not head an army on a night-march when I intend merely an evening stroll. But how, pray you, am I to be entertained otherwise than by going forth?"

The inn-keeper smiled with something like pity. "Sir, every night there meets here such a company of gay gentlemen, wits and poets as would dazzle the world, did it but hear one half of what they say over their pipes and their punch. I serve the distinguished company myself for I dare trust nobody's care in a matter so important to my house, and, I assure you, sir, I have at times been so doubled with mirth there was no life in me. Why, sir, Mr. Fullbil himself comes here at times!"

"Does he, indeed?" I cried although I never had heard of the illustrious man.

"Indeed and he does, sir," answered the inn-keeper pleased at my quick appreciation of this matter. "And then there is goings on, I warrant me. Mr. Bobbs be a'most always here and them two—ha, ha! Why sir, many great lords, sir, come here for a pipe and a bowl if they think Mr. Fullbil and Mr. Bobbs and the other gentlemen will be in spirits."

"I never doubt you," said I. "But is it possible for a private gentleman of no wit to gain admittance to this distinguished company?"

"Doth require a little managing, sir," said he, full of meaning.

"Pray you manage it then," said I, "for I have nought to do in London for at least two days and I would be seeing these famous men with whose names my country rings."

Early in the evening, the inn-keeper came to me, much pleased. "Sir, the gentlemen bid me bring you their compliments and I am to say they would be happy to have a pleasure in the honour of your presence. Mr. Fullbil himself is in the chair tonight. You are very fortunate sir."

"I am," said I. "Lead away and let us hope to find the great Fullbill in high feather."

CHAPTER XVIII

THE inn-keeper led me down to a large room the door of which he had flung open with a flourish. "The furrin' gentleman, may it please you, sirs," he announced and then retired.

The room was so full of smoke that at first I could see little but soon enough I made out a long table bordered with smoking and drinking gentlemen. A hoarse voice, away at the head of the board, was growling some words which convulsed most of the gentlemen with laughter. Many candles burned dimly in the haze.

I stood for a moment doubtful as to procedure, but a gentleman near the foot of the table suddenly arose and came toward me with great frankness and good-nature. "Sir," he whispered so that he would not interrupt the growls at the farther end of the room, "it would give me pleasure if you would accept a chair near me."

I could see that this good gentleman was moved solely by a desire to be kind to a stranger and I in another whisper gave my assent and thanks to his plan. He placed me in a chair next his own. The voice was still growling from the head of the table.

Very quickly, my eyes became accustomed to the smoke especially after I was handed a filled clay pipe by my new and excellent friend. I began to study the room and the people in it. The room was panelled in new oak and the chairs and the long table were all of new oak, well carved. It was the handsomest room I had ever been in.

Afterward I looked toward the growl. I saw a little old man in a chair much too big for him and in a wig much too big for him. His head was bent forward until his sharp chin touched his breast and out from under his darkling brows a pair of little eyes flashed angrily and arrogantly. All faces were turned toward him and all ears were open to his growls. He was the king; it was Fullbil.

His speech was all addressed at one man and I looked at the latter. He was a young man with a face both Roman and feminine, with that type of profile which is possessed by most of the popular actors in the reign of His Majesty of today. He had luxuriant hair and stung by the taunts of Fullbil, he constantly brushed it nervously from his brow while his sensitive mouth quivered with held-in retorts. He was Bobbs, the great dramatist.

And as Fullbil growled, it was a curiously mixed crowd which applauded and laughed. There were handsome lordlings from the very top of London cheek by cheek with sober men who seemed to have some intellectual occupation in life. The lordlings did the greater part of the sniggering. In the meantime, everybody smoked hard and drank punch harder. During occasional short pauses in Fullbil's remarks, gentlemen passed ecstatic comments one to another. "Ah, this indeed is a mental feast!" "Did ye ever hear him talk more wittily?" "Not I, 'faith; he surpasses even himself!" "Is it not a blessing to sit at table with such a master of learning and wit?" "Ah, these are the times to live in!"

I thought it was now opportune to say something of the same kind to my amiable friend and so I did it. "The old corpse seems to be saying a prayer," I remarked. "Why don't he sing it?"

My new friend looked at me, all agape, like a fish just over the side of the boat. " 'Tis Fullbil, the great literary master——" he began but at this moment, Fullbil, having recovered from a slight fit of coughing, resumed his growls and my friend subsided again into a worshipping listener.

For my part, I could not follow completely the words of the great literary master but I construed that he had pounced upon the drama of the time and was tearing its ears and eyes off.

At that time I knew little of the drama having never read nor seen a play in my life but I was all for the drama on account of poor Bobbs who kept chewing his lip and making nervous movements until Fullbil finished, a thing which I thought was not likely to happen before an early hour of the morning. But finish he did. Immediately, Bobbs, much impassioned, brought his glass heavily down on the table in a demand for silence. I thought he would get little hearing but much to my surprise I heard again the ecstatic murmur. "Ah, now, we shall hear Bobbs reply to Fullbil!" "Are we not fortunate?" " 'Faith, this will be over half London tomorrow!"

Bobbs waited until this murmur had passed away. Then he began, nailing an impressive fore-finger to the table. "Sir, you have been contending at some length that the puzzling situations which form the basis of our dramas of the day could not possibly occur in real life because five minutes of intelligent explanation between the persons concerned would destroy the silly mystery before anything at all could really happen. Your originality, sir, is famous—need I say it?—and when I hear you champion this opinion in all its majesty of venerable age and general acceptance, I feel stunned by the colossal imbecile strength of the whole proposition. Why, sir, you may recall all the mysterious murders which occurred in England since England had a name. The truth of them remains in unfathomable shadow. But, sir, any one of them could be cleared up in five minutes' intelligent explanation—by the murderer. There is no secret in the history of the world, sir, which could not be made plain in five minutes of intelligent explanation. Pontius Pilate could have been saved his blunder by far, far, far less than five minutes of intelligent explanation. But—mark ye—but who has ever heard five minutes of intelligent explanation? The complex interwoven mesh of life constantly, eternally, prevents people from giving intelligent explanations. You sit in the theatre and you say to yourself: 'Well, I could mount the stage and in a short talk to these people I could anticipate a further continuation of the drama.' Yes, you could; but you are an outsider. You have no relations with these characters. You arise like an angel. Nobody has been your enemy; nobody has been your mistress. You arise and give the five minutes of intelligent explanation; bah! There is not a situation in life which does not need five minutes of intelligent explanation; but it doesn't get it."

It could now be seen that the old man Fullbil was simply aflame with a destructive reply and even Bobbs paused under the spell of this anticipation of a gigantic answering. The literary master began very deliberately. "My good friend Bobbs," said he, "I see your nose gradually is turning red."

The drama immediately pitched into oblivion. The room thundered with a great shout of laughter that went to the ceiling. I could see Bobbs making angry shouts against an invulnerable bank of uncontrolled merriment. And amid his victory, old Fullbil sat with a faint vain smile on his cracked lips.

My excellent and adjacent friend turned to me in a burst of enthusiasm. "And did you ever hear a thing so well turned? Ha, ha! 'My good friend Bobbs,' quoth he, 'I see your nose gradually is turning red.' Ha, ha, ha! By my King, I have seldom heard a wittier answer."

"Bedad," said I, somewhat bewildered but resolved to appreciate the noted master of wit, "it stamped the drama down into the ground. Sure, never another play will be delivered in England after that tremendous over-throw."

"Aye," he rejoined, still shuddering with mirth, "I fail to see how the dramatists can survive it. It was like the wit of a new Shakespeare. It subsided Bobbs to nothing. I would not be surprised at all if Bobbs now entirely quit the writing of plays since Fullbil's words so closely hit his condition in the dramatic world. A dangerous dog, is this Fullbil."

"It reminds me of a story my father used to tell——" I began.

"Sir," cried my new friend hastily, "I beg of you! May I, indeed, insist? Here we talk only of the very deepest matters."

"Very good, sir," I replied amiably. "I will appear better no doubt as a listener but if my father was alive——"

"Sir," beseeched my friend, "the great Fancher, the immortal critic, is about to speak."

"Let him," said I, still amiable.

A portly gentleman of middle age now addressed Bobbs amid a general and respectful silence. "Sir," he remarked, "your words concerning the great age of what I shall call the Five-minutes'-intelligent-explanation theory have interested me deeply. You may care to hear that the theory was first developed by the Chinese and is contemporaneous I believe with their adoption of the custom of roasting their meat instead of eating it raw."

"Sir, I am interested and instructed," rejoined Bobbs.

Here old Fullbil let go two or three growls of scornful disapproval. "Fancher," said he, "my delight in your company is sometimes dimmed by my appreciation of your facilities for being entirely wrong. The great theory of which you speak so confidently, sir, was born no earlier than seven o'clock on the morning of this day. I was in my bed, sir; the maid had come in with my tea and toast. 'Stop,' said I, sternly. She stopped. And in those few moments of undisturbed reflection, sir, the thought came to life, the thought which you so falsely attribute to the Chinese, a savage tribe whose sole distinction is its ability to fly kites."

After the murmurs of glee had died away, Fancher answered with spirit. "Sir, that you are subject to periods of reflection, I will not deny, I cannot deny. Nor can I say honourably that I give my support to our dramatical friend's defense of his idea. But, sir, when you refer to the Chinese in terms which I cannot but regard as insulting, I am prepared, sir, to——"

There were loud cries. "Order! Order! Order!" The wrathful Fancher was pulled down into his chair by soothful friends and neighbors to whom he gesticulated and cried out during the uproar.

I looked toward old Fullbil expecting to see him disturbed or annoyed or angry. On the contrary he seemed pleased as a little boy who had somehow created a row. "The excellent Fancher," said he, "the excellent Fancher is wroth. Let us proceed, gentlemen, to more friendly topics. You, now, Doctor Chord, with what new thing in chemics are you ready to astound us?"

The speech was addressed to a little man near me who instantly blushed crimson, mopped his brow in much agitation, and looked at the table, unable for the moment to raise his eyes or speak a word. "One of the greatest scientists of the time," said my friend in my ear.

"Sir," faltered the little man in his bashfulness, "that part of the discourse which related to the flying of kites has interested me greatly and I am ready to contend that kites fly, not, as many say, through the influence of a demon or spirit which inhabits the materials, but through the pressure of the wind itself."

Fancher, now himself again, said: "I wish to ask the learned doctor whether he refers to Chinese kites?"

The little man hurriedly replied that he had not had Chinese kites in his mind at all.

"Very good, then," said the great critic. "Very good."

"But, sir," said Fullbil to little Chord, "how is it that kites may fly without the aid of demons or spirits if they are made by man? For it is known, sir, that man may not move in the air without the aid of some devilish agency and it is also known that he may not send aloft things formed of the gross materials of the earth. How then can these kites fly virtuously?"

There was a general murmur of approbation of Fullbil's speech and the little doctor cast down his eyes and blushed again, speechless.

It was a triumph for Fullbil and he received the congratulations of his friends with his faint vain smile implying that it was really nothing, you know, and that he could have done it much better if he had thought that anybody was likely to heed it.

The little Doctor Chord was so down-trodden that for the remainder of the evening he hardly dared raise his eyes from the table but I was glad to see him apply himself industriously to the punch.

To my great alarm, Fullbil now said: "Sirs, I fear we have suffered ourselves to forget we have with us tonight a strange gentleman from foreign parts. Your good fortune, sir," he added bowing to me over his glass. I bowed likewise but I saw his little piggish eyes looking wickedly at me. There went a titter around the board and I understood from it that I was the next victim of the celebrated Fullbil.

"Sir," said he, "may I ask from what part of Italy do you come?"

"I come from Ireland, sir," I answered decently.

He frowned. "Ireland is not in Italy, sir," said he. "Are you so good as to trifle with me, sir?"

"I am not, sir," said I.

All the gentlemen murmured; some looked at me with pity, some with contempt. I began to be frightened until I remembered that if I once drew my sword I could chase the whole roomful of philosophy into the next parish. I resolved to put on a bold front.

"Probably, sir," observed Fullbil, "the people of Ireland have heard so much of me, that I may expect many visits from Irish gentlemen who wish to hear what my poor mind may develope in regard to the only true philosophy of life?"

"Not in the least, sir," I rejoined. "Over there, they don't know you are alive and they are not caring."

Consternation fell upon that assembly like snow from a roof. The gentlemen stared at me. Old Fullbil turned purple at first but his grandeur could not be made to suffer long or seriously from my impudence. Presently he smiled at me a smile confident, cruel, deadly. "Ireland is a great country, sir," he observed.

" 'Tis not so great as many people's ignorance of it," I replied bluntly, for I was being stirred somewhat.

"Indeed!" cried Fullbil. Then he triumphantly added: "Then, sir, we are proud to have among us one so manifestly capable of giving us instruction."

There was a loud shout of laughter at this sally and I was very uncomfortable down to my toes but I resolved to hold a brave face and pretend that I was not minding their sneers. However, it was plain enough that old Fullbil had made me the butt of the evening.

"Sir," said the dramatist, Bobbs, looking at me, "I understand that in Ireland the pigs sit at table with even the best families."

"Sir," said the critic, Fancher, looking at me, "I understand that in Ireland the chastity of the women is so great that no child is born without a birth-mark in the shape of the initials of the legal husband and father."

"Sir," said old Fullbil, "I understand that in Ireland people go naked when it rains for fear of wetting their clothes."

Amid the uproarious merriment provoked by these speeches I sat in silence. Suddenly the embarrassed little scientist, Doctor Chord, looked up at me with a fine friendly sympathy. "A glass with you, sir," he said and as we nodded our heads solemnly over the rims I felt that there had come to my help one poor little frightened friend. As for my first acquaintance, he, seeing me attacked not only by the redoubtable Fullbil but also by the formidable Bobbs and the dangerous Fancher, had immediately begun to pretend that never in his life had he spoken to me.

Having a great knowledge of Irish character, I could see that trouble was brewing for somebody but I resolved to be very backward for I hesitated to create a genuine disturbance in these philosophical circles. However, I was saved this annoyance in a strange manner. The door opened and a newcomer came in bowing right and left to his acquaintances and finally taking a seat near Fullbil. I recognized him instantly; he was Sir Edmund Flixton, the gentleman who had had some thought of fighting me in Bath but who had refrained from it upon hearing that I had worsted Forister.

However he did not perceive me at that time. He chatted with Fullbil telling him evidently some very exciting news for I heard old Fullbil ejaculate: "By my soul, can it be possible!" Later Fullbil related some amusing things to Flixton and, upon an enquiry from Flixton, I was pointed out to him. I saw Flixton's face change; he spoke hastily to old Fullbil; old Fullbil turned pale as death. Swiftly some bit of information flashed around the board and I saw men's eyes open wide and white as they looked at me.

I have said that it was the age of bullies. It was the age when men of physical prowess walked down the street shouldering lesser men into the gutter and the lesser men had never a word to say for themselves. It was the age when if you expressed opinions contrary to those of a bully he was confidently expected to kill you or somehow maltreat you.

Of all that company of genius there now seemed to be only one gentleman who was not a-tremble. It was the little scientist, Doctor Chord. He looked at me with a bright and twinkling eye; suddenly he grinned broadly. I could not but burst into laughter when I noted the appetite with which he enjoyed the confusion and alarm of his friends.

"Come, Fullbil! Come, Bobbs! Come, Fancher! Where are all your pretty wits?" he cried for this timid little man's impudence increased mightily amid all this helpless distress. "Here's the dignity and power of learning for you, in gad's truth. Here's Knowledge enthroned, fearless, great! Have ye all lost your nimble tongues?"

And he was for going on to worry them but that I called out to him. "Sir," said I mildly, "if it please you, I would not have the gentlemen disturbed over any little misunderstanding of a pleasant evening. As regards quarrelling I am all milk and water

myself. It reminds me of an occasion in Ireland once when——"
Here I recounted a story which Father Donovan always began
on after more than three bottles and to my knowledge he had
never succeeded in finishing it. But this time I finished it. "And,"
said I, "the fellow was sitting there drinking with them and they
had had good fun with him when of a sudden he up and spoke.
Says he: ' 'Tis God's truth I never expected in all my life to be
an evening in the company of such a lot of scurvy rat-eaters,'
he says to them. 'And,' says he, 'I have only one word for that
squawking old masquerading pea-cock that sits at the head of
the table,' says he. 'What little he has of learning I could put in
my eye without going blind,' says he. 'The old curmudgeon,' says
he. And, with that, he arose and left the room, afterward becoming King of Galway and living to a great age."

This amusing tale created a sickly burst of applause in the
midst of which I bowed myself from the room.

CHAPTER XIX

ON my way to my chamber, I met the inn-keeper and I casually asked him after Paddy and Jem. He said he would send to have word of them and inform me as soon as possible. Later a drawer came to my door and told me that Paddy and Jem with three men-servants of gentlemen sleeping at the inn had sallied out to a mug-house.

"Mug-house?" said I. "What in the devil's name is a mug-house?"

"Mug-house, sir?" said the man staring. "Mug-house? Why, sir, 'tis—'tis a form of amusement, sir."

"It is, is it?" said I. "Very good. And does anyone here know to what mug-house they went?"

"The Red Slipper, I think, sir," said the man.

"And how do I get to it?" said I.

"Oh, sir," he cried, " 'tis impossible!"

"Is it?" said I. "And why is it? The inn-keeper said the same to me and I would like to hear all the reasons."

"Sir," said the man, "when it becometh dark in London there walk abroad many men of evil minds who are no respecters of persons but fall upon whomsoever they may, beating them sorely, having no regard for that part of the Holy Book in which it is written——"

"Let go," said I. "I see what you mean." I then bid him get for me a stout lad with a cudgel and a lantern and a knowledge of the whereabouts of the Red Slipper.

I, with the stout lad, had not been long in the streets before I understood what the landlord and the waiter had meant. In fact we were scarce out of the door before the man was menacing with his cudgel two human vultures who slunk upon us out of the shadow. I saw their pale wicked snarling faces in the glow of the lantern.

A little later, a great shindy broke out in the darkness and I heard voices calling loudly for a rally in the name of some guild or society. I moved closer but I could make out little save that it was a very pretty fight in which a company of good citizens were trying to put to flight a band of roughs and law-breakers. There was a merry rattling of sticks. Soon enough, answering shouts could be heard from some of the houses and with a great slamming of doors, men rushed out to do battle for the peace of the great city. Meanwhile all the high windows had been filled with night-capped heads and some of these people even went so far as to pour water upon the combatants. They also sent down cat-calls and phrases of witty advice. The sticks clattered together furiously; once, a man with a bloody face staggered past us; he seemed to have been whacked directly on the ear by some uneducated person; it was as fine a shindy as one could hope to witness and I was deeply interested.

Then suddenly a man called out hoarsely that he had been stabbed—murdered. There were yells from the street and screams from the windows. My lantern-bearer plucked me madly by the sleeve. I understood him and we hastily left the neighborhood.

I may tell now what had happened and what followed this affair of the night. A worthy citizen had been stabbed to death indeed. After further skirmishes his comrade citizens had taken several wretches into custody. They were tried for the murder and all acquitted save one. Of this latter it was proven that the brawl had started through his attempt to gain the purse of a passing citizen and forthwith he was sentenced to be hanged for murder. His companion rascals were sent to prison for long terms on the expectation that one of them really might have been the murderer.

We passed into another street where each well-lighted window framed one or more painted hussies who called out to us in jocular obscenity but when we marched stiffly on without replying, their mood changed and they delivered at us volley after volley of language incredibly foul. There were only two of these creatures who paid no heed and their indifference to us was due to the fact that they were deeply engaged in a duel of words, exchanging the most frightful blood-curdling epithets.

Confident drunken men jostled us from time to time and frequently I could see small ashy-faced ancient-eyed youths dodging here and there with food or wine. My lantern-bearer told me
that the street was not quite awake; it was waiting for the out-
pourings from the taverns and mug-houses. I bade him hurry
me to the Red Slipper as soon as possible for never have I had
any stomach for these tawdry evils, fit as they are only for clerks
and sailors.

We came at length to the creaking sign of the Red Slipper. A
great noise came from the place. A large company was roaring
out a chorus. Without many words, I was introduced into the
room in which the disturbance was proceeding. It was blue with
smoke and the thundering chorus was still unfinished. I sank
unnoticed into a quiet corner.

I was astonished at the appearance of the company. There
were many men who looked like venerable prelates and many
men who looked like the heads of old and noble houses. I
laughed in my sleeve when I remembered I had thought to find
Paddy and Jem here. And at the same time I saw them up near
the head of the table, if it please you. Paddy had his hand on
the shoulder of a bishop and Jem was telling some tale into the
sympathetic ear of a marquis. At least this is the way matters
appeared to my stupefied sense.

The singing ceased and a distinguished peer at my elbow resumed a talk which evidently had been broken by the chorus.
"And so the Duke spoke with somewhat more than his accustomed vigour," said the distinguished peer. My worst suspicions
were confirmed. Here was a man talking of what had been said
by a duke. I cast my eye toward my happy pair of rogues and
wondered how I could ever extricate them from their position.

Suddenly there was a loud pounding upon the table and in
the ensuing quiet, the grave and dignified voice of the chair-
man could be heard. "Gentlemen," he said, "we crave your attention to a song by Mr. John Snowdon." Whereupon my very
own Jem Bottles arose amidst a burst of applause and began to
sing a ballad which had been written in Bristol or Bath in celebration of the notorious scoundrel, Jem Bottles.

Here I could see that if impudence could serve us, we would

not lack success in England. The ballad was answered with wild cheers of appreciation. It was the great thing of the evening. Jem was strenuously pressed to sing again but he buried his face in his mug and modestly refused. However they devoted themselves to his chorus and sang it over and over with immense delight. I had never imagined that the nobility were so free and easy.

During the excitement over Jem's ballad, I stole forward to Paddy. "Paddy," I whispered, "come out of this now. 'Tis no place for you here among all these reverend fathers and gentlemen of title. Shame on you."

He saw my idea in a flash. "Whist, sir," he answered. "There are being no reverend fathers or gentlemen of title here. They are all after being footmen and valets."

I was extremely vexed with myself. I had been in London only a brief space but Paddy had been in the city no longer. However, he had already managed his instruction so well that he could at once tell a member of the gentry from a servant. I admired Paddy's cleverness but at the same time I felt a certain resentment against the prelates and nobles who had so imposed upon me.

But, to be truthful, I have never seen a finer display of manners. These menials could have put courtiers to the blush. And from time to time somebody would speak out loud and clear an opinion pilfered verbatim from his master. They seldom spoke their own thought in their own way; they sent forth as their own whatever they could remember from the talk of their masters and other gentlemen. There was one man who seemed to be the servant of some noted scholar and when he spoke, the others were dumbfounded into quiet.

"The loriot," said he with a learned frown, "is a bird. If it is looked upon by one who has the yellow jaundice, the bird straightway dies but the sick person becomes well instantly. 'Tis said that lovage is used but I would be luctuous to hear of anybody using this lothir weed for 'tis no pentepharmacon but a mere simple and not worth a raspatory."

This utterance fairly made their eyes bulge and they sat in stunned silence. But I must say that there was one man who did not fear. "Sir," said Paddy respectfully but still with his own dignity, "I would be hearing more of this bird and we all would be feeling honoured for a short description."

"In colour he is ningid," said the learned valet.

"Bedad!" cried Paddy. "That's strange!"

" 'Tis a question full of tenebrosity," remarked the other, leaning back in his chair. "We poor scholars grow madarosis reflecting upon it. However I may tell you that the bird is simous; yblent in the sun-light but withal strenuous-eyed; its blood inclined to intumescence. However, I must be breviloquent for I require a enneadecaterides to enumerate the true qualities of the loriot."

"By gor," said Paddy, "I'll know that bird if I see him ten years from now. Thank you kindly, sir. But we would be late for breakfast if you took the required time; and that's true for me."

Afterward I reflected that I had attended the meetings of two scholarly bodies in this one evening but for the life of me I couldn't decide which knew the least.

CHAPTER XX

BY the following Sunday I judged that the Earl of Westport and his family had returned to London and so I walked abroad in the hope of catching a glimpse of some of them among the brilliant gentry who on this day thronged in the public gardens. I had both Jem Bottles and Paddy accompany me for I feared they would get into mischief if I left them to themselves. The inn-keeper had told me that Kensington Gardens was the place where the grand people mostly chose to walk and flirt and show their clothes on a clear Sunday. It was a long way to these Gardens but we footed out bravely although we stopped once to see a fight between five drunken apprentices as well as several times for much-needed refreshment.

I had had no idea that the scene at the Gardens would be so splendid. Outside, the road was a block of gleaming chariots and coaches with servants a-blaze in their liveries. Here I left Paddy and Jem to amuse themselves as suited them.

But the array of carriages had been only a forecast of what my eyes would encounter in the Gardens itself. I was involved at once in a swarm of fashionable people. My eyes were dazzled with myriad colours and my nostrils, trained as they were to peat smoke, were saluted by a hundred delicious perfumes. Priceless silks and satins swept against my modest stockings.

I suffered from my usual inclination to run away but I put it down with an iron will. I soon found a more retired spot from which I could review the assemblage at something like my leisure. All the highly fashionable folk knew each other intimately, it appeared, and they kept off with figurative pikes attempts of a certain class not quite so high and mighty who seemed forever trying to edge into situations which would benefit them on the social ladder. Their failures were dismal but not so dismal as the heroic smiles with which they covered their little noiseless defeats.

I saw a lady, sumptuously arrayed, sweep slowly along with her daughter, a beautiful girl who greatly wished to keep her eyes fixed on the ground. The mother glanced everywhere with half-concealed eagerness and anxiety. Once she bowed impressively to a dame with a cold pale aristocrat's face around whom were gathered several officers in the uniform of His Majesty's Guards. The grand dame lifted her lorgnette and stared coolly at that impressive bow; then she turned and said something amusing to one of the officers who smilingly answered. The mother with her beautiful daughter passed on, both pairs of eyes now on the ground.

I had thought the rebuff would settle this poor misguided creature but in the course of an hour I saw three more of her impressive bows thrown away against the icy faces of other women.

But as they were leaving the Gardens they received attention from members of the very best society. One lordling nudged another lordling and they stared into the face of the girl as if she had been a creature of the street. Then they leisurely looked her up and down from head to toe. No tailor could have taken her measurements so completely. Afterward they grinned at each other and one spoke behind his hand, his insolent speculative eyes fixed on the retiring form of the girl. This was the social reward of the ambitious mother.

It has always been clear to me why the women turn out in such cohorts to any sort of a function. They wish to see the frocks and they are insistent that their own frocks shall be seen. Moreover they take great enjoyment in hating such of their enemies as may come under their notice. They never have a really good time but of this fact they are not aware since women are so constituted that they are able to misinterpret almost every one of their emotions.

The men, knowing something of their own minds at times, stealthily avoid such things unless there are very special reasons. In my own modest experience I have seen many a popular hostess hunting men with a net. However it was plain why so many men came to Kensington Gardens on a Sunday afternoon.

It was the display of feminine beauty. And when I say "display" I mean it. In my old age the fashion balloons a lady with such a sweep of wires and trellises that no Irishman could marry her because there is never a door in all Ireland through which his wife could pass. In my youth, however the fashion required all dresses to be cut very low and all skirts to cling so that if a four-legged woman entered a drawing-room everybody would know it. It would be so easy to count them. At present a woman could have eight legs and nobody be the wiser.

It was small wonder that the men came to ogle at Kensington Gardens on a fine Sunday afternoon. Upon my word, it was worth any young gentleman's time. Nor did the beauties blush under the gaze of banks of fastidious beaus who surveyed them like men about to bid at a horse-fair. I thought of my father and how he would have enjoyed the scene. I wager he would have been a gallant with the best of them, bowing and scraping and dodging ladies' skirts. He would have been in his very element.

But as for me I had come to gain a possible glimpse of Lady Mary. Beyond that, I had no warm interest in Kensington Gardens. The crowd was too high and fine; many of the people were altogether too well-bred. They frightened me.

However, I turned my head by chance to the left and saw near me a small plain man who did not frighten me at all. It was Doctor Chord, the little scientist. He was alone and seemed to be occupied in studying the crowd. I moved over to him. "A good day to you, sir," I said extending my hand.

When he recognized me, his face broke into a beaming smile. "Why, sir," he cried, "I am very glad to see you, sir. Perchance like me you have come here for an hour's quiet musing on fashionable folly."

"That's it, sir," said I. "You've hit it exactly."

I have said that he was a bashful man but it seemed that his timidity was likely to show itself only in the presence of other great philosophers and scientists. At any rate, he now rattled on like a little engine, surveying the people keenly and discoursing upon their faults. "There goes Lady Lucy Ninth. 'Tis said she has had a child by—ahem. The tale is an outrageous falsehood. However, that don't matter. No; that don't matter a groat. She might just as well have had the child, poor thing.

Nobody believes in her virtue anyhow. If I was her I would have the child, I would, indeed! 'Tis a shame, it is, a cruel shame."

"And who repeats these libels, Doctor?" said I. "Has she no father living or brothers to hunt out these evil-tongued creatures and punish them?"

" 'Twould be a conflict with the half of London in which there are many indestructible dowagers," said he wagging his head. "No; she can only bear it and smile."

"But," I cried, "I see many grand persons rushing to speak to her! That great lady just called her, 'You dear thing'! How is this if she bears an ill name?"

"My son," answered the venerable philosopher gently, "in the minds of many people, a woman's chastity is in no wise affected by the fact that she has had a child by an exalted personage."

"Bedad," said I, "they don't think that way in Ireland. However, I remember my father saying that, in France, there was some such view."

"There's the old Marquis of Stubbington," observed my friend. "He beats his wife with an ebony stick. 'Tis said she always carries a little bottle of liniment in the pocket of her skirt. Poor thing, her only pleasure in life is to talk scandal but this she does on such a heroic scale that it occupies her time completely. There is young Lord Gram walking again with that soap-boiler and candle-maker. 'Tis disgraceful! The poor devil lends Gram money and Gram repays him by allowing him to be seen in his company. Gram gambles away the money but I don't know what the soap-boiler does with his distinguished honours. However you can see that the poor wretch is delighted with his bargain. There are the three Banellie girls, the most ill-tempered ugly cats in England. But each will have a large marriage-portion so they have no fears, I warrant me. I wonder the eldest has the effrontery to show her face here so soon if it is true that the waiting-woman died of her injuries. There is little Wax talking to them. He needs one of those marriage-portions. Aye, he needs all three what with his very boot-maker almost inclined to be insolent to him. I see that foreign Count is talking to the Honourable Mrs. Trasky. He is no more nor less than a gambler by trade and they say he came here from Paris because he was caught cheating there and kicked and caned with such intense publicity that he was forced to leave in the dead of night. However, he found many young birds here eager to be plucked and devoured. 'Tis little they care so long as they may play till dawn. Did you hear about Lady Prefent. She went after her son to the Count's rooms at night. In her younger days she lived rather a gay life herself, 'tis rumoured, and so she was not to be taken in by her son's lies as to where he spent his evenings and his money. Ha, I see the Countess Cheer. There is a citadel of virtue! It has been stormed and taken so many times that I wonder it is not in ruins and yet here it is defiant, with banners flying. Wonderful. She——"

"Hold!" I cried. "I have enough. I would have leave to try and collect my wits. But one thing I would know at once. I thought you were a shy scholar and here you clatter away with the tongue of an old rake. You amaze me. Tell me why you do this. Why do you use your brain to examine this muck?"

" 'Tis my recreation," he answered simply. "In my boy-hood I was allowed no games and in the greater part of my manhood I have been too busy. Of late years, I have more leisure and I often have sought here a little innocent amusement, something to take one's mind off one's own affairs and yet not of such an arduous nature as would make one's head tired."

"By my faith, it would make my head tired," I said. "What with remembering the names of the people and all the different crimes, I should go raving mad." But what still amazed me was the fact that this little man, habitually meek, frightened and easily trodden down in most ordinary matters, should be able to turn himself upon occasion into a fierce and howling wolf of scandal, baying his betters, waiting for the time when an exhausted one fell in the snow and then burying his remorseless teeth in him. What a quaint little Doctor Chord.

"But tell me truly," said I. "Is there no virtuous lady or honest gentleman in all this great crowd?"

He stared, his jaw dropping. "Stap me, the place is full of them," he ejaculated. "They are thick as flies in a fish-market."

"Well, then," said I, "let us talk of them. 'Tis well to furbish and burnish our minds with tales of rectitude and honour."

But the little Doctor was no longer happy. "There is nought to say," he answered gloomily. "They are as quiet as bibles. They make no recreation for me. I have scant interest in them."

"Oh, you little rogue, you," I cried. "What a precious little bunch of evil it is! 'They make no recreation for me,' quoth he. Here's a great bold out-spoken monster. But, mark you, sir, I am a younger man but I too have a bold tongue in my head and I am saying that I have friends among ladies in London and if I catch you so much as whispering their names in your sleep, I'll cut off your ears and eat them. I speak few words, as you may have noted, but I keep my engagements, you little brew of trouble, you."

"Stap me," whimpered the little Doctor, plucking feverishly at the buttons of his coat, rolling his eyes wildly, not knowing at all what he did. "The man's mad! The man's mad!"

"No," said I, "my blood is cold, very cold."

The little Doctor looked at me with the light of a desperate inspiration in his eye. "If your blood is cold, sir," said he, "I can recommend a gill of port wine."

I needs must laugh. "Good," I cried, "and you will join me."

CHAPTER XXI

I DON'T know if it was the gill of comforting port but at any rate I was soon enough convinced that there was no reason for speaking harshly to Doctor Chord. It served no purpose; it accomplished nothing. The little old villain was really as innocent as a lamb. He had no dream of wronging people. His prattle was the prattle of an unsophisticated maiden lady. He did not know what he was talking. These direful intelligences ran as easily off his tongue as water runs off the falling wheel. When I had indirectly informed him that he was more or less of a dangerous scandal-monger, he had cried: "The man is mad!" Yes; he was an innocent old thing.

But then it is the innocent old scandal-mongers, poor old placid-minded well-protected hens, who are the most harmful. The vicious gabblers defeat themselves very often. I remember my father once going to a fair and kissing some girls there. He kissed them all turn by turn as was his right and his duty and then he returned to a girl near the head of the list and kissed her five times more because she was the prettiest girl in all Ireland and there is no shame to him there. However there was a great hullaballoo. The girls who had been kissed only once led a regular crusade against the character of this other girl and, before long, she had a bad name and the odious sly lads with no hair on their throats winked as she passed them and numerous mothers thanked God that their daughters were not fancied by the lord of that region. In time these tales came to the ear of my father and he called some of his head men to meet him in the dining-room. "I'll have no trifling," said he. "The girl is a good girl for all I know and I have never seen her before nor since. If I can trace a bad word to any man's mouth I'll flog him till he can't move. 'Tis a shame, taking away the girl's name for a few kisses by the squire at a fair with every-

body looking on and laughing. What do the blackguards mean?"
Every man in the dining-room took oath he had never said
a word and they all spoke truth. But the women clamoured on
without pausing for wind and refused to take word of the men-
folk, who were gifted with the power of reason. However the
vicious people defeated themselves in time. People began to
say to a lass who had been kissed only once: "Ah, now, you
would be angry because you were not getting the other five."
Everything seemed to grow quiet and my father thought no
more about it having thought very little about it in the first place
save enough to speak a few sharp words. But, would you believe
it, there was an old woman living in a hovel not a mile from
the castle who kept up the scandal for twelve more months.
She had never been married and, as far as anyone knew, she
had never wished to be. She had never moved beyond Father
Donovan's church in one direction and a little peat-heap in the
other direction. All her days she had seen nothing but the
wind-swept moors and heard nothing but the sea lashing the
black rocks. I am mistaken; once she came to the castle hearing
that my mother was ill. She had a remedy with her, poor soul,
and they poured it in the ashes when her back was turned.
My mother bade them give her some hot porridge and an old
cloth gown of her own to take home. I remember the time
distinctly. Well, this poor thing couldn't tell between a real sin
and an alligator. Bony, withered, aged, this crone might have
been one of the highest types of human perfection. She wronged
nobody; she had no power to wrong. Nobody wronged her; it
was never worth it. She really was at peace with all the world.
This obeys the most exalted injunctions. Every precept is kept
here. But this tale of the squire and the girl took root in her
head. She must have been dazzled by the immensity of the
event. It probably appealed to her as would a grand picture of
the Burning of Rome or a vivid statue of Lot's wife turning to
look back. It reached the dimensions of great history. And so
this old woman who had always lived the life of a nun dreamed
of nothing but the colossal wrong which had come within her
stunted range of vision. Before and after church she talked of
no other thing for almost eighteen months. Finally, my father
in despair rode down to her little cottage.

"Mollie," said he calling from the road, "Mollie, come out."
She came out. "Mollie," said my father, "you know me?"
"Aye," said she, "you are The O'Ruddy and you are a rogue."
"True for you, Mollie," said my father pleasantly. "You know
it and I know it. I am indeed a grand rogue. But why would
you be tearing to tatters the name of that poor girl in Bally-
goway?" " 'Tis not me who has said more than three words,"
she cried astonished, "and before I speak ill of anybody I hope
the devil flies away with me." Well my father palavered on for
a long time telling her that he would take away the pension of
twenty-five shillings a year which he had given her because he by
accident had shot her second cousin in the leg twelve years before
that time. She steadfastly answered that she would never speak
ill of anybody but the girl was a brazen-faced wench and he was
no better. My father came away and I have no doubt the scandal would still be alive if the old woman had not died, may the
saints rest her.

And so I was no longer angry with Doctor Chord but spoke
to him pleasantly. "Come," said I, "I would have you point me
out the great swordsmen, if it please you. I am eager to see
them and the talk will be cleanly, also."

"Aye," said my friend. "Nothing could give me more pleasure.
And now, look you! The tall straight grave young man there
is Ponsonby who flashes the wisest blade in England unless
Reginald Forister is better. Anyhow Forister is not here today.
At least I don't see him. Ponsonby fought his last duel with a
gentleman named Vellum because Vellum said flatly that Mrs.
Catharine Wainescorte was a——"

"Stop there," said I, "and get to the tale of the fighting."

"Well, Ponsonby won without difficulty," said the Doctor,
"but it is said that he took an unfair advantage——"

"Stop again!" I cried. "Stop again! We will talk no more of
swordsmen. Somehow I have lost my interest. I am put to it to
think of a subject for talk and we may have to do with a period
of silence but that will do your jaw no injury at any rate."

But I was mistaken in thinking that the little man could
forego his recreation for more than a moment. Suddenly he
burst out with a great spleen. "Titles!" he cried. "Empty
titles! Husks, husks, husks! 'Tis all they care for, this mob!

Honourable manhood goes a-begging while the world worships
at the feet of pimply lords! Pah! Lovely girls, the making of
fine wives and mothers, grow old while the world worships at
the feet of some old horse-headed duchess! Pah! Look at these
pick-thanks and flatterers, cringing at the boots of the people
of fashion. Upon my life, before I would so demean myself,
I——" He ceased suddenly, his eye having caught sight of
some people in the crowd. "Ah," said he, while a singularly vain
and fatuous smile settled upon his countenance. "Ah, the
Countess of Westport and her charming daughter, the Lady
Mary, have arrived. I must go and speak to them." My eye
had followed his glance quickly enough, you may be sure.
There, true enough, was the formidable figure of the old Countess and at her side was the beautiful Lady Mary.

With an absent-minded murmur of apology, Doctor Chord
went mincing toward them, his face still spread with its
idiotic smile.

He cantered up to them with the grace of a hobbled cow.
I expected him to get a rebuff that would stun him into the
need of a surgeon but to my surprise the Countess received
him affably, bending her head to say some gracious words.
However I had more eyes for Lady Mary than for the capers
of little Chord.

It was a great joy to be able to look at her. I suffered from a
delicious trembling and frequently my vision became dim
purely from the excitement. But later I was moved by another profound emotion. I was looking at her; I must have her
look at me. I must learn if her eye would light, if her expression
would change, when she saw me. All this sounds very boyish
but it is not necessary to leave it out for that reason because, as
my father often said, every Irishman is a boy until he has
grand-children. I do not know if he was perfectly right in this
matter but at any rate it is a certain advantage in a love
affair to have the true boyish ardour which is able to enshrine
a woman in one's heart to the exclusion of everything, believing her to be perfection and believing life without her a hell
of suffering and woe. No man of middle-age experience can
ever be in love. He may have his illusions. He may think he is

in love. A woman may gain the power to bind him hand and foot and drag him wherever she listeth but he is not in love. That is his mistaken idea. He is only misinterpreting his feelings. But, as my father said, it is very different with Irishmen, who are able to remain in love to a very great age. If you will note, too, climatic conditions, and other unpleasant matters, have practically no effect upon them, so little indeed that you may find streets named after them in Italian cities and many little German children speak with a slight brogue. My father often said that one great reason for an Irishman's success with the ladies was his perfect willingness to get married. He was seldom to be seen scouting for unfair advantages in intrigue. If the girl was willing, be she brown, yellow or white, he was always for the priest and the solemn words. My father also contended that in every marriage contracted on the face of the earth in which neither man nor maid could understand the other's national speech, the bride-groom was an Irishman. He was the only man who was able to make delightful love with the aid of mere signals.

However I must be going on with my story although it is a great pleasure to talk of my countrymen. They possess a singular fascination for me. I cannot forget that I too am an Irishman.

The little Doctor was still cutting antics; the old Countess was still saying agreeable things; Lady Mary was smiling in gentle amusement. As I moved out to catch Lady Mary's eye, I did not at all lose sight of the fact that if the pugnacious mother of my innamorata took one glimpse of me there might result a scene which could end in nothing but my ignominious flight. I edged toward the group, advancing on the Countess' port quarter as she was talking animatedly over her starboard bow at the entranced little Doctor. At times Lady Mary looked about her still smiling her smile which no doubt was born of the ridiculous performances of Chord. Once I thought she looked squarely at me and my heart beat like a drum so loudly that I thought people must hear. But her glance wandered on casually over the throng and then I felt truly insignificant like a man who could hide behind the nail of his own thumb.

Perceiving that I was so insignificant, I judged it prudent as well as advantageous to advance much closer. Suddenly Lady Mary's clear virgin eye met mine, met it fully.

Now, I don't know what was in this glance we exchanged. I have stopped myself just on the verge of a full explanation of the thrills, quivers, hopes, fears, dreams which assailed me as I looked back into the beautiful face of Lady Mary. I was also going to explain how the whole scene appeared. But I saw soon enough that my language would not be appropriate to the occasion. But anyhow we looked each other point-blank in the eye. It was a moment in which the very circling of the earth halted and all the suns of the universe poised ready to tumble or rise. Then Lady Mary lowered her glance and a pink blush suffused her neck and cheek.

The Countess, Lady Mary and Doctor Chord moved slowly on through the throng and I followed. The great question now was whether Lady Mary would look back. If she looked back, I would feel that I was making grand way with her. If she did not look back, I would know myself as a lost man. One can imagine how eagerly I watched her. For a long time it was plain that she had no intention whatever of looking back. Indeed, one could imagine a certain irrevocable feminine determination not to look back. I decided that she would not look back. I lugubriously arranged my complete downfall. Then, at the very moment of my despair, she gazed studiously off to her extreme left for a certain time and then suddenly cast one short glance behind her. Only heaven knows what value I placed upon this brief look. It appeared for the moment to me that I had won her, won everything. I bravely forged ahead until I was quite insistently under the eye of Lady Mary and then she again looked toward me but it was a look so repelling and frigid that it went through me as if I had been a paper ring in a circus. I slunk away through the crowd, my thoughts busy with trying to find out what had happened to me.

For three minutes, I was a miserable human being. At the end of that time, I took heart again. I decided that Lady Mary had frowned at me because she was afraid she had been too good to me with her look and smile. You know what I mean. I have seen a young girl give a young man a flower and at very next moment be seemingly willing to give her heart's blood to get that flower back, overcome with panic terror that she had passed—in his opinion, mind you—beyond the lines of the best behaviour. Well I said to myself that Lady Mary had given me the hard look for similar reasons. It was rational to make this judgment for certainly she had no cause for an active dislike. I had never been even so much as a nuisance to her.

Fortified with these philosophic decisions, I again followed the trio and I was just in time to find Chord handing them into a splendid chariot. I stood out boldly for I knew if I could not get one more look from Lady Mary I would die.

Seated beside her mother, her eye wandered eagerly over the crowd. I was right, by the saints! She was looking for me.

And now here came the stupid laws of convention. Could I yell? Could I even throw my hat in the air to guide her eye aright? No; I was doomed to stand there as still as a bottle on a shelf.

But she saw me! It was at the very last moment. There was no time for coquetry. She allowed her glance to linger and God knows what we said to each other in this subtle communication through all the noise and hub-bub of the entrance-place. Then suddenly the coachman's reins tightened; there were some last bows; the chariot whirled away.

CHAPTER XXII

CHORD ambled back, very proud indeed and still wearing his fatuous smile. He was bursting with a sense of social value and to everybody he seemed to be saying: "Did you see me?" He was over-joyed to find me waiting for him. He needed a good listener at once. Otherwise he would surely fly to pieces.

"I have been talking to the Countess of Westport and her daughter Lady Mary Strepp," said he pompously. "The Countess tells that the Earl has been extremely indisposed during their late journey in the West." He spoke of the Earl's illness with an air of great concern as if the news had much upset him. He pretended that the day was quite over-gloomed for him. Dear, dear; I doubted if he would be able to eat any supper.

"Have a drop of something, old friend," said I sympathetically. "You can't really go on this way. 'Twill ruin your nerves. I am surprised that the Countess did not break the news to you more gently. She was very inconsiderate, I am sure."

"No, no, don't blame the poor lady," cried Chord. "She herself was quite distracted. The moment she saw me she ran to me —did you see her run to me?"

"I did that," said I with emphasis.

"Aye, she ran to me," said the little fool, "and says she, 'Oh, my dear Doctor, I must tell you at once the condition of the Earl.' And when I heard everything I was naturally cut up, as you remarked, being an old friend of the family, ahem, yes, an old friend of the family."

He rattled on with his nonsensical lies and in the meantime I made up my mind to speak plainly to him as I intended to make him of great service to me. "Stop a moment," said I good-naturedly. "I will hear no more of this rubbish from you,

you impudent little impostor. You care no more for the Earl of Westport's illness than you do for telling the truth and I know how much you care for that. Listen to me now and I'll see if I can't knock some sense into your little addled head. In the first place, the Earl of Westport and my father were old friends and companions-in-arms in the service of the French king and I came over from Ireland especially to take a dying message and a token from my father to the Earl. That is all you need know about that but I would have you leave off your prate of your friend the Earl of Westport for I understand full well you couldn't distinguish between him and a church door although 'tis scandalously little you know of church doors. So we will stop there on that point. Then I will go on to the next point. The next point is that I am going to marry Lady Mary Strepp."

The little Doctor had been choking and stuttering in a great spasm but my last point bid fair to flatten him out on the floor. I took the over-powered philosopher and led or carried him to another drink. "Stap me," he cried, again and again. "The man is mad!"

I surveyed him with a bland smile. "Let it sink into you," said I soothingly. "Don't snarl and wrangle at it. It is all heaven's truth and in time you will come to your senses and see what I am telling you."

Well, as soon as he had fully recovered his wind, he fell upon me with thousands of questions for one may see that he would have plenty of interest in the matter as soon as he was assured that there was much veracity involved in one way or another in my early statement. His questions I answered as it pleased me but I made clear enough to him that although Lady Mary was well disposed toward me, neither her father nor her mother would even so much as look at me if I applied for a position as under-footman, I was that low in their estimate. "However," said I, "I can re-arrange all that very easily. And now, my bucko, here is where your fortune meets mine. You are fitted by nature more to attend other people's affairs than to take a strict interest in your own. All kinds of meddling and interference come easily to you. Well, then, here is a chance to exercise your gifts inoffensively and yet in a way which may make two people happy for life. I will tell you now that I don't even know where is the Earl's town house. There is where your importance appears at once. You must show me the house. That is the first thing. After that we will arrange all the details about ladders and garden walls and, mayhap, carrier-doves. As for your reward, it will appear finally in the shape of a bowing recognition by people of fashion which is what you most desire in the world, you funny little man."

Again I had stunned him. For a time, I could see his brain swimming in a perfect sea of bewilderment. But, as before, sense gradually came to him and he again volleyed questions at me. But what stuck in his crop was the thought that Lady Mary could prefer me. He tried his best to believe it but he would always end up by saying: "Well, *if* Lady Mary cares for you, the affair is not too difficult." Or, "Well, if you are *sure* Lady Mary loves you——" I could have broken his head a thousand times. "Bad luck to you, Doctor," I cried. "Don't you know such croaking would spoil the peace of any true lover? Is ever any worthy man able not to be anxious in such matters? 'Tis only foppery coxcombs who have great confidence and they are usually misled, thank the lord. Be quiet, now, and try to take everything for granted."

Then the spirit of the adventure came upon him and he was all for it, heels over head. As I had told him, this sort of meddling was his proper vocation. He who as a recreation revelled in the mere shadows of the intrigues of people of quality, now was really part of one, an actor in it, the repository of its deep secret. I had to curb his enthusiasm. He had such a sense of the importance of my news and of his distinction in having heard it that I think he wished to tell the secret to the entire world.

As soon as the afternoon grew late, I suggested a walk to that part of London in which was situate the Earl's town house. I did not see why we should not be moving at once on the campaign. The Doctor assented and we went forth to look for Jem Bottles and Paddy. We found them at an ale-house which was the resort of the chairmen, footmen and coachmen of the grand people. The two rogues had evidently passed a pleasant afternoon. Jem Bottles was still making love to a very pretty girl, some part of whose easy affection or interest he had won; and Paddy, it seems, had had a rip-roaring fight with two lackeys, worsted them with despatch, and even pursued them some distance. At sight of me, they dropped their occupations and came docilely. To my stern interrogation in regard to the pretty girl, Jem Bottles stoutly rejoined that she was his second cousin whom he had not seen for many years. To this I made no reply for it does no good to disturb the balance of a good liar. If at times he is led to tell the truth, he becomes very puzzling. In all the years Jem Bottles has been in my service, I have never reprimanded him for lying. I would confuse matters to no purpose inasmuch as I understand him perfectly.

"And how," said I to Paddy, "did you come to engage in this disgraceful brawl of a Sunday?"

"Your honour," answered Paddy, "there was two of these men with fat legs came here and says one looking hard at me, 'Here's a furriner,' he says. 'Furriner yourself, you fish-faced ditch-lurker,' says I and with that he takes up his fists and hits me a knock. There was a little shindy and afterward they ran away bawling and I was pursuing them only I feared to lose my way in these strange parts."

The walk to Lord Westport's house was a long one. It seems that he had built a great new mansion at a place outside of the old city gates where other nobles and great brewers had built fine houses, surrounding them all with splendid gardens.

One must not suppose that I had any idea of taking the mansion by storm. My first idea was to dream a lover's dream as I gazed upon the abode of my treasure. This, I believe, is a legitimate proceeding in all careers. Every lover worthy of the name is certain to pilgrimage, muffled in his cloak, to moon over the home of his adored one. Otherwise there can be no real attachment.

In the second place, I wished to develope certain plans for gaining speech of Lady Mary. I will not deny that I purposed on a near day to scale the garden wall and hold speech of my sweetheart as she walked alone among the flowers. For my success I depended upon the absolute conventionality of the idea. In all history no lover has ever been chased out of a garden by an under-gardener with a hoe.

When we arrived at the house I found that it was indeed a

gorgeous mansion. It was surrounded on all sides by high brick walls but through the elaborate tracery of one of the iron-work gates I saw Lady Mary's home standing amid sweeping green lawns.

We reconnoitred all sides and at the back I found a lonely avenue lined with oaks. Here a small door pierced the wall for the use apparently of the gardeners or grooms. I resolved that here I would make my attack.

As we passed the iron gates on our way back to town, we saw window after window light up with golden radiance. I wondered which part of that vast edifice hid the form of my Mary.

I had asked Doctor Chord to sup with me at the inn and on the way thither, he proved somewhat loquacious. "I see in you, sir," said he, "a certain instinct of true romance which is infrequently encountered in this hum-drum commercial age. Allow me to express to you, sir, my warm admiration. I did not think that a gallant of this hum-drum commercial age could prove such a free spirit. In this hum-drum commercial age——"

"I am an Irishman," said I, "and in Ireland we are always hum-drum but we are never commercial for the reason that we have not the tools."

"Aye," said he, "you must be a great people. Strangely enough you are the first Irishman I have ever seen although I have seen many blackamoors. However I am edified to find you a gentleman of great learning and experience. And in this hum-drum commercial age——"

"Let go," said I. "I can do very well without your opinion as to my learning and experience. In regard to this being a hum-drum commercial age, you will find that all ages say the same thing of themselves. I am more interested in the winning of Lady Mary."

" 'Twas to that subject I was just about to turn the talk," said the Doctor. "I need not express again to you the interest I feel and if it is true, as you say, that Lady Mary really loves you——"

"May the devil fly away with you," I cried in a great rage. "Are you never to have done? You are an old frog. I ask you to help me and you do nothing but dispirit me with these doubts. I'll not put up with it."

"I am very sorry to displease you, sir," answered my friend. "If you examine my intentions with a dispassionate eye, sir, I am convinced you will have found nothing in me which should properly cause these outbursts of disapprobation. When I say, 'If Lady Mary really loves you,' I am referring to the strange mishaps and misconstructions which attend human thought at all times and when I say——"

"Let go again," I cried. "When I misunderstand you, don't enlighten me for I find these explanations very hard to bear."

To my surprise the little man answered with great spirit. "I am unable to gain any approval for my deep interest in your affairs, sir," he cried. "Perchance, it would be better if I could affect a profound indifference. I am certainly at a loss for words when each sentence of mine is made the subject of wrathful objection."

"You are right," said I. "But you will understand how ten thousand emotions beset and haggle a lover and I believe he always revenges himself upon his dearest friends. Forgive me."

"With all my heart," answered the little Doctor. "I am aware, sir, that at the present time you are in many ways like a highly-tightened fiddle which any breeze frets into murmurings. Not being absolutely certain of the devotion of your beloved, you naturally——"

"By the ten lame pipers of Ballydehob," I shouted, "let go of that talk. I can't be having it. I warn ye. 'Tis either a grave for me or quiet for you and I am thinking it is quiet for you."

"Inasmuch," said the Doctor, "as my most judicious speeches seem to inflame your passions, sir, I am of the opinion that a perfect silence on my part becomes almost necessary and, to further this end, I would recommend that you refrain from making interrogations or otherwise promulgating opportunities when an expression of candid opinion seems expected and desired."

"You've hit it," said I. "We will have no more interrogations. However, I would much like to know how you became so intimate with Lord Westport's family."

Doctor Chord blushed with something of his earlier manner.

" 'Tis a matter which I did not expect to have leap at me out of the darkness in this fashion," he said bashfully. "However I am convinced of how well you know these people and I will traffic no more with hollow pretence. As you know, I deal much in chemical knowledge which I am able to spread to almost every branch of human use and need."

" 'Tis an ill work," said I, sourly. "I doubt if Father Donovan would care to hear you be speaking in this way. He always objected to scientific improvements as things which do harm to the Church."

"In regard to the estimable friend you mention," said the Doctor, "I unhesitatingly state my profound assurances of respect."

"Quite so," I answered. "He will be pleased to hear of it. And now we will return to the other matter."

"I will obediently proceed," said he. "Five years back, the Countess of Westport was thrown from her carriage. Physicians rushed to her rescue. I too appeared, being at the time out for a walk. They wished to immediately bleed her but I waved them aside and, recognizing me as a figure in the great world of science, they fell back, abashed. I prescribed a small drink of hot rum. The lady took it. Almost immediately she recovered. She offered me a guinea. I refused curtly. She enquired, here and there, for my condition. Afterward she apologized to me for not offering more than a guinea. Since that time we have been warm friends. She knows me as a great scientist who came to her assistance in time of trouble when numerous quacks wished to bleed her and I over-powered them and gave her a drink of rum. 'Tis true that after she reached her own bed, the Earl's physician bled her but she did not seem to appreciate it although he drew twenty-five ounces, I think. But she has remained always grateful for the hot rum. This matter of bleeding is the true basis of all surgery but I think there may happen cases where a warm drink or a kick in the breeches may suffice as well as bleeding."

"Well and good," said I, "talk of bleeding if you like. Now that I know the reason of your affectionate relations with the Countess, I am no longer hard after information and we may just as well talk about bleeding."

"Well, sir," said the Doctor, "the Countess afterward put her faith in me and one day I myself was called to the house and I bled Lady Mary in the leg——"

"The leg! You hound!" I cried. "And what part of the leg?"

"The thigh," said he.

"The thigh," I shouted, rubbing my fist in his eye. "O, impudence unparalleled! O, impudence immeasurable! O, infinity of impudence."

"Science," said Doctor Chord primly, "does not regard these matters."

CHAPTER XXIII

AT supper that evening, Doctor Chord amplified some of
his views. "A few staunch retainers could quickly aid
you to scale the walls of the castle," said he. "But, I
have forgotten," he added blankly. " 'Tis not a castle. 'Tis is a
house."

"If you would take some of these ancient ideas and bury them
in the garden," said I, "they might grow in time to be some
new kind of turnip or other valuable food. But at the present
moment they do not seem to me to serve much purpose. Supposing that the house is not a castle? What of that?"

"Castles——" said he. "Castles lend themselves——"

"Castles!" I cried. "Have done with castles. All castles may be
Jews, as you say. But this is a house."

"I remarked that it was a house," he answered gently. "It
was that point that I was making."

"Very good," said I. "We will now proceed to definite matters.
Do you know if Lady Mary walks in the garden? It is absolutely
necessary that Lady Mary should walk in the garden."

"She does," he replied at once. "At this season of the year,
Lady Mary walks in the garden on every fine day at about ten
of the clock."

"Then," I cried, smiting the table, "our course is clear. I feel
elate. My only regret is that my father is not here to give me a
word now and then for 'tis a game he would know down to the
ground."

"Although I am not your father," said Doctor Chord modestly,
"I may be able to suggest some expedient way of gaining entrance to the castle."

"House," said I.

"House," said he.

"However," said I, "we must lower ourselves to extremely practical matters. Can you climb a tree?"

"A tree?" said he. "Climb a tree? Stap me!"

" 'Tis all very well to stap yourself in this fashion," said I rather warmly, "but the climbing of trees appears here as an important matter. In my part of Ireland there are few trees and so climbing trees did not enter into my education. However, I am willing to attempt the climbing of a tree for the sake of my true love and if I fall—how high was this wall? Do you remember?"

" 'Twas at least ten feet," answered the Doctor. "And there was a murderous row of spikes at the top. But," he added, "the more spikes, and all that, make them the more convinced that the garden is perfectly safe from intrusion."

"That is a word of sense out of you," I cried. "The spikes convince them the garden is safe from intrusion and so they give over their watchfulness. So now in the morning we will go there and I will climb one of the oak trees bordering the wall—may the saints aid me."

"You were asking if I could climb a tree," remarked the Doctor. "I will point out to you that it is a question of no importance. It is you yourself who must climb the tree for even if I succeeded in the arduous and painful task I could not pay your vows to Lady Mary and for such purpose primarily the tree is to be climbed."

"True for you, Doctor," I answered with a sigh. "True for you. I must climb the tree. I can see that. I had some thought of making Paddy climb it but, as you say, a man must do his own love-making and by the same token, I would break the head of anyone who tried to do it for me. I would that. In this world, people must climb their own trees. Now that I think of it seriously, it was ridiculous in me to plan that Paddy should climb the tree."

" 'Second thoughts are always best,' " said the little Doctor piously. " 'Tis a phrase from one of the greatest writers of the day. And at any rate I myself because of age and debility would not be able to climb a tree."

"Let us say no more of it," said I. "I see my mistake. But, tell me one thing. I know you are a man with a great deal on your mind. Can you spare the time for this adventure?"

But on this point, the Doctor was very clear and emphatic. I think that if I had said he could not have a place in the plot, he would have died immediately of a broken heart. " 'Tis true I have not finished my treatise proving that the touchstone is fallible," he cried eagerly, "but it would give me pleasure to delay the work indefinitely if in the meantime I can be of assistance."

"That is a man's talk," said I. "Well, then, in the morning, we will go forth to do or die. And now a glass to success."

That night I slept very heartily for some of my father's soldier training is in my veins and on the eve of hard or precarious work I am always able to get sound rest. My father often said that on the night before a battle in which he would stand seventy-seven chances of being killed he always slept like a dog in front of the fire.

At dawn, I was up and ready. My first move was to have Paddy and Jem sent to me and to give them such information as would lead them to an intelligent performance of their duties during the day. "Mind ye now," said I, "here's where the whole thing may be won or lost. There is a lovely lady inside the walls of that garden which I was showing you yesterday. She lives in the big house. She is the lady who made you feel ashamed when you took the old Earl's—well, never mind. I hope we are all properly repentant over it. However, I had better be getting on with the matter in hand. She lives there and if I can find no way to gain speech of her, we all three of us will have to take to the thickets and that's the truth."

"If I could but lay my fingers on her throttle," said Jem Bottles in a blood-curdling voice, "she soon enough would——"

"Stop!" I cried. "You misunderstood me."

"Aye he does," spoke in Paddy. "But I know what your honour is meaning. You are meaning that the young lady—aye, didn't I see her and didn't she give me a look of her eye? Aye, I know what your honour is meaning."

"You are knowing it precisely," said I. "The young lady is more to me than three Irelands. You understand? Well, then, in the first place I must gain speech of her. Today, we march out and see what I can accomplish by climbing trees. In the meantime you two are to lay in waiting and assist me when necessary."

"I am foreseeing that everything will be easy," cried Paddy jubilantly.

"You are an Irishman," I responded in anger.

"Aye," he replied bitterly, "and another is within reach of my stick if it weren't for my respect for my betters although such a thing never could happen, praise God."

"No bold talk," said I. "You may do that after." I bade Jem Bottles load his pistols and carry them handy but to keep them well concealed. Paddy preferred to campaign with only a stout stick. I took one pistol and of course my sword.

These preparations deeply stirred Jem Bottles and Paddy.

"Your honour," said Paddy, "if I see a man pulling you by the leg when you would be climbing the tree, may I hit him one lick?"

"Aye," growled Jem Bottles, "and if I get a pistol against his head, he'll find out the difference between gun-powder and sand."

"Stop," I cried. "You have the wrong idea entirely. This talk of carnage startles me and alarms me. Remember we are in London. In London, even the smallest massacre arouses great excitement. There are to be no killings nor even any sound thrashings. It is all to be done with dainty gloves. Neither one of the pair of you looks fitted for the work but I am obliged to make you serve by hook or crook. 'Tis too late to scour the country looking for good comrades. I must put up with ye since I can get no better."

They were well pleased at the prospect of spirited adventures although Paddy made some complaints because there was no chance of a great ogre which he could assail. He wished to destroy a few giants in order to prove his loyalty to the cause. However, I soothed him out of this mood, showing him where he was mistaken, and presently we were all prepared and only waited for the coming of Doctor Chord.

When the little philosopher appeared however I must truly say that I fell back a-gasping. He had tied some sort of a red turban about his head and pulled a black cocked hat down over it until his left eye was wickedly shaded. From beneath his sombre cloak, a heavy scabbard protruded. "I have come. I am ready," said he in a deep voice.

"Bedad, you have," cried I sinking into a chair. "And why didn't a mob hang you on the road, little man? How did you reach here safely? London surely never could stand two glimpses of such a dangerous-looking pirate. You would give a sedan-chair the vapours."

He looked himself over ruefully. "'Tis a garb befitting the dangerous adventure upon which I engage," said he, somewhat stiff in the lip.

"But let me make known to you," I cried, "that when a man wears a garb befitting his adventure, he fails surely. He should wear something extraneous. When you wish to do something evil, you put on the coat of a parson. That is the clever way. But here you are looking like a gallows bird of the greatest claim for the rope. Stop it; take off the red thing, tilt your hat until you look like a gentleman and let us go to our adventure respectably."

"I was never more surprised in my life," said he sincerely. "I thought I was doing a right thing in thus arraying myself for an experience which cannot fail to be thrilling and, mayhap, deadly. However I see you in your accustomed attire and in the apparel of your men-servants I see no great change from yesterday. May I again suggest to you that the adventure upon which we proceed may be fraught with much danger?"

"A red rag around your temples marks no improvement in our risks," said I. "We will sally out as if we were off to a tea-party. When my father led the forlorn hope at the storming of Würstenhausenstaffenberg, he wore a lace collar and he was a man who understood these matters. And I may say that I wish he was here. He would be a great help."

In time, the Doctor removed his red turban and gradually and sadly emerged from the more sanguine part of his paraphernalia and appeared as a simple little philosopher. Personally I have no objection to a man looking like a brigand but my father always contended that clothes served no purpose in real warfare. Thus I felt I had committed no injustice in depriving Chord of his red turban.

We set out. I put much faith in the fact that we had no definite plans but to my great consternation Doctor Chord almost immediately began to develope well-laid schemes. As we moved toward the scene of our adventure, he remarked them to me. "First of all," said he, "a strong party should be stationed at the iron gates not only to prevent a sally of the garrison but to prevent an intrepid retainer from escaping and alarming the city. Furthermore——"

"My gallant warrior," said I, interrupting him, "we will drop this question to the level of a hum-drum commercial age. I will try to compass my purpose by a simple climbing of a tree and to that end all I could need from you is a stout lift and a good word. Then we proceed in the established way of making signs over a wall. All this I explained to you fully. I would not have you think that I am about to bombard my lady-love's house."

With a countenance of great mournfulness he grumbled: "No fascines have been prepared."

"Very good," said I. "I will climb the tree without the aid of fascines."

As luck would have it, there was a little inn not very far from the Earl's house and on the lonely avenue lined with oaks. Here I temporarily left Jem Bottles and Paddy for I feared their earnestness which was becoming more terrible every minute. In order to keep them pacified I gave instructions that they should keep a strict watch up the avenue and if they saw any signs of trouble they were to come a-running and do whatever I told them. These orders suggested serious business to their minds and so they were quite content. Their great point was that if a shindy was coming, they had a moral right to be mixed up in it.

Doctor Chord and I strolled carelessly under the oaks. It was still too early for Lady Mary's walk in the garden and there was an hour's waiting to be worn out. In the meantime, I was moved to express some of my reflections. " 'Tis possible—nay, probable —that this is a bootless quest," said I dejectedly. "What shadow of an assurance have I that Lady Mary will walk in the garden on this particular morning? This whole thing is absolute folly."

"At any rate," said the Doctor, "now that you already have walked this great distance, it will be little additional trouble to climb a tree."

He had encouraged me to my work at exactly the proper moment. "You are right," said I, taking him warmly by the hand. "I will climb the tree, in any case."

As the hour approached, we began to cast about for the proper oak. I am sure they were all the same to me but Doctor Chord was very particular. " 'Tis logical to contend," said he, "that the question of the girth of the tree will enter importantly into our devices. For example, if a tree be so huge that your hands may not meet on the far side of it, a successful ascension will be impossible. On the other hand, a very slim tree is like to bend beneath your weight and even precipitate you heavily to the ground, which disaster might retard events for an indefinite period."

"Science your science, then," said I. "And tell me what manner of tree best suits the purpose of a true lover."

"A tree," said the Doctor, "is a large vegetable arising with one woody stem to a considerable height. As to the appearance and quality of a tree, there are many diversifications and this fact in itself constitutes the chief reason for this vegetable being of such great use to the human family. Ships are made of nought but trees and if it were not for ships we would know little of the great world of which these English islands form less than a half. Asia itself is slightly larger than all Scotland and if it were not for ships we would be like to delude ourselves with the idea that we and our neighbors formed the major part of the world."

With such wise harangues the Doctor entertained my impatience until it was time for me to climb a tree. And when this time came, I went at my work without discussion and delay. "There," said I resolutely, "I will climb this one if it kills me." I seized the tree; I climbed. I will not say there was no groaning and puffing but anyhow I at last found myself astride of a branch and looking over the wall into the Earl of Westport's garden.

But I might have made myself less labour and care by having somebody paint me a large landscape of this garden and surveyed it at my leisure. There I was high in a tree dangling my legs and staring at smooth lawns, ornamental copses and brilliant flower-beds without even so much as a dog to enliven the scene. "O'Ruddy," said I to myself after a long time, "you've hung yourself here in mid-air like bacon to a rafter and I'll not say much to you now. But if you ever reach the ground without breaking your neck, I'll have a word with you for my feelings are sorely stirred."

I do not know how long I sat in the tree engaged in my bitter meditations. But finally I heard a great scudding of feet from near the foot of the tree and I then saw the little Doctor bolting down the road like a madman, his hat gone, his hair flying, while his two coat-tails stuck out behind him straight as boards.

My excitement and interest in my ally's flight was so great that I near fell from my perch. It was incomprehensible that my little friend could dust the road at such speed. He seemed only to touch the ground from time to time. In a moment or two, he was literally gone like an arrow shot from the bow.

But, upon casting my bewildered glance downward, I found myself staring squarely into the mouth of a blunderbuss. The mouth of this blunderbuss, I may say, was of about the width of a fair-sized water-pitcher; in colour it was bright and steely. Its appearance attracted me to such an extent that I lost all idea of the man behind the gun. But presently I heard a grim slow voice say: "Climb down, ye thief."

The reason for little Doctor Chord's hasty self-removal from the vicinity was now quite clear and my interest in his departure was no longer speculative.

CHAPTER XXIV

CLIMB down, ye thief," said the grim slow voice again. I looked once more into the mouth of the blunderbuss. I decided to climb. If I had had my two feet square on the ground, I would have taken a turn with this man, artillery or no artillery, to see if I could get the upper hand of him. But neither I nor any of my ancestors could ever fight well in trees. Foliage incommodes us. We like a clear sweep for the arm and everything on a level space and neither man in a tree. However a sensible man holds no long discussions with a blunderbuss. I slid to the ground, arriving in a somewhat lacerated state. I thereupon found that the man behind the gun was evidently some kind of keeper or gardener. He had a sour face, deeply chiselled with mean lines but his eyes were very bright, the lighter parts of them being steely blue, and he rolled the pair of them from behind his awful weapon.

"And for whom have you mistaken me, rascal?" I cried as soon as I had come ungracefully to ground and found with whom I had to deal.

"Have mistaken ye for nought," replied the man proudly. "Ye be the thief of the French pears, ye be."

"French pears—French—French what?" I cried.

"Aye, ye know full well," said he, "and now ye'll just march."

Seeing now plainly that I was in the hands of one of Lord Westport's gardeners who had mistaken me for some garden-thief for whom he had been on the look-out, I began to expostulate very pointedly. But always this man stolidly faced me with the yawning mouth of the blunderbuss. "And now ye'll march," said he and despite everything I marched. I marched myself through the little door in the wall and into the gardens of the Earl of Westport. And the infernal weapon was clamped against the small of my back.

But still my luck came to me even then like basket falling out of a blue sky. As, in obedience to my captor's orders, I rounded a bit of shrubbery I came face to face with Lady Mary. I stopped so abruptly that the rim of the on-coming blunderbuss must have printed a fine pink ring on my back. I lost all my intelligence. I could not speak. I only knew that I stood before the woman I loved while a man firmly pressed the muzzle of a deadly fire-arm between my shoulder-blades. I flushed with shame as if I really had been guilty of stealing the French pears.

Lady Mary's first look upon me was one of pure astonishment. Then she quickly recognized the quaint threat expressed in the attitude of the blunderbuss. "Strammers," she cried rushing forward, "what would you be doing to the gentleman?"

" 'Tis no gentleman, your la'ship," answered the man confidently. "He be a low-born thief o'pears, he be."

"Strammers," she cried again and wrested the blunderbuss from his hands. I will confess that my back immediately felt easier. "And now sir," she said turning to me haughtily, "you will please grant me an explanation of to what my father is indebted for this visit to his private grounds?"

But she knew; no fool of a gardener and a floundering Irishman could keep pace with the nimble wits of a real woman. I saw the pink steal over her face and she plainly appeared not to care for an answer to her peremptory question. However I made a grave reply which did not involve the main situation. "Madam may have noted a certain deluded man with a bell-mouthed howitzer," said I. "His persuasions were so pointed and emphatic that I was induced to invade these gardens wherein I have been so unfortunate as to disturb a lady's privacy, a thing which only causes me the deepest regret."

"He be a pear thief," grumbled Strammers from a distance. "Don't ye take no word o' his, your la'ship, after me bringing 'im down from out a tree."

"From out a tree?" said Lady Mary and she looked at me and I looked at her.

"The man is right, Lady Mary," said I significantly. "I was in a tree looking over the garden wall."

"Strammers," said she with decision, "wait for me in the

rose-garden and speak no single word to anybody until I see you again. You have made a great mistake." The man obediently retired after saluting me with an air of slightly dubious apology. He was not yet convinced that I had not been after his wretched French pears.

But with the withdrawal of this Strammers, Lady Mary's manner changed. She became frightened and backed away from me, still holding the gardener's blunderbuss. "Oh, sir," she cried in a beautiful agitation, "I beg of you to leave at once. Oh, please."

But here I saw it was necessary to treat the subject in a bold Irish way. "I'll not leave, Lady Mary," I answered. "I was brought here by force and only force can make me withdraw."

A glimmer of a smile came to her face and she raised the blunderbuss, pointing it full at my breast. The mouth was still the width of a water-jug and in the fair inexperienced hands of Lady Mary it was like to go off at any moment and blow a hole in me as big as a platter. "Charming huntress," said I, "shoot!"

For answer, she suddenly flung the weapon to the grass and, burying her face in her hands, began to weep. "I'm afraid it's l-l-loaded," she sobbed out.

In an instant I was upon my knees at her side and had taken her hand. Her fingers resisted little but she had turned away her head. "Lady Mary," said I softly, "I am a poor devil of an Irish adventurer, but—I love you. I love you so that if I was dead you could bid me rise. I am a worthless fellow; I have no money and my estate you can hardly see for the mortgages and trouble upon it; I am no fine suitor but I love you more than them all; I do, upon my life."

"Here approaches Strammers in quest of his blunderbuss," she answered calmly. "Perhaps we had better give it him."

I sprang to my feet and, sure enough, the thick-headed nine-pin of a gardener was nearing us. "Don't ye trust 'im, your la'ship," he cried. "I caught 'im in a tree, I did, and he be a bad lot."

Lady Mary quelled him and he at once went away with his blunderbuss, still muttering his many doubts. But still one cannot drop a love declaration and pick it up again with the facility of a tailor resuming his work on a waistcoat. One can't say: "Where was I? How far had I gone before this miserable interruption came?" In a word, I found myself stammering and stuttering and wasting moments too precious for words. "Lady Mary——" I began. "Lady Mary—I love you, Lady Mary. Lady Mary——" It was impossible for me to depart from this rigmarole and express the many things with which my heart was full. It was a maddening tongue-tie. The moment seemed for me the crisis of my existence and yet I could only say: "Lady Mary, I love you." I know that in many cases this statement has seemed to be sufficient but as a matter of fact I was full of things to say and it was plain to me that I was losing everything through the fact that my silly tongue clung to the roof of my mouth.

I do not know how long the agony endured but at any rate it was ended by a thunderous hammering upon the little door in the garden wall. A high Irish voice could be heard. "And if ye be not leaving him out immediately, we will be coming over the wall if it is ten thousand feet high, ye murdering rogues."

Lady Mary turned deadly pale. "Oh, we are lost," she cried.

I saw at once that the interview was ended. If I remained doughtily, I remained stupidly. I could come back some other day. I clutched Lady Mary's hand and kissed it. Then I ran for the door in the garden wall. In a moment I was out and I heard her frantically bolting the door behind me.

I confronted Paddy and Jem. Jem had in his hands a brace of pistols which he was waving determinedly. Paddy was wetting his palms and resolutely swinging a club. But when they saw me their ferocity gave way to an outburst of affectionate emotion. I had to assert all my mastership to keep Paddy from singing. He would sing. Sure, if they had never heard an Irish song it was time they did. "Paddy," said I, "my troubles are on me. I wish to be thinking. Remain quiet."

Presently we reached the little inn and from there the little Doctor Chord flew out like a hawk at a sparrow. "I thought you were dead," he shouted wildly. "I thought you were dead."

"No," said I, "I am not dead but I am very thirsty." And, although they were murmuring this thing and that thing, I would have no word with them until I was led to the parlour of the inn and given a glass. "Now," said I, "I penetrated to the garden and afterward I came away and I can say no more."

The little Doctor was very happy and proud. "When I saw the man with the blunderbuss," he recounted, "I said to him boldly: 'Sirrah, remove that weapon! Exclude it from the scene! Eliminate it from the situation!' But his behaviour was extraordinary. He trained the weapon in such a manner that I myself was in danger of being eliminated from the situation. I instantly concluded that I would be of more benefit to the cause if I temporarily abandoned the vicinity and withdrew to a place where the climatic conditions were more favourable to prolonged terms of human existence."

"I saw you abandoning the vicinity," said I, "and I am free to declare that I never saw a vicinity abandoned with more spirit and finish."

"I thank you for your appreciation," said the Doctor, simply. Then he leaned to my ear and whispered, barring his words from Jem and Paddy who stood respectfully near our chairs. "And the main object of the expedition?" he asked. "Was there heavy firing and the beating down of doors? And I hope you took occasion to slay that hideous monster who flourished the blunderbuss? Imagine my excitement after I had successfully abandoned the vicinity! I was trembling with anxiety for you. Still, I could adopt no steps which would not involve such opportunities for instant destruction that the thought of them brought to mind the most terrible ideas. I pictured myself lying butchered, blown to atoms by a gardener's blunderbuss. Then the spirit of self-sacrifice arose in me, and, as you know, I sent your two servants to your rescue."

The little man was looking through the window at this moment. Suddenly he started back, flinging up his hands. "My soul, he is again upon us," he cried. I hastily followed his glance and saw the man Strammers making peaceful way toward the inn. Apparently he was going to the tap-room for an early pint. The Doctor flurried and dove until I checked him in fear that he would stand on his head in the fire-place. "No," said I, "calm yourself. There will be no blunderbusses. On the other hand, I see here a great chance for a master stroke. Be quiet now and try to hold yourself in a chair and see me deal

with the situation. When it comes to a thing like this, it is
all child's play for me. Paddy," said I. "Jem," said I, "there is
a gardener in the tap-room. Go and become his warm friends.
You know what I mean. A tuppence here and there won't matter. But, of course, always treat him with the profound consideration which is due to so distinguished a gardener."

They understood me at once and grinned. But even then I
was struck with their peculiar reasons for understanding at
once. Jem Bottles understood at once because he had been a
highwayman; Paddy understood at once because he was an
Irishman. One had been all his life a rogue; the other had been
born on an intelligent island. And so they comprehended me
with equal facility.

They departed on their errand and when I turned I found
myself in the clutches of a maddened Doctor Chord. "Monster," he screamed, "you have ordered him to be killed!"

"Whist," said I, "it would never do to order him to be killed.
He is too valuable."

CHAPTER XXV

YOU appear more at your ease when you are calm," said I to the Doctor as I squashed him into a chair. "Your ideas of murder are juvenile. Gardeners are murdered only by other gardeners, over some question of a magnolia tree. Gentlemen of position never murder gardeners."

"You are right, sir," he responded frankly. "I see my mistake. But, really, I was convinced that something dreadful was about to happen. I am not familiar with the ways of your nationality, sir, and when you gave the resolute directions to your men, it was according to my education to believe that something sinister was at hand although no one could regret more than I that I have made this foolish mistake."

"No," said I, "you are not familiar with the ways of my nationality and it will require an indefinite number of centuries to make your countrymen understand the ways of my nationality and, when they do, they will only pretend that after great research they have discovered something very evil indeed. However in this detail I am able to fully instruct you. The gardener will not be murdered. His fluency with a blunderbuss was very annoying but in my opinion it was not so fluent as to merit death."

"I confess," said Doctor Chord, "that all peoples save my own are great rascals and natural seducers. I cannot change this national conviction for I have studied politics as they are known in the King's Parliament and it has been thus proved to me."

"However, the gardener is not to be murdered," said I, "and although I am willing to cure you in that particular ignorance, I am not willing to take up your general cure as a life work. A glass of wine with you."

After we had adjusted this slight misunderstanding we occupied our seats comfortably before the fire. I wished to give Paddy and Jem plenty of time to conciliate Strammers but I must say that the wait grew irksome. Finally, I arose and went into the corridor and peered into the tap-room. There was Paddy and Jem with their victim, the three of them seated affectionately in a row on a bench, drinking from quart-pots of ale. Paddy was clapping the gardener on the shoulder. "Strammers," he cried, "I am thinking more of you than of my own cousin Mickey who was that gay and that gallant—it would make you wonder. Although I am truthful in saying they killed him for the peace of the parish. But he had the same bold air with him and devil the girl in the country-side but didn't know who was the lad for her."

Strammers seemed greatly pleased but Jem Bottles evinced deep disapproval of Paddy's Celtic methods. "Let Master Strammers be," said he. "He be a-wanting a quiet draught. Let him have his ale with no talking here and there."

"Aye," said Strammers, now convinced that he was a great man and a philosopher, "a quiet draught o' old ale is a good thing."

"True for you, Master Strammers," cried Paddy enthusiastically. "It is in the way of being of a good thing. There you are now. Aye, that's it. 'A good thing'! Sure."

"Aye," said Strammers, deeply moved by this appreciation which he had believed should always really have existed. "Aye, I spoke well."

"Well would be no name for it," responded Paddy fervidly. "By gor, and I wish you were knowing Father Corrigan. He would be the only man to near match you. 'A quiet draught o' old ale is a good thing,' says you and, by the piper, 'tis hard to say Father Corrigan could have done it that handily. 'Tis you that are a wonderful man."

"I have a small way o' my own," said Strammers, "which even some o' the best gardeners has accounted most wise and humorous. The power o' good speech be a great gift." Whereupon the complacent Strammers lifted his arm and buried more than half his face in his quart-pot.

"It is," said Paddy earnestly. "And I am doubting if even the best gardeners would be able to improve it. And says you: 'A quiet draught o' old ale is a good thing.' 'Twill take a grand gardener to beat that word."

"And besides the brisk way of giving a word now and then," continued the deluded Strammers, "I am a great man with flowers. Some of the finest beds in London are there in my master's park."

"Are they so?" said Paddy. "I would be liking to see them."

"And ye shall," cried the gardener with an out-burst of generous feeling. "So ye shall. On a Sunday we may stroll quietly and decently in the gardens and ye shall see."

Seeing that Paddy and Jem were getting on well with the man, I returned to Doctor Chord. " 'Tis all right," said I. "They have him in hand. We have only to sit still and the whole thing is managed." Later I saw the three men in the road, Paddy and Jem embracing the almost tearful Strammers. These farewells were touching. Afterward my rogues appeared before me, each with a wide grin.

"We have him," said Paddy, "and 'tis us that has an invitation to come inside the wall next Sunday. 'I have some fine flowers in the gardens,' said he. 'Have ye so?' said I. 'Well then 'tis myself will be breaking your head if you don't leave us inside to see them.' 'Master Paddy,' said he, 'you are a gentleman, or if not you are very like one, and you and your handsome friend, Master Jem, as well as another friend or two, is welcome to see the gardens whenever I can make certain the master and mistress is out.' And with that I told him he could go home."

"You are doing well," I said, letting the scoundrel see in my face that I believed his pleasant tale and he was so pleased that he was for going on and making a regular book out of it. But I checked him. "No," said I. "I am fearing that I would become too much interested and excited. I am satisfied with what you've been telling me. 'Twas more to my mind to have beaten that glass-eyed man but we have taken the right course. And now we will be returning to where we lodge."

During the walk back to the Pig and Turnip, Doctor Chord took it upon himself to discourse in his usual style upon the recent events. "Of course, sir, I would care to hear of the tragic scenes which must have transpired soon after I—I——"

"Abandoned the vicinity?" said I.

"Precisely," he responded. "Although I was not in the exact neighborhood during what must have been a most tempestuous part of your adventure, I can assure you I had lost none of my former interest in the affair."

"I am believing you," said I, "but let us talk now more of the future. I am much absorbed in the future. It appears to me that it will move at a rapid pace."

I did not tell him about my meeting with Lady Mary because I knew if occasion arose he would spread the news over half-London. No consideration would have been great enough to bridle the tongue of the little gossip from use of the first bit of news which he had ever received warm from the fire. Besides, after his behaviour in front of the enemy, I was quite certain that an imparting of my news could do nothing in the way of impairing his inefficiency. Consequently it was not necessary to trouble him with dramatic details.

"As to the part of the adventure which took place in the garden you are consistently silent, I observe, sir," said the Doctor.

"I am," said I. "I come of a long line of silent ancestors. My father was particularly notable in this respect."

"And yet, sir," rejoined the Doctor, "I had gained an impression that your father was quite willing to express himself in a lofty and noble manner on such affairs as attracted his especial notice."

"He was that," said I, pleased. "He was, indeed. I am only wishing I had his talent for saying all that was in his mind so fast that even the priest could not keep up with him and goodness knows Father Donovan was no small talker."

"You prove to me the limitations of science, sir," said he. "Although I think I may boast of some small education of a scientific nature, I think I will require some time for meditation and study before I will be able to reconcile your last two statements."

" 'Tis no matter," I cried amiably. "Let it pass."

For the rest of that week there was conference following conference at the Pig and Turnip and elsewhere. My three companions were now as eager as myself for the advent of the critical Sunday when I, with Paddy and Jem, were to attempt our visit to Strammers's flower-gardens. I had no difficulty in persuading the Doctor that his services would be invaluable at another place; for the memory of the blunderbuss seemed to linger with him. I had resolved to disguise myself slightly, for I had no mind to have complications arising from this gardener's eyes. I think a little disguise is plenty unless one stalks mysteriously and stops and peers here and there. A little unostentatious minding of one's own affairs is a good way to remain undiscovered. Then nobody looks at you and demands: "Who is this fellow?" My father always said that when he wished to disguise himself he dressed as a common man, and although this gained him many a hard knock of the fist and blow of the stick from people who were really his inferiors, he found his disguise was perfection. However, my father only disguised when on some secret mission from King Louis, for it does not become a gentleman to accept a box on the ears from anybody unless it is in the service of his sovereign.

I remember my father saying also these tours as a common man taught him he must ever afterward ride carefully through the streets of villages and towns. He was deeply impressed by the way in which men, women and children had to scud for their lives to keep from under the hoofs of the chargers of these devil-may-care gentlemen who came like whirlwinds through narrow crowded streets. He himself often had to scramble for his life, he said.

However, that was many years back, and I did not fear any such adventures in my prospective expedition. In such a case I would have trembled for what might happen. I have no such philosophy of temper as had my father. I might take the heel of a gay cavalier and throw him out of the saddle, and then there would be a fine uproar. However, I am quite convinced that it is always best to dodge. A good dodger seldom gets into trouble in this world, and lives to a green old age, while the noble patriot and others of his kind die in dungeons. I remember an honest man who set out to reform the parish in the matter of drink. They took him and—but, no matter; I must be getting on with the main tale.

CHAPTER XXVI

ON Saturday night I called the lads to my room and gave them their final instructions.

"Now, you rogues," said I to them, "let there be no drinking this night, and no trapesing of the streets, getting your heads broke just at the critical moment; for, as my father used to say, although a broken head is merrily come by, a clear head's worth two of it when business is to be transacted. So go to your beds at once, the two of you, if there's any drinking to be done, troth it's myself that'll attend to it."

With that I drove them out and sat down to an exhilarating bottle, without ever a thought of where the money was to come from to pay for it. It is one of the advantages of a public house frequented by the nobility that if you come to it with a bold front, and one or two servants behind your back, you have at least a clear week ahead before they flutter the show of a bill at you and ask to see the colour of your gold in exchange for their ink and paper.

My father used to say that a gentleman with money in his pocket might economize and no disgrace to him; but when stomach and purse are both empty, go to the best house in the town, where they will feed you, and lodge you, and drink you, before asking questions. Indeed I never shed many salt tears over the losses of a publican, for he shears so closely those sheep that have plenty of wool that he may well take care of an innocent lamb like myself, on which the crop is not yet grown.

I was drinking quietly and thinking deeply on the wisdom of my father, who knew the world better than ever his son will know it, when there was an unexpected knock at the door, and in walked Doctor Chord. I was not too pleased to see the little man, for I had feared he had changed his mind and wanted to come with us in the morning, and his company was something I had no desire for. He was a coward in a pinch, and a distrustful man in peace, ever casting doubt on the affection I was sure sometimes that Lady Mary held for me; and if he wasn't talking about that, sure he went rambling on—great discourses on science which held little interest for a young man so deeply in love as I was. The proper study of mankind is womankind, said a philosopher that my father used to quote with approval, but whose name I'm forgetting at this moment. Nevertheless I welcomed the little Doctor and said to him:

"Draw you up a chair, and I'll draw out a cork."

The little man sat him down, and I placed an open bottle nice and convenient to his elbow.

Whether it was the prospect of good wine, or the delight of better company, or the thought of what was going to happen on the morrow, I could not tell; but it seemed to me the little Doctor laboured under a great deal of excitement, and I became more and more afraid that he would insist on bearing us company while the Earl and the Countess were away at church. Now it was enough to have on my hands two such models of stupidity as Paddy and Jem without having to look after Doctor Chord as well, and him glancing his eyes this way and that in apprehension of a blunderbuss.

"Have you made all your plans, O'Ruddy?" he inquired, setting down his cup a good deal emptier than when he lifted it.

"I have," said I.

"Are you entirely satisfied with them?" he continued.

"My plans are always perfect plans," I replied to him, "and trouble only comes in the working of them. When you have to work with such raw material as I have to put up with, the best of plans have the unlucky habit of turning round and hitting you in the eye."

"Do you expect to be hit in the eye tomorrow?" asked the Doctor, very excited, which was shown by the rattle of the bottle against the lip of his cup.

"I'm only sure of one thing for tomorrow," said I, "and that is the certainty that if there's blunder to be made one or other of my following will make it. Still, I'm not complaining, for it's good to be certain of something."

"What's to be your mode of procedure?" said the Doctor, giving me a touch of his fine language.

"We wait in the lane till the church bells have stopped ringing, then Paddy and Jem go up to the little door in the wall, and Paddy knocks nice and quietly, in the expectation that the door will be opened as quietly by Strammers, and thereupon Jem and Paddy will be let in."

"But won't ye go in with them?" inquired the little Doctor very hurriedly.

"Doctor Chord," said I, lifting up my cup, "I have the honour to drink wine with you, and to inform you that it's myself that's outlining the plan."

"I beg your pardon for interrupting," said the Doctor; then he nodded to me as he drank.

"My two villains will go in alone with Strammers, and when the door is bolted, and they have passed the time of day with each other, Paddy will look around the garden and exclaim how it excels all the gardens that ever was, including that of Eden; and then Jem will say what a pity it was they couldn't have their young friend outside to see the beauty of it. It is my expectation that Strammers will rise to this, and request the pleasure of their young friend's company; but if he hesitates Paddy will say that the young friend outside is a free-handed Irishman who would no more mind a shilling going from his pocket into that of another man than he would the crooking of an elbow when a good drink is to be had. But be that as it may, they're to work me in through the little door by the united diplomacy of England and Ireland, and, once inside of the walls, it is my hope that I can slip away from them and see something of the inside of the house as well."

"And you have the hope that you'll find Lady Mary in the withdrawing-room," said the Doctor.

"I'll find her," says I, "if she's in the house; for I'm not going from room to room on a tour of inspection to see whether I'll buy the mansion or not."

"It's a very good plan," said the Doctor, drawing the back of his hand across his lips. "It's a very good plan," he repeated, nodding his head several times.

"Now, by the Old Head of Kinsale, little man," said I, "what do you mean by that remark and that motion of the head? What's wrong with the plan?"

"The plan's a good one, as I have said," reiterated the Doctor. But I saw there was something on his mind, and told him so, urging him to be out with it.

"Do you think," said I, "that Lady Mary will be in church with her father and mother?"

"I do not," muttered the Doctor, cautiously bringing his voice down to a whisper; "but I want to warn you that there's danger here in this room while you're lurking around my Earl's palace."

"How can danger harm me here when I am somewhere else?" I asked.

A very mysterious manner fell upon the little man, and he glanced, one after the other, at the four corners of the room, as if he heard a mouse moving and wanted to detect it. Then he looked sternly at the door, and I thought he was going to peer up the chimney, but instead he leaned across the table and said huskily:

"The papers!"

"What papers?" I asked, astonished.

"Your thoughts are so intent on the young lady that you forget everything else. Have you no recollection of the papers the Earl of Westport is so anxious to put himself in possession of?"

I leaned back in my chair and gazed steadily at Doctor Chord; but his eyes would not bring themselves to meet mine, and so he made some pother about filling up his cup again, with the neck of the bottle trembling on the edge, as if its teeth were chattering.

Now my father used to say when a man is afraid to meet your eye, be prepared to have him meet your fist. I disremembered saying anything to the Doctor about these same papers, which, truth to tell, I had given but little thought to recently, with other things of more importance to crowd them out of mind.

"How come you to know anything about the papers?" I said at last.

"Oh, your memory is clean leaving you!" cried the little

Doctor, as if the cup of wine he drank had brought back his courage to him. "You told me all about the papers when we were in Kensington Gardens."

"If I did," says I, "then I must have further informed you that I gave them as a present to Lady Mary herself. Surely I told you that?"

"You told me that, of course; but I thought you said they had come back into your possession again. If I'm wrong, it's no matter at all, and there's nothing to be said about them. I'm merely speaking to you by way of a friend, and I thought if you had the papers here in your room it was very unsafe to leave them unprotected by yourself or someone you can trust. I was just speaking as your well-wisher, for I don't want to hear you crying you are robbed, and us at our wit's end not getting either the thief or the booty."

He spoke with great candour and good humour, and the only thing that made me suspicious at first was that for the life of me I could not ever remember mentioning the papers to him, yet it was very likely that I did; for, as my father used to say, an Irishman talks more than the recording angel can set down in his busiest day, and therefore it is lucky that everything he says is not held against him. It seemed to me that we talked more of scandal than of papers in the park, but still I might be mistaken.

"Very good, Doctor," I cried, genially. "The papers it is, and, true for you, the Earl would like to get his old claws on them. Have you any suggestions to make?"

"Well, it seems to me, O'Ruddy, that if the Earl got wind of them it would be the easiest thing in the world to have your apartment rifled during your absence."

"That is true enough," I agreed, "so what would you do about the papers if you were in my boots?"

"If I had a friend I could trust," said Doctor Chord slowly, "I would give the papers to him and tell him to take good care of them."

"But why not carry them about in my own pocket?" I asked.

"It seemed to me they were not any too safe last time they were there," said the Doctor, pleasantly enough. "You see,

O'Ruddy, you're a marked man if once the Earl gets wind of your being in town. To carry the papers about on your own person would be the unsafest thing you could do, ensuring you a stab in the back, so that little use you'd have for the papers ever after. I have no desire to be mixed further in your affairs than I am at the present moment, but nevertheless I could easily take charge of the packet for you; then you would know where it was."

"But would I be sure to know where *you* were?" said I, my first suspicion of him returning to me.

The little Doctor laughed.

"I am always very easily found," he said; "but when I offered to take the papers it was merely in case a stranger like yourself should not have a faster friend beside him than I am. If you have any such, then I advise you to give custody of the papers to him."

"I have no real friend in London that I know of," said I, "but Paddy."

"The very thing," cried the Doctor, joyously, at once putting to rest all my doubts concerning him. "The very thing. I would give the papers to Paddy and tell him to protect them with his life. I'm sure he'll do it, and you'll know where to find both them and him when you want them. But to go away from the Pig and Turnip right across to the other end of the town, taking your two servants with you, leaving nobody to guard papers that are of importance to you, strikes me as the height of folly. I'll just fill up another cup, and so bid you good-night, and good luck for the morrow."

And with that the little man drained the bottle, taking his leave with great effusion, and begging my pardon for even so much as mentioning the papers, saying they had been on his mind for the last day or two, and, feeling friendly toward me, he wished to warn me not to leave them carelessly about.

After he left I thought a good deal about what the Doctor had said, and I wondered at myself that I had ever misdoubted him; for, although he was a man given greatly to talk, yet he had been exceedingly friendly with me from the very first night I had met him, and I thought shame of myself that I was losing trust in my fellow man here in this great city of London, because in Ireland we trust each other entirely; and indeed we are under some compulsion in that same matter, for there is so little moncy about that if you do not take a man's word now and then there's nothing else for you to take.

CHAPTER XXVII

I SLEPT well that night, and it was broad daylight when I awoke. A most beautiful morning it seemed to me, and just the time for a lonely stroll in the beautiful gardens, so long as there was someone with you that you thought a great deal of. I made a good breakfast, and then took out the papers and placed them on the table before me. They were all safe so far. I could not comprehend how the Earl would know anything of my being in London, unless, indeed, he caught sight of me walking in his own gardens with his own daughter, and then, belike, he was so jealous a man that he would maybe come to the conclusion I was in London as well as himself.

After breakfast Paddy and Jem came in, looking as bold as Blarney Castle; and when I eyed them both I saw that neither one nor the other was a fit custodian for papers that might make the proudest Earl in England a poor man or a rich man, depending which way they went. So I put the documents in my own pocket without more ado, and gave up my thoughts to a pleasanter subject. I changed my mind about a disguise, and put on my back the best clothes that I had to wear. I wished I had the new suits I had been measured for, but the spalpeen of a tailor would not let me have them unless I paid him some of the money they cost. When I came to think over it I saw that Strammers would surely never recognize me as a gay spark of fashion when he had merely seen me once before, torn and ragged, coming down from a tree on top of his blunderbuss. So I instructed Paddy to say that he and Jem were servants of the best master in the world, who was a great lover of gardens; that he was of immense generosity, and if Strammers allowed him to come into the gardens by the little door he would be a richer man when the door was opened than he would be if he kept it shut. I had been long enough in London to learn the golden method of persuasion; anyhow I could not bring myself to the chance of meeting with my lady, and me dressed worse than one of her own servants.

We were all in the lane when the church bells ceased to ring, and if anyone had seen us he would simply have met a comely young Irish gentleman taking the air of a Sunday morning with two faithful servants at his heels. I allowed something like ten impatient minutes to crawl past me, and then, as the lane was clear and everyone for the church within its walls, I tipped a nod to Paddy, and he, with Jem by his side, tapped lightly at the door, while I stood behind the trunk of the tree up which I had climbed before. There was no sign of Doctor Chord in the vicinity, and for that I was thankful, because up to the last moment I feared the little man could not help intruding himself on what was somebody else's business.

The door was opened with some caution, letting Paddy and Jem enter; then it was closed, and I heard the bolts shot into their places. But I was speedily to hear more than bolts that Sunday morning. There was a sound of thumping sticks, and I heard a yell that might well have penetrated to the Pig and Turnip itself, although it was miles away. I knew Paddy's cry, and next there came some good English cursing from Jem Bottles, while a shrill voice called out:

"Catch the red-haired one; he's the villain we want!"

In the midst of various exclamations, maledictions, and other constructions of speech, mingled, I thought, with laughter, I flung my shoulder against the door, but I might as well have tried to batter down the wall itself. The door was as firm as Macgillicuddy Reeks. I know when I am beat as well as the next man, and, losing no more time there, I ran as fast as I could along the wall, out of the lane, and so to the front of the house. The main entrance was protected by great gates of wrought iron, which were opened on occasion by a man in a little cubby of a cabin that stood for a porter's lodge. The man wasn't there, and the gates were locked; but part of one of the huge wings of wrought iron was a little gate that stood ajar. This I pushed open, and, unmolested, stepped inside.

The trees and shrubbery hid from me the scene that was taking place inside the little wooden door. I dashed through the underbrush and came to the edge of a broad lawn, and there was going on as fine a scrimmage as any man could wish to see. Jem Bottles had his back against the wooden door, and was laying about him with a stout stick; half a dozen tall fellows in livery making a great show of attack, but keeping well out of range of his weapon. Poor Paddy had the broad of his back on the turf, and it looked like they were trying to tear the clothes off him, for another half-dozen were on top of him; but I can say this in his favour, Paddy was using his big feet and doing great execution with them. Every now and then he planted a boot in the well-fed front of a footman or under-gardener, and sent him flying. The whole household seemed to be present, and one could hardly believe there was such a mob in a single mansion. The Earl of Westport was there, and who stood beside him but that little villain, Doctor Chord.

But it was the Countess herself that was directing operations. She had an ebony stick in her hands, and when Paddy kicked one of her underlings the vigorous old lady smote the over-turned servant to make him to the fray again. It was an exciting scene, and Donnybrook was nothing to it. Their backs were all toward me, and I was just bubbling with joy to think what a surprise I was about to give them—for I drew my sword and had a yell of defiance on my lips—when a cry that nobody paid the least attention to turned my mind in another direction entirely.

One of the first-floor windows was open, and over the sill leaned Lady Mary herself, her face aflush with anger.

"Father! Mother!" she cried. "Are not you ashamed of yourselves, making this commotion on a Sunday morning? Call the servants away from there! Let the two poor men go! Oh, shame, shame upon you."

She wrung her hands, but, as I was saying, nobody paid the slightest heed to her, and I doubt if any of them heard her, for Paddy was not keeping silence by any manner of means. He was taking the worst of all the blows that fell on him in a vigorous outcry.

"Murther! murther!" he shouted. "Let me on my feet, an' I'll knock yez all into the middle of county Clare."

No one, however, took advantage of this generous offer, but

they kept as clear as they could of his miscellaneous feet, and the Countess poked him in the ribs with the point of her ebony stick whenever she wasn't laying it over the backs of her servants.

Now, no man can ever say that I was a laggard when a good old-fashioned contest was going on, and the less indolence was observable on my own part when friends of mine were engaged in the fray. Sure I was always eager enough, even when it was a stranger's debate, and I wonder what my father would think of me now, to see me veer from the straight course of battle and thrust my unstruck sword once more into its scabbard. It was the face in the window that made me forget friend and foe alike. Lady Mary was the only member of the household that was not on the lawn, and was protesting unheard against the violence to two poor men who were there because they had been invited to come by the under-gardener.

I saw in the twinkling of an eye that the house had been deserted on the first outcry. Doors were left wide open for the whole world to enter. I dodged behind the trees, scuttled up the gravelled driveway, leaped the stone steps three at a time, and before you could say "Ballymuggins" I was in the most superb hall in which I ever set my foot. It was a square house with the stairway in the middle. I kept in my mind's eye the direction of the window in which Lady Mary had appeared. Quick as a bog-trotter responds to an invitation to drink, I mounted that grand stairway, turned to my right, and came to a door opposite which I surmised was the window through which Lady Mary was leaning. Against this door I rapped my knuckles, and speedily I heard the sweet voice of the most charming girl in all the world demand with something like consternation in its tones:

"Who is there?"

"It's me, Lady Mary!" said I. "The O'Ruddy, who begs the privilege of a word with you."

I heard the slam of a window being shut, then the sound of a light step across the floor, and after that she said with a catch in her voice:

"I'll be pleased you should come in, Mr. O'Ruddy."

I tried the door, but found it locked.

"How can I come in, Lady Mary," says I, "if you've got bolts held against me?"

"There are no bolts," said Lady Mary; "the key should be on the outside. I am locked in. Look for the key and open the door."

Was ever a more delightful sentence spoken to a man? My heart was in my throat with joy. I glanced down, and there, sure enough, stuck the key. I turned it at once, then pulled it out of the lock and opened the door.

"Lady Mary," says I, "with your permission, it seems to me a door should be locked from the inside."

With that I thrust the key through the far side of the door, closed it, and locked it. Then I turned round to face her.

The room, it was plain to be seen, was the parlour of a lady—a boudoir, as they call it in France, a word that my father was very fond of using, having caught it when he was on the campaign in that delightful country. The boudoir was full of confections and charming little dainties in the way of lace, and easy chairs, and bookcases, and little writing-desks, and a work-basket here and there; but the finest ornament it possessed was the girl who now stood in the middle of the floor with a frown on her brow that was most becoming. Yes, there was a frown on her brow, although I expected a smile on her lips because of the cordial invitation she had given me to come in.

It would seem to either you or me that if a lady suffered the indignity of being locked in her room, just as if she was a child of six years old, she would welcome with joy the person who came and released her. Now, my father, who was the wisest man since Solomon—and indeed, as I listened to him, I've often thought that Solomon was overpraised—my father used to say there was no mystery at all about women. "You just think," he would say, "of what a sensible man would do on a certain occasion; then configure out in your mind the very opposite, and that's what a woman will do." A man who had been imprisoned would have held out his hand and have said, "God bless you, O'Ruddy; but I'm glad to see you." And here stood this fine lady in the middle of her room, looking at me as if I were the dirt beneath her feet, and had forced my way into her presence, instead of being invited like a man of honour to enter.

"Well, Mr. O'Ruddy," she said, throwing back her head,

haughty-like, "Why do you stand dallying in a lady's bower when your followers are being beaten on the lawn outside?"

I cannot give you Lady Mary's exact words, for I was so astonished at their utterance; but I give you a very good purport of them.

"Is it the beating of my men?" I said. "Troth, that's what I pay them for. And whoever gives them a good drubbing saves me the trouble. I saw they had Paddy down on the turf, but he's a son of the ould sod, and little he'll mind being thrown on his mother. But if it's Jem Bottles you're anxious about, truth to tell I'm more sorry for those that come within range of his stick than for Jem with his back to the wall. Bottles can take care of himself in any company, for he's a highwayman in an excellent way of business."

I always like to mention anything that's in favour of a man, and so I told her what profession Bottles followed. She gave a toss of her head, and gave me a look that had something like contempt in it, which was far from being pleasant to endure. Then she began walking up and down the room, and it was plain to see that my Lady was far from being pleased with me.

"Poor fellows! Poor faithful fellows! That's what comes of having a fool for a master."

"Indeed, your ladyship," said I, drawing myself up to my full height, which wasn't so very much short of the door itself, "there are worse things than blows from a good honest cudgel. You might better say, 'This is what comes to a master with two fools for servants.'"

"And what comes to a master?" she demanded. "Sure no one asks you to be here."

"That shows how short your ladyship's memory is," said I with some irritation. "Father Donovan used to tell me that the shortest thing in the world was the interval between an insult and a blow in Ireland, but I think a lady's memory is shorter still. 'Turn the key and come in,' says you. What is that, I would like to know, but an invitation."

It appeared to me that she softened a bit, but she continued her walk up and down the room and was seemingly in great agitation. The cries outside had stopped, but whether they had murdered both Jem Bottles and Paddy I had no means at that moment of knowing, and I hope the two will forgive me when I say that my thoughts were far from them.

"You will understand," said Lady Mary, speaking still with resentment in her voice, "that the papers you held are the key to the situation. Have you no more sense than to trust them to the care of a red-headed clown from whom they can be taken as easy as if they were picked up off the street?"

"Indeed, believe me, Lady Mary, that no red-headed clown has any papers of mine."

"Indeed, and I think you speak the true word there. The papers are now in my father's possession, and he will know how to take care of them."

"Well, he didn't know that the last time he had them," I cried, feeling angry at these unjust accusations, and not being able to bear the compliment to the old man, even if he was an Earl. "The papers," said I, "are as easily picked from me as from the street, like you were saying just now; but it isn't a pack of overfed flunkeys that will lift them from me. Lady Mary, on a previous occasion I placed the papers in your hands; now, with your kind permission, I lay them at your feet"—and, saying this with the most courteous obeisance, I knelt with one knee on the floor and placed the packet of papers where I said I would place them.

Now, ever since that, the Lady Mary denies that she kicked them to the other end of the room. She says that as she was walking to and fro the toe of her foot touched the packet and sent it spinning; and, as no real Irishman ever yet contradicted a lady, all I will say is that the precious bundle went hurtling to the other end of the room, and it is very likely that Lady Mary thought the gesture of her foot a trifle too much resembled an action of her mother, the Countess, for her manner changed in the twinkling of an eye, and she laughed like her old self again.

"Mr. O'Ruddy," she said, "you put me out of all patience. You're as simple as if you came out of Ireland yesterday."

"It's tolerably well known," said I, "by some of your expert swordsmen, that I came out the day before."

Again Lady Mary laughed.

"You're not very wise in the choice of your friends," she said.

"I am, if I can count you as one of them," I returned.

She made no direct reply to this, but continued:

"Can't you see that that little Doctor Chord is a traitor? He has been telling my father all you have been doing and all you have been planning, and he says you are almost simple enough to have given the papers into his own keeping no longer ago than last night."

"Now, look you, Lady Mary, how much you misjudged me. The little villain asked for the papers, but he didn't get them; then he advised me to give them to a man I could trust, and when I said the only man I could trust was red-headed Paddy out yonder, he was delighted to think I was to leave them in his custody. But you can see for yourself I did nothing of the kind, and if your people thought they could get anything out of Paddy by bad language and heroic kicks they were mistaken."

At that moment we had an interruption that brought our conversation to a standstill and Lady Mary to the door, outside which her mother was crying:

"Mary, Mary! where's the key?"

"Where should it be?" said Lady Mary, "but in the door."

"It is not in the door," said the Countess wrathfully, shaking it as if she would tear it down.

"It is in the door," said Lady Mary positively; and quite right she was, for both of us were looking at it.

"It is not in the door," shouted her mother. "Some of the servants have taken it away."

Then we heard her calling over the banisters to find out who had taken away the key of Lady Mary's room. There was a twinkle in Mary's eye, and a quiver in the corners of her pretty mouth that made me feel she would burst out laughing, and indeed I had some ado to keep silence myself.

"What have you done with those two poor wretches you were maltreating out in the garden?" asked Lady Mary.

"Oh, don't speak of them," cried the Countess, evidently in no good humour. "It was all a scandal for nothing. The red-headed beast did not have the papers. That little fool, Chord, has misled both your father and me. I could wring his neck for him, and now he is palavering your father in the library and saying he will get the papers himself or die in the attempt. It serves us right for paying attention to a babbling idiot like him.

I said in the first place that that Irish baboon of an O'Ruddy was not likely to give them to the ape that follows him."

"Tare-an-ounds!" I cried, clenching my fists and making for the door; but Lady Mary rattled it so I could not be heard, and the next instant she placed her snow-flake hand across my mouth, which was as pleasant a way of stopping an injudicious utterance as ever I had been acquainted with.

"Mary," said the Countess, "your father is very much agitated and disappointed, so I'm taking him out for a drive. I have told the butler to look out for the key, and when he finds it he will let you out. You've only yourself to blame for being locked in, because we expected the baboon himself and couldn't trust you in his presence."

It was now Lady Mary's turn to show confusion at the old termagant's talk, and she coloured as red as a sunset on the coast of Kerry. I forgave the old hag her discourteous appellation of "baboon" because of the joyful intimation she gave me through the door that Lady Mary was not to be trusted when I was near by. My father used to say that if you are present when an embarrassment comes to a lady it is well not to notice it, else the embarrassment will be transferred to yourself. Remembering this, I pretended not to see Lady Mary's flaming cheeks, and, begging her pardon, walked up the room and picked from the corner the bundle of papers which had, somehow or other, come there, whether kicked or not. I came back to where she was standing and offered them to her most respectfully, as if they, and not herself, were the subject of discussion.

"Hush," said Lady Mary in a whisper; "sit down yonder and see how long you can keep quiet."

She pointed to a chair that stood beside a beautifully polished table of foreign wood, the like of which I had never seen before, and I, wishing very much to please her, sat down where she told me and placed the bundle of papers on the table. Lady Mary tiptoed over, as light-footed as a canary-bird, and sat down on the opposite side of the table, resting her elbows on the polished wood, and, with her chin in her hands, gazed across at me, and a most bewildering scrutiny I found it, rendering it difficult for me to keep quiet and seated, as she had requested. In a minute or two we heard the crunch of wheels on the gravel in front, then the carriage drove off, and the big gates clanked together.

Still Lady Mary poured the sunshine of her eyes upon me, and I hope and trust she found me a presentable young man, for under the warmth of her look my heart began to bubble up like a pot of potatoes on a strong fire.

"You make me a present of the papers, then?" said Lady Mary at last.

"Indeed and I do, and of myself as well, if you'll have me. And this latter is a thing I've been trying to say to you every time I met you, Mary acushla, and no sooner do the words come to my lips than some doddering fool interrupts us; but now, my darling, we are alone together, in that lover's paradise which is always typified by a locked door, and at last I can say the things——"

Just here, as I mentioned the word "door," there came a rap at it, and Lady Mary started as if someone had fired a gun.

"Your ladyship," said the butler, "I cannot find the key. Shall I send for a locksmith?"

"Oh, no," said Lady Mary, "do not take the trouble. I have letters to write, and do not wish to be disturbed until my mother returns."

"Very good, your ladyship," returned the butler, and he walked away.

"A locksmith!" said Lady Mary, looking across the table at me.

"Love laughs at them," said I.

Lady Mary smiled very sweetly, but shook her head.

"This is not a time for laughter," she said, "but for seriousness. Now, I cannot risk your staying here longer, so will tell you what I have to say as quickly as possible. Your repeatedly interrupted declaration I take for truth, because the course of true love never did run smooth. Therefore, if you want me, you must keep the papers."

At this I hastily took the bundle from the table and thrust it in my pocket, which action made Lady Mary smile again.

"Have you read them?" she asked.

"I have not."

"Do you mean to say you have carried these papers about for so long and have not read them?"

"I had no curiosity concerning them," I replied. "I have something better to look at," I went on, gazing across at her; "and when that is not with me the memory of it is, and it's little I care for a pack of musty papers and what's in them."

"Then I will tell you what they are," said Lady Mary. "There are in that packet the title-deeds to great estates, the fairest length of land that lies under the sun in Sussex. There is also a letter written by my father's own hand, giving the property to your father."

"But he did not mean my father to keep it," said I.

"No, he did not. He feared capture, and knew the ransom would be heavy if they found evidence of property upon him. Now all these years he has been saying nothing, but collecting the revenues of this estate and using them, while another man had the legal right to it."

"Still he has but taken what was his own," said I, "and my father never disputed that, always intending to come over to England and return the papers to the Earl; but he got lazy-like, by sitting at his own fireside, and seldom went farther abroad than to the house of the priest; but his last injunctions to me were to see that the Earl got his papers, and indeed he would have had them long since if he had but treated me like the son of an old friend."

"Did your father mention that the Earl would give you any reward for returning his property to him?"

"He did not," I replied with indignation. "In Ireland, when a friend does a friend's part, he doesn't expect to be paid for it."

"But don't you expect a reward for returning them?"

"Lady Mary," said I, "do you mean to be after insulting me? These papers are not mine, but the Earl of Westport's, and he can have them without saying as much as 'Thank you kindly' for them."

Lady Mary leaned back in her chair and looked at me with half-closed eyes, then she stretched forth her hand and said:

"Give me the papers."

"But it's only a minute since," I cried, perplexed, "that you held them to be the key of the situation, and said if I didn't keep them I would never get you."

"Did I say that?" asked Lady Mary with the innocence of a three-year-old child. "I had no idea we had come to such a conclusion. Now do you want a little advice about those same papers?"

"As long as the advice comes from you, Mary darling, I want it on any subject."

"You have come into England brawling, sword-playing, cudgel-flinging, and never till this moment have you given a thought to what the papers are for. These papers represent the law."

"Bad cess to it," said I. "My father used to say, have as little to do with the law as possible, for what's the use of bringing your man into the courts when a good shillelah is speedier and more satisfactory to all concerned."

"That may be true in Ireland, but it is not true in England. Now, here is my advice. You know my father and mother, and if you'll just quit staring your eyes out at me, and think for a minute, you may be able to tell when you will get their consent to pay your addresses to me without interruption." Here she blushed and looked down.

"Indeed," said I, "I don't need to take my eyes from you to answer *that* question. It'll be the afternoon following the Day of Judgment."

"Very well. You must then stand on your rights. I will give you a letter to a man in the Temple, learned in the law. He was legal adviser to my aunt, who left me all her property, and she told me that if I ever was in trouble I was to go to him; but instead of that I'll send my trouble to him with a letter of introduction. I advise you to take possession of the estate at Brede, and think no more of giving up the papers to my father until he is willing to give you something in return. You may then ask what you like of him; money, goods, or a farm"—and again a bright red colour flooded her cheeks. With that she drew toward her pen and paper and dashed off a letter which she gave to me.

"I think," she said, "it would be well if you left the papers with the man in the Temple; he will keep them safely, and no one will suspect where they are; while, if you need money, which is likely, he will be able to advance you what you want on the security of the documents you leave with him."

"Is it money?" said I, "sure I couldn't think of drawing money on property that belongs to your good father, the Earl."

"As I read the papers," replied Lady Mary, very demurely, casting down her eyes once more, "the property does not belong to my good father, the Earl, but to the good-for-nothing young man named O'Ruddy. I think that my father, the Earl, will find that he needs your signature before he can call the estate his own once more. It may be I am wrong, and that your father, by leaving possession so long in the hands of the Earl, may have forfeited his claim. Mr. Josiah Brooks will tell you all about that when you meet him in the Temple. You may depend upon it that if he advances you money your claim is good, and, your claim being good, you may make terms with even so obstreperous a man as my father."

"And if I make terms with the father," I cried, "do you think his comely daughter will ratify the bargain?"

Lady Mary smiled very sweetly, and gave me the swiftest and shyest of glances across the table from her speaking eyes, which next instant were hidden from me.

"May be," she said, "the lawyer could answer that question."

"Troth," I said, springing to my feet, "I know a better one to ask it of than any old curmudgeon poring over dry law-books, and the answer I'm going to have from your own lips."

Then, with a boldness that has ever characterized the O'Ruddys, I swung out my arms and had her inside o' them before you could say Ballymoyle. She made a bit of a struggle and cried breathlessly:

"I'll answer, if you'll sit in that chair again."

"It's not words," says I, "I want from your lips, but this"—and I smothered a little shriek with one of the heartiest kisses that ever took place out of Ireland itself, and it seemed to me that her struggle ceased, or, as one might say, faded away, as my lips came in contact with hers; for she suddenly weakened in my arms so that I had to hold her close to me, for I thought she would sink to the floor if I did but leave go, and in the excite-

ment of the moment my own head was swimming in a way
that the richest of wine had never made it swim before. Then
Lady Mary buried her face in my shoulder with a little sigh of
content, and I knew she was mine in spite of all the Earls and
Countesses in the kingdom, or estates either, so far as that
went. At last she straightened up and made as though she
would push me from her, but held me thus at arms' length,
while her limpid eyes looked like twin lakes of Killarney on a
dreamy misty morning when there's no wind blowing.

"O'Ruddy," she said, solemnly, with a little catch in her voice,
"you're a bold man, and I think you've no doubt of your answer;
but what has happened makes me the more anxious for your
success in dealing with those who will oppose both your wishes
and mine. My dear lover, is what I call you now; you have
come over in tempestuous fashion, with a sword in your hand,
striving against everyone who would stand up before you. After
this morning, all that should be changed, for life seems to
have become serious and momentous. O'Ruddy, I want your
actions to be guided, not by a drawn sword, but by religion and
by law."

"Troth, Mary-acushla, an Irishman takes to religion of his own
nature, but I much misdoubt me if it comes natural to take to
the law."

"How often have you been to mass since you came to England,
O'Ruddy?"

"How often?" says I, wrinkling my brow, "indeed you mean,
how many times?"

"Yes; how many times?"

"Now, Mary, how could you expect me to be keeping count of
them?"

"Has your attendance, then, been so regular?"

"Ah, Mary, darling; it's not me that has the face to tell you a
lie, and yet I'm ashamed to say that I've never set foot in a
church since I crossed the channel, and the best of luck it is
for me that good old Father Donovan doesn't hear these same
words."

"Then you will go to church this very day and pray for
heaven's blessing on both of us."

"It's too late for the mass this Sunday, Mary, but the churches are open, and the first one I come to will have me inside of it."

With that she drew me gently to her, and herself kissed me, meeting none of that resistance which I had encountered but a short time before; and then, as bitter ill luck would have it, at this delicious moment we were startled by the sound of carriage-wheels on the gravel outside.

"Oh!" cried Lady Mary in a panic; "how time has flown!"

"Indeed," said I, "I never knew it so fast before."

And she, without wasting further time in talking, unlocked the door, whipped out the key, and placed it where I had found it in the beginning. She seemed to think of everything in a moment, and I would have left her letter and the papers on the table if it hadn't been for that cleverest of all girls, who, besides her lips of honey, had an alert mind, which is one of the things appreciated in Ireland. I then followed her quickly down a narrow back stairway and out into a glass house, where a little door at the end led us into a deliciously shaded walk, free from all observation, with a thick screen of trees on the right hand and the old stone wall on the left.

Here I sprang quickly to overtake her, but she danced away like a fairy in the moonlight, throwing a glance of mischief over her shoulder at me, with her finger on her lips. It seemed to me a pity that so sylvan a dell should merely be used for the purposes of speed, but in a jiffy Mary was at the little door in the wall and had the bolts drawn back, and I was outside before I understood what had happened, listening to bolts being thrust back again, and my only consolation was the remembrance of a little dab at my lips as I passed through, as brief and unsatisfactory as the peck of a sparrow.

CHAPTER XXVIII

IT was a beautiful day, as lovely as any an indulgent Providence had ever bestowed upon an unthankful generation.

Although I wished I had had an hour or two to spend with Mary wandering up and down that green alley through which we had rushed with such indecent haste, all because two aged and angry members of the nobility might have come upon us, yet I walked through the streets of London as if I trod on the air, and not on the rough cobble-stones of the causeway. It seemed as if I had suddenly become a boy again, and yet with all the strength and vigour of a man, and I was hard put to it not to shout aloud in the sunlight, or to slap on the back the slow and solemn Englishmen I met, who looked as if they had never laughed in their lives. Sure it's a very serious country, this same land of England, where their dignity is so oppressive that it bows down head and shoulders with thinking how grand they are; and yet I'll say nothing against them, for it was an Englishwoman that made me feel like a balloon. Pondering over the sobriety of the nation, I found myself in the shadow of a great church, and, remembering what my dear Mary had said, I turned and went in through the open door, with my hat in my hand. It was a great contrast to the bright sunlight I had left, and to the busy streets with their holiday-making people. There were only a few scattered here and there in the dim silence of the church, some on their knees, some walking slowly about on tiptoe, and some seated meditating in chairs. No service was going forward, so I knelt down in the chapel of Saint Patrick himself; I bowed my head and thanked God for the day and for the blessing that had come with it. As I said, I was like a boy again, and to my lips, too long held from them, came the prayers that had been taught me. I was glad I had not forgotten them, and I said them over and over with joy in my heart. As I raised my head, I saw standing and looking at me a priest, and, rising to my feet, I made my bow to him, and he came forward, recognizing me before I recognized him.

"O'Ruddy," he said, "if you knew the joy it gives to my old heart to meet you in this sacred place and in that devout attitude, it would bring some corresponding happiness to yourself."

"Now by the piper that played before Moses, Father Donovan, and is this yourself? Sure I disrecognized you, coming into the darkness, and me just out of the glare beyond"—and I took his hand in both of mine and shook it with a heartiness he had not met since he left the old turf. "Sure and there's no one I'd rather meet this day than yourself"—and with that I dropped on one knee and asked for his blessing on me and mine.

As we walked out of the church together, his hand resting on my shoulder, I asked how such a marvel came to pass as Father Donovan, who never thought to leave Ireland, being here in London. The old man said nothing till we were down the steps, and then he told me what had happened.

"You remember Patsy O'Gorman," he said.

"I do that," I replied, "and an old thief of the world and a tight-fisted miser he is."

"Whist," said Father Donovan, quietly crossing himself. "O'Gorman is dead and buried."

"Do you tell me that!" said I, "then rest his soul. He would be a warm man and leave more money than my father did, I'm thinking."

"Yes, he left some money, and to me he left three hundred pounds, with the request that I should accomplish the desire of my life and take the pilgrimage to Rome."

"The crafty old chap, that same bit of bequestation will help him over many a rough mile in purgatory."

"Ah, O'Ruddy, it's not our place to judge. They gave a harder name to O'Gorman than he deserved. Just look at your own case. The stories that have come back to Ireland, O'Ruddy, just made me shiver. I heard that you were fighting and brawling through England, ready to run through any man that looked cross-eyed at you. They said that you had taken up with a highwayman; that you spent your nights in drink and breathing out smoke; and here I find you, a proper young man, doing credit to your country, meeting you, not in a tavern, but on your knees with bowed head in the chapel of Saint Patrick, giving the lie to the slanderer's tongue."

The good old man stopped in our walk, and with tears in his eyes shook hands with me again, and I had not the heart to tell him the truth.

"Ah well," I said, "Father Donovan, I suppose nobody, except yourself, is quite as good as he thinks, and nobody, including myself, is as bad as he appears to be. And now, Father Donovan, where are you stopping, and how long will you be in London?"

"I am stopping with an old college friend, who is a priest in the church where I found you. I expect to leave in a few days' time and journey down to the seaport of Rye, where I am to take ship that will land me either in Dunkirk or in Calais. From there I am to make my way to Rome as best I can."

"And are you travelling alone?"

"I am that, although, by the blessing of God, I have made many friends on the journey, and everyone I met has been good to me."

"Ah, Father Donovan, you couldn't meet a bad man if you travelled the world over. Sure there's some that carry such an air of blessedness with them that everyone they meet must, for very shame, show the best of his character. With me it's different, for it seems that where there's contention I am in the middle of it, though, God knows, I'm a man of peace, as my father was before me."

"Well," said Father Donovan slowly, but with a sweet smile on his lip, "I suppose the O'Ruddys were always men of peace, for I've known them before now to fight hard enough to get it."

The good father spoke a little doubtfully, as if he were not quite approving of our family methods, but he was a kindly man who always took the most lenient view of things. He walked far with me, and then I turned and escorted him to the place where he resided, and, bidding good-bye, got a promise from him that he would come to the Pig and Turnip a day later and have a bite and sup with me, for I thought with the assistance of the landlord I could put a very creditable meal before him, and Father Donovan was always one that relished his meals, and he enjoyed his drink too, although he was set against too much of it. He used to say, "It's a wise drinker that knows when geniality ends and hostility begins, and it's just as well to stop before you come to the line."

With this walking to and fro the day was near done with when I got back to the Pig and Turnip and remembered that neither a bit of pig nor a bit of turnip had I had all that long day, and now I was ravenous. I never knew anything make me forget my appetite before; but here had I missed my noonday meal, and not in all my life could I overtake it again. Sure there was many an experience crowded together in that beautiful Sunday, so, as I passed through the entrance to the inn, I said to the obsequious landlord:

"For the love of Heaven, get placed on my table all you have in the house that's fit to eat, and a trifle of a bottle or two, to wash it down with."

So saying, I passed up the creaking old oaken stair and came to my room, where I instantly remembered there was something else I had forgotten. As I opened the door there came a dismal groan from Paddy, and something that sounded like a wicked oath from Jem Bottles. Poor lads! that had taken such a beating that day, such a cudgelling for my sake; and here I stood at my own door in a wonder of amazement, and something of fright, thinking I had heard a banshee wail. The two misused lads had slipped out of my memory as completely as the devil slipped off Macgillicuddy Reeks into the pond beneath when Saint Patrick had sent the holy words after him.

"Paddy," said I, "are you hurted? Where is it you're sore?"

"Is it sore?" he groaned. "Except the soles of my feet, which they couldn't hit with me kickin' them, there isn't an inch of me that doesn't think it's worse hurted than the rest."

"It's sorry I am to hear that," I replied, quite truthfully, "and you, Jem, how did you come off?"

"Well, I gave a better account of myself than Paddy here, for I made most of them keep their distance from me; but him they got on the turf before you could say Watch me eye, and the whole boiling of them was on top of him in the twinkling of the same."

"The whole boiling of them?" said I, as if I knew nothing of the occurrence, "then there was more than Strammers to receive you?"

"More!" shouted Jem Bottles, "there was forty if there was one."

Paddy groaned again at the remembrance, and moaned out:

"The whole population of London was there, and half of it on top of me before I could wink. I thought they would strip the clothes off me, and they nearly did it."

"And have you been here alone ever since? Have you had nothing to eat or drink since you got back?"

"Oh," said Jem, "we had too much attention in the morning, and too little as the day went on. We were expecting you home, and so took the liberty of coming up here and waiting for you, thinking you might be good enough to send out for someone who would dress our wounds; but luckily that's not needed now."

"Why is it not needed?" I asked. "I'll send at once."

"Oh, no," moaned Paddy, "there was one good friend that did not forget us."

"Well," said Jem, "he seemed mighty afeerd of coming in. I suppose he thought it was on his advice that we went where we did, and he was afeerd we thought badly of him for it; but of course we had no blame to put on the poor little man."

"In Heaven's name, who are you talking of?" said I.

"Doctor Chord," answered Jem. "He put his head inside the door and inquired for us, and inquired specially where you were; but that, of course, we couldn't tell him. He was very much put out to find us mis-handled, and he sent us some tankards of beer, which are now empty, and we're waiting for him because he promised to come back and attend to our injuries."

"Then you didn't see Doctor Chord in the gardens?"

"In what gardens?" asked Bottles.

"You didn't see him among that mob that set on you?"

"No fear," said Jem, "wherever there's a scrimmage Doctor Chord will keep away from it."

"Indeed and in that you're wrong," said I. "Doctor Chord has been the instigator of everything that has happened, and he stood in the background and helped to set them on."

Paddy sat up with wild alarm in his eyes.

"Sure, master," says he, "how could you see through so thick a wall as that?"

"I did not see through the wall at all; I was in the house. When you went through the back door, I went through the front gate, and what I am telling you is true. Doctor Chord is the cause of the whole commotion. That's why he was afraid to come in the room. He thought perhaps you had seen him, and, finding you had not, he'll be back here again when everything is over. Doctor Chord is a traitor, and you may take my word for that."

Paddy rose slowly to his feet, every red hair in his head bristling with scorn and indignation; but as he stood erect he put his hand to his side and gave a howl as he limped a step or two over the floor.

"The black-hearted villain," he muttered through his teeth. "I'll have his life."

"You'll have nothing of the sort," said I, "and we'll get some good attendance out of him, for he's a skillful man. When he has done his duty in repairing what he has inflicted upon you, then you can give him a piece of your mind."

"I'll give him a piece of my boot; all that's left of it," growled Jem Bottles, scowling.

"You may take your will of him after he has put some embrocation on your bruises," said I; and as I was speaking there came a timorous little knock at the door.

"Come in," I cried, and after some hesitation the door opened, and there stood little Doctor Chord with a big bottle under his arm. I was glad there was no supper yet on the table, for if there had been I must have asked the little man to sit down with me, and that he would do without a second's hesitation, so I could not rightly see him maltreated who had broken a crust with me.

He paid no attention to Jem or Paddy at first, but kept his cunning little eye on me.

"And where have you been to-day, O'Ruddy?" he asked.

"Oh," said I, "I accompanied these two to the door in the wall, and when they got through I heard yells fit to make a hero out of a nigger; but you know how stout the bolts are and I couldn't get to them, so I had just to go out of hearing of their bellowings. On the way back I happened to meet an old friend of mine, Father Donovan, and——"

Here Paddy, forgetting his good manners, shouted out:

"Thank God there's a holy father in this hole of perdition; for I know I'm goin' t' die to-morrow at the latest."

"Stop your nonsense," said I. "You'll have to hold on to life at least a day longer; for the good father is not coming here until two days are past. You're more frightened than hurt, and the Doctor here has a lotion that will make you meet the priest as a friend and not as a last counsellor.

"As I was saying, Doctor Chord, I met Father Donovan, and we strolled about the town, so that I have only now just come in. The father is a stranger in London, on a pilgramage to Rome. And sure I had to show him the sights."

"It was a kindly action of you," said Doctor Chord, pulling the cork of the medicine-bottle. "Get those rags off," he called to Paddy, "and I'll rub you down as if you were the finest horse that ever followed the hounds."

There was a great smell of medicine in the air as he lubricated Paddy over the bruised places; then Jem Bottles came under his hands, and either he was not so much hurt as Paddy was, or he made less fuss about it, for he glared at the Doctor all the time he was attending him, and said nothing.

It seemed an inhospitable thing to misuse a man who had acted the good Samaritan so arduously as the little Doctor with three quarters of his bottle gone, but as he slapped the cork in it again I stepped to the door and turned the key. Paddy was scowling now and then, and groaning now and again, when the cheerful Doctor said to him, as is the way with physicians when they wish to encourage a patient:

"Oh, you're not hurt nearly as bad as you think you are. You'll be a little sore and stiff in the morning, that's all, and I'll leave the bottle with you."

"You've never rubbed me at all on the worst place," said Paddy angrily.

"Where was that?" asked Doctor Chord—and the words were hardly out of his mouth when Paddy hit him one in the right eye that sent him staggering across the room.

"There's where I got the blow that knocked me down," cried Paddy.

Doctor Chord threw a wild glance at the door, when Jem Bottles, with a little run and a lift of his foot, gave him one behind that caused the Doctor to turn a somersault.

"Take that, you thief," said Jem; "and now you've something that neither of us got, because we kept our faces to the villains that set on us."

Paddy made a rush, but I cried:

"Don't touch the man when he's down."

"Sure," says Paddy, "that's when they all fell on me."

"Never strike a man when he's down," I cried.

"Do ye mean to say we shouldn't hit a man when he's down?" asked Jem Bottles.

"You knew very well you shouldn't," I told him. "Sure you've been in the ring before now."

"That I have," shouted Bottles, pouncing on the unfortunate Doctor. He grabbed him by the scruff of the neck and flung him to his feet, then gave him a bat on the side of the head that sent him reeling up toward the ceiling again.

"That's enough, Jem," I cautioned him.

"I'm not only following the Doctor," said Jem, "but I'm following the Doctor's advice. He told us to take a little gentle exercise and it would allay the soreness."

"The exercise you're taking will not allay the soreness on the Doctor's part. Stop it, Jem! Now leave him alone, Paddy; he's had enough to remember you by, and to learn that the way of the traitor is the rocky road to Dublin. Come now, Doctor, the door is open; get out into the passage as quick as you can, and I hope you have another bottle of that excellent lotion at home."

The threatening attitude of both Jem and Paddy seemed to paralyse the little man with fear, and he lay on the boards glaring up at them with terror in his eyes.

"I'm holding the door open for you," said I, "and remember I may not be able to hold Paddy and Jem as easily as I hold the door; so make your escape before they get into action again."

Doctor Chord rolled himself over quickly, but, not daring to get on his feet, trotted out into the passage like a big dog on his hands and knees; and just then a waiter, coming up with a tray and not counting on this sudden apparition in the hallway, fell over him; and if it were not for my customary agility and presence of mind in grasping the broad metal server, a good part of my supper would have been on the floor. The waiter luckily leaned forward when he found himself falling, holding the tray high over his head, and so, seizing it, I saved the situation and the supper.

"What are ye grovelling down there for, ye drunken beast?" shouted the angry waiter, as he came down with a thud. "Why don't you walk on your two feet like a Christian?"

Doctor Chord took the hint and his departure, running along the passage and stumbling down the stairway like a man demented. When he got down into the courtyard he shook his fist at my window and swore he would have the law of us; but I never saw the little man again, although Paddy and Jem were destined to meet him once more, as I shall tell later on.

The supper being now laid, I fell at it and I disremember having ever enjoyed a meal more in my life. I sent Paddy and Jem to their quarters with food and a bottle of good wine to keep them company, and I think they deserved it, for they said the lotion the Doctor had put on the outside of them was stinging, so they thought there should be something in the inside to counteract the inconvenience.

I went to sleep the moment I touched the pillow, and dreamed I was in the most umbrageous lover's walk that ever was, overhung with green branches through which the sunlight flickered, and closed in with shrubbery. There I chased a flying nymph that always just eluded me, laughing at me over her shoulder and putting her finger to her lips, and at last, when I caught her, it turned out to be Doctor Chord, whereupon I threw him indignantly into the bushes, and then saw to my dismay it was the Countess. She began giving her opinion of me so vigorously that I awoke and found it broad daylight.

CHAPTER XXIX

AFTER a comforting and sustaining breakfast I sent for Paddy and Jem, both of whom came in limping.

"Are you no better this morning?" I asked them.

"Troth, we're worse," said Paddy with a most dismal look on his face.

"I'm sorry to hear it," said I; "but I think the trouble will wear off to-day if you lie snug and quiet in the inn. Here's this bottle of embrocation, or what is left of it, so you may take it with you and divide it fairly between you, remembering that one good rub deserves another, and that our chief duty on this earth is to help our fellow man; and as there's nothing like easy employment for making a man forget his tribulations, Jem will rub Paddy, and Paddy will rub Jem, and thus, God blessing you both, you will pass the time to your mutual bene-fit."

"Yer honour," sniffed Jem Bottles, "I like your own prescriptions better than Doctor Chord's. I have but small faith in the liniment; the bottle of wine you gave us last night—and I wish it had been as double as it made us see—was far better for our trouble than this stuff."

"I doubt it, Jem," said I, "for you're worse this morning than you were last night; so I'll change the treatment and go back to Doctor Chord's remedy, for sure the Doctor is a physician held in high esteem by the nobility of London. But you're welcome to a double mug of beer at my expense, only see that you don't take too much of that."

"Yer honour," said Jem, "it's only when we're sober that we fall upon affliction. We had not a drop to drink yesterday morn-ing, and see what happened us."

"It would have made no differ," I said, "if you had been as tipsy as the Earl himself is when dinner's over. Trust in Providence, Jem, and rub hard with the liniment, and you'll be a new man by the morrow morn."

With this I took my papers and the letter of introduction, and set out as brave as you please to find the Temple, which I thought would be a sort of a church, but which I found to be a most sober and respectable place very difficult for a stranger to find his way about in. But at last I came to the place where Mr. Josiah Brooks dispensed the law for a consideration to ignorant spalpeens like myself, that was less familiar with the head that had a gray wig on than with cracking heads by help of a good shillelah that didn't know what a wig was. As it was earlier in the morning than Mr. Brooks's usual hour I had to sit kicking my heels in a dismal panelled anteroom till the great lawyer came in. He was a smooth-faced serious-looking man, rather elderly, and he passed through the anteroom without so much as casting a look at me, and was followed by a melancholy man in rusty black who had told me to take a chair, holding in his hand the letter Lady Mary had written. After a short time the man came out again, and, treating me with more deference than when he bade me be seated, asked me kindly if I would step this way and Mr. Brooks would see me.

"You are Mr. O'Ruddy, I take it," he said in a tone which I think he thought was affable.

"I am."

"Have you brought with you the papers referred to in this letter?"

"I have."

And with that I slammed them down on the table before him. He untied the bundle and sorted out the different documents, apparently placing them in their right order. After this he adjusted his glasses more to his liking and glanced over the papers rapidly until he came to one that was smaller than the rest, and this he read through twice very carefully. Then he piled them up together at his right hand very neatly, for he seemed to have a habit of old maid's precision about him. He removed his glasses and looked across the table at me.

"Are you the son of the O'Ruddy here mentioned?"

"I am."

"His eldest son?"

"His only son."

"You can prove that, I suppose?"

"Troth, it was never disputed."

"I mean there would be no difficulty in getting legal and documentary proof."

"I think not, for my father said after my first fight, that it might be questioned whether I was my mother's son or no— there was no doubt that I was his."

The legal man drew down his brows at this, but made no comment as, in tones that betrayed little interest in the affair, he demanded:

"Why did your father not claim this property during his lifetime?"

"Well, you see, Mr. Brooks, my father was an honest man, and he never pretended the property was his. From what I remember of his conversation on the subject the Earl and him was in a tight place after a battle in France, and it was thought they would both be made prisoners. The Earl had his deeds with him, and if he were caught the enemy would demand a large ransom for him, for these would show him to be a man of property. So he made the estate over to my father, and my father ran the risk of being captured and taken for the Earl of Westport. Now that I have been made happy by the acquaintance of his lordship, I'm thinking that if my father had fallen into the hands of the enemy he might have remained there till this day without the Earl raising a hand to help him. Nobody in England would have disputed the Earl's ownership of his own place, which I understand has been in his family for hundreds of years, so they might very well have got on without the deeds, as in fact they have done. That's all I know about it."

"Then, sir," said Mr. Brooks, "do you intend to contest the ownership of the property on the strength of these documents?"

"I do," said I firmly.

"Very well. You must leave them with me for a few days until I get opinion upon them. I may say I have grave doubts of your succeeding in such litigation unless you can prove that your father gave reasonable consideration for the property made over to him."

"Troth, he'd no consideration to give except his own freedom and the loan of a pair of breeches, and it seems that the Earl never troubled his head whether he gave the first-named or not. He might have given his life for all the thanks his son got from my Lord of Westport."

"From a rapid glance at these instruments I can see that they may be of great value to his lordship, but I doubt their being of any value at all to you; in fact you might find the tables turned upon you, and be put in the position of a fraudulent claimant or a levier of blackmail."

"It's not blackmail I'm going to levy at all," cried I, "but the whitest of white mail. I have not the slightest intention of going into the courts of law; but, to tell you the plain truth about it, Lady Mary and me are going to get married in spite of all the Earls that ever drank, or all the Countesses that ever scolded. Now this dear girl has a great confidence in you, and she has sent me to you to find what's best to be done. I want nothing of this property at all. Sure I've estates enough of my own in Ireland, and a good castle forby, save that the roof leaks a little in places; but a bundle of straw will soon set that to rights, only old Patsy is so lazy through not getting his money regular. Now it struck me that if I went boldly to Brede Castle, or whatever it is, and took possession of it, there would first be the finest scrimmage any man ever saw outside of Ireland, and after that his lordship the Earl would say to me:

" 'O'Ruddy, my boy, my limbs are sore; can't we crack a bottle instead of our heads over this, and make a compromise?'

" 'Earl of Westport,' I'll say to him, 'a bottle will be but the beginning of it. We'll sit down at a table and settle this debate in ten minutes if you're reasonable.'

"He'll not be reasonable, of course, but you see what I have in my mind."

"Brede Place," said the lawyer slowly, "is not exactly a castle, but it's a very strong house and might be held by a dozen determined men against an army."

"Then once let me get legally inside, and I'll hold it till the

Earl gets more sense in his head than is there at the present moment."

"Possession," said Mr. Brooks, "is nine points of the law."

"It is with a woman," said I, thinking of something else.

"It is with an estate," answered Josiah severely.

"True for you," I admitted, coming back to the point at issue, for it was curious, in spite of the importance of the interview, how my mind kept wandering away to a locked room in the Earl of Westport's house, and to a shady path that ran around the edge of his garden.

"I intend to get possession of the Brede estate if I have to crack the crown of every man at present upon it. But I am an Irishman, and therefore a person of peace, and I wish to crack the crowns in accordance with the law of England, so I come to you for directions how it should be done."

"It is not my place," said Brooks, looking very sour, "to counsel a man to break either heads or the law. In fact it is altogether illegal to assault another unless you are in danger of your own life."

"The blessing of all the saints be upon you," said I, "yet, ever since I set foot in this land, coming across the boiling seas, entirely to do a kindness to the Earl of Westport, I have gone about in fear of my life."

"You have surely not been assaulted?" demanded Mr. Brooks, raising his eyebrows in surprise.

"Assaulted, is it? I have been set upon in every manner that is possible for a peace-lover to be interfered with. To tell you the truth, no longer ago than yesterday morning, as quiet and decent a Sunday as ever came down on London, my two innocent servants, garrulous creatures that wouldn't hurt a fly, were lured into the high walled garden of the Earl of Westport to see the flowers which both of them love, and there they were pounced upon by the whole bodyguard of my lord the Earl, while himself and his quiet-mannered Countess were there to urge them on. Doctor Chord, a little snobbish creature, basking in the smiles of their noble countenances, stood by and gave medical advice showing where best to hit the poor innocent unfortunates that had fallen into their hands."

"Tut, tut!" said Josiah Brooks, his face frowning like a storm-cloud over the hills of Donegal. "If such is indeed the case, an action would lie——"

"Oh, well and as far as that goes, so would Doctor Chord, and all the rest that was there. My poor lads lie now, bruised and sore, in the upper rooms of the stable at the Pig and Turnip. They want no more action, I can tell you, nor lying either."

"You can prove, then," said the lawyer, "that you have suffered violence from the outset."

"Indeed and I could."

"Well, well, we must look into the matter. You recite a most curious accumulation of offences, each of which bears a serious penalty according to the law of England. But there is another matter mentioned in Lady Mary's letter which is even more grave than any yet alluded to."

"And what is that?" I asked in surprise.

"She says that she wishes to have advanced to you, upon the security of these papers, five hundred golden guineas."

"Do you tell me that now?" I cried with delight. "Sure I have always said that Mary was the most sensible girl within the boundaries of this realm."

"That may all be; but women, you see, know little of money or the methods of obtaining it."

"You're right in that," I admitted. "It's the other end of the stick they hold; they know a good deal of the way of spending it."

"You will understand," went on Mr. Brooks, "that if money is to be raised on the security of these documents, your rights in possessing them must be severely scrutinized, while—you will pardon my saying so—the security of your estates in Ireland might be looked at askance by the money-lenders of London."

"Oh, don't let the estates in Ireland trouble you, for the money-lenders of Dublin have already mortgaged them a foot deep. You can raise little on my estates in Ireland but the best turf you ever burned, and that's raised with a spade."

"Very well," said Josiah Brooks, gathering up the papers and tying them together with a bit of red ribbon which he took out of his drawer, ignoring the Irish cord that had held them through all their emergencies. "Very well, I shall seek advice and let you know the result."

"Seek advice," I cried. "Sure a man of your attainments doesn't need to seek advice of anyone. Aren't you learned in the law yourself?"

"I must have counsel's opinion," said Josiah solemnly, as if he were speaking of the decisions of Providence.

"Well, you astonish me, Mr. Brooks, for I thought you knew it all, and that's why I came to you; but perhaps it's only your own modesty that makes you reluctant to speak of your attainments, though I suppose what you really mean is that you want to take a pipe in your mouth and a glass of good liquor at your elbow and read the papers at your leisure."

Mr. Josiah Brooks was a solemn man, and he did not appear to relish the picture I so graphically drew of him, when in truth I was thinking only of his own comfort; so I changed the subject with an alertness of mind which perhaps he was incapable of appreciating.

"How far from London is this estate of Brede?" I asked, "and how do you get to it?"

"It is fifty or sixty miles away," he said, "and lies in the county of Sussex, close to the sea, but not on it. If you wish to visit Brede estate," he went on, as if I had not been telling him I was going to do that very thing in force, "if you wish to visit Brede estate, the best plan is to go to Rye and there engage a guide who will lead you to it."

"Rye," said I in astonishment, wondering where I had heard the name before; then, suddenly remembering, I said:

"Rye is a seaport town, is it not?"

"It is," agreed Mr. Brooks.

"Rye is the spot," rejoined I, "where Father Donovan will embark on his pilgrimage to Rome. Sure, and I'm glad to hear that, for the good old man and I will travel there together, and the blessing of Providence will surround me, which I hope will be helpful if the Earl's cut-throats bar the way, as is more than likely."

"Very well, Mr. O'Ruddy, as you are doubtless impatient to know the result, you may call upon me tomorrow afternoon at four o'clock, and I may be in a position to give you more information than I can offer at present."

I took that as a dismissal, and, getting up, shook him warmly by the hand, although his arm was as stiff as a pump handle, and he seemed to take little pleasure in the farewell. And so I left the Temple, that was as lonely as the road between Innishannon and the sea, and trudged out into Fleet Street, which was as lively as Skibbereen Fair. I was so overjoyed to find that my journey lay in the same direction as Father Donovan's that I tramped on westward till after some trouble I found the priest's house in which he was stopping, to tell the good father that I would go part of the way to Rome with him. He was indeed delighted to see me, and introduced me to his host, Father Kilnane, nearly as fine a man and as good a priest as Father Donovan himself.

We had dinner there all together at mid-day, and I invited Father Donovan to come out and see the town with me, which he did. The peaceful father clung to my arm in a kind of terror at what he was witnessing, for he was as innocent of the ways of a big town as if he had been a gossoon from a hedge-school in Ireland. Yet he was mightily interested in all he saw, and asked me many thousand questions that day, and if I did not know the correct answer to them, it made no differ to Father Donovan, for he did not know the answer himself and took any explanation as if it was as true as the gospels he studied and preached.

Daylight was gone before we got back to the house he lodged in, and nothing would do but I must come in and have a bit of supper, although I told him that supper would be waiting for me at the Pig and Turnip. It had been agreed between us that we would travel together as far as Rye, and that there I should see him off on his tempestuous voyage to Dunkirk or Calais, as the case might be. The old man was mightily delighted to find that our ways lay together through the south of England. He was pleased to hear that I had determined on my rights through the courts of law, with no more sword-playing and violence, which, to tell the truth, until it reached its height, the old man was always against; although, when a quarrel came to its utmost interesting point, I have seen Father

Donovan fidget in his cassock, and his eyes sparkle with the glow of battle, although up till then he had done his best to prevent the conflict.

It was getting late when I neared the Pig and Turnip, and there was a good deal of turmoil in the streets. I saw one or two pretty debates, but, remembering my new resolution to abide by law and order, I came safely past them and turned up the less-frequented street that held my inn, when at the corner, under the big lamp, a young man with something of a swagger about him, in spite of the meanness of his dress, came out from the shadow of the wall and looked me hard in the face.

"Could you direct me, sir, to a hostelry they call the Pig and Turnip?" he asked with great civility.

"If you will come with me," said I, "I'll bring you to the place itself, for that's where I'm stopping."

"Is it possible," he said, "that I have the honour of addressing The O'Ruddy?"

"That great privilege is yours," said I, coming to a standstill in the middle of the street, as I saw the young man had his sword drawn and pressed close against his side to allay suspicion. I forgot all about law and order, and had my own blade free of the scabbard on the instant; but the young man spoke smoothly and made no motion of attack, which was very wise of him.

"Mr. O'Ruddy," he says, "we are both men of the world and sensible men and men of peace. Where two gentlemen, one down on his luck and the other in prosperity, have a private matter to discuss between them, I think this discussion should take place quietly and in even tones of voice."

"Sir," said I, giving my sword-hand a little shake, so that the weapon settled down into its place, "Sir, you express my sentiments exactly, and as you are a stranger to me perhaps you will be good enough to announce the subject that concerns us."

"I may say at the outset," he remarked almost in a whisper, so polite he was, "that I have eight good swordsmen at my back, who are not visible until I give the signal; therefore you see, sir, that your chances are of the slightest if I should be compelled to call upon them. I know the fame of The O'Ruddy as a swordsman, and you may take it as a compliment, sir, that I should hesitate to meet you alone. So much for saving my own skin, but I am a kindly man and would like to save your skin as well. Therefore if you will be kind enough to hand to me the papers which you carry in your pocket, you will put me under strong obligations, and at the same time sleep peaceably tonight at the Pig and Turnip instead of here in the gutter, to be picked up by the watch, for I can assure you, sir, as a man that knows the town, the watch will not be here to save you whatever outcry you may make."

"I am obliged to you, sir, for your discourse and your warning, to both of which I have paid strict attention; and in the interests of that peace which we are each of us so loath to break I may announce to you that the papers you speak of are not in my possession."

"Pardon me, sir, but they must be; for we have searched your room thoroughly, and we have also searched your servants."

"A thief of the night," cried I with mighty indignation, "may easily search an honest man's room; and his poor servants, beaten and bruised by your master's orders, would fall easy victims to the strength and numbers of your ruffians; but you will find it a difficult matter to search me."

"Sir," he replied, bowing as polite as Palermo, "I grieve to state that you are in error. The searching of both your servants and your rooms was accomplished, not through the employment of force, but by the power of money. Your servants insisted they had nothing on their persons but liniment, and they accepted one gold piece each to allow me to verify their statements. Another gold piece gave me, for a time, the freedom of your room. If you have not the papers upon you, then there is no harm in allowing me to run my hand over your clothes, because the package is a bulky one and I will speedily corroborate your statement."

"Sir," said I, not to be outdone in courtesy by this gentleman of the gutter, "I will tell you truthfully that I have nothing on me but my sword, and to that you are quite welcome if you leave to me the choice of which end I hold and which I present to you"—and with that I sprang with my back to the wall, under the lamp, leaving myself partially in shadow, but having spread in front of me a semicircle of light which any assailant attacking must cross, or indeed remain in its effulgence if he would keep free of the point of my blade.

"It grieves me to find that you are a man of violence," replied the scoundrel in the mildest of tones, "and you will bear witness afterward that I did my best to keep you from harm."

"I freely acknowledge it now," said I. "Bring on your men."

To tell the truth, I had no belief at all in the existence of his force, and thought he was playing a game on me, hoping to take me unawares; for if the man knew anything at all he must have known what a swordsman I was, and it was no charge of cowardice against him that he was loath to come to close quarters with me. I speedily discovered, however, that all he said was true; for he gave a low whistle, and out of the darkness instantly sprang seven or eight as malicious-looking villains as a man would care to see, each one with a sword in his hand.

As many erroneous and exaggerated accounts of this encounter have been given in the coffee-houses, and even in the public prints, it is well that I should now tell the truth about it. No man that has the hang of his blade need fear the onset of a mob except in one case, and that is this—if the whole eight set upon me at once with every sword extended, there was a chance that though I might, by great expertness, disable half of them, the other half would run me through. But it should never be forgotten that these men were fighting for money, and I was fighting for my life, and that makes all the difference in the world. Each man makes a show of attack, but he holds off, hoping that one of the others will dare to thrust. This is fatal to success, but not necessarily fatal to their intended victim. An active man with a wall at his back can generally account for all that comes in front of him if he is deeply in earnest and has not too much liquor in him. It astonished London that I was able to defeat eight men, each one of whom was armed as efficiently as myself; but, as my father used to say, if you are not wholly taken up with the determination to have a man's life, you may pink him in what spot you choose if you give a little thought to the matter. The great object is the disarming of the enemy. Now, if you give a man a jab in the knuckles, or if you run your blade delicately up his arm from the wrist to the elbow, this is what happens. The man involuntarily yells out, and as involuntarily drops his sword on the flags. If you prick a man on the knuckle-bone, he will leave go his sword before he has time to think, it being an action entirely unconscious on his part, just like winking your eye or drawing your breath; yet I have seen men run through the body who kept sword in hand and made a beautiful lunge with it even as they staggered across the threshold of death's door.

Now I had no desire for any of these men's lives, but I determined to have their swords. I glittered my own shining blade before their eyes, flourishing a semicircle with it, and making it dart here and there like the tongue of an angry snake; and instantly every man in front of me felt uncomfortable, not knowing where the snake was going to sting, and then, as I said before, they were fighting for money and not for honour. When I had dazzled their eyes for a moment with this sword-play and bewildered their dull brains, I suddenly changed my tactics and thrust forward quicker than you can count one, two, three, four, five, six, seven, eight—and each man was holding a bleeding fist to his mouth, while the swords clattered on the cobbles like hail on the copper roof of a cathedral. It was the most beautiful and complete thing I ever saw. I then swept the unarmed men back a pace or two with a flirt of my weapon, and walked up the pavement, kicking the swords together till they lay in a heap at my feet. The chief ruffian stood there dazed, with his sword still in his hand, for he had stepped outside the circle, he acting as captain, and depending on the men to do the work.

"Drop that," I shouted, turning on him, and he flung his sword in the street as if it was red hot.

"Sir," said I to him, "a sword in your hand is merely an inconvenience to you; see if you don't look better with an armful of them. Pick up these nine blades in a bundle and walk on before me to the Pig and Turnip. When we come into the courtyard of that tavern, you are to turn round and make me the lowest bow you can without rubbing your nose against the pavement. Then you will say, as gracefully as the words can be uttered:

" 'Mr. O'Ruddy,' you say, 'these swords are yours by right of conquest. You have defeated nine armed men tonight in less than as many minutes, so I present you with the spoil.' Then you will bow to the people assembled in the courtyard—for there is aways a mob of them there, late and early—and you will make another low obeisance to me. If you do all this acceptably to my sense of politeness, I will let you go unmolested; but if you do otherwise, I will split your gullet for you."

"Sir," said the captain, "I accept your terms."

With that he stooped and picked up the bundle of weapons, marching on stolidly before me till he came to the Pig and Turnip. All the rest had disappeared in the darkness, and had gone to their dens, very likely to nurse sore knuckles and regret the loss of good stout blades.

Our coming to the tavern caused a commotion, as you may well imagine; and although I don't make too much of the encounter, yet it is my belief that such an incident never happened in London before. The captain carried out his part of the presentation with an air of deference and a choice of good language that charmed me; then he backed out under the archway to the street, bowing six or seven times as he went. I had never any fault to find with the man's manner. Paddy and Jem, now seemingly quite recovered from their misusage of Sunday, stood back of the group with eyes and mouths open, gazing upon me with an admiration I could not but appreciate.

"Come out of that," said I, "and take this cutlery up to my room," and they did.

I sat down at the table and wrote a letter to Mr. Brooks.

"Sir," said I in it, "I don't know whether I am plaintiff or defendant in the suit that's coming on, but whichever it is here's a bundle of legal evidence for your use. You mentioned the word 'violence' to me when I had the pleasure of calling on you. This night I was set upon by nine ruffians, who demanded from me the papers now in your possession. I took their knives from them, so they would not hurt themselves or other people, and I send you these knives to be filed for reference."

I tied up the swords in two bundles, and in the morning sent Paddy and Jem off with them and the letter to the Temple, which caused great commotion in that peaceable quarter of the city, and sent forth the rumour that all the lawyers were to be at each other's throats next day.

CHAPTER XXX

IN the afternoon I went slowly to the Temple, thinking a good deal on the way. It's truth I tell, that in spite of the victory of the night before I walked to the Temple rather downhearted. Whether Josiah Brooks was an attorney, or a barrister, or a solicitor, or a plain lawyer, I don't know to this day, and I never could get my mind to grasp the distinction that lies between those names in that trade; but whichever it was it seemed to me he was a cold, unenthusiastic man, and that he thought very little indeed of my game. There is small pleasure in litigation in England as compared with the delight of the law in the old Ark. If I had gone to see a lawyer in Dublin or Cork he would have been wild with excitement before I had got half through my story. He would have slapped me on the back and shook me by the hand, and cried "Whurroo" at the prospect of a contest. My quarrel would have been his before I had been ten minutes in his presence, and he would have entered into the spirit of the fight as if he were the principal in it instead of merely acting for him; but in this gloomy country of England, where they engage upon a lawsuit, not with delight, but as if they were preparing for a funeral, there is no enjoyment in the courts at all at all. I wished I could transfer the case to the old turf, where there is more joy in being defeated than there is in winning in England; for I have seen the opposing lawyers rise from the most gentlemanly and elegant language you ever heard to a heated debate; then fling books at each other, and finally clench, while the judge stood up and saw fair play. But this man Brooks was so calm and collected and uninterested that he fairly discouraged me, and I saw that I was going to get neither the money I needed nor the support I expected from him.

As I went up his dark stairway in the Temple and came to

the passage that led to the outer room, I saw standing in a corner the two bundles of swords I had sent him, as if he had cast them out, which indeed he had done. After some delay in the outer room, the melancholy man in rusty black asked me, would I go in, and there sat Josiah Brooks at his table as if he had never left it since I took my departure the day before. He looked across at me with a scrutiny which seemed to be mingled with dislike and disapproval.

"Mr. O'Ruddy," he said, quiet-like, "it is not customary to send to a law office a number of swords, which are entirely out of place in such rooms. They have been counted and are found to number nine. I shall be obliged if you sign this receipt for them, accept delivery of the same, and remove them from the premises at your earliest convenience."

So I signed the receipt without a word and handed it back to him. Then I said:

"I will send my servant for the swords as soon as I return to the inn."

He inclined his head the merest trifle, drew some papers toward him, and adjusted his glasses.

"It is my duty to tell you, Mr. O'Ruddy, that if you go into the courts with this case you will assuredly be defeated, and the costs will follow. There is also a possibility that when the civil proceedings are determined a criminal action against yourself may ensue."

"I told you, sir," said I, with my heart sinking, "I had no intention of troubling the courts at all at all. In the land I come from we are more inclined to settle a case with a good stout blackthorn than with the aid of a lawyer's wig. These papers say in black and white that I am the owner of Brede estate, and I intend to take possession of it."

"It is only right to add," continued Brooks, with that great air of calm I found so exasperating, "it is only right to add that you are in a position to cause great annoyance to the Earl of Westport. You can at least cast doubt on his title to the estate; and he stands this jeopardy, that if contrary to opinion your cause should prove successful—and we must never forget that the law is very uncertain—the Earl would have to account for the moneys he has drawn from the estate, which would run into many thousands of pounds, and, together with the loss of the property, would confront his lordship with a most serious situation. Your case, therefore, though weak from a strictly legal point of view, is exceptionally strong as a basis for compromise."

These words cheered me more than I can say, and it is an extraordinary fact that his frozen, even tone, and his lack of all interest in the proceedings had an elevating effect upon my spirits which I could not have believed possible.

"As it is a compromise that I'm after," said I, "what better case can we want?"

"Quite so," he resumed; "but as there is no encouragement in the strictly legal aspect of the plea, you will understand that no money-lender in London will advance a farthing on such unstable security. Even though I am acting in your interests, I could not take the responsibility of advising any capitalist to advance money on such uncertain tenure."

This threw me into the depths again; for, although I never care to meet trouble half way, I could not conceal from myself the fact that my bill at the Pig and Turnip had already reached proportions which left me no alternative but to slip quietly away in liquidation of the account. This was a thing I never liked to do; and when I am compelled to make that settlement I always take note of the amount, so that I may pay it if I am ever that way again and have more money than I need at the moment. Even if I succeeded in getting away from the inn, what could I do at Brede with no money at all, for in that part of the country they would certainly look upon the Earl of Westport as the real owner of the property, and on me as a mere interloper; and if I could not get money on the documents in London, there was little chance of getting credit even for food at Brede.

"It is rather a blue look-out then," said I as cheerfully as I could.

"From a legal standpoint it is," concurred Mr. Brooks, as unconcerned as if his own payment did not depend on my raising the wind with these papers. "However, I have been instructed by a person who need not be named, who has indeed stipulated that no name shall be mentioned, to advance you the sum of five hundred guineas, which I have here in my drawer, and which I will now proceed to count out to you if you, in the meantime, will sign this receipt, which acquits me of all responsibility and certifies that I have handed the money over to you without rebate or reduction."

And with that the man pulled open a drawer and began to count out the glittering gold.

I sprang to my feet and brought my fist down on the table with a thump. "Now, by the Great Book of Kells, what do you mean by chopping and changing like a rudderless lugger in a ten-knot breeze? If the expedition is possible, and you had the money in your drawer all the time, why couldn't you have spoken it out like a man, without raising me to the roof and dropping me into the cellar in the way you've done?"

The man looked unruffled across the table at me. He pushed a paper a little farther from him, and said without any trace of emotion:

"Will you sign that receipt at the bottom, if you please?"

I sat down and signed it, but I would rather have jabbed a pen between his close-set lips to give him a taste of his own ink. Then I sat quiet and watched him count the gold, placing it all in neat little pillars before him. When it was finished, he said:

"Will you check the amount?"

"Is that gold mine?" I asked him.

"It is," he replied.

So I rose up without more ado and shovelled it into my pockets, and he put the receipt into the drawer after reading it over carefully, and arched his eyebrows without saying anything when he saw me pocket the coins uncounted.

"I wish you good afternoon," said I.

"I have to detain you one moment longer," he replied. "I have it on the most trustworthy information that the Earl of Westport is already aware of your intention to proceed to the country estate alleged to be owned by him. Your outgoings and incomings are watched, and I have to inform you that unless you proceed to Rye with extreme caution there is likelihood that you may be waylaid, and perchance violence offered to you."

"In that case I will reap a few more swords; but you need not fear, I shall not trouble you with them."

"They are out of place in a solicitor's chamber," he murmured gently. "Is there anything further I can do for you?"

"Yes," I said, "there is one thing more. I would be obliged if you could make me a bundle of legal-looking papers that are of no further use to you: a sheet of that parchment, and some of the blue stuff like what I carried. The Earl seems determined to have a packet of papers from me, and I would like to oblige him, as he's going to be my father-in-law, although he doesn't know it. I'd like some writing on these papers—Latin for preference."

Josiah Brooks thought steadily for a few moments, then he called out and the melancholy rusty man came in. He took a few instructions and went out again. After a long time he entered once more and placed on the table a packet I would have sworn was my own. This the lawyer handed to me without a word, and the rusty man held open the door for me. So, with the bogus papers in my pocket, not to mention the genuine gold, I took my leave of Josiah and the Temple.

As soon as I was outside I saw at once that there was no time to be lost. If the Earl had guessed my intention, as was hinted, what would he do? Whenever I wish to answer a question like that to myself, I think what would I do if I were in the position of the other man. Now what I would have done, was this, if I were the Earl of Westport. I would send down to Brede all the ruffians at my disposal and garrison the house with them; and if the Earl did this, I would be on the outside, and he on the inside with advantage over me accordingly. Most men fight better behind stone walls than out in the open; and, besides, a few men can garrison a barracks that five hundred cannot take by assault. However, as it turned out, I was crediting the Earl with brains equal to my own, which in truth neither he nor any of his followers had below their bonnets. He trusted to intercepting me on the highway, just as if he hadn't already failed in that trick. But it takes a score of failures to convince an Englishman that he is on the wrong track altogether, while an Irishman has so many plans in his head that there's never time to try one of them twice in succession. But if I was wrong about the Earl, I was right about his daughter, when I suspected that she gave the lawyer the information about the Earl's knowledge of my plans, and I was also right when I credited the dear girl with drawing on her own funds to give me the golden guineas—"and may each one of them," said I to myself, "prove a golden blessing on her head."

At any rate, there was no time to be lost, so I made straight to Father Donovan and asked him would he be ready to begin the journey to Rye after an early breakfast with me at the Pig and Turnip.

You never saw a man in your life so delighted at the prospect of leaving London as was Father Donovan, and indeed I was glad to get away from the place myself. The good father said the big town confused him; and, although he was glad to have seen it, he was more happy still to get out of it and breathe a breath of fresh country air once more. So it was arranged that he would come to the Pig and Turnip next morning between six and seven o'clock. I then turned back to the shop of a tailor who for a long time had had two suits of clothing waiting for me that were entirely elegant in their design. The tailor, however, would not take the word of a gentleman that payment would follow the delivery of the costumes; for a little later would be more convenient for me to give him the money, and this made me doubt, in spite of the buttons and gold lace, if the garments were quite the fashionable cut, because a tailor who demands money on the spot shows he is entirely unaccustomed to deal with the upper classes; but I needed these clothes, as the two suits I possessed were getting a little the worse for wear.

When I went into his shop he was inclined to be haughty, thinking I had come to ask credit again; but when he saw the glitter of the money the man became obsequious to a degree that I never had witnessed before. I was affable to him, but distant; and when he offered me everything that was in his shop, I told him I would take time and consider it. He sent a servant following behind me with the goods, and so I came once more to the Pig and Turnip, where I ordered Paddy and Jem to go to the Temple and fetch away the swords.

There seemed to be a pleased surprise on the face of the

landlord when I called for my bill and paid it without question, chiding him for his delay in not sending it before. I engaged a horse for Father Donovan to ride on the following morning, and ordered breakfast ready at six o'clock, although I gave my commands that I was to be wakened an hour before daylight.

I spent the rest of the day in my room with Paddy and Jem, trying to knock into their heads some little notion of geography, wishing to make certain that they would sooner or later arrive in Rye without stumbling in on Belfast while on the way. My own knowledge of the face of the country was but meagre, so the landlord brought in a rough map of the south of England, and I cautioned the lads to get across London Bridge and make for the town of Maidstone, from where they could go due south, and if they happened on the coast they were to inquire for Rye and stay there until further orders. Jem Bottles, who thought he had brains in his head, said he would not be so open in telling everyone we were going to Rye if he was me, because he was sure the Earl had people on the look-out, and money was plenty with his lordship. If everyone knew when we were taking our departure, there would be no difficulty in following us and overcoming us on some lonely part of the road.

"Jem," said I, "that's all very true; but when they attacked us before they got very little change for their trouble; and if you are afraid of some slight commotion on the road, then you can stay back here in London."

"I am not afraid at all," said Jem, "but if there's anything particular you would like to see in Rye, there's no use in blocking the road to it."

"Sure, Jem, then be quiet about it."

Turning to the landlord, who was standing by, I said to him:

"My men fear we are going to be intercepted, so I think if I began the journey some time before daylight, and they followed me soon after, I might slip away unnoticed."

The landlord scratched his head and crinkled up his brow, for to think was unusual with him.

"I don't see," he said at last, "what you have to gain by going separately. It seems to me it would be better to go in a body, and then, if you are set on, there are three instead of one."

"Very well," said I, "I'll take your caution into consideration, and act upon it or not as seems best when the time comes."

I told Paddy and Jem to sleep that night on the floor of my own room, and cautioned them to wake me an hour before daylight at the latest. Jem slept through until I had to kick him into consciousness; but poor Paddy, on the other hand, wakened me four times during the night—the first time two hours after I had gone to sleep, and I could have cudgelled him for his pains, only I knew the lad's intentions were good. The last time I could stand it no longer, although it was still earlier than the hour I had said, so I got up and dressed myself in one of my new suits.

"And here, Paddy," said I, "you will wear the costume I had on yesterday."

"I couldn't think of it," said Paddy, drawing back from the grandeur.

"You are not to think, you impudent gossoon, but to do as I tell you. Put them on, and be as quick as you can."

"Troth, yer honour," said Paddy, still shrinking from them, "they're too grand for the likes o' me, an' few will be able to tell the differ atween us."

"You conceited spalpeen, do ye think there's no difference between us but what the clothes make? Get into them. I intend certain other people to take you for me in the dark, and I can warrant you these clothes, grand as you think them, will be very soundly beaten before this day is done with."

"Ochone, ochone," moaned Paddy, "am I to get another beating already, and some of the bruises not yet off my flesh?"

"Put on the coat now, and don't do so much talking. Sure it's all in the day's work, and I promise you before long you'll have your revenge on them."

"It's not revenge I'm after," wailed Paddy, "but a whole skin."

"Now you're transformed into a gentleman," said I, "and many a lad would take a beating for the privilege of wearing such gorgeous raiment. Here is a packet of paper that you're to keep in your pocket till it's taken away from you. And now I'll help you to saddle the horse, and once you're across London Bridge you'll likely come upon Maidstone and Rye some time in your life, for you can't get back over the river again except by the same bridge, so you'll know it when you come to it."

And so I mounted Paddy in the courtyard; the sleepy watchman undid the bolts in the big gate in the archway; and my man rode out into the darkness in no very cheerful humour over his journey. I came back and took forty winks more in the arm-chair, then, with much difficulty, I roused Jem Bottles. He also, without a murmur, but with much pride in his dressing, put on the second of my discarded suits, and seemed to fancy himself mightily in his new gear. With plenty of cord I tied and retied the two bundles of swords and placed them across the horse in front of his saddle, and it was not yet daylight when Jem jingled out into the street like a moving armoury. Two huge pistols were in his holsters, loaded and ready to his hand.

"By the saints," said Jem proudly, "the man that meddles with me shall get hot lead or cold steel for his breakfast," and with that he went off at a canter, waking the echoes with the clash of his horse's shoes on the cobble-stones.

I went up stairs again and threw myself down on the bed and slept peacefully with no Paddy to rouse me until half-past-six, when a drawer knocked at the door and said that a priest that was downstairs would be glad to see me. I had him up in a jiffy, and a hot breakfast following fast on his heels, which we both laid in in quantities, for neither of us knew where our next meal was to be. However, the good father paid little thought to the future as long as the present meal was well served and satisfactory. He had no more idea than a spring lamb how we were to get to Rye, but thought perhaps a coach set out at that hour in the morning. When I told him I had a horse saddled and waiting for him, he was pleased, for Father Donovan could scamper across the country in Ireland with the best of them. So far as I could judge, the coast was clear, for everyone we met between the Pig and Turnip and the bridge seemed honest folk intent on getting early to their work. It was ten minutes past seven when we clattered across the bridge and set our faces toward Rye.

CHAPTER XXXI

LOOKING back over my long life I scarcely remember any day more pleasant than that I spent riding side by side with Father Donovan from London to Rye. The fine old man had a fund of entertaining stories, and although I had heard them over and over again there was always something fresh in his way of telling them, and now and then I recognized a narrative that had once made two separate stories, but which had now become welded into one in the old man's mind. There was never anything gloomy in these anecdotes, for they always showed the cheerful side of life and gave courage to the man that wanted to do right; for in all of Father Donovan's stories the virtuous were always made happy. We talked of our friends and acquaintances, and if he ever knew anything bad about a man he never told it; while if I mentioned it he could always say something good of him to balance it, or at least to mitigate the opinion that might be formed of it. He was always doing some man a good turn or speaking a comforting word for him.

"O'Ruddy," he said, "I spent most of the day yesterday writing letters to those that could read them in our part of Ireland, setting right the rumours that had come back to us, which said you were fighting duels and engaged in brawls, but the strangest story of all was the one about your forming a friendship with a highwayman, who, they said, committed robberies on the road and divided the spoil with you, and here I find you without a servant at all at all, leading a quiet, respectable life at a quiet, respectable inn. It's not even in a tavern that I first come across you, but kneeling devoutly, saying a prayer in your mother church. I see you leaving your inn having paid your bill like a gentleman, when they said you took night-leave of most of the hostelries in England. Dear me, and there was the landlord bowing to you as if you were a prince, and all his servants in a row with the utmost respect for you. Ah, O'Ruddy, it's men like you that gives the good name to Ireland, and causes her to be looked up to by all the people of the world."

I gave Father Donovan heartfelt thanks for his kindness, and prayed to myself that we would not come upon Jem Bottles on the road, and that we would be left unmolested on our journey until we saw the seacoast. Of course, if we were set upon, it would not be my fault, and it's not likely he would blame me; but if we came on Bottles, he was inclined to be very easy in conversation, and, in spite of my warnings, would let slip words that would shock the old priest. But when a day begins too auspiciously, its luck is apt to change before the sun sets, as it was with me.

It was nearing mid-day, and we were beginning to feel a trifle hungry, yet were in a part of the country that gave little promise of an inn, for it was a lonely place with heath on each side of the road, and, further on, a bit of forest. About half-way through this wooded plain an astonishing sight met my eyes. Two saddled horses were tied to a tree, and by the side of the road appeared to be a heap of nine or ten saddles, on one of which a man was sitting, comfortably eating a bit of bread, while on another a second man, whose head was tied up in a white cloth, lay back in a recumbent position, held upright by the saddlery. Coming closer, I was disturbed to see that the man eating was Jem Bottles, while the other was undoubtedly poor Paddy, although his clothes were so badly torn that I had difficulty in recognizing them as my own. As we drew up Jem stood and saluted with his mouth full, while Paddy groaned deeply. I was off my horse at once and ran to Paddy.

"Where are ye hurted?" said I.

"I'm killed," said Paddy.

"I've done the best I could for him," put in Jem Bottles. "He'll be all right in a day or two."

"I'll not," said Paddy, with more strength than one would suspect; "I'll not be all right in a day or two, nor in a week or two, nor in a month or two, nor in a year or two; I'm killed entirely."

"You're not," said Bottles. "When I was on the highway I never minded a little clip like that."

"Hush, Bottles," said I, "you talk altogether too much. Paddy," cried I, "get on your feet, and show yer manners here to Father Donovan."

Paddy got on his feet with a celerity which his former attitude would not have allowed one to believe possible.

"My poor boy!" said the kindly priest; "who has misused you?" and he put his two hands on the sore head.

"About two miles from here," said Paddy, "I was set on by a score of men——"

"There was only nine of them," interrupted Jem, "count the saddles."

"They came on me so sudden and unexpected that I was off my horse before I knew there was a man within reach. They had me down before I could say my prayers, and cudgelled me sorely, tearing my clothes, and they took away the packet of papers you gave me, sir. Sure I tried to guard it with my life, an' they nearly took both."

"I am certain you did your best, Paddy," said I; "and it's sorry I am to see you injured."

"Then they rode away, leaving me, sore wounded, sitting on the side of the road," continued Paddy. "After a while I come to myself, for I seemed dazed; and, my horse peacefully grazing beside me, I managed to get on its back, and turned toward London in the hope of meeting you; but instead of meeting you, sir, I came upon Jem with his pile of saddles, and he bound up my head and did what he could to save me, although I've a great thirst on me at this moment that's difficult to deal with."

"There's a ditch by the side of the road," said the priest.

"Yes," said Paddy sadly; "I tried some of that."

I went to my pack on the horse and took out a bottle and a leather cup. Paddy drank and smacked his lips with an ecstasy that gave us hope for his ultimate recovery. Jem Bottles laughed, and to close his mouth I gave him also some of the wine.

"I hope," said Father Donovan with indignation, "that the miscreant who misused you will be caught and punished."

"I punished them," said Jem, drawing the back of his hand across his mouth.

"We'll hear about it another time," said I, having my suspicions.

"Let the good man go on," begged Father Donovan, who is not without human curiosity.

Jem needed no second bidding.

"Your Reverence," he said, "I was jogging quietly on as a decent man should, when, coming to the edge of this forest, I saw approach me a party of horsemen, who were very hilarious and laughed loudly. If you look up and down the road and see how lonely it is, and then look at the wood, with no hedge between it and the highway, you'll notice the place was designed by Providence for such a meeting."

"Sure the public road is designed as a place for travellers to meet," said the father, somewhat bewildered by the harangue.

"Your Reverence is right, but this place could not afford better accommodation if I had made it myself. I struck into the wood before they saw me, tore the black lining from my hat, punched two holes in it for the eyes, and tied it around my forehead, letting it hang down over my face; then I primed my two pistols and waited for the gentlemen. When they were nearly opposite, a touch of the heels to my horse's flank was enough, and out he sprang into the middle of the road.

" 'Stand and deliver!' I cried, pointing the pistols at them, the words coming as glibly to my lips as if I had said them no later ago than yesterday. 'Stand and deliver, ye——' " and here Jem glibly rattled out a stream of profane appellatives which was disgraceful to listen to.

"Tut, tut, Jem," I said, "you shouldn't speak like that. Anyway we'll hear the rest another time."

"That's what I called them, sir," said Jem, turning to me with surprise, "you surely would not have me tell an untruth."

"I wouldn't have you tell anything. Keep quiet. Father Donovan is not interested in your recital."

"I beg your pardon, O'Ruddy," said Father Donovan, looking at me reproachfully; "but I am very much interested in this man's narrative."

"As any good man should be," continued Jem, "for these were arrant scoundrels; one of them I knew, and his name is Doctor Chord. He fell off his horse on the roadway at once and pleaded for mercy. I ordered the others instantly to hold their hands above their heads, and they did so, except one man who began fumbling in his holster, and then, to show him what I could do with a pistol, I broke his wrist. At the sound of the shot the horses began to plunge, nearly trampling Doctor Chord into the dust.

" 'Clasp your hands above your heads, ye——' "

Here went on another stream of terrible language again, and in despair I sat down on the pile of saddles, allowing things to take their course. Jem continued:

"The lesson of the pistol was not misread by my gentlemen, when they noticed I had a second loaded one; so, going to them one after the other, I took their weapons from them and flung them to the foot of that tree, where, if you look, you may see them now. Then I took a contribution from each one, just as you do in church, your Reverence. I'm sure you have a collection for the poor, and that was the one I was taking up this day. I have not counted them yet," said the villain turning to me, "but I think I have between sixty and seventy guineas, which are all freely at your disposal, excepting a trifle for myself and Paddy there. There's no plaster like gold for a sore head, your Reverence. I made each one of them dismount and take off his saddle and throw it in the pile; then I had them mount again and drove them with curses toward London, and very glad they were to escape."

"He did not get the papers again," wailed Paddy, who was not taking as jubilant a view of the world as was Jem at that moment.

"I knew nothing of the papers," protested Bottles. "If you had told me about the papers, I would have had them, and if I had been carrying the papers these fellows would not have made away with them."

"Then," said the horrified priest, "you did not commit this action in punishment for the injury done to your friend? You knew nothing of that at the time. You set on these men thinking they were simple travellers."

"Oh, I knew nothing of what happened to Paddy till later, but you see, your Reverence, these men themselves were thieves and robbers. In their case it was nine men against one poor half-witted Irish lad——"

"Half-witted yourself," cried Paddy angrily.

"But you, sir," continued his Reverence, "were simply carrying out the action of a highwayman. Sir, you *are* a highwayman."

"I was, your Reverence, but I have reformed."

"And this pile of saddles attests your reformation!" said the old man, shaking his head.

"But you see, your Reverence, this is the way to look at it——"

"Keep quiet, Jem!" cried I in disgust.

"How can I keep quiet," urged Bottles, "when I am unjustly accused? I do not deny that I was once a highwayman, but Mr. O'Ruddy converted me to better ways——"

"Highways," said Paddy, adding, with a sniff, "Half-witted!"

"Your Reverence, I had no more intention of robbing those men than you have at this moment. I didn't know they were thieves themselves. Then what put it into my head to jump into the wood and on with a mask before you could say, Bristol town? It's the mysterious ways of Providence, your Reverence. Even I didn't understand it at the time, but the moment I heard Paddy's tale I knew at once I was but an instrument in the hand of Providence, for I had not said, 'Stand and deliver!' this many a day, nor thought of it."

"It may be so; it may be so," murmured the priest, more to himself than to us; but I saw that he was much troubled, so, getting up, I said to Paddy:

"Are you able to ride farther on today?"

"If I'd another sup from the cup, sir, I think I could," whereat Jem Bottles laughed again, and I gave them both a drink of wine.

"What are you going to do with all this saddlery?" said I to Bottles.

"I don't know anything better than to leave it here; but I think, your honour, the pistols will come handy, for they're all very good ones, and Paddy and me can carry them between us, or I can make two bags from these leather packs, and Paddy could carry the lot in them, as I do the swords."

"Very well," I said. "Make your preparations as quickly as you can and let us be off, for this latest incident, in spite of you, Jem, may lead to pursuit and get us into trouble before we are ready for it."

"No fear, sir," said Jem confidently. "One thief does not lay information against another. If they had been peaceable travellers, that would be another thing; but, as I said, Providence is protecting us, no doubt because of the presence of his Reverence here, and not for our own merits."

"Be thankful it is the reward of someone else's merits you reap, Bottles, instead of your own. No more talk now, but to horse and away."

For some miles Father Donovan rode very silently. I told him something of my meeting with Jem Bottles and explained how I tried to make an honest man of him, while this was the first lapse I had known since his conversion. I even pretended that I had some belief in his own theory of the interposition of Providence, and Father Donovan was evidently struggling to acquire a similar feeling, although he seemed to find some difficulty in the contest. He admitted that this robbery appeared but even justice; still he ventured to hope that Jem Bottles would not take the coincidence as a precedent, and that he would never mistake the dictates of Providence for the desires of his own nature.

"I will speak with the man later," he said, "and hope that my words will make some impression upon him. There was a trace of exaltation in his recital that showed no sign of a contrite spirit."

On account of the delay at the roadside it was well past twelve o'clock before we reached Maidstone, and there we indulged in a good dinner that put heart into all of us, while the horses had time to rest and feed. The road to Rye presented no difficulties whatever, but under ordinary conditions I would have rested a night before travelling to the coast. There would be a little delay before the Earl discovered the useless nature of the papers which he had been at such expense to acquire, but after the discovery there was no doubt in my mind that he would move upon Brede as quickly as horses could carry his men, so I insisted upon pressing on to Rye that night, and we reached the town late with horses that were very tired. It was a long distance for a man of the age of Father Donovan to travel in a day, but he stood the journey well, and enjoyed his supper and his wine with the best of us.

We learned that there was no boat leaving for France for several days, and this disquieted me, for I would have liked to see Father Donovan off early next morning, for I did not wish to disclose my project to the peace-loving man. I must march on Brede next day if I was to get there in time, and so there was no longer any possibility of concealing my designs. However, there was no help for it, and I resolved to be up bright and early in the morning and engage a dozen men whom I could trust to stand by me. I also intended to purchase several cartloads of provisions, so that if a siege was attempted we could not be starved out. All this I would accomplish at as early an hour as possible, get the carts on their way to Brede, and march at the head of the men myself; so I went to bed with a somewhat troubled mind, but fell speedily into a dream-less sleep nevertheless, and slept till broad daylight.

CHAPTER XXXII

I FOUND Rye a snug little town, and so entirely peaceable-looking that when I went out in the morning I was afraid there would be nobody there who would join me in the hazardous task of taking possession of the place of so well-known a man as the Earl of Westport. But I did not know Rye then as well as I do now: it proved to be a great resort for smugglers when they were off duty and wished to enjoy the innocent relaxation of a town after the comparative loneliness of the seacoast, although, if all the tales they tell me are true, the authorities sometimes made the seashore a little too lively for their comfort. Then there were a number of seafaring men looking for a job, and some of them had the appearance of being pirates in more prosperous days.

As I wandered about I saw a most gigantic ruffian, taking his ease with his back against the wall, looking down on the shipping.

"If that man's as bold as he's strong," said I to myself, "and I had half a dozen more like him, we'd hold Brede House till the day there's liberty in Ireland"; so I accosted him.

"The top o' the morning to you," said I genially.

He eyed me up and down, especially glancing at the sword by my side, and then said civilly:

"The same to you, sir. You seem to be looking for someone?"

"I am," said I, "I'm looking for nine men."

"If you'll tell me their names I'll tell you where to find them, for I know everybody in Rye."

"If that's the case you'll know their names, which is more than I do myself."

"Then you're not acquainted with them?"

"I am not; but if you'll tell me your name I think then I'll know one of them."

There was a twinkle in his eye as he said:

"They call me Tom Peel."

"Then Tom," said I, "are there eight like you in the town of Rye?"

"Not quite as big perhaps," said Tom, "but there's plenty of good men here, as the French have found out before now— yes, and the constables as well. What do you want nine men for?"

"Because I have nine swords and nine pistols that will fit that number of courageous subjects."

"Then it's not for the occupation of agriculture you require them?" said Peel with the hint of a laugh. "There's a chance of a cut in the ribs, I suppose, for swords generally meet other swords."

"You're right in that; but I don't think the chance is very strong."

"And perhaps a term in prison when the scrimmage is ended?"

"No fear of that at all at all; for if anyone was to go to prison it would be me, who will be your leader, and not you, who will be my dupes, do you see?"

Peel shrugged his shoulders.

"My experience of the world is that the man with gold lace on his coat goes free, while they punish the poor devil in the leather jacket. But, turn the scheme out bad or ill, how much money is at the end of it?"

"There'll be ten guineas at the end of it for each man, win or lose."

"And when will the money be paid?"

"Half before you leave Rye, the other half in a week's time, and perhaps before—a week's time at the latest; but I want men who will not turn white if a blunderbuss happens to go off."

The rascallion smiled and spat contemptuously in the dust before him.

"If you show me the guineas," said he, "I'll show you the men."

"Here's five of them, to begin with, that won't be counted against you. There'll be five more in your pocket when we leave Rye, and a third five when the job's ended."

His big hand closed over the coins.

"I like your way of speaking," he said. "Now where are we to go?"

"To the strong house of Brede, some seven or eight miles from here. I do not know how far exactly, nor in what direction."

"I am well acquainted with it," said Peel. "It was a famous smuggler's place in its time."

"I don't mean a smuggler's place," said I. "I am talking of the country house of the Earl of Westport."

"Yes, curse him, that's the spot I mean. Many a nobleman's house is put to purposes he learns little of, although the Earl is such a scoundrel he may well have been in with the smugglers and sold them to the government."

"Did he sell them?"

"Somebody sold them."

There was a scowl on Peel's face that somehow encouraged me, although I liked the look of the ruffian from the first.

"You're an old friend of his lordship's, then?" said I.

"He has few friends in Rye or about Rye. If you're going to do anything against Westport, I'll get you a hundred men for nothing if there's a chance of escape after the fight."

"Nine men will do me, if they're the right stuff. You will have good cover to sleep under, plenty to eat and drink, and then I expect you to hold Brede House against all the men the Earl of Westport can bring forward."

"That's an easy thing," said Peel, his eye lighting up. "And if worse comes to the worst I know a way out of the house that's neither through door or window nor up a chimney. Where will I collect your men?"

"Assemble them on the road to Brede, quietly, about half a mile from Rye. Which direction is Brede from here?"

"It lies to the west, between six and seven miles away as the crow flies."

"Very well, collect your men as quickly as you can, and send word to me at the Anchor. Tell your messenger to ask for The O'Ruddy."

Now I turned back to the tavern sorely troubled what I would do with Father Donovan. He was such a kindly man that he would be loath to shake hands with me at the door of the inn, as he had still two or three days to stop, so I felt sure he would insist on accompanying me part of the way. I wished I could stop and see him off on his ship; but if we were to get inside of Brede House unopposed, we had to act at once. I found Paddy almost recovered from the assault of the day before. He had a bandage around his forehead, which, with his red hair, gave him a hideous appearance, as if the whole top of his head had been smashed. Poor Paddy was getting so used to a beating each day that I wondered wouldn't he be lonesome when the beatings ceased and there was no enemy to follow him.

Father Donovan had not yet appeared, and the fire was just lit in the kitchen to prepare breakfast, so I took Jem and Paddy with me to the eating shop of the town, and there a sleepy-looking shopkeeper let us in, mightily resenting this early intrusion, but changed his demeanour when he understood the size of the order I was giving him, and the fact that I was going to pay good gold; for it would be a fine joke on The O'Ruddy if the Earl surrounded the house with his men and starved him out. So it was no less than three cartloads of provisions I ordered, though one of them was a cartload of drink, for I thought the company I had hired would have a continuous thirst on them, being seafaring men and smugglers, and I knew that strong, sound ale was brewed in Rye.

The business being finished, we three went back to the Anchor, and found an excellent breakfast and an excellent man waiting for me, the latter being Father Donovan, although slightly impatient for closer acquaintance with the former.

When breakfast was done with, I ordered the three horses saddled, and presently out in the courtyard Paddy was seated on his nag with the two sacks of pistols before him, and Jem in like manner with his two bundles of swords. The stableman held my horse, so I turned to Father Donovan and grasped him warmly by the hand.

"A safe journey across the Channel to you, Father Donovan, and a peaceful voyage from there to Rome, whichever road you take. If you write to me in the care of the landlord of this inn I'll be sending and sending till I get your letter, and when you return I'll be standing and watching the sea, at whatever point you land in England, if you'll but let me know in time. And so good-bye to you, Father Donovan, and God bless you, and I humbly beseech your own blessing in return."

The old man's eyes grew wider and wider as I went on talking and talking and shaking him by the hand.

"What's come over you, O'Ruddy?" he said, "and where are you going?"

"I am taking a long journey to the west and must have an early start."

"Nonsense," cried Father Donovan, "it's two or three days before I can leave this shore, so I'll accompany you a bit of the way."

"You mustn't think of it, Father, because you had a long day's ride yesterday, and I want you to take care of yourself and take thought on your health."

"Tush, I'm as fresh as a boy this morning. Landlord, see that the saddle is put on that horse I came into Rye with."

The landlord at once rushed off and gave the order, while I stood there at my wit's end.

"Father Donovan," said I, "I'm in great need of haste at this moment, and we must ride fast, so I'll just bid good-bye to you here at this comfortable spot, and you'll sit down at your ease in that big arm-chair."

"I'll do nothing of the kind, O'Ruddy. What's troubling you, man? and why are you in such a hurry this morning, when you said nothing of it yesterday?"

"Father, I said nothing of it yesterday, but sure I acted it. See how we rode on and on in spite of everything, and did the whole journey from London to Rye between breakfast and supper. Didn't that give you a hint that I was in a hurry?"

"Well, it should have done, it should have done, O'Ruddy; still, I'll go a bit of the way with you and not delay you."

"But we intend to ride very fast, Father."

"Ah, it's an old man you're thinking I'm getting to be. Troth, I can ride as fast as any one of the three of you, and a good deal faster than Paddy."

At this moment the landlord came bustling in.

"Your Reverence's horse is ready," he said.

And so there was nothing for it but to knock the old man

down, which I hadn't the heart to do. It is curious how stubborn some people are; but Father Donovan was always set in his ways, and so, as we rode out of Rye to the west, with Paddy and Jem following us, I had simply to tell his Reverence all about it, and you should have seen the consternation on his countenance.

"Do you mean to tell me you propose to take possession of another man's house and fight him if he comes to claim his own?"

"I intend that same thing, your Reverence"; for now I was as stubborn as the old gentleman himself, and it was not likely I was going to be put off my course when I remembered the happiness that was ahead of me; but there's little use in trying to explain to an aged priest what a young man is willing to do for the love of the sweetest girl in all the land.

"O'Ruddy," he said, "you'll be put in prison. It's the inside of a gaol, and not the inside of a castle, you'll see. It's not down the aisle of a church you'll march with your bride on your arm, but it's hobbling over the cobbles of a Newgate passage you'll go with manacles on your legs. Take warning from me, my poor boy, who would be heart-broken to see harm come to you, and don't run your neck into the hangman's noose, thinking it the matrimonial halter. Turn back while there's yet time, O'Ruddy."

"Believe me, Father Donovan, it grieves me to refuse you anything, but I cannot turn back."

"You'll be breaking the law of the land."

"But the law of the land is broken every day in our district of Ireland, and not too many words said about it."

"Oh, O'Ruddy, that's a different thing. The law of the land in Ireland is the law of the alien."

"Father, you're not logical. It's the alien I'm going to fight here"—but before the father could reply we saw ahead of us the bulky form of Tom Peel, and ranged alongside of the road, trying to look very stiff and military-like, was the most awkward squad of men I had ever clapped eyes on; but determined fellows they were, as I could see at a glance when I came fornenst them, and each man pulled a lock of his hair by way of a salute.

"Do you men understand the use of a sword and a pistol?" said I.

The men smiled at each other as though I was trying some kind of a joke on them.

"They do, your honour," answered Tom Peel on their behalf. "Each one of them can sling a cutlass to the king's taste, and fire a pistol without winking, and there are now concealed in the hedge half a dozen blunderbusses in case they should be needed. They make a loud report and have a good effect on the enemy, even when they do no harm."

"Yes, we'll have the blunderbusses," said I, and with that the men broke rank, burst through the hedge, and came back with those formidable weapons. "I have ammunition in the carts," I said, "did you see anything of them?"

"The carts have gone on to the west, your honour; but we'll soon overtake them," and the men smacked their lips when they thought of the one that had the barrels in it. Now Paddy came forward with the pistols, and Bottles followed and gave each man a blade, while I gave each his money.

"Oh dear! Oh dear!" groaned Father Donovan.

"There's just a chance we may be attacked before we get to Brede, and, Father, though I am loath to say good-bye, still it must be said. It's rare glad I'll be when I grip your hand again."

"All in good time; all in good time," said Father Donovan; "I'll go a bit farther along the road with you and see how your men march. They would fight better and better behind a hedge than in the open, I'm thinking."

"They'll not have to fight in the open, Father," said I, "but they'll be comfortably housed if we get there in time. Now, Peel, I make you captain of the men, as you've got them together, and so, Forward, my lads."

They struck out along the road, walking a dozen different kinds of steps, although there were only nine of them; some with the swords over their shoulders, some using them like walking-sticks, till I told them to be more careful of the points; but they walked rapidly and got over the ground, for the clank of the five guineas that was in each man's pocket played the right kind of march for them.

"Listen to reason, O'Ruddy, and even now turn back," said Father Donovan.

"I'll not turn back now," said I, "and, sure, you can't expect it of me. You're an obstinate man yourself, if I must say so, Father."

"It's a foolhardy exploit," he continued, frowning. "There's prison at the end of it for someone," he murmured.

"No, it's the House of Brede, Father, that's at the end of it."

"Supposing the Earl of Westport brings a thousand men against you—what are you going to do?"

"Give them the finest fight they have ever seen in this part of England."

In spite of himself I saw a sparkle in Father Donovan's eye. The nationality of him was getting the better of his profession.

"If it were legitimate and lawful," at last he said, "it would be a fine sight to see."

"It will be legitimate and lawful enough when the Earl and myself come to terms. You need have no fear that we're going to get into the courts, Father."

"Do you think he'll fight?" demanded the father suddenly, with a glint in his eyes that I have seen in my own father's when he was telling us of his battles in France.

"Fight? Why of course he'll fight, for he's as full of malice as an egg's full of meat; but nevertheless he's a sensible old curmudgeon, when the last word's said, and before he'll have it noised over England that his title to the land is disputed he'll give me what I want, although at first he'll try to master me."

"Can you depend on these men?"

"I think I can. They're old smugglers and pirates, most of them."

"I wonder who the Earl will bring against you?" said Father Donovan, speaking more to himself than to me. "Will it be farmers or regular soldiers?"

"I expect they will be from among his own tenantry; there's plenty of them, and they'll all have to do his bidding."

"But that doesn't give a man courage in battle?"

"No, but he'll have good men to lead them, even if he brings them from London."

"I wouldn't like to see you attacked by real soldiers; but I think these men of yours will give a good account of themselves if there's only peasantry brought up against them. Sure, the peasantry in this country is not so warlike as in our own"—and there was a touch of pride in the father's remark that went to my very heart.

After riding in silence for a while, meditating with head bowed, he looked suddenly across at me, his whole face lighted up with delicious remembrance.

"Wouldn't you like to have Mike Sullivan with you this day," he cried, naming the most famous fighter in all the land, noted from Belfast to our own Old Head of Kinsale.

"I'd give many a guinea," I said, "to have Mike by my side when the Earl comes on."

The old father suddenly brought down his open hand with a slap on his thigh.

"I'm going to stand by you, O'Ruddy," he said.

"I'm glad to have your blessing on the job at last, Father," said I; "for it was sore against me to go into this business when you were in a contrary frame of mind."

"You'll not only have my blessing, O'Ruddy, but myself as well. How could I sail across the ocean and never know which way the fight came out; and then, if it is to happen in spite of me, the Lord pity the frailness of mankind, but I'd like to see it. I've not seen a debate since the Black Fair of Bandon."

By this time we had overtaken the hirelings with their carts, and the men were swinging past them at a good pace.

"Whip up your horses," said I to the drivers, "and get over the ground a little faster. It's not gunpowder that's in those barrels, and when we reach the house there will be a drink for every one of you."

There was a cheer at this, and we all pushed on with good hearts. At last we came to a lane turning out from the main road, and then to the private way through fields that led to Brede House. So far there had been no one to oppose us, and now, setting spurs to our horses, we galloped over the private way, which ran along the side of a gentle hill until one end of the mansion came into view. It seemed likely there was no suspicion who we were, for a man digging in the garden stood up and took off his cap to us. The front door looked like the Gothic entrance of a church, and I sprang from my horse and knocked loudly against the studded oak. An old man opened the door without any measure of caution, and I stepped inside. I asked him who he was, and he said he was the caretaker.

"How many beside yourself are in this house?"

He said there was only himself, his wife, and a kitchen wench, and two of the gardeners, while the family was in London.

"Well," said I, "I'd have you know that I'm the family now, and that I'm at home. I am the owner of Brede estate."

"You're not the Earl of Westport!" said the old man, his eyes opening wide.

"No, thank God, I'm not!"

He now got frightened and would have shut the door, but I gently pushed him aside. I heard the tramp of the men, and, what was more, the singing of a sea song, for they were nearing the end of their walk and thinking that something else would soon pass their lips besides the tune. The old man was somewhat reassured when he saw the priest come in; but dismay and terror took hold of him when the nine men with their blunderbusses and their swords came singing around a corner of the house and drew up in front of it. By and by the carts came creaking along, and then every man turned to and brought the provisions inside of the house and piled them up in the kitchen in an orderly way, while the old man, his wife, the wench, and the two gardeners stood looking on with growing signs of panic upon them.

"Now, my ancient caretaker," said I to the old man, in the kindest tones I could bring to my lips, so as not to frighten him more than was already the case, "what is the name of that little village over yonder?" and I pointed toward the west, where, on the top of a hill, appeared a church and a few houses.

"That, sir," he said, with his lips trembling, "is the village of Brede."

"Is there any decent place there where you five people can get lodging; for you see that this house is now filled with men of war, and so men of peace should be elsewhere? Would they take you in over at the village?"

"Yes, sir, it is like they would."

"Very well. Here is three guineas to divide among you, and in a week or thereabouts you will be back in your own place, so don't think disaster has fallen on you."

The old man took the money, but seemed in a strange state of hesitancy about leaving.

"You will be unhappy here," I said, "for there will be gun-firing and sword-playing. Although I may not look it, I am the most bloodthirsty swordsman in England, with a mighty uncertain temper on me at times. So be off, the five of you!"

"But who is to be here to receive the family?" he asked.

"What family?"

"Sir, we had word last night that the Earl of Westport and his following would come to this house today at two of the clock, and we have much ado preparing for them; for the messenger said that he was bringing many men with him. I thought at first that you were the men, or I would not have let you in."

"Now the saints preserve us," cried I, "they'll be on us before we get the windows barricaded. Tom Peel," I shouted, "set your men to prepare the defence at once, and you'll have only a few hours to do it in. Come, old man, take your wife and your gardeners, and get away."

"But the family, sir, the family," cried the old man, unable to understand that they should not be treated with the utmost respect.

"I will receive the family. What is that big house over there in the village?"

"The Manor House, sir."

"Very well, get you gone, and tell them to prepare the Manor House for the Earl of Westport and his following; for he cannot lodge here tonight"—and with that I was compelled to drag them forth, the old woman crying and the wench snivelling in company. I patted the ancient wife on the shoulder and told her there was nothing to be feared of; but I saw my attempt at consolation had little effect.

Tom Peel understood his business; he had every door barred and stanchioned, and the windows protected, as well as the means to his hand would allow. Up stairs he knocked out some of the diamond panes so that the muzzle of a blunderbuss would go through. He seemed to know the house as if it was his own; and in truth the timbers and materials for defence which he conjured up from the ample cellars or pulled down from the garret seemed to show that he had prepared the place for defence long since.

"Your honour," he said, "two dangers threaten this house which you may not be aware of."

"And what are those, Tom?" I asked.

"Well, the least serious one is the tunnel. There is a secret passage from this house down under the valley and out and up near the church. If it was not guarded they could fill this house unknown to you. I will stop this end of it with timber if your honour gives the word. There's not many knows of it, but the Earl of Westport is certain to have the knowledge, and some of his servants as well."

"Lead me to this tunnel, Tom," said I, astonished at his information.

We came to a door in one of the lower rooms that opened on a little circular stone stairway, something like a well, and, going down to the bottom, we found a tunnel in which a short man could stand upright.

"Thunder and turf, Tom!" said I, "what did they want this for?"

"Well, some thought it was to reach the church, but no one ever lived in this house that was so anxious to get to church that he would go underground to it. 'Faith, they've been a godless lot in Brede Place until your honour came, and we were glad to see you bring a priest with you. It put new heart in the men; they think he'll keep off Sir Goddard Oxenbridge."

"Does he live near here? What has he to do with the place?"

"He is dead long since, sir, and was owner of this house. Bullet wouldn't harm him, nor steel cut him, so they sawed him in two with a wooden saw down by the bridge in front. He was a witch of the very worst kind, your honour. You hear him groaning at the bridge every night, and sometimes he walks through the house himself in two halves, and then everybody leaves the place. And that is our most serious danger, your honour. When Sir Goddard takes to groaning through these rooms at night, you'll not get a man to stay with you, sir; but as he comes up from the pit by the will of the Devil we expect his Reverence to ward him off."

Now this was most momentous news, for I would not stop in the place myself if a ghost was in the habit of walking through it; but I cheered up Tom Peel by telling him that no imp of Satan could appear in the same county as Father Donovan, and he passed on the word to the men, to their mighty easement.

We had a splendid dinner in the grand hall, and each of us was well prepared for it; Father Donovan himself, standing up at the head of the table, said the holy words in good Latin, and I was so hungry that I was glad the Latins were in the habit of making short prayers.

Father Donovan and I sat at table with a bottle for company, and now that he knew all about the situation, I was overjoyed to find him an inhabitant of the same house; for there was no gentleman in all the company, except himself, for me to talk with.

Suddenly there was a blast of a bugle, and a great fluttering outside. The lower windows being barricaded, it was not possible to see out of them, and I was up the stair as quick as legs could carry me; and there in front were four horses harnessed to a great carriage, and in it sat the old Earl and the Countess, and opposite them who but Lady Mary herself, and her brother, Lord Strepp. Postilions rode two of the horses, and the carriage was surrounded by a dozen mounted men.

Everybody was looking at the house and wondering why nobody was there to welcome them, and very forbidding this stronghold must have seemed to those who expected to find the doors wide open when they drove up. I undid the bolts of one of the diamond-paned windows, and, throwing it open, leaned with my arms on the sill, my head and shoulders outside.

"Good day to your ladyship and your lordship," I cried—and then all eyes were turned on me—"I have just this day come into my inheritance, and I fear the house is not in a state to receive visitors. The rooms are all occupied by desperate men and armed; but I have given orders to your servants to prepare the Manor House in the village for your accommodation; so, if you will be so good as to drive across the valley, you will doubtless meet with a better reception than I can give you at this moment. When you come again, if there are no ladies of the party, I can guarantee you will have no complaint to make of the warmth of your reception."

His lordship sat dumb in his carriage, and for once her ladyship appeared to find difficulty in choosing words that would do justice to her anger. I could not catch a glimpse of Lady Mary's face at all at all, for she kept it turned toward the village; but young Lord Strepp rose in the carriage, and, shaking his fist at me, said:

"By God, O'Ruddy, you shall pay for this"; but the effect of the words was somewhat weakened by reason that his sister, Lady Mary, reached out and pulled him by the coat-tails, which caused him to be seated more suddenly than he expected; then she gave me one rapid glance of her eye and turned away her face again.

Now his lordship, the great Earl of Westport, spoke, but not to me.

"Drive to the village," he said to the postilions; then horsemen and carriage clattered down the hill.

We kept watch all that night, but were not molested. In the southern part of the house Father Donovan found a well-furnished chapel, and next morning held mass there, which had a very quieting effect on the men, especially as Oxenbridge had not walked during the night. The only one of them who did not attend mass was Jem Bottles, who said he was not well enough and therefore would remain on watch. Just as mass was finished Jem appeared in the gallery of the chapel and shouted excitedly:

"They're coming, sir; they're coming!"

I never before saw a congregation dismiss themselves so speedily. They were at their posts even before Tom Peel could give the order. The opposing party was leaving the village and coming down the hill when I first caught sight of them from an upper window. There seemed somewhere between half a dozen and a dozen horsemen, and behind them a great mob of people on foot that fairly covered the hillside. As they crossed the brook and began to come up, I saw that their leader was young Lord Strepp himself, and Jem whispered that the horsemen behind him were the very men he had encountered on the road between London and Maidstone. The cavalry were well in advance, and it seemed that the amateur infantry took less and less pleasure in their excursion the nearer they drew to the gloomy old house, so much so that Lord Strepp turned back among them and appeared to be urging them to make haste. However, their slow progress may be explained by the fact that a certain number of them were carrying a huge piece of timber, so heavy that they had to stagger along cautiously.

"That," said Tom Peel, who stood at my elbow, "is to batter in the front door and take us by storm. If you give the word, your honour, we can massacre the lot o' them before they get three blows struck."

"Give command to the men, Peel," said I, "not to shoot anyone if they can help it. Let them hold their fire till they are within fifty yards or so of the front, then pass the word to fire into the gravel of the terrace; and when you shoot let every man yell as if he were a dozen, and keep dead silence till that moment. I'll hold up my hand when I want you to fire."

There was a deep stillness over all the beautiful landscape. The bushes and the wood, however, were an exception to this, although the songs of the birds among the trees and singing of the larks high in the air seemed not to disturb the silence; but the whole air of the countryside was a suggestion of restful peace, at great variance with the designs of the inhabitants, who were preparing to attack each other.

Father Donovan stood beside me, and I saw his lips moving in prayer; but his eyes were dancing with irredeemable delight, while his breath came quick and expectant.

"I'm afraid those chaps will run at the first volley," he said, smiling at me. "They come on very slowly and must be a great trial to the young lord that's leading them."

It was indeed a trial to the patience of all of us, for the time seemed incredibly long till they arrived at the spot where I had determined they should at least hear the report of the blunderbusses, although I hoped none of them would feel the effects of the firing. Indeed, the horsemen themselves, with the exception of Lord Strepp, appeared to take little comfort in their position, and were now more anxious to fall behind and urge on the others on foot than to lead the band with his lordship.

I let them all get very close, then held up my hand, and you would think pandemonium was let loose. I doubt if all the cannon in Cork would have made such a noise, and the heathen Indians we read of in America could not have given so terrifying a yell as came from my nine men. The blunderbusses were more dangerous than I supposed, and they tore up the gravel into a shower of small stones that scattered far and wide, and made many a man fall down, thinking he was shot. Then the mob ran away with a speed which made up for all lost time coming the other direction. Cries of anguish were heard on every side, which made us all laugh, for we knew none of them were hurted. The horses themselves seemed seized with panic; they plunged and kicked like mad, two riders being thrown on the ground, while others galloped across the valley as if they were running away; but I suspect that their owners were slyly spurring them on while pretending they had lost control of them. Lord Strepp and one or two others, however, stood their ground, and indeed his lordship spurred his horse up opposite the front door. One of my men drew a pistol, but I shouted at him:

"Don't shoot at that man, whatever he does," and the weapon was lowered.

I opened the window and leaned out.

"Well, Lord Strepp," cried I, " 'tis a valiant crowd you have behind you."

"You cursed highwayman," he cried, "what do you expect to make by this?"

"I expect to see some good foot-racing; but you are under an error in your appellation. I am not a highwayman; it is Jem Bottles here who stopped nine of your men on the Maidstone road and piled their saddles by the side of it. Is it new saddlery you have, or did you make a roadside collection?"

"I'll have you out of that, if I have to burn the house over your head."

"I'll wager you'll not get any man, unless it's yourself, to come near enough to carry a torch to it. You can easily have me out of this without burning the house. Tell your father I am ready to compromise with him."

"Sir, you have no right in my father's house; and, to tell you the truth, I did not expect such outlawry from a man who had shown himself to be a gentleman."

"Thank you for that, Lord Strepp; but, nevertheless, tell your father to try to cultivate a conciliatory frame of mind, and let us talk the matter over as sensible men should."

"We cannot compromise with you, O'Ruddy," said Lord Strepp in a very determined tone, which for the first time made me doubt the wisdom of my proceedings; for of course it was a compromise I had in mind all the time, for I knew as well as Father Donovan that if he refused to settle with me my position was entirely untenable.

"We cannot compromise with you," went on the young man. "You have no right, legal or moral, to this place, and you know it. I have advised my father to make no terms with you. Good day to you, sir."

And with that he galloped off, while I drew a very long face as I turned away.

"Father Donovan," I said, when I had closed the window, "I am not sure but your advice to me on the way here was nearer right than I thought at the time."

"Oh, not a bit of it," cried Father Donovan cheerfully. "You heard what the young man said, that he had advised his father not to make any terms with you. Very well, that means terms have been proposed already; and this youth rejects the wisdom of age, which I have known to be done before."

"You think, then, they will accept a conference?"

"I am sure of it. These men will not stand fire, and small blame to them. What chance have they? As your captain says, he could annihilate the lot of them before they crushed in the front door. The men who ran away have far more sense than that brainless spalpeen who led them on, although I can see he is brave enough. One or two more useless attacks will lead him to a more conciliatory frame of mind, unless he appeals to the law, which is what I thought he would do; for I felt sure a sheriff would be in the van of attack. Just now you are opposed only to the Earl of Westport; but, when the sheriff comes on, you're fornenst the might of England."

This cheered me greatly, and after a while we had our dinner in peace. The long afternoon passed slowly away, and there was no rally in the village, and no sign of a further advance; so night came on and nothing had been done. After supper I said good-night to Father Donovan, threw myself, dressed as I was, on the bed, and fell into a doze. It was toward midnight when Tom Peel woke me up; that man seemed to sleep neither night nor day; and there he stood by my bed, looking like a giant in the flicker of the candle-light.

"Your honour," he said, "I think there's something going on at the mouth of the tunnel. Twice I've caught the glimpse of a light there, although they're evidently trying to conceal it."

I sat up in bed and said:

"What do you propose to do?"

"Well, there's a man inside here that knows the tunnel just as well as I do—every inch of it—and he's up near the other end now. If a company begins coming in, my man will run back without being seen and let us know. Now, sir, shall I timber this end, or shall we deal with them at the top of the stair one by one as they come up. One good swordsman at the top of the stair will prevent a thousand getting into the house."

"Peel," said I, "are there any stones outside, at the other end of the tunnel?"

"Plenty. There's a dyke of loose stones fronting it."

"Very well; if your man reports that any have entered the tunnel, they'll have left one or two at the other end on guard; take you five of your most trusted men, and go you cautiously a roundabout way until you are within striking distance of the men on guard. Watch the front upper windows of this house; and if you see two lights displayed, you will know they are in the tunnel. If you waited here till your man comes back, you would be too late; so go now, and, if you see the two lights, overpower the men at the mouth of the tunnel unless they are too many for you. If they are, then there's nothing to do but retreat. When you have captured the guard, make them go down into the tunnel; then you and your men tear down the dyke and fill the hole full of stones; I will guard this end of the passage."

Tom Peel pulled his forelock and was gone at once, delighted with his task. I knew that if I got them once in the tunnel there would no longer be any question of a compromise, even if Lord Strepp himself was leading them. I took two lighted candles with me and sat patiently at the head of the stone stairway that led, in circular fashion, down into the depths. Half an hour passed, but nothing happened, and I began to wonder whether or not they had captured our man, when suddenly his face appeared.

"They are coming, sir," he cried, "by the dozen. Lord Strepp is leading them."

"Will they be here soon, do you think?"

"I cannot tell. First I saw torches appear, then Lord Strepp came down and began giving instructions, and, after counting nearly a score of his followers, I came back as quick as I could."

"You've done nobly," said I. "Now stand here with this sword and prevent any man from coming up."

I took one of the candles, leaving him another, and lighted a third. I went up the stair and set them in the front window; then I opened another window and listened. The night was exceedingly still—not even the sound of a cricket to be heard. After a few minutes, however, there came a cry, instantly smothered, from the other side of the valley; another moment and I heard the stones a rolling, as if the side of a wall had tumbled over, which indeed was the case; then two lights were shown on the hill and were waved up and down; and although Peel and I had arranged no signal, yet this being the counterpart of my own, I took to signify that they had been successful, so, leaving the candles burning there, in case there might have been some mistake, I started down the stair to the man who was guarding the secret passage.

"Has anything happened?"

"Nothing, sir."

I think the best part of an hour must have passed before there was sign or sound. Of course I knew if the guards were flung down the hole, they would at once run after their comrades and warn them that both ends of the tunnel were in our possession. I was well aware that the imprisoned men might drag away the stones and ultimately win a passage out for themselves; but I trusted that they would be panic-stricken when they found themselves caught like rats in a trap. In any case it would be very difficult to remove stones from below in the tunnel, because the space was narrow and few could labour at a time; then there was every chance that the stones might jam, when nothing could be done. However, I told the man beside me to go across the valley and ask Peel and his men to pile on rocks till he had a great heap above the entrance, and, if not disturbed, to work till nearly daylight, so I sat on the top of the circular stair step with my rapier across my knees, waiting so long that I began to fear they all might be smothered, for I didn't know whether the stopping of air at one end would prevent it coming in at the other, for I never heard my father say what took place in a case like that. Father Donovan was in bed and asleep, and I was afraid to leave the guarding of the stair to anyone else. It seemed that hours and hours passed, and I began to wonder was daylight never going to come, when the most welcome sound I ever heard was the well-known tones of a voice which came up from the bottom of the well.

"Are you there, Mr. O'Ruddy?"

There was a subdued and chastened cadence in the inquiry that pleased me.

"I am, and waiting for you."

"May I come up?"

"Yes, and very welcome; but you'll remember, Lord Strepp, that you come up as a prisoner."

"I quite understand that, Mr. O'Ruddy."

So, as I held the candle, I saw the top of his head coming round and round and round, and finally he stood before me stretching out his sword, hilt forward.

"Stick it in its scabbard," said I, "and I'll do the same with mine." Then I put out my hand, "Good morning to your lordship," I said. "It seems to me I've been waiting here forty days and forty nights. Will you have a sup of wine?"

"I would be very much obliged to you for it, Mr. O'Ruddy."

With that I called the nearest guard and bade him let nobody up the stair without my knowing it.

"I suppose, my lord, you are better acquainted with this house than I am; but I know a spot where there's a drop of good drink."

"You have discovered the old gentleman's cellar, then?"

"Indeed, Lord Strepp, I have not. I possess a cellar of my own. It's you that's my guest, and not me that's yours on this occasion."

I poured him out a flagon, and then one for myself, and as we stood by the table I lifted it high and said:

"Here's to our better acquaintance."

His lordship drank, and said with a wry face, as he put down the mug:

"Our acquaintance seems to be a somewhat tempestuous one; but I confess, Mr. O'Ruddy, that I have as great a respect for your generalship as I have for your swordsmanship. The wine is good and revivifying. I've been in that accursed pit all night, and I came to this end of it with greater reluctance than I expected to when I entered the other. We tried to clear away the stones; but they must have piled all the rocks in Sussex on top of us. Are your men toiling there yet?"

"Yes, they're there, and I gave them instructions to work till daylight."

"Well, Mr. O'Ruddy, my poor fellows are all half dead with fright, and they fancy themselves choking; but although the place was foul enough when we entered it, I didn't see much difference at the end. However, I did see one thing, and that was that I had to come and make terms. I want you to let the poor devils go, Mr. O'Ruddy, and I'll be parole that they won't attack you again."

"And who will give his parole that Lord Strepp will not attack me again?"

"Well, O'Ruddy,"—I took great comfort from the fact that he dropped the Mr.—"Well, O'Ruddy, you see we cannot possibly give up this estate. You are not legally entitled to it. It is ours and always has been."

"I'm not fighting for any estate, Lord Strepp."

"Then, in Heaven's name, what are you fighting for?"

"For the consent of the Earl and Countess of Westport to my marriage with Lady Mary, your sister."

Lord Strepp gave a long whistle; then he laughed and sat down in the nearest chair.

"But what does Mary say about it?" he asked at last.

"The conceit of an Irishman, my lord, leads me to suspect that I can ultimately overcome any objections she may put forward."

"Oho! that is how the land lies, is it? I'm a thick-headed clod, or I would have suspected something of that sort when Mary pulled me down so sharply as I was cursing you at the front door." Then, with a slight touch of patronage in his tone, he said:

"There is some difference in the relative positions of our families, Mr. O'Ruddy."

"Oh, I'm quite willing to waive that," said I. "Of course it isn't usual for the descendant of kings, like myself, to marry a daughter of the mere nobility; but Lady Mary is so very charming that she more than makes up for any discrepancy, whatever may be said for the rest of the family."

At this Lord Strepp threw back his head and laughed again joyously, crying,—

"King O'Ruddy, fill me another cup of your wine, and I'll drink to your marriage."

We drank, and then he said:

"I'm a selfish beast, guzzling here when those poor devils think they're smothering down below. Well, O'Ruddy, will you let my unlucky fellows go?"

"I'll do that instantly," said I, and so we went to the head of the circular stair and sent the guard down to shout to them to come on, and by this time the daylight was beginning to turn the upper windows grey. A very bedraggled stream of badly frightened men began crawling up and up and up the stairway, and as Tom Peel had now returned I asked him to open the front door and let the yeomen out. Once on the terrace in front, the men seemed not to be able to move away, but stood there drawing in deep breaths of air as if they had never tasted it before. Lord Strepp, in the daylight, counted the mob, asking them if they were sure everyone had come up, but they all seemed to be there, though I sent Tom Peel down along the tunnel to find if any had been left behind.

Lord Strepp shook hands most cordially with me at the front door.

"Thank you for your hospitality, O'Ruddy," he said, "although I came in by the lower entrance. I will send over a flag of truce when I've seen my father; then I hope you will trust yourself to come to the Manor House and have a talk with him."

"I'll do it with pleasure," said I.

"Good morning to you," said Lord Strepp.

"And the top o' the morning to you, which is exactly what we are getting at this moment, though in ten minutes I hope to be asleep."

"So do I," said Lord Strepp, setting off at a run down the slope.

CHAPTER XXXIII

ONCE more I went to my bed, but this time with my clothes off, for if there was to be a conference with the Earl and the Countess at the Manor House, not to speak of the chance of seeing Lady Mary herself, I wished to put on the new and gorgeous suit I had bought in London for that occasion, and which had not yet been on my back. I was so excited and so delighted with the thought of seeing Lady Mary that I knew I could not sleep a wink, especially as daylight was upon me, but I had scarcely put my head on the pillow when I was as sound asleep as any of my ancestors, the old Kings of Kinsale. The first thing I knew Paddy was shaking me by the shoulder just a little rougher than a well-trained servant should.

"Beggin' your pardon," says he, "his lordship, the great Earl of Westport, sends word by a messenger that he'll be pleased to have account with ye, at your early convenience, over at the Manor House beyond."

"Very well, Paddy," said I, "ask the messenger to take my compliments to the Earl and say to him I will do myself the honour of calling on him in an hour's time. Deliver that message to him; then come back and help me on with my new duds."

When Paddy returned I was still yawning, but in the shake of a shillelah he had me inside the new costume, and he stood back against the wall with his hand raised in amazement and admiration at the glory he beheld. He said after that kings would be nothing to him, and indeed the tailor had done his best and had won his guineas with more honesty than you'd expect from a London tradesman. I was quietly pleased with the result myself.

I noticed with astonishment that it was long after mid-day, so it occurred to me that Lord Strepp must have had a good sleep himself, and sure the poor boy needed it, for it's no pleasure to spend life underground till after you're dead, and his evening in the tunnel must have been very trying to him, as indeed he admitted to me afterward that it was.

I called on Father Donovan, and he looked me over from head to foot with wonder and joy in his eye.

"My dear lad, you're a credit to the O'Ruddys," he said, "and to Ireland," he said, "and to the Old Head of Kinsale," he said.

"And to that little tailor in London as well," I replied, turning around so that he might see me the better.

In spite of my chiding him Paddy could not contain his delight, and danced about the room like an overgrown monkey.

"Paddy," said I, "you're making a fool of yourself."

Then I addressed his Reverence.

"Father Donovan," I began, "this cruel war is over and done with, and no one hurt and no blood shed, so the Earl——"

At this moment there was a crash and an unearthly scream, then a thud that sounded as if it had happened in the middle of the earth. Father Donovan and I looked around in alarm, but Paddy was nowhere to be seen. Toward the wall there was a square black hole, and, rushing up to it, we knew at once what had happened. Paddy had danced a bit too heavy on an old trap-door, and the rusty bolts had broken. It had let him down into a dungeon that had no other entrance; and indeed this was a queer house entirely, with many odd nooks and corners about it, besides the disadvantage of Sir Goddard Oxenbridge tramping through the rooms in two sections.

"For the love of Heaven and all the Saints," I cried down this trap-door, "Paddy, what has happened to you?"

"Sure, sir, the house has fallen on me."

"Nothing of the kind, Paddy. The house is where it always was. Are you hurted?"

"I'm dead and done for completely this time, sir. Sure I feel I'm with the angels at last."

"Tut, tut, Paddy, my lad; you've gone in the wrong direction altogether for them."

"Oh, I'm dying, and I feel the flutter of their wings," and as he spoke two or three ugly blind bats fluttered up and butted their stupid heads against the wall.

"You've gone in the right direction for the wrong kind of

angels, Paddy; but don't be feared, they're only bats, like them in my own tower at home, except they're larger."

I called for Tom Peel, as he knew the place well.

"Many a good cask of brandy has gone down that trap-door," said he, "and the people opposite have searched this house from cellar to garret and never made the discovery Paddy did a moment since."

He got a stout rope and sent a man down, who found Paddy much more frightened than hurt. We hoisted both of them up, and Paddy was a sight to behold.

"Bad luck to ye," says I; "just at the moment I want a presentable lad behind me when I'm paying my respects to the Earl of Westport, you must go diving into the refuse heap of a house that doesn't belong to you, and spoiling the clothes that does. Paddy, if you were in a seven years' war, you would be the first man wounded and the last man killed, with all the trouble for nothing in between. Is there anything broken about ye?"

"Every leg and arm I've got is broken," he whimpered, but Father Donovan, who was nearly as much of a surgeon as a priest, passed his hand over the trembling lad, then smote him on the back, and said the exercise of falling had done him good.

"Get on with you," said I, "and get off with those clothes. Wash yourself, and put on the suit I was wearing yesterday, and see that you don't fall in the water-jug and drown yourself."

I gave the order for Tom Peel to saddle the four horses and get six of his men with swords and pistols and blunderbusses to act as an escort for me.

"Are you going back to Rye, your honour?" asked Peel.

"I am not. I am going to the Manor House."

"That's but a step," he cried in surprise.

"It's a step," said I, "that will be taken with dignity and consequence."

So, with the afternoon sun shining in our faces, we set out from the house of Brede, leaving but few men to guard it. Of course I ran the risk that it might be taken in our absence; but I trusted the word of Lord Strepp as much as I distrusted the designs of his father and mother, and Strepp had been the captain of the expedition against us; but if I had been sure the mansion was lost to me, I would have evaded none of the pomp of my march to the Manor House in the face of such pride as these upstarts of Westports exhibited toward a representative of a really ancient family like the O'Ruddy. So his Reverence and I rode slowly side by side, with Jem and Paddy, also on horseback, a decent interval behind us, and tramping in their wake that giant, Tom Peel, with six men nearly as stalwart as himself, their blunderbusses over their shoulders, following him. It struck panic in the village when they saw this terrible array marching up the hill toward them, with the sun glittering on us as if we were walking jewellery. The villagers, expecting to be torn limb from limb, scuttled away into the forest, leaving the place as empty as a bottle of beer after a wake. Even the guards around the Manor House fled as we approached it, for the fame of our turbulence had spread abroad in the land. Lord Strepp tried to persuade them that nothing would happen to them, for when he saw the style in which we were coming he was anxious to make a show from the Westport side and had drawn up his men in line to receive us. But we rode through a silent village that might have been just sacked by the French. I thought afterward that this desertion had a subduing effect on the old Earl's pride, and made him more easy to deal with. In any case his manner was somewhat abated when he received me. Lord Strepp himself was there at the door, making excuses for the servants, who he said had gone to the fields to pick berries for their supper. So, leaving Paddy to hold one horse and Jem the other, with the seven men drawn up fiercely in front of the Manor House, Father Donovan and myself followed Lord Strepp into a large room, and there, buried in an arm-chair, reclined the aged Earl of Westport, looking none too pleased to meet his visitors. In cases like this it's as well to be genial at the first, so that you may remove the tension in the beginning.

"The top of the morning—I beg your pardon—the tail of the afternoon to you, sir, and I hope I see you well."

"I am very well," said his lordship, more gruffly than politely.

"Permit me to introduce to your lordship, his Reverence,

Father Donovan, who has kindly consented to accompany me that he may yield testimony to the long-standing respectability of the House of O'Ruddy."

"I am pleased to meet your Reverence," said the Earl, although his appearance belied his words. He wasn't pleased to meet either of us, if one might judge by his lowering countenance, in spite of my cordiality and my wish to make his surrender as easy for him as possible.

I was disappointed not to see the Countess and Lady Mary in the room, for it seemed a pity that such a costume as mine should be wasted on an old curmudgeon, sitting with his chin in his breast in the depths of an easy-chair, looking daggers though he spoke dumplings.

I was just going to express my regret to Lord Strepp that no ladies were to be present in our assemblage, when the door opened, and who should sail in, like a full-rigged man-o'-war, but the Countess herself, and Lady Mary, like an elegant yacht floating in tow of her. I swept my bonnet to the boards of the floor with a gesture that would have done honour to the Court of France; but her Ladyship tossed her nose higher in the air, as if the man-o'-war had encountered a huge wave. She seated herself with emphasis on a chair, and says I to myself, "It's lucky for you, you haven't Paddy's trap-door under you, or we'd see your heels disappear, coming down like that."

Lady Mary very modestly took up her position standing behind her mother's chair, and, after one timid glance at me, dropped her eyes on the floor, and then there were some moments of silence, as if everyone was afraid to begin. I saw I was going to have trouble with the Countess, and although I think it will be admitted by my enemies that I'm as brave a man as ever faced a foe, I was reluctant to throw down the gage of battle to the old lady.

It was young Lord Strepp that began, and he spoke most politely, as was his custom.

"I took the liberty of sending for you, Mr. O'Ruddy, and I thank you for responding so quickly to my invitation. The occurrences of the past day or two, it would be wiser perhaps to ignore——"

At this there was an indignant sniff from the Countess, and

I feared she was going to open her batteries, but to my amazement she kept silent, although the effort made her red in the face.

"I have told my father and mother," went on Lord Strepp, "that I had some conversation with you this morning, and that conditions might be arrived at satisfactory to all parties concerned. I have said nothing to my parents regarding the nature of these conditions, but I gained their consent to give consideration to anything you might say, and to any proposal you are good enough to make."

The old gentleman mumbled something incomprehensible in his chair, but the old lady could keep silence no longer.

"This is an outrage," she cried, "the man's action has been scandalous and unlawful. If, instead of bringing those filthy scoundrels against our own house, those cowards that ran away as soon as they heard the sound of a blunderbuss, we had all stayed in London, and you had had the law of him, he would have been in gaol by this time and not standing brazenly there in the Manor House of Brede."

And after saying this she sniffed again, having no appreciation of good manners.

"Your ladyship has been misinformed," I said with extreme deference. "The case is already in the hands of dignified men of law, who are mightily pleased with it."

"Pleased with it, you idiot," she cried. "They are pleased with it simply because they know somebody will pay them for their work, even if it's a beggar from Ireland, who has nothing on him but rags."

"Your ladyship," said I, not loath to call attention to my costume, "I assure you these rags cost golden guineas in London."

"Well, you will not get golden guineas from Brede estate," snapped her ladyship.

"Again your ladyship is misinformed. The papers are so perfect, and so well do they confirm my title to this beautiful domain, that the money-lenders of London simply bothered the life out of me trying to shovel gold on me, and both his lordship and your ladyship know that if a title is defective there is no money to be lent on it."

"You're a liar," said the Countess genially, although the Earl looked up in alarm when I mentioned that I could draw money on the papers. Again I bowed deeply to her ladyship, and, putting my hands in my pockets, I drew out two handfuls of gold, which I strewed up and down the floor as if I were sowing corn, and each guinea was no more than a grain of it.

"There is the answer to your ladyship's complimentary remark," said I with a flourish of my empty hands; and, seeing Lady Mary's eyes anxiously fixed on me, I dropped her a wink with the side of my face farthest from the Countess, at which Lady Mary's eyelids drooped again. But I might have winked with both eyes for all the Countess, who was staring like one in a dream at the glittering pieces that lay here and there and gleamed all over the place like the little yellow devils they were. She seemed struck dumb, and if anyone thinks gold cannot perform a miracle, there is the proof of it.

"Is it gold?" cried I in a burst of eloquence that charmed even myself, "sure I could sow you acres with it by the crooking of my little finger from the revenues of my estate at the Old Head of Kinsale."

"O'Ruddy, O'Ruddy," said Father Donovan very softly and reprovingly, for no one knew better than him what my ancestral revenues were.

"Ah well, Father," said I, "your reproof is well-timed. A man should not boast, and I'll say no more of my castles and my acres, though the ships on the sea pay tribute to them. But all good saints preserve us, Earl of Westport, if you feel proud to own this poor estate of Brede, think how little it weighed with my father, who all his life did not take the trouble to come over and look at it. Need I say more about Kinsale when you hear that? And as for myself, did I attempt to lay hands on this trivial bit of earth because I held the papers? You know I tossed them into your daughter's lap because she was the finest-looking girl I have seen since I landed on these shores."

"Well, well, well, well," growled the Earl, "I admit I have acted rashly and harshly in this matter, and it is likely I have done wrong to an honourable gentleman, therefore I apologize for it. Now, what have you to propose?"

"I have to propose myself as the husband of your daughter,

Lady Mary, and as for our dowry, there it is on the floor for the picking up, and I'm content with that much if I get the lady herself."

His lordship slowly turned his head around and gazed at his daughter, who now was looking full at me with a frown on her brow. Although I knew I had depressed the old people, I had an uneasy feeling that I had displeased Lady Mary herself by my impulsive action and my bragging words. A curious mildness came into the harsh voice of the old Earl, and he said, still looking at his daughter:

"What does Mary say to this?"

The old woman could not keep her eyes from the gold, which somehow held her tongue still, yet I knew she was hearing every word that was said, although she made no comment. Lady Mary shook herself, as if to arouse herself from a trance, then she said in a low voice:

"I can never marry a man I do not love."

"What's that? what's that?" shrieked her mother, turning fiercely round upon her, whereat Lady Mary took a step back. "Love, love? What nonsense is this I hear? You say you will not marry this man to save the estate of Brede?"

"I shall marry no man whom I do not love," repeated Lady Mary firmly.

As for me, I stood there, hat in hand, with my jaw dropped, as if Sullivan had given me a stunning blow in the ear; then the old Earl said sternly:

"I cannot force my daughter: this conference is at an end. The law must decide between us."

"The law, you old dotard," cried the Countess, rounding then on him with a suddenness that made him seem to shrink into his shell. "The law! Is a silly wench to run us into danger of losing what is ours? He *shall* marry her. If you will not force her, then I'll coerce her"; and with that she turned upon her daughter, grasped her by her two shoulders and shook her as a terrier shakes a rat. At this Lady Mary began to weep, and indeed she had good cause to do so.

"Hold, madam," shouted I, springing toward her. "Leave the girl alone. I agree with his lordship, no woman shall be coerced on account of me."

My intervention turned the Countess from her victim upon me.

"You agree with his lordship, you Irish baboon? Don't think she'll marry you because of any liking for you, you chattering ape, who resemble a monkey in a show with those trappings upon you. She'll marry you because I say she'll marry you, and you'll give up those papers to me, who have sense enough to take care of them. If I have a doddering husband, who at the same time lost his breeches and his papers, I shall make amends for his folly."

"Madam," said I, "you shall have the papers; and as for the breeches, by the terror you spread around you, I learn they are already in your possession."

I thought she would have torn my eyes out, but I stepped back and saved myself.

"To your room, you huzzy," she cried to her daughter, and Mary fled toward the door. I leaped forward and opened it for her. She paused on the threshold, pretending again to cry, but instead whispered:

"My mother is the danger. Leave things alone," she said quickly. "We can easily get poor father's consent."

With that she was gone. I closed the door and returned to the centre of the room.

"Madam," said I, "I will not have your daughter browbeaten. It is quite evident she refuses to marry me."

"Hold your tongue, and keep to your word, you idiot," she rejoined, hitting me a bewildering slap on the side of the face, after which she flounced out by the way her daughter had departed.

The old Earl said nothing, but gazed gloomily into space from out the depths of his chair. Father Donovan seemed inexpressibly shocked, but my Lord Strepp, accustomed to his mother's tantrums, laughed outright as soon as the door was closed. All through he had not been in the least deceived by his sister's pretended reluctance, and recognized that the only way to get the mother's consent was through opposition. He sprang up and grasped me by the hand and said:

"Well, O'Ruddy, I think your troubles are at an end, or," he cried, laughing again, "just beginning, but you'll be able to say more on that subject this time next year. Never mind my mother; Mary is, and always will be, the best girl in the world."

"I believe you," said I, returning his handshake as cordially as he had bestowed it.

"Hush!" he cried, jumping back into his seat again. "Let us all look dejected. Hang your head, O'Ruddy!" and again the door opened, this time the Countess leading Lady Mary, her long fingers grasping that slim wrist.

"She gives her consent," snapped the Countess, as if she were pronouncing sentence. I strode forward toward her, but Mary wrenched her wrist free, slipped past me, and dropped at the feet of Father Donovan, who had risen as she came in.

"Your blessing on me, dear Father," she cried, bowing her head, "and pray on my behalf that there may be no more turbulence in my life."

The old father crossed his hands on her shapely head, and for a moment or two it seemed as if he could not command his voice, and I saw the tears fill his eyes. At last he said simply and solemnly:—

"May God bless you and yours, my dear daughter."

We were married by Father Donovan with pomp and ceremony in the chapel of the old house, and in the same house I now pen the last words of these memoirs, which I began at the request of Lady Mary herself, and continued for the pleasure she expressed as they went on. If this recital is disjointed in parts, it must be remembered I was always more used to the sword than to the pen, and that it is difficult to write with Patrick and little Mary and Terence and Kathleen and Michael and Bridget and Donovan playing about me and asking questions, but I would not have the darlings sent from the room for all the writings there is in the world.

THE TEXT: HISTORY AND ANALYSIS

THE TEXT: HISTORY AND ANALYSIS

THE documentary records for the text of *The O'Ruddy* are comparatively full. They comprise (1) the original holograph manuscript of chapters I–XXV (less the final page), (2) a typescript and three carbons of chapter XXIV, (3) a holograph list of the numbers and headings for the first four chapters, (4) a brief dictated summary of the proposed continuation beyond chapter XXV, (5) a set of the author's page proofs for Robert Barr's part, chapters XXVI to the end, (6) the serialized text in the *Idler*, and (7) the first English edition and its reprint from the same plates in the United States. A missing document, and it is an important one, is the typescript used as printer's copy.

The manuscript, owned by Mr. and Mrs. Donald S. Klopfer of New York City, previously recorded only by David A. Randall, *Dukedom Large Enough* (New York, 1969), pp. 228–229, comprises 102 leaves of cheap wove ruled foolscap, unwatermarked, measuring 264 × 208 mm., the rules 9 mm. apart, the writing on one side of the paper only. It is autograph throughout except for a page and a half. In chapter X after Crane had started fol. 43 with the last two words of a sentence (*twice revised.*), an unidentified hand takes over, completes the chapter on fol. 44 and begins the next on fol. 45. (In the present edition this text runs from *Afterward we performed* [70.39] to *horsemen* [72.31].) The last leaf, which would have concluded chapter XXV, is missing. The leaves for chapters XXIV–XXV, which Crane sent to Pinker for typing in Cora's absence,[1] have

---

[1] See *Letters*, p. 266 (March 24, 1900): "The XXIV Chapter of the novel is finished but not yet typed. It will reach you on Tuesday." P. 266 (March 31?): "I enclose Chapter XXIV and XXV (4000 wds) of the Romance for typing." Cora to Pinker, *Letters*, p. 272 (about April 15): "Please send the last two Chapters (ms) of the Romance down. Mr. Crane sent them to you to be typed on March 31st." P. 277 (April 24?): "Please send by return Chapters XXIV and XXV of the Romance. Mr. Crane sent them to you to be typed when I was away."

been folded and are dog-eared. All the other leaves are unfolded. The ink is mostly black, but there are a few stretches of
blue ink near the beginning. For example, fol. 1 starts in black
and continues for twelve lines through *law-abiding* (3.12). Then
the line continues in a smaller script in blue, the color that
carries on to fol. 9, line 33, ending with *foreigner."* (16.2).
With the new paragraph that follows, the black ink returns.
After two more intervals of blue, the black ink inscribes the
rest of the manuscript starting on fol. 15 (24.10). At the start
of chapter xv is written the heading *Part II*, wanting in the
printed book. Some corrections and notations are made in pencil, apparently as a final review, but these are not in Crane's
hand and were probably made by Cora. This hand in pencil
wrote *Chapter 1* on fol. 1 and on the early folios added an *R*
(for Romance) at the upper left corner. Beginning with fol. 14
this *R*, in ink, is accompanied by the roman chapter number.
From this point Crane seems to have made these ink notations
in the upper left before he began to write out the page, since occasionally the text is indented around them. Crane's own notation *Typing stopped* on fol. 33 (55.3 after *infant?"*) has been
deleted in pencil. On fol. 99, line 17, after *thirsty."*, probably in
Cora's hand, is the pencil notation above a slant, *commence
here*. This corresponds to the end of the preserved typescript of
chapter xxiv.

Each chapter is numbered separately by Crane, starting
with 1, above a centered semicircle. In addition, for fols. 1–33,
the first seven chapters, Crane numbered the leaves consecu-
tively. Thereafter the consecutive numbering was added later
in pencil, presumably by Cora. In the text the wordage is
marked off by hundreds in pencil and on the verso of each leaf
is noted in ink the count for that page and the cumulative total
for the chapter. On the verso of each leaf ending a chapter appears the running total for the manuscript, in addition. On the
verso of fol. 102 the count for chapter xxv at that point is
given as 1,405 words, which would bring the total to 62,575.
The missing last page would have brought chapters xxiv
(2,200 words) and xxv close to the 4,000 word total for the two
remarked in Crane's letter to Pinker of *c*. March 27–31 (*Letters*,
p. 266).

Only a few notations other than the word counts appear on the versos. On fol. 10ᵛ (fol. 4ᵛ of chapter II) Crane wrote the following note:

Eng.	U.S.
Harper's Magazine	
The Anglo-Saxon Review	
Pall Mall Magazine	
Strand	
English Illustrated	Phil. Sat. Ev. Post
The Gentlewoman	

These are magazines which had taken his Spanish-American War stories, except for *Harper's*, which had published the Whilomville series. On fol. 68ᵛ (the first leaf of chapter XII) he noted *Pig and Turnip;* and on fol. 97ᵛ (the first leaf of chapter XXIV) he began, with paragraph indention, on what would have been the original recto, 'The majestic name of the Mississippi lent to New Or-|leans', undoubtedly a trial start for "The Brief Campaign Against New Orleans" in *Great Battles of the World,* which was published in *Lippincott's Magazine,* LXV (March, 1900), 405–411.

Professor Levenson has analyzed the circumstances of the production of the typescript and three carbons for most of chapter XXIV preserved in the Columbia University Libraries Special Collections, as well as the Columbia list of the first four chapter headings. The typescript consists of four leaves of foolscap paper, with three carbons in black. The leaves are numbered from 1 to 4 within centered parentheses; typed in the upper left corner of each page is *R. Chap. XXIV.).* The chapter number, underlined, heads page 1. In all four copies someone, perhaps Cora, has corrected the typing by adding letters and punctuation omitted in the right margin upon reaching the end of the line without margin release. Alterations are not made in the text, however. The typing manifestly derives from the manuscript and concludes where the manuscript had the inscription in Cora's hand, *commence here.* A list of the variants, printed after the Historical Collation, suggests that all of the departures from manuscript are typing errors without authority. Following this list, to complete the record, a list is provided of the changes made while typing and of the alterations in ink. Textually, the typescript has no authority, because of the primary authority of the manuscript and the lack of any revision in the four pages. However, the variants made in the typing would provide some insight into the source of corruption in the printed texts if we could be certain that Cora had typed the main manuscript (which seems most probable) and—what is perhaps somewhat less certain—if she were the typist of this chapter XXIV. In all likelihood either Helen Crane or Cora was the typist of the chapter. On the basis of one of her favorite misspellings, *betwen*, it may well have been Cora, although as a whole the spelling (while not impeccable) is superior to her usual habits.

Professor Matthew J. Bruccoli owns a previously unrecorded set of page proofs of Robert Barr's conclusion, starting with chapter XXVI and continuing to the end, stapled in plain tan wrappers. Across the top of the first page is inscribed: 'To Miss A. E. Trant in Buffalo. Here follows the part of "The O'Ruddy" which I wrote, with my own American fountain pen, the same with which "These here" words are written. Robert Barr of London Sept 30 1904.' The proofs are pulled in sheets folded in 4's, the text printed on rectos only. Each gathering of four such leaves is signed from 1 to 32. The typesetting is the same as that of the book version, although in an uncorrected state, but the number of lines per page differs, these proofs having only 32 lines whereas the book has 33. It is clear that before imposition for the manufacture of the plates these type-pages were rearranged to conform to the book format as we have it. Centered at the top of each page is '2d' in pencil (five of these in blue ink) and at the foot are written the initials 'CWB' in pencil. Thirty-five corrections have been marked in these proofs by a proofreader and thirteen queries entered. Many of the corrections are of technical matters such as the adjustment of wrong spacing, the supplying of missing heading capitals, and the setting right of typos. Others supply correct punctuation and add internal single quotes to a speech within dialogue. Necessary words that had been skipped are added three times; once a word is removed, this an error that Barr did not recognize since he did not replace it.[2] Otherwise no substantive variants appear except for a setting right of Barr's slip *most* by the substitution of *more* (250.2). On the evidence of the book text, Barr accepted almost all of the queries and made the necessary alterations which the proofreader by underlining and a question mark had called to his attention. He brought noun and verb into agreement four times, he removed *Doctor* before *Chord* at 176.25 (the query is an odd one), mended such queried spellings as *postillion,* added a necessary 'a' before *difficult* (213.23) and also added *lad* where another missing word had been queried (260.12), altered *O'Donovan* to *Donovan* (267.29). From this specimen it is clear that the proofreader generally was content to deal with printing faults but had an eye for questions of punctuation and of grammar and for such disruptions of sense as were caused by skipped words. Ordinarily, if there were doubt, a question mark directed the author's attention to the reading. However, the proofreader twice took it upon himself to alter words for sense. Once, at 250.2 he was right; once, at 175.33 he created an error that stuck.

Collation discloses that another round of corrections was marked in the lost master proofs, since the first edition shows 48 differences exclusive of those noted in the Bruccoli proofs. A number of these correct mechanical errors overlooked by the proofreader, but various must be authorial revisions, such as the substitution of *the lads* for *my lads* (173.1); the deletion of *this night* after *done* (173.9); the substitution of *frequented by* for *endeared to* (173.13), of *great* for *good* (174.17), of *before* for *against* (193.16), of *town* for *place* (235.1); or the addition of *while I gave each his money* (241.19). Revisions are not confined to the language: at 188.25 the syntax is smoothed by the transfer of *whether kicked or not* from its position after *other* to after *there.* It seems evident that the *2d* written at the head of the present proofs refers to a second or duplicate set of

---

[2] This was a misunderstanding on the part of the proofreader, who did not comprehend O'Ruddy's ironic understatement at 175.33, ' "I'll find her," says I, "if she's in the house; for I'm not going from room to room on a tour of inspection to see whether I'll buy the mansion or not." ' Here the proofreader removed the first 'not', with the result that the remark makes nonsense in the book.

marked pages sent the author with the first, and that Barr had returned the first set to the publisher, adding these 48 to the number already marked or queried by the proofreader but not troubling to record them in the duplicate set that he later gave away. These variants, then, attest to careful authorial proofreading but, more important, to a willingness to tinker with meaning and syntax at the proof stage. Both stages of proof-correction have been recorded in the List of Emendations for this section of the novel.

The O'Ruddy was serialized in *The Idler*, in England, in seven installments, in January, 1904, xxiv, 351–377; February, xxiv, 469–488; March, xxiv, 635–664; April, xxv, 65–90; May, xxv, 171–187; June, xxv, 307–326; and July, xxv, 413–435. The illustrations, variously dated 1903 and 1904, are by Bertram Gilbert. The chapter numbers differ from those in the manuscript and book owing to various cuts made for periodical publication. Beginning with the second installment and continuing through the sixth, a synopsis of the previous action was provided. The copyright notice for Methuen and for Stokes begins with the third installment.

The book was set for Methuen by Morrison & Gibb, Ltd., of Edinburgh, and plates were sent to Stokes in the United States, although the publication of the English edition was delayed until the conclusion of the *Idler* serialization and so followed the American appearance by some months. This Stokes edition may be described as follows:

[within spaced double rules] THE O'RUDDY | *A ROMANCE* | BY | STEPHEN CRANE | *Author of "The Red Badge of Courage," "Active | Service," "Wounds in the Rain,"* etc. | AND | ROBERT BARR | *Author of "Tekla," "In the Midst of Alarms," | "Over the Border," "The Victors,"* etc. | *With frontispiece by* | C. D. WIL-LIAMS | [type-ornament] | NEW YORK | FREDERICK A. STOKES COMPANY | PUBLISHERS

Collation: 1–22⁸ 23⁴ (signed on third leaf throughout), pp. [i–iv] [1] 2–356 + frontispiece; leaf measures 7 ¹³⁄₃₂ × 5″, all edges trimmed; wove paper, endpapers are text wove paper.

Contents: p. i: half-title, 'THE O'RUDDY'; p. ii: blank; front. in color, 'Copyright, 1903, by Frederick A. Stokes Company. | "A

WOMAN'S MEDDLING OFTEN RESULTS IN THE DESTRUC-
TION OF | THOSE SHE—THOSE SHE DOESN'T CARE TO HAVE
KILLED." | —*Page 83.*'; p. iii: title; p. iv: '*Copyright, 1903,* | BY
FREDERICK A. STOKES COMPANY | *All rights reserved* | Published
in October, 1903 || UNIVERSITY PRESS · JOHN WILSON | AND
SON · CAMBRIDGE, U.S.A.'; p. 1: text, headed '|| THE O'RUDDY
|| CHAPTER I', ending on p. 356.

Binding: Gray-yellow (90.gy.Y) fine crisscross cloth. Front: '[green
(very dark yellowgreen 138.v.d.yG) outlined in black] The |
O'Ruddy | [full-length figure to left in same green and black]
| [black] By | Stephen Crane | and. . . . | Robert Barr'. *Spine*:
'[black] The | O'Ruddy | [shamrock ornament] | [green] *Stephen
| Crane | & | Robert | Barr* | [black] STOKES'. *Back*: blank.

Price: $1.50. Copyright applied for October 27, 1903, and deposit
made November 2. Announced in the *Publishers' Weekly*, December 5, 1903.

Copies: University of Virgina-Barrett (551446); Harvard (with endpapers of heavier wove stock).

Variants: In the Barrett Collection of the University of Virginia
Library is an advance copy (551448), signed in pencil on p. iv:
'From Paul R. Reynolds, | 70, 5th Av N Y'. Identical with the first
edition, bound, except that it wants the frontispiece and endpapers
and is bound in gray-green wrappers.
  In the Barrett Collection, also, is a copy (551447) in a special
binding of very deep red (14.v.deep Red) fine vertical-ribbed cloth,
the lettering in gold within a blind single rule frame. *Front*:
'[within blind single rules] The O'Ruddy ||| *Stephen Crane and
Robert Barr*'. *Spine*: || The | O'Ruddy | *Crane and Barr* || '. *Back*:
blind single rule frame. The text is the same wove paper, but the
endpapers are of heavier and smoother stock; the leaf measures
7³⁄₃₂ × 4¹¹⁄₁₆", all edges trimmed. This may represent a trial binding.

In order to secure early copyright, Methuen imported Stokes
advance copies like that preserved in the Barrett Collection and
doctored them for the statutory deposit. The British Museum
copy (012707.a.22) is date-stamped November 12, 1903. A
cancel slip has been pasted on the title-page, obscuring the
Stokes text, starting with the line '*With frontispiece by*' and
reading 'METHUEN & CO. | 36 ESSEX STREET W.C. | LON-
DON' in a different typesetting from the imprint in the 1904

Methuen regular edition. Also, on p. iv the copyright notice has been scraped out. The British Museum copy has been rebound in brown boards with cloth spine, but the Bodleian Library deposit copy (2561 e. 2090), date-stamped 19 November, 1903, retains the original gray-green wrappers. Its cancel slip is in two parts: the original slip covered the ornament and Stokes imprint only, but a second was then pasted on to cover the frontispiece notice.

The Methuen London edition may be described as follows:

THE O'RUDDY | A ROMANCE | BY | STEPHEN CRANE | AND | ROBERT BARR | METHUEN & CO. | 36 ESSEX STREET W.C. | LONDON | 1904

Collation: π^2 1–22^8 23^2, pp. [i–iv] [1] 2–356 + publisher's catalogue A^{20}, signing A5 as A2 and A9 as A3; pages [1–2] 3–40. Leaf measures 7½ × 5", top edge trimmed, fore edge rough trimmed, bottom edge untrimmed; wove paper text and endpapers.

Contents: p. i: half-title, 'THE O'RUDDY'; p. ii: book lists, 'BY STEPHEN CRANE | THE RED BADGE OF COURAGE | WOUNDS IN THE RAIN | BY ROBERT BARR | TEKLA | IN THE MIDST OF ALARMS | OVER THE BORDER | THE VICTORS'; p. iii: title; p. iv: blank; p. 1: text, ending on p. 356 with colophon, '*Printed by* MORRISON & GIBB LIMITED, *Edinburgh*'.

Binding: Fine vertical-ribbed dark red (16.d.Red) cloth, lettering in gold. *Front*: '[within single rules] THE | O'RUDDY | BY | STEPHEN | CRANE | AND | ROBERT | BARR'. *Spine*: '[within single rules] THE | O'RUDDY | STEPHEN | CRANE | AND | ROBERT | BARR | [within single rules] METHUEN'. *Back*: blank.

Price: six shillings. British Museum deposit copy stamped July 7, 1904. Announced in the *Publishers' Circular of* July 16.

Copies: University of Virginia-Barrett (551449); British Museum (012629.bbb.3); London Library.

The Barrett advance copy of the Stokes edition has been collated on the Hinman Machine against the Barrett regular Stokes copy and also against the Methuen copy without signs of any textual variation in the Methuen plates. The printed first-edition text, thus, appears to be invariant.

The progress of the novel's composition is recorded with some fullness in the correspondence with Pinker analyzed by Professor Levenson, whose account shows that it was customary for Cora to have the chapters typed up one by one, or two by two, as finished (probably by herself, as Mrs. Frewen recalled on one occasion), and sent to Pinker. On January 22, 1900, Pinker acknowledged receipt of chapters VI and VII, and after stating that he would deliver these to Methuen he continued, 'It would be as well to let me have the third copy, as Mrs. Crane suggests, so that I may see if we can get a serial opening for it.' If 'the third copy' is to be taken literally, Pinker would have been sent the ribbon and a carbon but was aware that an extra copy had been retained at Brede. In early February, Pinker in a hand-written letter acknowledges receipt of 'Chapter X of the Romance, and also the three typewritten copies of the 26,610 words.' (The word count of 26,610 appears on the verso of the last leaf of chapter X in the manuscript.) In this letter the 'three' of 'three typewritten copies' is written over 'two'. The language is far from clear, but it seems a reasonable conjecture that in acknowledging the 26,610 words Pinker is actually stating that he has received the ribbon copy and two carbons of chapter X; and presumably also the extra carbon of chapters I to IX he had requested on January 22 so as to have a third copy to send about for magazine serialization. (One copy would have been for Methuen and the second for Stokes, with the third copy now to be used for magazine sale.) A carbon copy, presumably, would have been retained at Brede. Only on one occasion, when Cora was in Paris, did Crane himself dispatch copy to Pinker: this was the manuscript itself for chapters XXIV and XXV which Pinker was to have typed for him. It would seem that the difficulty that Cora experienced in having this copy returned to her led her to the retyping of most of chapter XXIV when the manuscript was sent back, presumably so that she would have a typed copy as well as the manuscript in her possession.[3]

The major textual problem in *The O'Ruddy* concerns the

---

[3] The typing stops at the point where she noted on the manuscript, *commence here*. This notation was presumably for the guidance of the person who was to continue the typing. It is uncertain whether the rest of the chapter (and also chapter XXV?) was retyped but the pages lost, although this last would seem improbable. The typing ends at the foot of a page, perhaps the reason it was suspended and the notation made in the manuscript at that point. Possibly the retyping was given over if a carbon was unexpectedly returned of Pinker's typescript. At any rate, this ribbon copy with its three carbons does not appear ever to have been used.

status of the substantive variants between the manuscript and the first edition, for convenience referred to as E1, the Methuen edition. If some of these variants, at least, appeared in the book because they faithfully reproduced Crane's own revisions made in the typescript that served as printer's copy, they would be authoritative and would need to be adopted as emendations of the manuscript copy-text insofar as they could be identified. On the other hand, unless a master typescript had been retained at Brede such revision could not have taken place, barring a hasty reading over of copy before mailing it to Pinker. Or even if such a carbon had been retained, evidence would be required that Crane actually revised it with a view to its future use as printer's copy. Otherwise some other source for these variants must be sought, in which case they could not be authoritative, whatever their origin. Hence it is incumbent on an editor to examine in detail what evidence may be recovered that appears to bear on the origin and nature of these variants, with particular reference to what can be determined about the nature of the typescript that was used as printer's copy.

Collation of the *Idler* text establishes that its first installment comprising chapters I–V, printed in the number for January, 1904, was set from different copy from that used for the second in February and for all later installments. That is, in chapter VI to XXV the vast majority of the *Idler* substantive variants from the manuscript are shared by the book (E1), and very few common variants are found in which the *Idler* and MS agree against E1 unique variance. On the contrary, in the first five chapters of the initial installment the majority of the *Idler* variants that disagree with E1 concur with MS, and relatively few join E1 against MS. The evidence—especially when the *Idler* agrees with E1 in error—effectively demonstrates that starting with chapter VI the *Idler* was set up from E1 proofs or sheets, or both, but that the copy for the first five chapters could not have been E1. The normal inference follows that this copy was a typescript. Moreover, if the majority of the E1 variants may be taken as originating in the revisory markings in the typescript that was its printer's copy and not as inserted during the reading of the proof (a fair hypothesis), then the typescript that set the *Idler* chapters I–V must have been a different copy from that which set the corresponding text in E1.

Analysis of the unique variants in the *Idler*, chapters i–v, differing both from MS and from Ei, establishes that they fall into a few relatively well-defined categories. The most prominent is that of censorship. All references to swearing are toned down or removed, as by the substitution of *cursing* for MS,Ei *damning* at 5.26, or the omission of *damned* at 37.23. Anything to do with sexuality is modified or excised. The description of Lady Mary's beauty as *both ascetic and deeply sensuous* (30.8) is sacrificed, as is Jem Bottles' injured outcry, *Do you think me an illegitimate child?* (25.33); and in his *I repulse with scorn any man's suggestion that I am illegitimate* (25.36–37) the phrase *have no mother* chastely substitutes for *am illegitimate*. Violence and coarseness are similarly deleted. At 8.25–26 *at each other's bellies* is modified to *at each other,* and at 24.35–37 O'Ruddy's threat to Bottles, *and, ripping out your bowels, shall sprinkle them on the road for the first post-horses to mash and trample* is excised. These acts of censorship for the journal's family audience are repeated on subsequent occasions when the book is the printer's copy, and hence they cannot be a special characteristic of the typescript that was used as copy for the first installment.[4] In other matters what appear to be simple errors bulk large, such as the *Idler* reading *be* for *lie* (4.24), or *hands* for *hand* (11.8), or *the corner of a field* for *a corner of the field* (18.13). Common, too, are simple sophistications of copy, difficult sometimes to distinguish from inadvertent departures, such as *an attack* for *attack* (11.26), *skilled* for *skilful* (17.6), or *this* for *his* (20.10). Included here are such stylistic adjustments as the unsplitting of Crane's usual split infinitives at 3.16 and 18.12–13 or the transposition of *he again* to *again he* (19.20).

No reading in the *Idler* that varies from MS appears to have any authority. An anomaly, however, is the statement at 6.5 that the Earl of Westport's lands to which the papers relate were *in the South* whereas in MS and Ei the reading is *in the North* (MS: *north*). That the lands were indeed in the south is not revealed until in Barr's part they are identified with Brede. This assignment is a Barr invention, for Crane's dictated notes in-

---

[4] For the sake of the record, one may remark that, later, the *Idler* cuts in Barr's part switch to a removal or a lightening of what might be thought to be aspersions on Roman Catholicism, especially in the person of Father Donovan as too unworldly (or stupid) and, simultaneously, too **hard drinking**.

dicate that he had intended Brede to be Forister's residence. Another interesting *Idler* variation occurs at 53.28 where MS and E1 place the Forister-Nell episode in Bristol, which is clearly a slip for Bath; and indeed at 56.1 MS shows *Bristol* deleted and *Bath* interlined. However, the *Idler* correctly assigns it to *Bath* throughout. Since this correction occurs in the second installment where E1 (reading *Bristol*) furnished printer's copy for the *Idler* (reading *Bath*), we cannot assign the alteration to Barr going over the copy for the *Idler* either here, or, presumably, for *South*. On the other hand, the *Idler* editor seems to have remembered and to have altered the two errors first in the typescript and then later when the printer's copy changed to the proofs for E1. The reading over of copy by the editor would, in fact, have been a twofold one, it would seem. That is, he would have read the typescript for acceptance. But as he marked the copy (whether typescript or proofs) for his printer, with particular regard for censorship of offensive material, and—on the evidence—with some occasional regard for stylistic improvement, he would have been able to alter these two irregularities as they came to his attention.[5]

If the change from *North* to *South* (and later of *Bristol* to *Bath*) were editorial, then no *Idler* reading in the first five chapters (or indeed elsewhere) appears to have any authority independent of the original copy. Moreover, for chapters i–v the copy was very clearly a carbon of the original typescript that was not the same as the edited ribbon pages presumably used for the manufacture of E1. Further, it would seem that this carbon used for the *Idler* had not been revised in any identifiable manner—except by the editor for his own purposes—from the form represented by its original transcript of the manuscript. That is, although not all of the *Idler* variants can be assigned to the compositor or editor—for some no doubt originated in the typing—the evidence suggests that the number of typescript variants from MS was few.

Variation in the typescript from the manuscript would be detected by common readings in the *Idler* and E1 differing from MS. Not all such readings can be positively assigned to the type-

<hr/>

[5] Alert as this editor was to catch such a small point as *North* for *South*, he overlooked the change that MS, and presumably the typescript, later made from *O'Donovan* to *Donovan*, and at 4.17 the *Idler* reading is *O'Donovan*.

script, however, for some must represent the correction of errors so obvious that the alteration would have been made independently by *Idler* and E1 in case the typescript and carbons had followed the MS slip and had not been altered on review. Of such nature are *Idler*, E1 *gentlemen* for MS *gentleman* (10.11 *et seq.*), *quiet* for *quite* (15.21), or the addition of *the* (30.12) or of *at* (39.36). At the opposite pole—although fortuitous correction cannot be ruled out—we may reasonably take it that the addition of *that* at 5.10, the omission of *to* before *strangle* at 30.26, and the substitution of *sword* for *sword's* at 42.15, represent readings in which *Idler* and E1 follow typescript variants from MS. The unsplitting of an infinitive by *Idler* and E1 at 3.16 and 18.12–13, or the change from the plural to the singular possessive at 41.19, may or may not represent independent styling; perhaps the alteration to *blackguard* of MS *blagaurd* is similar (13.32, 21.3). Whether *waiting* in both texts for MS *awaiting* (27.5), or *said* for the odd MS *sang* (42.32) or *an'* (E1: *an*) for MS *and* (19.17) are independent or are reproductions of the typescript is less certain. Of course, a mistaken unique variant in *Idler*, or in E1, might represent an error in the typescript automatically corrected by the other so that its origin in the typescript could never be demonstrated, such as the possibility (although far from the probability) that a reading like *Idler's come* for MS,E1 *came* (41.10) derives from the typescript but was corrected in E1. Such possibilities appear to be few in the first five chapters and need not be taken seriously. But occasionally variants do disclose a typescript reading that followed the MS error. Such a one is MS,E1 *judge* for the corrected *Idler's judged* (34.31), or MS *finger. Be careful, Idler's finger, be careful!*, but E1's correct *finger be careful* (34.23).

The evidence for the substantive fidelity of the unannotated *Idler* and E1 basic typescript copies to the manuscript original is strong, therefore; and, indeed, the incidence of error is markedly less than the departures that may be observed in the four pages of the preserved retyping of part of chapter xxiv.[6] We do

---

[6] These are TMs *discussion* for MS *discussions* (162.9), *the ground* for *ground* (162.17), *baskets* for *basket* (163.1), *woman that I* for *woman I* (163.7), *express* for *expressed* (163.12), *letting* for *leaving* (165.18), *come come* for *could come* (165.22), and the omission of MS *from* (165.34) and of *little* (165.34). The full account of all variants is given after the Historical Collation appendix.

not know, of course, how much if any the typist of chapter xxiv worked on the regular typescript. What develops, however, is excellent evidence that the form of the typescript used as printer's copy for chapters i–v of the *Idler* represented a relatively faithful reproduction of the substantives of the manuscript and was without authorial revision that can be detected. In short, before this typescript was annotated by the *Idler's* editor, it is a fair conjecture that the copy was unannotated by Crane or Cora except, very likely, for such corrections of obvious typing errors as may be seen in the typescript for chapter xxiv.

The inference follows that the *Idler* text for chapters i–v has no authority independent of the manuscript; and that wherever it departs from MS the variants are, in the majority, *Idler* editorial markings or compositorial mistakes and, in the minority, the reproduction of typescript errors. Finally, the conclusion is evident that whatever authoritative annotation may or may not have been given to the typescript that was sent to the Methuen printer, any such annotation was not present in whole or in part in the typescript copy sent to the *Idler*, which was, in fact, in its pristine condition without change other than Cora's usual mending.

One small question of textual transmission remains. It seems clear that independent typescript copies (i.e., a ribbon and a carbon) were assembled for Methuen and for the *Idler*, these probably being the same copies submitted when negotiations for sale were in process and retained by the publisher and the magazine for their uses. Stokes in the United States was able to publish his edition from Methuen plates as early as October, 1903, even though Methuen held off publication until July, 1904, in order to permit completion of the serialization that was Barr's payment for his work. We do not know the exact date at which Methuen had its own sheets printed and bound, but typesetting and proofreading had had to be completed in time for plates to be manufactured that could be sent across the Atlantic to produce a book published in late October, 1903.[7] Early September of 1903, then, is as good a date as any to fix as a definite *terminus ad quem* for the manufacture of the plates. Thus since

---

[7] The inscription *September 30, 1904*, on Barr's set of proofs is only the date of presentation and bears no relation to the date of receipt, of course.

typesetting for the *Idler* would probably have started no earlier than October–November, 1903, for the January, 1904, number, proof from Methuen should have been available as printer's copy for the first installment. That, instead, the typescript was used as copy (fortunately for us) indicates that the *Idler* office was not aware of the early production of the plates. That this ignorance was rectified by the time the second installment was set for the February issue is clear, even though we cannot know the exact circumstances that led to the change in printer's copy. Perhaps Barr, who had an interest in the *Idler*, had not been aware of the situation until the first installment appeared and thereupon made immediate provision for the remainder to be set from what would have been considered the superior Methuen-edited text. The one pertinent point for the textual transmission is that—given the dates of production for book and for magazine—it is a certainty that the second and subsequent installments of the *Idler* would have been set from final proofs pulled from the Methuen plates. Under these circumstances it would be useless to examine the *Idler* variants from E1 starting with chapter VI in the hope of discovering E1 proof-alterations in any part of the *Idler* copy that might have been set from uncorrected Methuen proofs.[8]

The problem of the *Idler* copy having been examined, we may turn to the more difficult but crucial evidence bearing on the nature of the copy sent to the printer of E1. No external evidence assists that has very much weight. Some difficulty seems to have developed after Crane's death in getting together copies to send to the various writers who were being solicited to finish the novel. On June 13,1900, Barr wrote Cora that he would return to her the original manuscript that he had; but on July 4 that he would leave the typewritten manuscript with Pinker. Probably these were not the same. Yet in the summer Cora wrote Pinker several times demanding a typescript so that she could try to make arrangements for a dramatization, and once remarked that Barr had said he had lent Pinker his copy. At one time there

---

[8] That the *Idler* follows the error omitting *not* at 175.33, a reading that originated in the corrected E1 proof, demonstrates the nature of the copy at this late point. Given the dates of production, no reason exists to conjecture that the copy for earlier installments of the *Idler* would have differed.

seem to have been two copies circulating in the United States.[9] On the whole, it would appear that four typed copies were in existence, that one of these was kept at Brede but was given to Barr to read after Crane's death, that Cora did not recover this from Pinker and, after Crane's death, probably had no copy of her own save, for a time, the manuscript.[10] So far as the evidence goes, then, up to the time of Crane's death it is almost certain that a typescript carbon was kept at Brede, even though it was later pressed into service.[11] No copy other than this could have contained authorial revisions in case Crane was moved to make them in the text after it was in typescript. However, in the various correspondence about the completion of the novel or its publication no mention is ever made to indicate that any copy existed that was superior in its text to the others.[12] It is a fair

[9] The documentation and analysis of these letters may be found in Professor Levenson's Introduction.

[10] Her ultimate possession of this manuscript is doubtful since in that case it should have become a part of the collection of Crane's papers and books that she later sold and is now preserved at Columbia University. As Professor Levenson reconstructs the case, the manuscript itself was in circulation eventually.

[11] However, it is not demonstrable what actual copy of the typescript eventually became the Methuen printer's copy. Pinker sent Methuen the typed chapters as received, presumably in the ribbon copy. While Barr was first thinking of carrying on the novel, he was given what was probably the Brede copy of the typescript, but then returned it to Pinker. Considerably later, when he finally accepted the commission, we have no information as to what copy he worked on. One would suppose that he eventually would have received the Methuen file copy, which could not have been authorially revised, but no certainty is possible. The supply of copies was not unlimited. Before Barr went ahead with the conclusion, Methuen had a copy, Stokes had a copy, a copy was with Reynolds for serial sale, and a copy was circulating in England in search of serialization. One of these—but not the Methuen one—would have been the Brede copy. So far as the evidence goes, indeed, the Methuen would seem to have been the only copy that would have been available for Barr to use once he started work. Of course, if the Brede copy had had special annotations no doubt it could have been traded for the Methuen, which could then have been used for negotiations about English serialization. But until Barr accepted, it would seem that for well over a year this Brede copy was used by Pinker for ordinary purposes of circulation if indeed it had not been sent to Reynolds. Professor Levenson's account must be taken as authoritative.

[12] It may be that when Barr saw Crane at Dover he was given the 'original manuscript' that in a letter of June 13, 1900, he proposed to return to Cora before she left for the United States with Crane's body. Since Cora would treasure the manuscript, it may have been on that occasion that she exchanged for it the typewritten copy that he had in his possession, as indicated in the July 4 letter to Cora in the United States, and that he proposed to leave with Pinker. This, then, would have been the Brede carbon. Yet in August, Cora (back in London) is writing to Pinker that she must have a typescript in order

statement, at any rate, that external evidence is wanting to suggest revision of a typescript on the scale found in the E1 variants from MS and, in the first five chapters, from the *Idler*.

It would be useless to appeal to probability, whether Crane—who on the available evidence made very few changes in the typescripts of his short stories—would engage himself to a rather large series of stylistic and other revisions of his novel at a time when, seemingly, every ounce of his failing energy was going toward the production of fresh copy against payments, in addition to such work as *Great Battles of the World*, his other continuing project during the last hectic months when he was pushing ahead on *The O'Ruddy*. Some very slight revision does indeed exist, but it is in the manuscript itself. A total of nineteen readings are found in which MS was altered but E1 agrees with the original reading. When the owner of the hand can be determined, it is Crane himself who made the changes; but in the nature of the case not every one can be guaranteed as his. These are all relatively minor stylistic changes natural to make on casual reading over. All that they disclose is that Crane occasionally was moved to make a few revisions after the typescript of the chapters had left his hand, and he noted these in the manuscript, apparently as his sole master copy. Evidence from the *Idler* text does not indicate that any of these readings got into the typescript behind that copy. That they were ever transferred to one of the two other typescripts that were not used for printer's copy is, of course, scarcely to be determined.[13]

---

to negotiate for a dramatization, and she states that she knows Pinker has a copy that Barr had 'lent' to him. Once more, no special value is placed on this specific copy. Indeed, if it were the actual copy that Cora received from Pinker and sent to Belasco in New York—for which he acknowledged receipt on September 5, 1900—revisions in it are rather unlikely.

[13] In sixteen of these readings the revised MS form is unique and both the *Idler* and E1 follow the uncorrected version, although only one of these occurs where the *Idler* is an independent witness in the first five chapters. The readings are 5.37 MS(c) *Tisn't* vs. MS(c)+ *It isn't*; 53.11 MS(c) *acts for me* omitted; 66.6 *lady* vs. *Lady*; 70.39 MS(c) *another* vs. *a*; 81.18 MS(c) *principle* vs. *principal*; 82.27 MS(c) *whom* vs. *who*; 83.33 *calling* vs. *calling out*; 83.33 *a* vs. *his*; 98.14 *woman* vs. *lady*; 105.1 *Mass* vs. *Masses* in MS(u),E1 but omitted in I; 120.39 *Immediately* vs. *and immediately*; 126.34 *Knowledge* vs. *knowledge*; 129.11 *upon* vs. *down upon*; 131.24 *would* omitted in MS(u),E1 (this forms part of large cut in I); 156.13 *hard* vs. *a hard*; 169.34 *o'* vs. *of*. In three readings the *Idler* agrees with MS(c) against MS(u) and E1, the first two when it was setting from typescript. Given the nature of these variants, and especially of the third, it

Whether, independent of these few alterations in the manuscript, any authorial revisions found their way into the typescript used as Methuen copy is a question susceptible of analysis and assessment only from the text itself. On the whole the evidence of substantive variation does not yield to statistical analysis. That is, although some chapters are more heavily altered than others, the qualitative differences are more important than the quantitative in view of the fact that some considerable amount of nonauthorial alteration is manifestly present throughout. Yet a statistical survey is not without its uses. For example, if the E1 variants were in general the result of authorial changes in a copy of the typescript used for E1, one might suppose that the last two chapters that Crane was able to write would differ in this respect from earlier sections. If Crane were too ill to write a word beyond the end of chapter xxv, despite his need for money, one might take it that he would be unlikely to devote himself to stylistic revision of these last chapters. But chapters XXIV and XXV have twelve and thirteen substantive variants, respectively, between E1 and MS.[14] If this does not altogether compare with the approximately thirty-seven in chapter I and thirty-two in chapter II, the statistical disparity is of little account when compared with the approximately thirteen variants in chapter III and fourteen in chapter IV. (Incidentally, a two-month gap inter-

---

is a reasonable conjecture that they represent independent *Idler* editorial or compositorial variants that fortuitously agree with the corrected readings of the manuscript and are not indicative of the *Idler* typescript. These are 6.6 MS(c),I *he* vs. MS(u),E1 *as he*; 19.32 *staunching* vs. *stanching*; 56.1 *Bath* vs. *Bristol*. In two readings, within the second and third chapters, the *Idler* and the unrevised manuscript agree against E1 and the revised MS. Given the nature of these two readings it is safe to conjecture that the *Idler* variant is a fortuitous editorial or compositorial change and that the MS correction occurred before the typescript was made up. These are 17.4 MS(c),E1 *manners* vs. MS(u),I *manner*; 21.18 MS(c),E1 *at* vs. MS(u),I *by*.

[14] In chapter XXIV these are MS *to ground* but E1 *ground* (162.17), MS *my intelligence* but E1 *intelligence* (163.6), MS *noted* but E1 *noticed* (163.27), *huntress* but E1 *mistress* (164.18), *had turned* but *turned* (164.24), *I am* but *I'm* (164.25), *him* but *to him* (164.32), *moment* but *moments* (165.8), *said* but *said to him* (166.4), *that* but *the* (166.21), and *terrible* but *horrible* (166.26). In chapter xxv they are MS *magnolia-bed* but E1 *magnolia-tree* (168.5), *to fully instruct you* but E1 *to instruct you fully* (168.19), *was* but E1 *were* (169.5), *my own cousin* but *my cousin* (169.9–10), *wonder. Although* but *wonder, although* (169.11), *is* but *be* (169.20), *being of a* but *being a* (169.23), *really have* but *have* (169.26), *Donovan* but *Corrigan* (169.29,32), *o'* but *of* (169.35), *I am* but *I'm* (169.39), and *'Twill* but *'Twould* (170.1).

vened between chapters II and III.) Qualitatively, no particular differences in kind appear between the alterations in these final chapters and the earlier ones, even at the start, such as might lead to a conjecture that the agent of one was not the agent of the other: they are pretty much of a piece throughout. It follows that the variants may be analyzed as a whole, without regard for their position in the romance, and what is applicable to one chapter is likely to be applicable to another. This being so, it is convenient to concentrate on the first five chapters where a control exists in the *Idler* text that will distinguish variants from MS in the E1 typescript made by annotation (or by compositorial slip) from variants in the typing. In this area appear well over a hundred substantive differences between MS and E1 that cannot be imputed to the typing.

A certain number of cuts are of immediate interest. The rationale for these is usually apparent. For instance, at 38.17–19 two sentences of Paddy's instructions to the stable boys hoisting him on his horse are excised because of Paddy's reference to his foot caught in the stirrup. It is clearly improper for him to use the word *stirrup* when he is so ignorant of horsemanship that at 38.25 he calls reins *straps* and speaks of steering the horse.[15] Three cuts appear to be made for reasons of decorum. The most obvious is that at 31.1–2 when O'Ruddy, impressed at being called *your lordship* by the landlord at Bath, innocently confesses, *I was almost resolved to delay for a time at this charming inn.* This manifest absurdity when he is in frantic search of his stolen papers would strike any editor as out of keeping with the narrative situation. With this cut as a clue, one can then note that the extreme nervousness of Lord Strepp when he calls upon O'Ruddy might seem out of character and indecorous not only for a man of his position but also for one who in his other words and actions betrays no lack of calm and easy confidence.[16] Thus at 7.12–13 *He looked at me and blushed and hesitated* is sacri-

---

[15] One may comment in passing—although it is not evidence—that a cut like this resembles an editorial more than an authorial procedure. If Crane on reviewing the typescript had seen the impropriety of Paddy's use of *stirrup*, he might easily have found a substitute, like *straps* for reins, instead of removing the offending sentence.

[16] For a cut for what seem to be similar reasons, see the omission of Strepp's "Sir," he said, "you will pardon me at 16.14.

ficed. This requires the further excision of *then——" he asked at last. You are.* The cuts are awkwardly made, for somehow the *at last* that applied to Strepp's hesitant speech gets itself preserved and inappropriately is hitched to O'Ruddy's *" 'Tis not a question for your father's son, my lord," I answered bluntly at last,* when no pause on O'Ruddy's part is possible. Moreover, shortly at 7.16 *And I now saw why he was embarrassed* hinges on the deleted description of Strepp. An author might make such a clumsy excision if he were concerned about changing the impression Strepp was to make upon the reader, and the floating *at last* error might have occurred in his typescript alteration; but an editor may seem to be the more appropriate agent, particularly since this is not the only cut that leaves anomalies in the context.[17]

One of the several reasons for cuts seems to be a desire to tighten the narrative by removing repetitions or lengthy dwelling on similar material. The first deletion at 3.28 is typical, for the father's command *Take them to him in England* is scarcely necessary, coming after *do you return them to him.* A similar motive may perhaps account for the omission at 20.18–20 of *As we walked back toward the inn, I admonished him so severely that he gave over most of his high airs but not without commentary,* which introduces the commentary itself. Interesting implications are present in another excision that seems due to an attempt at condensation. At 9.22–23 E1 cuts MS *it being known through Forister no doubt that the duel* before continuing *was to be fought at day-break.* At first sight the omitted remark would seem to be quite superfluous: Forister is discussing the duel and it might seem obvious that it was he who had told his hearers of it. But of course—whether intended or not—the omission by removing the source of the information as Forister leaves open other agents. Moreover, the cut removes something of a slur on Forister's loose tongue, a change that could scarcely be

---

[17] Just so, in the cut at 31.1–2 already remarked, the E1 text reads: *I was so pleased with his calling me "your lordship" that I hesitated a moment. But I was recalled to sense by the thought that although Jem Bottles and I* etc. Here the reason for the momentary hesitation is not altogether clear (it could have been that O'Ruddy was taken aback), and certainly the remark about being recalled to sense has no meaning at all without the deleted preceding *I was almost resolved to delay for a time at this charming inn,* which would have been taking leave of his senses.

Crane's intention given the emphasis on it elsewhere. On the whole this alteration looks less like an author's second thoughts than a somewhat mechanical piece of editing.

A tightening of the style by minor deletion seems to motivate the omission in E1 of such phrases, which are indeed awkward, as MS *be glad to* in *I am instructed to be glad to meet any terms which you may suggest* (16.24) and of *compelled to* in *he will not wish to be compelled to be spared, I feel sure* (20.2). Simple repetitions are likely to go, like *a mere nothing* in O'Ruddy's stammered *don't speak of it—a nothing—a mere nothing* (40.10). At 36.7–8 the statement that Forister laughed seemed to the annotator to be sufficient, so that he cut the illustrative *Ha, ha, ha!*

In some circumstances the annotator could add. He particularly did not like Crane's habit of introducing dialogue without some bridge. Thus at 15.15 he inserted *and said*, at 18.13 *where he exclaimed*, and *and cried* at 37.20. He did not care for Crane's typical series without an *and*: at 11.36, for example, MS *they were simply limp, helpless with laughter* is altered to *limp and helpless*, which alters the syntax from apposition to a series; and at 30.3 *I thought of a cloaked figure, a pair of shining eyes* becomes *figure and a pair*. He also disliked Crane's characteristic designed repetitions of words and phrases. At 21.12–13 repeated *These papers* becomes *They*; at 23.6 repeated *this man's* is changed to *his*; and at 37.36 repeated *My business* becomes *which*. Crane's tenses always called forth editorial interference, in this case exemplified by the change of *heard* to *had heard* (5.28), *are* to *were* (8.23), *comes . . . hems and haws* to *came . . . hemmed and hawed* (9.9–10), *had* to *have* (13.16), and *had had* to *had* (31.38). Perhaps it was the proofreader who (as he was to do with Barr in the preserved proofs) altered or queried *was* to *were* (10.39). Proofreader or annotator, Crane's split infinitives did not survive, as at 18.12–13, 39.38, and 42.3. Other of Crane's syntactical mannerisms were smoothed out: for instance, *me it* is changed to *it me* (11.1–2), *would only* to *only would* (16.37), *been told since* to *since been told* (22.11), *near to* to *near* (23.3), *and yet is* to *is yet* (27.38), and *of exactly* to *exactly of* (42.12). Some attempts are made to alter Crane's language. Rather oddly the annotator had such a strong preference for *to see* that he altered *find* to *see* (16.13) and *met* to *saw* (23.2), a characteristic that is found later as well, along with his favorite *immediately* to which *instantly* had been changed at 42.3. For no ascertainable reason *one day* becomes *once* (6.5), *was going* is altered to *wanted to go* (7.2), *in short* to *in fact* (8.38), *best* to *finest* (17.5), *whirled*—a Crane favorite—to *wheeled* (21.17), *intimation* is coarsened to *information* (16.37), *coldly* to *coolly* (41.7), and *plied* to *applied* (41.33). E1's *chocking* for MS *choking* (40.9) is a misprint; but whether *creeping* for *creaking* (28.39) is also a compositorial error, and *fearfully* for *tearfully* (31.24–25), is less certain. The last is in the class of *time* for *times* (3.9), *quay* for *quays* (12.15), and *coin* for *coins* (13.15). The annotator's or compositor's tinkering with idiom leads away from Crane in the alteration of *taken seat* to *taken his seat* (34.32) and in the refusal at 17.23 and 34.27 to begin a sentence with *And*. The sophistication of *Here are* to *Here, you* (40.13) seems to show a misunderstanding of the meaning. It is probably significant that when at 33.16 E1 mends a positive error in MS where a word or two had been omitted, it discards the MS language *a distance* in favor of a complete reconstruction, *as I had reached a place*. E1 is correct to alter *O'Donovan* to *Donovan* at 4.17, a change the proofreader was to call to Barr's attention at the very end of the novel.

A number of these alterations go contrary to Crane's stylistic and linguistic habits, some betray a misunderstanding of the text, and many seem intent on mere normalizing and smoothing. No single change is so characteristic of Crane, or indeed of authorial revision, as to require us to assign the variants to Crane's revision of the typescript. Taken with the lack of external evidence for revision—and indeed some negative evidence in the circumstances—and considering the almost unique attention to a typescript required in conditions that were far from leisurely —the nature of the variants themselves seems to support the working theory that in the surveyed five chapters no E1 variant can be traced to an authoritative source.

A similar examination applied to any other section of the book would yield similar results. Indeed, in at least one respect alterations elsewhere are quite demonstrably not authorial. This refers not so much to the frequent stylistic changes away from

Crane's known characteristics but more to a few quite serious, lengthy cuts. One of these cuts is similar to that made at 31.1–2 in that it involves decorum: that O'Ruddy would have got drunk if he had stopped at the country inn to join Strepp and Royale, at 74.28–31, introduces a discordant note, for O'Ruddy is never shown inebriated. The others delete matters that have sexual references. The book is not so dainty in this respect as is the *Idler*, but Crane's frankness for the period passed the strict limits that were imposed. At 80.29–82.18 a relatively lengthy conversation between O'Ruddy and Bottles about Forister's mistress Nell and her way of life is excised, and so is the talk with Doctor Chord in Kensington Gardens about the scandal surrounding Lady Lucy Ninth (135.36–136.17). Although E1 had printed O'Ruddy's agitation at Royale's account of Lady Mary as a baby in her bath which the *Idler* removed (65.27–28; 65.34–66.4), the book cuts an amusing account of Doctor Chord's bleeding Lady Mary because he made the incision in her thigh (152.32–153.10).

When one regards the stylistic and other forms of editing that the *Idler* imposed on the typescript text for chapters I–V, the E1 editing throughout does not appear to be unusual in its presence or very different in its nature. The *O'Ruddy* manuscript was written at top speed and obviously represents the original composition, not a revised fair copy. That a writer like Barr and a publisher like Methuen—forced to deal with what is in some respects a draft manuscript left incomplete by a dead author whose style at best offered irresistible temptation to editorial tinkering—would as an act of piety preserve all the roughnesses, real or fancied, is a fantastic proposition. Methuen would certainly require printer's copy that was not only complete but also in publishable shape. Whether it was Barr or a Methuen reader (with some small help finally from the proofreader) who edited the typescript for publication cannot be ascertained, although one might guess that everyone concerned had a hand in it. Whatever the sources, it is clear that a consistent effort was made to bring the typescript into conformity with what was considered to be a suitable correctness and smoothness of style, with parallel attention to any incidents in the narrative that violated the standards of the day. That in some respects a surface improvement by conventional standards resulted from this editorial process is undeniable; but that this improvement originated with the author is so highly doubtful from every point of view as to be an unacceptable guide to editorial procedure in a critical edition that is more concerned with what Crane actually wrote than with what Methuen or Barr thought he should have written. Under these circumstances the editorial position is that although some useful alterations of manuscript errors resulted from the preparation of the E1 typescript for publication [18]—and these are adopted when they constitute necessary corrections, not simply fancied improvements—no demonstrable authority inheres to any change made in the *Idler* or in E1. The copy-text, by necessity, is the Klopfer manuscript since it represents Crane's own accidentals texture. But since the *Idler* and the E1 substantive variants are assessed as unauthoritative, very little emendation of the copy-text is accepted from them or, indeed, in any respect. Thus the present edition, for Crane's part (3.0–171.30) is made up from a close transcript of the manuscript's substantives as well as its accidentals, with such corrections and normalizing as are customary in a critical text. Where the last manuscript page is missing (171.31–172.38) E1 necessarily is the only textual authority.

For Barr's part (173.1–267.31) the Bruccoli uncorrected proofsheets are the natural copy-text since they are the closest of any preserved document to the lost Barr manuscript. These are emended by reference first to the proofreader's marked corrections which were accepted by Barr and then by reference to E1, which reproduces—in theory—the finally corrected proofsheets to which had been added the Barr alterations [19] marked in the set of proofs he had returned to Methuen. The identification of the final E1 readings, variant from the proofsheets, with Barr's independent corrections and revisions is conjectural, of course, for no copy exists to determine whether the printer or

---

[18] As for instance the normalizing of Crane's original *O'Donovan* to *Donovan*, his later choice, which had been inconsistent in the manuscript, or the editorially alert identification of Paddy's priest as *Father Corrigan* (as at 105.11), not *Donovan* as the manuscript carelessly had it at 169.29,32. But see the E1 perpetuation of the Bristol-Bath confusion.

[19] These are more numerous than his acceptances of the proofreader's changes and queries marked in the second set which has been preserved.

the publisher reread the revises and made further changes that were not submitted to Barr for approval since they would have been considered to be necessary corrections. Certain of these alterations, such as the addition of required closing quotation marks at 187.24 and 188.13, or the necessary change of single to double quotes at 207.2 and 209.6–7, are corrections of mechanical errors that had escaped the proofreader in the preserved set of proofs. Whether these were caught and marked by Barr or were discovered upon reading revises is not to be determined. The change of unmarked *bannisters* in the proof to E1 *banisters* is doubtful as an authorial correction, given the proofreader's marked query of *postillions* at 248.21, which comes out in E1 as *postilions*. In view of the real possibility for the presence in E1 of unauthoritative changes never approved by Barr, some question must always apply to minor punctuation changes in E1 such as the substitution of a question mark and dash for the proofsheet comma after *all* at 220.27. The substitution in E1 of a question mark for a correct semicolon at 243.22 seems even more mechanically motivated and is without parallel elsewhere in Barr's part. At 218.20 the rigid substitution of a semicolon for a comma after *funeral* is, in fact, quite wrong. One cannot demonstrate that these were not Barr's own markings, but a strong possibility exists against their authority. If this is true for certain of the accidentals, it may apply as well to some of the substantives. Under these conditions the uncorrected proofsheets may offer a sounder copy-text than the possibly sophisticated E1. A further convenience is present in this choice in that without cluttering the Historical Collation with rejected accidentals variants, or the duplication of most of the information from the collational apparatus in a special list of proofchanges, the history of the transmission of the text from proofs to finally printed form can be conveniently managed in one place in the List of Emendations.[20]

---

[20] Only one change in procedure is necessary here. Ordinarily, the List of Emendations records only the changes accepted in the copy-text, leaving the rejected substantive readings for the Historical Collation and ignoring the rejected accidentals variants when no emendation has been made. But here it is important for the record to have a complete listing. Hence an exception has been made, and the few accepted variant accidentals readings from the copy-text are also listed, together with the rejected readings of E1.

In Crane's part, edited from the manuscript as copy-text, the only silent changes in this edition involve the ambiguous positioning of quotation marks in relation to associated punctuation. Like many authors Crane sometimes carelessly placed the quotation marks directly above a comma or period, or even sometimes slightly in front of it, even though his normal intention agreed with conventional placement. These variable relationships are all inadvertent and hence are normalized silently.[21] A considerable amount of other correction and normalization proved necessary, as in the editing of most literary manuscripts, a detailed record of which would have swelled the List of Emendations to monstrous proportions. Crane had certain relatively fixed misspellings, such as *recieved* or *foriegn*, and a fixed habit of placing quotation marks before instead of after a concluding dash.[22] He almost invariably used the apostrophe form *it's* for the possessive pronoun. All such corrected details are listed on their first appearance, with the page-line number followed by *et seq.*, meaning that this emendation applies to all subsequent appearances that are not specifically noted otherwise as correct in the copy-text. This method is as accurate, ultimately, and is certainly more convenient than the alternative system of carefully listing the page-line in a string of numbers for all subsequent occurrence. Other normalization, such as that of hyphenated compounds, is recorded regularly as it occurs.

In Barr's part conventional E1 spacing present throughout the book such as *was n't, I 'll, 't is, they 're* is silently normalized to the present-day forms. A problem arises when a certain amount of housestyling in E1, which was editorially rejected when Crane's manuscript was the copy-text, now in Barr's chap-

[21] Any other treatment would be pedantic. The exact positioning of the quote mark, whether directly above or very slightly to the left or to the right, is sometimes almost impossible to determine in a commonly acceptable manner; and to attempt to record such arbitrarily decided positions could never result in true accuracy, even if any useful purpose were to be served thereby—which it is not.

[22] This last is not an error, for it had an honorable history in the eighteenth century and is occasionally found in the nineteenth century, indeed a few times in Crane's magazine texts. But it differs from the conventional printing-house style of the time and, though worth recording as a characteristic of the manuscript, is not worth preserving in any printed text except for a diplomatic reprint.

ters becomes a copy-text characteristic. Typical examples concern the frequent E1 use of a comma and dash to introduce dialogue instead of a colon, or the use of commas in connection with parenthetical dashes, or the division of *every one, any one, some one*, or of *to-night, to-morrow, to-day*. Partly for the sake of uniformity between the two sections in a reading text, and partly because some indications exist that Barr's copy in certain respects at least might have differed from this housestyling,[23] the present edition alters these conventions to agree with those adopted in the first twenty-five chapters, but notes the changes.

In the List of Emendations the treatment of the authorities differs in the first five chapters from that in the remaining chapters of Crane's part. Although the *Idler* and E1 are technically equal in authority in this first installment, being set from duplicate typescripts, the *Idler* typescript was less systematically edited than that for E1 and is therefore usually nearer to MS. Thus if an emendation of MS is necessary, the primary source of the emendation will be the *Idler*, not E1. However, since substantives have an independent interest, the substantive emendations in the first five chapters will always record the readings of all three authorities. On the other hand, beginning with chapter VI the situation changes. In this section the *Idler* is derived immediately from E1 and has no authority apart from E1; thus E1 alone becomes the next authority to MS. Under such conditions the rationale of the notation changes, since in these later chapters E1 is taken as the primary source of emendation.

Throughout, the book form of the text is noted as E1. Despite the fact that the United States edition appeared before the English, this Stokes edition was printed unaltered from the Methuen (E1) plates. Hence the *textual* transmission was directly from MS to typescript to E1, and more clarity as to the Methuen editing will be achieved if the collations reflect the actual transmission and not a textually meaningless priority in publication of the Stokes printing.

Unless it is a question of emendation of the manuscript copy-text, the collations omit the listing of variant paragraph-

[23] Although it must be remarked that in Barr's letters to Cora what appears to be a definite spacing does appear in *any one*.

ing. The manuscript frequently does not paragraph dialogue, but with almost complete regularity E1 sets off all dialogue from narrative by paragraphs. (The *Idler* is somewhat less regular in this restyling.) The evidence suggests that variation in paragraphing between the two printed editions and the manuscript is not to be referred to the typescript and whatever authority it might have but instead is a pure matter of house-styling, without authority. Since the styling of manuscript and of E1, especially, in this matter of paragraphing is at opposite poles, rejected *Idler* and E1 paragraphing has been classified as a simple variation in the system of 'accidentals,' and therefore not recordable in the Historical Collation. In this respect the treatment agrees with the procedures adopted for derived texts in other volumes of this edition.

F.B.

ADDENDUM: Professor M. J. Bruccoli owns a copy of the Stokes first edition with the dust jacket, which may be described as follows:

Black printing on tan wove paper. Front: 'THE O'RUDDY | BY STEPHEN CRANE | and ROBERT BARR ||| With Frontispiece in Color by C. D. WILLIAMS ||| [underlined] A rattling romance, full of humor, dash and | incident. | [underlined] The hero, The O'Ruddy, is an inimitable | Irish blade, witty, audacious and irresistible. | [rest without underline] All the world knows that Stephen Crane | was at work on the MS. of this novel, of which | he had completed the greater part. When he | started for the Continent, Robert Barr, his friend, | went with him as far as the Channel and bade | him good-bye there. Before separating they had | a long detailed talk over the novel and its com-|pletion. Crane thought that he would never get | well and expressed the strongest desire that Barr | should finish "The O'Ruddy" if he himself | should not live to do so. | *Afterwards Barr was so occupied with | writing "Over the Border," that he was not | able to do anything with the story, but has | now yielded to the urgent requests of his | publishers, and has carried his old friend's | novel to a triumphant conclusion.* | —*The Publishers.* ||| FREDERICK A. STOKES | COMPANY, PUBLISHERS'. Spine: 'THE | O'RUDDY || STEPHEN CRANE | and | ROBERT BARR | STOKES'. Back, and front and back flaps: book advertisements.

Professor Bruccoli's collection also includes a copy of the second printing of the Stokes edition, noted on the verso of the titlepage as 'Second Edition', and a copy of the second Methuen edition of 1921 (reset), the copyright page of which lists three printings in 1904. (See *Stephen Crane, 1871–1971: An Exhibition from the Collection of Matthew J. Bruccoli* [Dept. of English, University of South Carolina, Bibliographical Series No. 6, 1971], p. 9.)

APPENDIXES

TEXTUAL NOTES

3.28 Take . . . England.] The unnecessary repetitiousness of this sentence may have led to its deletion by the E1 editor. That the general typescript had it is indicated by its presence in the *Idler*.

6.5 one day] The change in E1 to 'once' is not felicitous and it is hard to believe that it was a special typescript alteration. The reason may perhaps be found in the E1 addition of 'as', later in the same line, before 'he was then'. The present editor's conjecture is that in order to insert this word in proof, 'one day' was reduced to 'once'. If these two changes were made in proof, they would lack all authority against the agreement of MS and I.

7.11 bluntly] E1 reads 'bluntly at last.', which in context makes little sense. When one sees the cut that E1 made in the MS text, the reason for the error is clear, for 'the last' actually was appended to Lord Strepp's question, ' "You are, then——" he asked at last.', and by accident was not deleted with it. This cut may have been made in the E1 typescript, but eyeskip in E1 is as probable, on the evidence of the 'at last' and the repeated ' "You are, then. . .".'

11.32 sang] This slightly unusual verb in MS for the conventional 'rang' of I and E1 indicates that the change was made in the typescript. That MS probably represents what Crane wanted is suggested by another typescript change at 42.32 in which I and E1 agree in the conventional 'said' against MS 'sang', again an unusual idiom here. Reference may be made to "This Majestic Lie," TALES OF WAR, *Works*, VI, 204.13–14, for another confusion in the texts between 'sang' and 'rang' in which the first emendation to 'rang' may be in some doubt. That a reading originated in the *O'Ruddy* typescript entitles it to respect but not to the same authority as possessed by the manuscript because it is unlikely—given the haste in which the chapters were sent off to Pinker—that Crane read over the typescript with any care to alter the less obvious typist sophistications. Moreover, Cora's conjectured care with checking the typescript does not preclude her making unauthoritative changes.

16.14 "Sir," he said . . . me.] The reason for the E1 omission of this sentence is obscure. Without it, Lord Strepp's opening words are discourteous in their abruptness, and it is appropriate that O'Ruddy should answer at 16.27 with the same form in which he had been addressed.

38.17–19 Well, then . . . stirrup?] The reason for this E1 cut may well be that if Paddy did not know the name for *reins* (38.24–25), he would be unlikely to speak so familiarly here of the *stirrup*. The cut leaves a small jagged edge, for 'ready again' in the next sentence depends upon the first try interrupted by the caught foot.

39.36–37 gazed at me] Although 'gaze' as a transitive verb is recorded in the *O.E.D.*, its use is stated to be poetical, and the last illustration offered dates from 1839. Under these circumstances, it is more probable that Crane inadvertently omitted the 'at' than that he was cognizant of the rare transitive usage and was trying to give the illusion of eighteenth-century language. He is not deliberately archaic in this manner elsewhere.

43.4 All the same] Since MS reads 'At the same I wished' there is a strong pull to conjecture that the MS error lies not in 'At' but in the omission of 'time' after 'same', and that 'All the same' is a typescript sophistication passed on to E1. However, O'Ruddy's use of the phrase 'all the same' at 6.34–35 may prove decisive in assigning the MS mistake to 'At' and emending properly from E1.

54.31–33 Now . . . knowledge.] The omission of this sentence in E1 (and thence in I) leaves a jagged edge, as in some other such excisions. That O'Ruddy will be silent is a promise directly dependent upon the omitted statement that he now knows the secret.

70.9 women] On the analogy of Crane's frequent confusion in writing 'gentleman' for 'gentlemen' (as at 53.26, 78.5, or 83.12), it is quite possible that he intended the plural here, as in E1, though inscribing the singular. The context is not absolute in any requirement, but the plural fits a trifle more naturally. Whatever the authority of the typescript, it could have read 'women'; although it is true that the E1 editor was quite capable of making the change on his own.

77.8 highwayman.] In the manuscript a horizontal line above and below the deleted passage, extending slightly between the lines of text, appears to make a proposed excision that was, apparently, ignored in the typescript. The repetition scarcely seems designed. It might have occurred if Crane at this point were making a fair copy of a draft. E1 retained the passage but the *Idler* editor seems to have recognized the error and cut it properly.

131.24 would speak] Crane wrote only 'speak' in error; the 'would' has been supplied in pencil in a strange hand. The E1 'spoke' may be a sophistication, possibly in the typescript, from the example of 'spoke' at 131.25.

140.4 refused] The E1 reading 'refused' for MS 'refusing' is a necessary correction. Crane got himself into trouble by not observing parallel structure, and as a result 'refusing' as he wrote the sentence becomes parallel with 'pausing' (not with 'clamoured') and so subject to modification by 'without', which makes nonsense. A strong pause after 'wind' as an emendation (with 'and' deleted) would help to set right the syntax but would not be characteristic of Crane's punctuation system. On the whole, the E1 variant is best adopted (though presumably without authority) as a correction, not a revision.

175.33 not] The E1 proof read, 'I'm not going . . . on a tour of inspection to see whether I'll buy the mansion or not', but the proofreader marked the 'not' for deletion. The marking must be wrong. The O'Ruddy ironically means that he will not stroll through the rooms but instead will find Lady Mary directly, without delay (as indeed he does). It may be that Barr was not thinking of the sense when he failed to restore the deleted 'not' and instead was momentarily confused.

263.27 if] The line is loose in E1 and it would seem that the word fell out before plates were made. The presence of 'if' in I means that I was set from a copy with it, like the proof. This appearance vouches for its correctness, unless it was a last-minute correction in E1 (which is nonsense), or an independent correction by the I editor (possible).

EDITORIAL EMENDATIONS IN THE COPY-TEXT

[NOTE: Every editorial change from the manuscript copy-text is recorded here except for the few silent alterations of typographical detail noted in the essay on "The Text." For the first five chapters, in which the *Idler* is an independent witness, emendations accepted from I–E1 agreement are credited to the *Idler*; but beginning with chapter VI when the *Idler* was set from E1 copy the order is reversed and emendations are credited to the Methuen edition (E1) as the primary source. An alteration assigned to the Virginia edition (V) is made for the first time in the present edition if by *the first time* is understood *the first time in respect to the texts chosen for collation*, which for the present text comprise only the manuscript, the *Idler* serialization, the Methuen first edition of 1904, the typescript of chapter XXIV, and the Barr uncorrected proofs. Asterisked readings are discussed in the Textual Notes. The notation *et seq.* signifies that all following occurrences are to be taken as identical unless specifically listed to the contrary. The wavy dash ~ represents the same word that appears to the left of the bracket and is used exclusively in recording punctuation and other accidentals variants. An inferior caret ∧ indicates the absence of a punctuation mark. E1(p) signifies the Barr proofsheets, which may be (u) in their original state, or (c) with the proofreader's markings.]

3.12 -abiding,] E1; -abideing∧ MS; ~ — I
3.18 *Martha Bixby*] I; Martha Bixby MS; 'Martha Bixby' E1
3.18 Indies,] I,E1; ~ ∧ MS
3.20 besides] E1; beside MS,I
3.26 *et seq.* don't] I,E1; dont MS
3.27 life,] I,E1; ~ ∧ MS
*3.28 Take . . . England.] *stet* MS,I
4.17 Donovan] MS(c), E1; O'Donovan MS(u),I
4.22 Bristol,] I,E1; ~ ∧ MS
5.16 tonight] V; to-night MS+
5.29; 6.13 Colonel's] I,E1; colonel's MS
5.33 humour] I,E1; humor MS
5.37 *et seq.* 'Tisn't] I; ∧Tisn't MS; 'T isn't E1 (*except* E1 5.37 It isn't)

5.38 *et seq.* its] I; it's MS,E1 (E1 *in error only at* 5.38)
5.39; 6.23; 7.28 Colonel] I,E1; colonel MS
5.39 *et seq.* 'Tis] I; ∧Tis MS; 'T is E1
6.5 South] I; north MS,E1 (E1: North)
*6.5 one day] *stet* MS,I
6.9 *et seq.* stole——"] I,E1; ~ " —— MS
6.13 colour] I,E1; color MS
6.14 lordship's] I,E1; Lordship's MS
6.15 time∧] E1; ~ , MS (*doubtfully*),I
6.15,22; 11.5 lordship] I,E1; Lordship MS
6.15 *et seq.* 'Twas] I; T'was MS(*occasionally* Twas); 'T was E1

6.21; 9.11 honourable] I,E1; honorable MS

6.28 crazy,] I; ~ ∧ MS; ~ ; E1

6.32 *et seq.* couldn't] I; couldnt MS; could n't E1

7.9,24; 18.13; 21.19,20,27 honour] I,E1; honor MS

*7.11 bluntly] *stet* MS,I

7.20 *et seq.* ¹Mr.] I,E1; Mr∧ MS

8.14 Donovan] V; O'Donovan MS+

8.27 coat!] E1; ~ ? MS; ~ . I

8.38 authoritatively] I,E1; authoritively MS

9.8 accommodation] I,E1; accomadation MS

9.24 hub-bub] V; hubbub MS+

10.11 gentlemen] I,E1; gentleman MS

10.22 cloaks,] I,E1; ~ ∧| MS

10.34 'tis] *stet* MS

11.25 Earl] I,E1; earl MS

*11.32 sang] *stet* MS

13.32, 21.3 blaguards] V; blagaurds MS; blackguards I,E1

13.38 *et seq.* 'twill] I; ∧twill MS(*occasionally* t'will); 't will E1

14.38 *et seq.* villain] I,E1; villian MS

15.21 quiet] I,E1; quite MS

15.27 appearance] I,E1; appearence MS

15.30 afterward] E1; afterwards MS,I

15.31 *et seq.* perceived] I,E1; percieved MS

15.32 *et seq.* foreigners] I,E1; foriegners MS

*16.14 "Sir," he said . . . me.] *stet* MS,I

16.14 "you] I;| ∧ ~ MS

16.20,21,22,24 'lashings'] I; " ~ " MS; ∧ ~ ∧ E1 (*except* 16.20: ' ~ ')

17.10 England,] I,E1; ~ ∧ MS

17.11 sword,] I; ~ ∧ MS; ~ ; E1

17.23–24,30 Colonel's] I,E1; colonel's MS

17.29 *et seq.* seized] I,E1; siezed MS

18.4 -arm,] I,E1; ~ ∧ MS

18.7–8 couldn't] *stet* MS

18.23 Colonel] I,E1; colonel MS

18.28 O] V; oh MS; Oh I,E1

19.11 afterward] V; afterwards MS

20.4 *et seq.* won't] I,E1; wont MS

20.14 was playing] I,E1; playing MS

20.21 King] E1; king MS,I

20.21 'tis] *stet* MS

20.32; 21.7 gentlemen] I,E1; gentleman MS

21.3 I'd] I; Id MS; I 'd E1

21.4 I'm] I,E1; Im MS

21.17 "Villain,"] I; " ~ ∧" MS; " ~ !" E1

21.20 wailed,] I; ~ ∧| MS; ~ : E1

22.21 landlord] I,E1; ~ - ~ MS

23.20 *et seq.* principal] I,E1; principle MS

24.25–26 contemptuously] I,E1; contemptuouly MS

25.3 *et seq.* wouldn't] I; wouldnt MS; would n't E1

25.3 *et seq.* didn't] I; didnt MS; did n't E1

25.6 *et seq.* foreign] I,E1; foriegn MS

26.25 Jem,∧] E1; ~ ," MS

26.26 ∧Not . . . them.∧] E1; " ~ . . .~ ." MS

26.27 ∧All] E1; " ~ MS

26.28 Bottles's] E1; Bottles' MS

26.33 ¶ Soon] I,E1; *no* ¶ MS

27.23 limber,] I,E1; ~ ∧| MS

28.4 shepherd] I,E1; sheperd MS

30.0 CHAPTER IV] E1; IV MS,I

30.3 eyes,] I,E1; ~ ∧ MS

30.12 the daughter] I,E1; daughter MS

31.10; 37.30 honour] I,E1; honor MS

32.24 liever] V; lever MS+

33.16 as we were] V; *omit* MS,I; as I had reached a place E1

34.23 finger ∧ be] E1; ~ . Be MS; ~ , be I
34.31 judged] I; judge MS,E1
37.12 Him] E1; He MS,I
37.28 henchmen] I,E1; henchman MS
37.37 said I,] I,E1; ~ ~ ∧ MS
37.37 down stairs] E1; ~ - ~ MS; ~ -| ~ I
38.9 stable-boys] I,E1; ~ ∧ ~ MS
*38.17–19 Well, then . . . stirrup?] stet MS,I
38.23 King] I; king MS,E1
39.8 today] V; to-day MS+
39.19 borne] I,E1; born MS
*39.36 at] I,E1; omit MS
40.20 Afterward] E1; Afterwards MS,I
40.30 mummified] I,E1; mumified MS
41.19 comrade's] I,E1; comrades' MS
41.25 splendour] I,E1; splendor MS
42.18 Earl] I,E1; earl MS
*43.4 All] I,E1; At MS

[The Idler from this point on is printed from E1 (proof) and emendations are therefore made directly from E1.]

44.15 parlour] E1,I; parlor MS
44.22; 46.4,32; 48.20,21,30,33,36; 50.12; 57.15; 65.13; 66.4,10; 67.3; 74.22 Colonel] E1,I; colonel MS
45.14 inexplicable] E1,I; enexplicable MS
45.23 forty] E1,I; fourty MS
45.27 brook] E1,I; broke MS
45.30 forthcoming."] E1,I; ~ .∧ MS
46.9 et seq. receive] E1,I; recieve MS
46.21 clamour] E1,I; clamor MS
47.14 kept] E1,I; keep MS
47.14 humour] E1,I; humor MS
47.17; 48.31 swordsmen] E1,I; swordsman MS

48.2 Britain] E1,I; Britian MS
48.36 et seq. haven't] I; havent MS; have n't E1
49.21 heels?] E1,I; ~ . MS
50.2 'Pon] E1,I; ∧ ~ MS
51.15 Donovan] MS(u),E1,I; O'Donovan MS(c)
51.20 short,] E1,I; ~ ∧| MS
51.30 fowl's] E1,I; fowls' MS
53.7–8 inasmuch] E1,I; ~ ∧ ~ ∧ ~ MS
53.22 belly full] E1,I; bellyful MS
53.26; 78.5; 83.12 gentlemen] E1,I; gentleman MS
53.28,39; 54.1,2,10,17,25 Bath] I; Bristol MS,E1
53.32 soothe] E1,I; sooth MS
54.10 I've] V; Ive MS; I have E1,I
54.20 you!] E1,I; you! MS
54.22 et seq. 'Twould] I; T'would MS; 'T would E1
54.25 sweetheart,] E1,I; ~ ∧| MS
*54.31–33 Now, . . . knowledge.] stet MS
55.4 answered] E1,I; answed MS
57.26 et seq. privileged] E1,I; previleged MS
58.23 salaam] E1,I; salamm MS
59.9 never] E1,I; neven MS
60.7 possession] E1,I; possesion MS
60.24 landlord] E1,I; ~ - ~ MS
60.33; 73.3; 89.39 its] stet MS
61.19 flicked] V; flecked MS+
61.20 harbour] E1,I; harbor MS
62.3 et seq. received] E1,I; recieved MS
62.30 et seq. deceive] E1,I; decieve MS
63.12 judgment,] E1,I; ~ ∧| MS
63.24 Moses'] E1; Moses∧ MS; Moses's I
64.5 et seq. 'Faith] E1,I; ∧Faith MS
64.9 wasn't] stet MS
64.18 believing] E1,I; beleiveing MS
64.35 et seq. acquaintance] E1,I; acquintance MS

65.25 you','] V; ~ ∧' " MS; ~ !' "
Eɪ,I

65.26; 71.15 candour] I; candor MS,Eɪ

66.6 lady] MS(u),Eɪ,I; Lady MS(c)

66.36 Aye] Eɪ,I; Ay MS

67.24 Whenever∧] Eɪ,I; ~ , MS

67.29 meditations] Eɪ,I; mediations MS

68.24 rapture.] Eɪ,I; ~ ∧ MS

69.4 tumultuously] Eɪ,I; tumultously MS

*70.9 women] Eɪ,I; woman MS

70.21 ladyship] Eɪ,I; ~ - ~ MS

[*Strange hand begins here with* 70.39 'Afterwards' *and continues to* 72.31 'horsemen.']

70.39 Afterward] V; Afterwards MS; *omit* Eɪ,I

71.4 believe] Eɪ,I; Believe MS

71.7 around] Eɪ,I; round MS

71.11; 72.3 behaviour] Eɪ,I; behavior MS

71.19 saints] I; Saints MS,Eɪ

71.21 Madam,] Eɪ,I; ~ ∧ MS

71.21 if] Eɪ,I; If MS

71.35 The] Eɪ,I; the MS

71.39 bystander] Eɪ,I; byestander MS

72.13 duelling] MS(u),Eɪ,I; dueling MS(c)

72.20 foreign] *stet* MS

72.22 pursued] Eɪ,I; persued MS

[Crane's *hand resumes*.]

73.2 look] V; looked MS

73.4 ²lady!] Eɪ,I; ~ , MS

73.27 shoot] Eɪ,I; shot MS

74.4 today] V; to-day MS+

74.8 *et seq.* ain't] Eɪ,I; aint MS

74.11 surprise] Eɪ,I; suprise MS

74.29 drunkenness] V; drunkeness MS

75.11 a flying] Eɪ,I; flying MS

75.24 heard] Eɪ,I; *omit* MS

75.27 swordsmen] Eɪ,I; swordsman MS

*77.8 highwayman.] I; highwayman. [¶] "Ahum," said Paddy. "Ahum! Are ye listening, Jem Bottles?" [¶] "I be," replied the highwayman. MS,Eɪ (Eɪ: Ahem)

77.19; 83.33; 84.11; 86.18; 90.6 Earl] Eɪ,I; earl MS

77.38 till] Eɪ,I; til MS

78.1 Thinking,] Eɪ,I; ~ ∧ MS

78.15 he,] Eɪ,I; ~ ∧ MS

80.12 treasury] Eɪ,I; treasurery MS

81.10 gentleman'!] V; ~ !' MS

81.18 principal] MS(u),Eɪ,I; principle MS(c)

81.28 philosophy] V; philosphy MS

82.3 borne] V; born MS

82.4 lover."] V; ~ .∧ MS

82.21 a-blaze] V; ablaze MS+

82.37 landlord] Eɪ,I; ~ - ~ MS

83.27 Announce] Eɪ,I; Annonce MS

84.16 *et seq.* Seize] Eɪ,I; Sieze MS

85.5 abruptly] Eɪ,I; abrubbly MS

85.24; 86.20 into] Eɪ,I; in to MS

85.26 *et seq.* doctor] Eɪ,I; docter MS

85.34 I've] Eɪ,I; Ive MS

86.10 quickly,] Eɪ,I; ~ ∧ MS

86.14 'Twas] *stet* MS

87.11 tutor——"] V; ~ ——∧ MS; ~ ." Eɪ,I

88.14; 94.4; 111.21 honour] Eɪ,I; honor MS

89.11 'Twould] *stet* MS

89.16 present,] Eɪ,I; ~ ∧ MS

89.28 bony] Eɪ,I; boney MS

89.32 King] Eɪ,I; king MS

89.39 ostrich] Eɪ,I; albatross MS

90.5 anyhow,] Eɪ,I; ~ ∧ MS

91.9 discreetly] Eɪ,I; discretely MS

91.9 waistcoat] Eɪ,I; ~ - ~ MS

91.12 head I] E1,I; head out I MS

91.14 respect] E1,I; repect MS

91.15 ²off!"] E1,I; ~ !ᴧ MS

91.16 familiar] E1,I; familar MS

91.38 highwaymen] E1,I; high-wayman MS

92.3 that] E1,I; than MS

92.5 Wasn't] *stet* MS

92.21 "Your *no* ¶] E1,I; ¶ MS

92.21,22,30(*twice*) ladyship] E1,I; Ladyship MS

93.28 ways] E1,I; way MS

95.28; 96.37 valance] E1,I; valence MS

96.19 seized] E1,I; siezed MS

96.23 King's] E1,I; king's MS

96.27 Countess] E1,I; countess MS

96.31 fast,] E1,I; ~ ; MS

98.13 ladies] E1,I; lady MS

99.10 blackguard] E1,I; bla-guard MS

99.15 knew] E1,I; know MS

103.3 adaptability] E1; adapti-bility MS

103.7 Skibbereen] E1; Skibereen MS

104.3 heaven] V; Heaven MS+

104.7 years'] E1; year's MS

104.27 it.] E1; ~ᴧ MS

105.6; 106.25 Church] E1; church MS

106.26 you,'] E1; ~ ," MS

106.30 vagabond."] E1; ~ .ᴧ MS

106.34 wrong,] E1; ~ᴧ MS

106.38 be] E1; *omit* MS

107.2 potatoes] E1; pototoes MS

107.4 a-blaze] V; ablaze MS+

107.7; 117.3 landlord] E1,I; ~ - ~ MS

107.9 honoured] E1,I; honored MS

107.11 marvellous] E1,I; mar-velous MS

108.21 gaping] E1,I; gapeing MS

108.26 pint pot] E1,I; ~ - ~ MS

109.13 till] E1,I; til MS

109.28 stickadoroᴧ] E1,I; ~ , MS

110.22 ¹of] E1,I; *omit* MS

112.13 inexplicable] E1; inex-plicible MS

112.14 -knows-] E1; -know- MS

112.20 livelihood] E1; livlihood MS

114.5; 119.27; 127.13; 149.18; 152.24; 166.2 Afterward] E1,I; Afterwards MS

114.7 curiosity] E1,I; curiousity MS

114.20 several] E1,I; serval MS

114.21 splendour] E1,I; splendor MS

114.22 *et seq.* deceiving] E1,I; decieving MS

115.7 course,] E1,I; ~ᴧ MS

115.9 odour] E1; odor MS

115.28 favourite] E1; favorite MS

115.29 alleys] E1; allies MS

116.21 accommodation] E1,I; accomadation MS

116.28 stable-boys] E1,I; ~ᴧ~ MS

116.29 horse's] E1,I; horses' MS

117.6 out of my] E1,I; out my MS

117.21 King's] E1,I; king's MS

117.29 gentlemen] E1,I; gentle-man MS

119.0 CHAPTER XVIII] E1; XVIII MS; XVII I

119.2 furrin'] E1,I; furrin MS

120.19 'faith] *stet* MS

120.29 fit] E1,I; *omit* MS (*end of line*)

121.3 'Faith] V; ᴧ~ MS+

121.4 tomorrow] V; ~ - ~ MS+

121.14 imbecile] E1,I; embicile MS

121.34 doesn't] V; doesnt MS; does not E1,I

122.8 King] E1,I; king MS

122.16 Shakespeare] E1,I; Shakspeare MS

123.25 mopped] V; moped MS; mopping E1,I

123.35 again,] E1,I; ~ᴧ MS

125.12 Then,] E1,I; ~ᴧ| MS

126.39 quarrelling] E1,I; quarreling MS
127.9 And,] E1,I; ~ ∧ MS
127.10 squawking] E1,I;
sqawking MS
127.12 blind,] E1,I; ~ ∧ MS
128.9 Why,] E1; ~ < > | MS
128.21 sorely,] E1; ~ ∧| MS
129.1 later] E1; latter MS
129.12 clattered] MS(u),E1;
clatered MS(c)
130.6 I had] E1; had I MS
130.23 stupefied] E1; stupified
MS
130.27 vigour] E1; vigor MS
*131.24 would speak] stet MS
132.18 couldn't] stet MS
133.8 chose] E1,I; choose MS
133.10 Gardens] E1,I; gardens
MS
133.18 Gardens] I; garden MS;
Garden E1
134.9 Guards] E1; gaurds MS
136.13 affected] V; effected MS
136.27 honours] E1,I; honors
MS
136.30 marriage-portion] V;
~ ∧ ~ MS+
136.32 effrontery] E1,I; affron-
tery MS
136.36 Count] V; count E1,MS
136.37 et seq. Mrs.] E1,I; Mrs∧
MS
137.6 Count's] E1; count's MS
137.7 rumoured] E1; rumored
MS
137.13 Hold!] E1; ~ ∧ MS
137.28 matters,] E1; ~ ∧ MS
138.1,13,17; 143.24,32; 151.29
Doctor] E1; docter MS
140.1 blackguards] E1; blagards
MS
*140.4 refused] E1; refusing MS
140.24 couldn't] stet MS
140.25 Bony] E1; Boney MS
140.33 Lot's] E1; Lots MS
141.1 ¶ "Mollie] E1; no ¶ MS
141.3 Aye] V; Ay MS
141.11 twenty-five] MS(c)(25),
E1; fifty MS(u)

142.7 of] E1,I; omit MS
142.13 of the] E1,I; of the | of
the MS
143.6 conditions,] V; ~ ∧ MS+
143.13 willing,] E1; ~ ∧| MS
144.1 Perceiving] E1,I; Perceiving MS
144.23 decided] E1,I; deceded
MS
145.10 them] E1,I; omit MS
145.21 communication] E1,I;
cummunication MS
145.22 hub-bub] V; hubbub M+
146.10 West] E1,I; west MS
147.14 Strepp."] E1,I; ~ . ∧ MS
147.30 nor] E1,I; or MS
148.36 chairmen,] E1,I; ~ ∧ MS
148.36 coachmen] E1,I; coachman MS
151.2 it."] E1,I; ~ .∧ MS
151.5 have] E1,I; omit MS
151.11 enlighten] E1,I; enlightened MS
152.10 Church] E1,I; church
MS
152.38 Countess] V; countess
MS
154.2 staunch] E1,I; stanch MS
155.13 spikes,] V; ~ ∧| MS; ~ ∧
E1,I
155.33 tree."] E1,I; ~ .∧ MS
156.33,36 your honour] E1,I;
Your Honour MS
157.15 honour] E1,I; Honour MS
157.17 lick?] E1,I; ~ . MS
158.10–11 somewhat∧] E1,I; ~ ,
MS
158.26 fraught] E1,I; frought
MS
159.10 hum-drum] V; humdrum
MS+
159.23 left] E1,I; omit MS
159.34 hour's] E1,I; hours MS
160.24 for] E1; omit MS
162.22 Aye] V; Ay MS,TMs,E1,I
165.4 wasting] E1,I; wasteing
MS
165.7 rigmarole] E1,I; rigama-
role MS,TMs

165.11 sufficient] E1,I; sufficent MS,TMs

165.12 losing] E1,I; loseing MS, TMs

165.17 garden wall] I; ~ - ~ MS,TMs,E1

165.23 Lady] TMs,E1,I; Lady's MS

166.5 boldly:] E1,I; ~ ∧| MS

166.11 favourable] E1,I; favorable MS

168.5 magnolia tree] I; ~ - ~ E1; magnolia-bed MS

169.19,25,26 Aye] V; Ay MS+

169.29,32 Corrigan] E1,I; Donovan MS

169.30 'A] E1,I; " ' ~ MS

169.31 piper,] V; ~ ∧ MS+

171.1 Abandoned] E1,I; Abondoned MS

171.16 inefficiency] E1,I; inefficency MS

[MS *ends with* 171.30 (talker.").]

171.38 *et seq.* ∧Pig and Turnip∧] V; " ~ ~ ~ " E1,I

172.22 women∧] I; ~ , E1

173.1 the lads] E1,I; my lads E1(p)

173.9 done,] E1,I; done this night, E1(p)

173.13 frequented by] E1,I; endeared to E1(p)

174.4 on∧—] I; ~ , — E1

174.17 great] E1,I; good E1(p)

174.31 round] E1,I; around E1 (p)

174.33 *et seq.* tomorrow] V; to-morrow E1,I

174.37 is] E1,I; *omit* E1(p)

*175.33 not] E1(p[u]); *omit* E1 (p[c]),I

176.19 huskily:] V; ~ , — E1; ~ : — I

176.25 Doctor] E1(p)(Dr.)(*queried*); *omit* E1,I

177.12 *et seq.* someone] I; ~ ∧ ~ E1

178.27 good-night] E1(p[c]),I; ~ ∧ ~ E1(p[u])

181.1 anyhow] I; ~ ∧ ~ E1

181.5 *et seq.* anyone] I; ~ ∧ ~ E1 (*except at* 264.15)

181.9 *et seq.* everyone] I (*except at* 193.16; 256.37); ~ ∧ ~ E1

181.23 out:] V; ~ : — E1,I

182.22–23 them— . . . lips—] I; ~ , — . . . ~ , — E1

183.31 tones:] V; ~ , — E1; ~ : — I

183.37 voice:] V; ~ , — E1; ~ : — I

184.13 lady∧—] I; ~ , — E1

184.28–29 Solomon — . . . overpraised—] I; ~ , — . . . ~ , — E1

186.20 feet∧"] I; ~ ," E1

187.17 crying:] V; ~ , — E1; ~ : — I

187.24 door,"] E1,I; ~ , ∧ E1(p)

187.26 banisters] E1,I; bannisters E1(p)

187.37 palavering] E1(p[c]),I; palvering E1(p[u])

188.13 presence."] E1,I; ~ . ∧ E1 (p)

188.25 other, come . . . not.] E1,I (other∧); other, whether kicked or not, come there. E1(p)

190.8 are] E1,I; is E1(p)(*queried*)

190.8 -deeds] E1(p), E1,I('s' *queried*)

191.34 farm∧"] V; ~ ," E1,I

192.33 this∧"—] V; ~ ,"—E1,I

193.15 fashion] E1,I; fashlon E1(p)

193.16 before] E1,I; against E1(p)

195.2 ever] E1,I; *omit* E1(p)

196.10 beyond∧"] V; ~ ," E1,I

196.13 yourself∧"] V; ~ ," E1,I

198.3 it's] I; its E1

198.12 inn,] V; ~ ∧ E1,I

200.13 with] E1,I; yith E1(p)

201.11 counsellor. ∧] I; ~ ." E1

201.37 Chord—] I; ~ , — E1

206.7 no—] I; ~ , — E1

207.2 him."] E1,I; ~ .' E1(p)

207.27 me:] V; ~ , — E1; ~ :
— I

208.20 *et seq.* saints] V; Saints
E1,I

209.6–7 ∧Pig and Turnip. ∧] V;
' ~ ~ ~ .' E1,I: " ~ ~ ~ ."
E1(p)

210.6 yourself?"] E1(p[c]),I; ~
? " E1(p[u])

212.31 the weapon] E1(p[c]),I;
weapon E1(p[u])

213.7 tonight] V; to-night E1,I

213.23 a difficult] E1(p[c]),I; difficult E1(p[u])

213.39 you∧"] V; ~ ," E1,I

214.20 have] E1,I; has E1(p)
(*queried*)

214.23 this—] I; ~ , — E1

215.22 eight—] I; ~ , — E1

215.34 said] E1(p[c]),I; sad E1
(p[u])

216.7–8 courtyard∧— . . . early∧
—] I; ~ , — . . . ~ , — E1

216.32 know] E1(p[c]),I; *omit*
E1(p[u])

218.1 IN] E1(p[c]); N E1(p[u])

218.20 funeral,] E1(p),I; ~ ;
E1

219.15 So (*2-em indent*)] E1
(p[c]); So (*1-em indent*) E1
(p[u])

219.16 said:] V; ~ , — E1; ~ :
— I

219.37–38 successful— . . . uncertain—] I; ~ , — . . . ~ ,
— E1

220.27 all,] E1(p[u]); ~ ? — E1
(p[c]),I

221.3 meantime] I; ~ ∧ ~ E1

221.12 drawer] E1,I; draw
E1(p)

222.4 "Is] E1(p[c]); " Is E1
(p[u])

222.11 papers—] I; ~ , — E1

223.5 guineas—] I; ~ , — E1

223.29 wear.] E1(p[c]),I; ~∧
E1(p[u])

225.7 night—] I; ~ , — E1

225.28 flesh?"] E1(p[c]),I; ~."
E1(p[u])

226.35 honest] E1;I; early honest E1(p)

226.35 getting] E1,I; going
E1(p)

229.33 ecstasy] E1(p[c]),I; ec-
stacy E1(p[u])

230.26 " 'Stand and deliver!'']
E1(p[c]),I; "∧ ~ ~ ~ !" E1
(p[u])

230.28 'Stand . . . ye——']
E1(p[c]),I; " ~ . . . ~ ——"
E1(p[u])

230.31–32 Anyway] V; ~ ∧ ~
E1,I

231.10 " 'Clasp . . . ye——' "]
E1(p[c]),I; "∧ ~ . . . ~ ——
∧" E1(p[u])

231.16 other,] V; ~ ∧ E1,I

232.1 Oh] I; O E1

232.25 'Stand and deliver!']
E1(p[c]),I; " ~ ~ ~ !" E1
(p[u])

233.3 "Make] E1(p[c]),I; ∧ ~
E1(p[u])

235.1 I] E1(p[c]); *omit* E1(p[u])

235.1 town] E1,I; place E1(p)

235.19 Ireland";] V; ~ ;" E1,I

236.6 now—] I; ~ , — E1

236.19 anyone] I; ~ ∧ ~ E1

236.31 before—] I; ~ , — E1

237.35 ∧Anchor. ∧] V; ' ~ .' E1,I;
" ~ ." E1(p)

238.4 Brede] I; Brede's E1

238.26 ∧Anchor,∧] V; " ~ ," E1,I

239.6 you,] E1 (p[c]),I; ~ ∧
E1(p[u])

240.10 Reverence";] V; ~ ;" E1,I

240.19 it's] V; its E1,I

240.33 here∧"] V; ~ ," E1,I

240.33; 242.20; 243.4,14 father]
E1; Father E1(p), I

241.19 while . . . money] E1,I;
omit E1(p)

241.20 (*twice*) Oh] V; O E1,I

242.3 back] E1,I; ack E1(p)

242.10 you—] I; ~ , — E1

243.3 own∧"] I; ~ ," E1

243.9 Sullivan] E1,I; O'Gorman
E1(p)

243.10 the land] EI,I; our land EI(p)

243.18 "for] EI,I; ∧ ~ EI(p)

243.22 out;] EI(p[u]); ~ ? EI(p[c]),I

245.32 tonight∧"] I; ~ ," EI

246.27 'Faith] V; ∧ ~ EI,I

246.37–38 everybody] I; ~ ∧ ~ EI

247.15 Father] EI,I; As Father EI(p)

247.23 were] EI,I; was EI(p) (*queried*)

247.30 seemed] EI,I; looked EI(p)

247.35 cried∧—] I; ~ , — EI

247.36 me∧—] V; ~ , — EI,I

248.13 this";] V; ~ ;" EI,I

248.20 me.] EI(p[c]),I; ~ : EI(p[u])

248.21 postilions] EI; postillions EI(p) (*queried*),I

248.21 postilions; then] EI,I; ~ , and EI(p)

248.24–25 -furnished] EI,I; -finished EI(p)

250.2 more] EI(p[c]),I; most EI(p[u])

251.17 legal] EI,I; civil EI(p)

252.19 do∧— . . . it∧—] I; ~ , — . . . ~ , — EI

252.27 Plenty.] EI(p[c]),I; ~ : EI(p[u]) (*queried*)

253.1 will] EI(p[c]); wlli EI(p[u])

253.23 still∧—] I; ~ , — EI

254.17 was afraid] EI(p[c]),I; afraid EI (p[u])

254.20 when] EI,I; and EI(p)

255.15 The] EI,I; That EI(p)

255.33 Mr.—] EI(p[u]),I; ~ ., — EI(p[c])

256.10 a slight] EI,I; some slight EI(p)

256.26 unlucky] EI,I; poor EI(p)

256.33 yeomen] EI,I; women EI(p)

256.36 mob, asking] EI,I; men and asked EI(p)

256.37 up] EI,I; *omit* EI(p)

258.25 tailor] EI(p[c]),I; talior EI(p[u])

259.12 "you're] EI(p[c]),I; ∧ ~ EI(p[u])

260.12 lad] EI,I; *omit* EI(p) (*queried*)

260.21 of falling had done] EI,I; would do EI(p)

261.21 us.] EI(p[c]),I; ~ ∧ EI (p[u])

262.27 were] EI,I; was EI(p) (*queried*)

*263.27 if] EI(p),I; *omit* EI

264.12 staring] EI(p[c]),I; staying EI(p[u])

264.17 gold?] EI(p[c]),I; ~ , EI(p[u])

264.24 Father] EI,I; father EI(p)

265.25 Sullivan] EI,I; O'Gorman EI(p)

265.33 her";] V; ~ ;" EI,I

266.3 baboon?] EI(p[c]),I; ~ . EI(p[u])

266.5 resemble] EI,I; resembles EI(p) (*queried*)

266.6 upon] EI,I; about EI(p)

267.20.1 *space*] EI,I; *no space* EI(p)

267.29 Donovan] EI,I; O'Donovan EI(p) (*queried*)

WORD-DIVISION

1. *End-of-the-Line Hyphenation in the Virginia Edition*

[NOTE: No hyphenation of a possible compound at the end of a line in the Virginia text is present in the manuscript or, after 173.0, E1(p) except for the following readings, which are hyphenated within the line in the manuscript. Hyphenated compounds in which both elements are capitalized are excluded.]

3.11	law-|abiding		130.4	out-|pourings
4.24	sailor-|men		135.6	four-|legged
8.28	rabbit-|pie		140.4	men-|folk
13.18	red-|headed		150.2	iron-|work
17.12	wood-|chopper's		150.26	hum-|drum
19.33	blood-|letting		158.28	tea-|party
22.30	inn-|yard		162.24	garden-|thief
24.20	well-|mounted		163.27	bell-|mouthed
27.38	plum-|stew		194.5	carriage-|wheels
28.16	snuff-|boxes		209.1	storm-|cloud
50.8	tad-|pole		211.36	sword-|playing
54.28	under-|jaw		226.21	-past-|six
81.25	sweet-|heart		235.1	peaceable-|looking
83.7	chicken-|breast		235.4	well-|known
97.11	plough-|horse		245.7	gun-|firing
122.30	-minute's-|intelligent-		248.24	well-|furnished
128.7	mug-|house			

2. *End-of-the-Line Hyphenation in the Copy-Texts*

[NOTE: The following compounds, or possible compounds, are hyphenated at the end of the line in the copy-texts. The form in which they have been transcribed in the Virginia text, listed below, represents the practice of the manuscript and E1 proof as ascertained by other appearances or by parallels, or—failing that—by the known characteristics of Crane as seen in his manuscripts.]

9.18	downpour		57.20	draw-back
23.1	overtook		61.22	summer-house
26.36	blood-marks		66.36	pleasant-minded
27.4	wind-broken		70.14	blood-shed
55.30	tomorrow		89.25	shiver-shavering

107.6	tap-room	208.34	quiet-mannered
130.2	ancient-eyed	213.7	tonight
130.3	lantern-bearer	221.29	eyebrows
136.29	ill-tempered	222.6	legal-looking
139.13	placid-minded	224.18	look-out
142.1	manhood	226.4	archway
145.2	overcome	227.30	night-leave
147.32	under-footmen	228.8	sea-coast
151.23	highly-tightened	235.10	seashore
158.7	dangerous-looking	239.16	Landlord
186.6	red-headed	240.22	hangman's
190.21	fireside	254.3	panic-stricken
191.9	sword-playing	255.16	revivifying
203.13	stairway	259.11	overgrown
205.14	serious-looking	264.24	well-timed
208.33	bodyguard		

3. *Special Cases*

[NOTE: In the following the compound is hyphenated at the end of the line in the copy-text and in the Virginia Edition.]

13.39	to-|night (i.e., tonight)		burnt-thatch)
104.10	burnt-|thatch (i.e.,	164.33	nine-|pin (i.e., nine-pin)

HISTORICAL COLLATION

[NOTE: Only substantive variants from the Virginia text are listed here, together with their appearances in the manuscript (MS), the *Idler* serialization (I), the Methuen first edition of 1904 (EI), the typescript of chapter XXIV (TMs), and the Barr proofs for chapters XXVI to the end, either uncorrected (u) or with the proofreader's notations (c). Collated texts not noted for any reading agree with the Virginia Edition.]

3.9   times] time EI
3.12   from the] from EI
3.16   to ever] ever to I,EI
3.18   *Martha Bixby*] Martha Bixby MS; 'Martha Bixby' EI
3.20   besides] beside MS,I
3.23   in] into I,EI
3.24   is] are I,EI
3.28   Take . . . England.] *omit* EI
4.7   Whenever] Wherever EI
4.17   Donovan] O'Donovan MS (u),I
4.17   old] Old I
4.17   Mickey] Mickey Clancy EI
4.24   lie] be I
4.32   ludship] lordship I
5.10   noise] noise that I,EI
5.26   damning] cursing I
5.28   heard] had heard EI
5.37   'Tisn't] It isn't MS(u),EI
6.4   carried rather recklessly] rather recklessly carried EI
6.5   South] north MS,EI (EI: North)
6.5   one day] once EI
6.6   he] as he MS(u),EI
6.12 *et seq.*   Everyone] Every one EI
6.19   wind] winds EI
6.32 *et seq.*   maybe] may be EI
6.36   o'] of EI
6.38   take] takes EI

7.2   was going] wanted to go EI
7.11   bluntly] bluntly at last EI
7.12–13   He looked . . . last.] *omit* EI
8.6   young] *omit* EI
8.14   Donovan] O'Donovan MS+
8.23   are] were EI
8.26   other's bellies] other I
8.28–29   Clang! . . . Cling!] Cling! . . . Clang! EI
8.38   short] fact EI
9.9–10   comes . . . hems and haws] came . . . hemmed and hawed EI
9.13   that] why EI
9.16 *et seq.*   anyhow] any how EI
9.17   was] were EI
9.22–23   , it being . . . duel] *omit* EI
9.23   was] that was EI
10.6   a] *omit* EI
10.11   gentlemen] gentleman MS
10.15   or] of I
10.31 *et seq.*   forever] for ever I,EI
10.39   was glad] were glad EI
11.1–2   me it] it me EI
11.3   that he] he EI
11.8   hand] hands I
11.16   came a] came the EI
11.16   as] *omit* EI
11.24   on] in I

11.26   attack] an attack I

11.32   sang] rang I,EI

11.34   a railing‸] a railing; EI

11.36   limp,] limp and EI

12.15   quays] quay EI

13.15   coins] coin EI

13.24   Burke] Burk EI

13.32; 21.3   blaguards] blagaurds MS; blackguards I,EI

13.33   either] neither EI

13.34   that] that that EI

14.19   giving] going EI

14.20   and] *omit* EI

15.15   bewildered.] bewildered, and said: EI

15.18   that] *omit* EI

15.20   for there] There EI

15.21   quiet] quite MS

15.30   thus] just EI

15.30   afterward] afterwards MS,I

16.1   a simple] the simple EI

16.13   find] see EI

16.14   "Sir, . . . me.] He said: EI

16.19   this] the EI

16.22   which] that I

16.24   be glad to] *omit* EI

16.26   lashings] lashing I

16.37   intimation] information EI

16.37   would only] only would EI

17.3   the duel] this duel EI

17.4   manners] manner MS(u),I

17.5   best] finest EI

17.6   skilful] skilled I

17.23   And at] *omit* EI

17.33   high and] high, EI

18.12–13   to forcibly] forcibly to I,EI

18.13   a corner of the] the corner of a I

18.13   field.] field, where he exclaimed: EI

18.28   O] oh MS; Oh I,EI

19.10   You are] You're EI

19.11–13   This rabble . . . begin.] *omit* EI

19.11   afterward] afterwards MS+

19.17   Aye] *omit* I,EI

19.17   and] an' I; an EI

19.20   he again] again he I

19.25   young] *omit* I,EI

19.32   staunching] stanching MS(u),EI

20.2   compelled to be] *omit* EI

20.8   an] *omit* EI

20.10   his] this I

20.14   was] *omit* MS

20.18–20   As . . . commentary.] *omit* EI

20.22   I] me EI

20.32; 21.7   gentlemen] gentleman MS

21.2–3   truthful] faithful I

21.12–13   These papers] They EI

21.17   whirled] wheeled EI

21.18   at] by MS(u),I

21.21   badly] so badly I

22.8   violently] so violently I

22.11   been told since] since been told EI

22.27   pled] pleaded EI

23.2   met] saw EI

23.3   near to] near EI

23.5   this tree] the tree I

23.6   this man's] his EI

23.20 *et seq.*   principal] principle MS

23.34–35   —may . . . devil] *omit* I

24.35–37   and, ripping . . . trample] *omit* I

25.3,4   Kinsale] Kinsole I

25.4   know] knew I

25.7   that] *omit* I

25.25   moodily] *omit* I

25.33   Do . . . child?] *omit* I

25.37   am illegitimate] have no mother I

25.37–38   the quarter] a quarter EI

26.7–33   Admirable . . . there."] *omit* I

26.38   one] a EI

27.5   awaiting] waiting I,EI

27.8   ho] no I

27.38   and yet is] is yet E1

28.1   rest of that] *omit* I

28.1   last] *omit* I

28.14   take] to take I,E1

29.6   a hangel] an angel I

30.3   figure,] figure and E1

30.8   which . . . sensuous] *omit* I

30.12   the daughter] daughter MS

30.15   in] to I

30.24 *et seq.* meantime] mean time E1

30.26   to strangle] strangle I,E1

30.27   reasons] reason I

31.1–2   I was . . . inn.] *omit* E1

31.20   futilely] furtively I

31.24–25   tearfully] fearfully E1

31.26   Taking] Thinking E1

31.38   had had] had E1

32.6   mingling] mingled E1

32.14   soul] souls I

33.2–3   more . . . goose] gratitude I

33.16   as we were] *omit* MS,I; as I had reached a place E1

33.16   a distance] *omit* E1

33.26   a] the I

33.27–28   out . . . dying."] you in pieces, and then——" I

33.29   about] *omit* I

33.32   looks] look I

34.1–2   me, . . . Leave] me; mind you, leave E1

34.23   finger be careful] finger. Be careful MS; finger, be careful! I

34.27   And] *omit* E1

34.31   judged] judge MS,E1

34.32   seat] his seat E1

34.33   me] us I

36.3   papers] papers that E1

36.7–8   Ha, ha, ha!] *omit* E1

36.25   have been always] always have been I,E1

37.1   of] in E1

37.3   lonely] *omit* I

37.12   Him] He MS,I

37.16   in a] in E1

37.17   on] upon E1

37.20   admiration.] admiration and cried: E1

37.21   he cried] *omit* E1

37.23   damned] *omit* I

37.28   henchmen] henchman MS

37.35   this] his I

37.36   My business] which E1

38.5   own] *omit* E1

38.12   a half-league] half a league E1

38.17–19   Well, then . . . stirrup?] *omit* E1

38.28   no] not I

38.29   as] *omit* E1

38.30   fellow-] *omit* E1

39.8   young my] my young E1

39.19; 82.3   borne] born MS

39.25,26   Was I to tell him] *omit* E1

39.31   to] into I

39.34   on] upon E1

39.36   at] *omit* MS

39.38   to thoroughly] thoroughly to E1

40.9   choking] chocking E1

40.10   —a mere nothing] *omit* E1

40.13   Here are] Here, you E1

40.20   Afterward] Afterwards MS,I

40.22   please] pleases E1

40.24   chamber] room I

40.25   moments] minutes I

40.27   to] *omit* I

40.29   Tompkins] Thompson I

41.4   sobbed] sobbed in I

41.6   old] *omit* E1

41.7   coldly] coolly E1

41.9   deliver] to deliver E1

41.10   come] came I

41.19   comrade's] comrades' MS

41.21   came] come I

41.22   here] *omit* E1

41.33   plied] applied E1

41.34–35   "You scoundrel, you . . . speak.] *omit* E1

41.38   purse] pursel E1

42.3   to instantly] immediately to E1

42.12   of exactly] exactly of E1
42.15   sword's] sword I,E1
42.24–25   who . . .   napkin]
   omit I

42.32   sang] said I,E1
43.1   chuckled] chucked I
43.4   All] At MS
43.6   that] *omit* E1

[The Idler *from this point on is printed from E1 proof and is therefore
derived and without authority.*]

44.2   wrestled] writhed E1,I
44.19   cried] screamed E1,I
44.20   ¹threatens— . . .   threatens me,] threatens *me*,—E1,I
45.10   meantime] *stet* MS+
45.14   politely] *omit* E1,I
45.16   replied] repeated E1,I
45.27   brook] broke MS
45.34   instant] moment E1,I
45.34   discussion]   conversation
   E1,I
45.37   sputter; he] sputter, and
   E1,I
45.38   of a] of E1,I
45.38–39   tossed; suddenly] tossed, and suddenly E1,I
46.1   up this packet] it up E1,I
46.7   toward] towards I
46.18–19   believed that] believe
   E1,I
46.24   life] life that E1,I
46.26   million] thousand E1,I
46.34   while] when E1,I
46.35   damned] *omit* I
47.5   expected] expect E1,I
47.14   kept] keep MS
47.17; 48.31   swordsmen] swordsman MS
47.38   with a] with I
48.9   not] never I
48.25–26   dejectedly] dejectly I
48.26   business of] business—
   E1,I
48.27   know] know that E1,I
48.34   to say] that E1,I
48.36   called] call E1,I
49.1   sometimes] something E1,I
49.27   twirl] twist E1,I
49.30   However] *omit* E1,I
50.3   they] it E1,I
50.8   Damn him!] *omit* I
50.12   simply] *omit* E1,I

51.6   an] my E1,I
51.12   England? As] England‸ as
   E1,I
51.15   Donovan]   O'Donovan
   MS(c)
51.19   what] that E1,I
51.24   Bottles'] Bottle's 1; Bottles's E1
51.30   fowl's] fowls' MS
51.30   wing] wings I
52.5   cannot] couldn't I
52.6   —I mean . . .   eyes.] *omit*
   E1,I
52.8   then] *omit* E1,I
52.18   appeared.] approached and
   said: E1,I
52.19–20   said the servant] *omit*
   E1,I
52.22   in order] *omit* E1,I
52.27   consorting for the mo-
   ment] for the moment consorting E1,I
52.29–30   My . . .   abrupt, Mr.
   O'Ruddy.] *omit* E1,I
52.39   lip] lips I
53.9   slightly.] slightly. I   continued: E1,I
53.11   acts for me] *omit* MS(u),
   E1,I
53.19   the devil] *omit* I
53.22   belly full] bellyful MS
53.26   gentlemen]   gentleman
   MS
53.28,39; 54.1,2,10,17,25   Bath]
   Bristol MS,E1
54.1   what] to E1,I
54.4–5   "If . . .   himself.] *omit*
   E1,I
54.9   in everlasting hell] *omit* I
54.10   I've] I have E1,I
54.20   *God rot you*] *Curse you* I
54.27   minutes] moments E1,I

54.30 indecent] *omit* I
54.31–33 Now, . . . knowledge.]
  omit E1,I
54.35 55.3 In fact . . . infant?"] *omit* I
54.39 excitement.] excitement as
  I said: E1,I
55.1 knew] know E1
55.23 said he] he said E1,I
55.24 think] think that E1,I
55.25 really] real E1,I
56.1 Bath] Bristol MS(u),E1
56.2 little] young I
56.4 given] given me E1,I
56.4 the sign of] *omit* E1,I
57.12 damn] curse I
57.14 others] other E1,I
57.20 always] *omit* E1,I
57.21 evidences] evidence E1,I
57.27 that] *omit* E1,I
57.29 these] such E1,I
58.1 only had] had only E1,I
58.4 which] that E1,I
58.6–7 back, lie] back, or E1,I
58.7 ?lie] and he could lie E1,I
58.21 Royale] Colonel Royale
  E1,I
58.23 one to] one E1,I
58.30–32 to the Colonel. . . .
  tendering of] to Colonel Royale, and the Colonel gorgeously presented E1,I
59.8 among] along I
59.9 never had] had never E1,I
59.12 another] the other E1,I
59.26 seat] a seat E1,I
60.1 in . . . -house] there E1,I
60.13 this,] this and E1,I
60.15 the talk] talk E1,I
60.25 Some] So E1,I
60.33 And] *omit* E1,I
61.2 prostrations] protestations
  E1,I
61.3 ultimate] intimate E1,I
61.9 the theatre] a theatre E1,I
61.14 shyly] slyly E1,I
61.19 flicked] flecked MS+
61.31 seems] seemed E1,I
61.34–35 I wanted . . . gentleman."] *omit* E1,I

61.37–38 cool soon] soon cool
  E1,I
62.1 she said] said she E1,I
62.20 clate] elated E1,I
62.30 ailing] *omit* E1,I
62.34 turned,] turned to me E1,I
62.35 to me] *omit* E1,I
62.38 placidly was] was placidly E1,I
63.16 the point of] *omit* E1,I
63.19 struck] was within an
  inch of E1,I
63.28 your own stomach] yourself I
63.31 all] *omit* I
64.1 tongs,] tongs and E1,I
64.3 "Eh . . . father.] *omit* E1,I
64.3 lance?"] lance?" said he
  E1,I
64.15 potato] spud E1,I
64.21 afterward] afterwards I
64.30 keep] help E1,I
64.31 in] into E1,I
64.31 your bowels] you I
64.38 she or] of E1,I
64.38–65.1 was born] were born
  E1,I
65.15 Damn] Hang I
65.18 he still] still he E1,I
65.27–28 When . . . bath.]
  omit I
65.34–66.4 I was . . . of me.]
  omit I
66.1–2 never, never, never]
  never, never E1,I
66.5 cried] added I
66.6 lady] Lady MS(c)
66.15 numb] dumb I
66.19–20 disadvantage] advantages E1; disadvantages I
66.28 now was] was now E1,I
66.37 called] called out E1,I
67.18 of] with E1,I
67.22 certain] some E1,I
67.25 thing] thing that E1,I
67.29 meditations] mediations
  MS
68.2 knew] know E1,I
68.14 Damn] Sink I
68.14 of a] of E1,I

68.18   and] or E1,I
69.22   is] be E1,I
70.3   oneself] one's self E1,I
70.9   women] woman MS
70.24   damn-my-eyes] *omit* I
70.39   Afterward]   Afterwards
        MS; *omit* E1,I
70.39   another] a MS(u),E1,I
71.2   to hurriedly] hurriedly to
        E1,I
71.7   around] round MS
71.9   that] *omit* E1,I
71.10   soon would] would soon
        E1,I
71.12   form . . . runs] formed
        . . . ran I
71.13   ladies] the ladies E1,I
71.19   at] to E1,I
71.21   about] round
71.33   pelican] old pelican E1,I
72.13–17 Forister's . . . fellow-
        being.] *omit* I
72.21   and] and to E1,I
72.28   away] *omit* E1,I
73.2   I don't . . . parrot.] *omit*
        E1,I
73.2   look] looked MS
73.3   bird; it] bird as it E1,I
73.4   hoarse] coarse E1,I
73.5   ⌃Plague the bird!⌃] "Plague
        the bird!" E1,I
73.5   I turned] I muttered as I
        turned E1,I
73.6   ²said I] *omit* I
73.16   ,once] when once E1,I
73.24   arrived] was arrived E1,I
73.27   shoot] shot MS
74.7   be] to be E1,I
74.19   that] *omit* E1,I
74.19   stiffened] stiffened him
        E1,I
74.20–21 said he] said that he
        E1
74.28–31 No . . . Bath.] *omit*
        E1,I
74.36   hung] hanged I
75.4   depths] depth E1,I
75.5–6 to Bath.] *omit* E1,I
75.11   a flying] flying MS
75.13   of a] of E1,I

75.20   been] been gazing E1,I
75.20   gazing] *omit* E1,I
75.24   mine ears] my ears E1,I
75.24   heard] *omit* MS
75.27   swordsmen]   swordsman
        MS
75.28   spirits] spirit E1,I
75.37   dragging . . . horse and]
        omit E1,I
76.13   to never] never to E1,I
76.22   great] *omit* E1,I
76.31–32 And . . . -tower."]
        omit I
76.33–34 with . . . eloquence]
        omit I
77.8   highwayman.]   highway-
        man. [¶] "Ahum," said Paddy.
        "Ahum! Are ye listening, Jem
        Bottles?" [¶] "I be," replied the
        highwayman. MS,E1 (E1:
        Ahem)
77.18   Bottles'] Bottles's E1,I
77.22   taken] had taken E1,I
77.32   them] the pair E1,I
77.38   till] til MS
78.5; 83.12 gentlemen] gentle-
        man MS
78.5   but] *omit* E1,I
78.19   those] these E1
78.27   easy] easy it E1,I
78.32–33 and I . . . church]
        omit I
79.1–3 as if . . . to me.] *omit*
        E1,I
79.23   the] that E1,I
79.25   over] over again E1,I
79.27   again. And] again and
        E1,I
79.29   By dad] Bedad I
80.18   cloths] cloth E1,I
80.29–82.18 My head . . . At]
        omit E1,I
81.18   principal]   principle
        MS(c)
82.27   whom] who MS(u), E1,I
82.28   damn him] *omit* I
82.31–32 'tis . . . ¹sir] *omit* I
83.2   And] *omit* E1,I
83.16–17 with his cushions] up
        E1,I

83.33 calling] calling out MS(u),E1,I

83.33 from a] from his MS(u), E1,I

84.4 heard] heard that E1,I

84.6 fine] firm E1,I

84.23 have I] I have E1,I

85.20 simply] simply appalled him and E1,I

85.20 amazed and appalled] *omit* E1,I

85.24; 86.20 into] in to MS

85.25 shoulders] shoulder E1,I

85.37 -matter air] -matter-sir E1,I

86.13 bit] *omit* E1,I

86.21 Would] Could E1,I

86.25 Straw, straw, straw] Straw, straw E1,I

86.36 propose,] propose to do E1,I

88.5 know] know how E1,I

88.17 country] people I

88.20 only had] had only E1,I

88.28 29 her mother not] not her mother E1,I

89.10 Will] Shall I

89.39 ostrich] albatross MS

90.3 Paris] France I

90.13 said he] he said E1,I

91.12 head I] head out I MS

91.13; 96.5 hell-cat] wild-cat I

91.30 I thought . . . reasons] for many reasons I thought it E1,I

91.31 quick] *omit* E1,I

91.33 quickly] *omit* E1,I

91.33 fists] fist E1,I

91.38 highwaymen] highwayman MS

91.39 devil] not I

92.3 that] than MS

92.7 servants] servant E1,I

92.15 heark] hearken E1,I

92.31 all] *omit* I

92.37 from] of E1,I

93.1 he] *omit* E1,I

93.5 and] an' E1,I

93.21 fire-place] fireplace and E1,I

93.28 ways] way MS

93.33 the platter] platter E1,I

95.13 Devil] Never I

95.18 Never] Not I

95.25 raise] rise I

96.7 , the . . . witch] *omit* I

96.10 now was] was now E1,I

96.18 backwards] backward E1,I

96.31; 110.7 And] An E1; An' I (*l.c. at* 110.7)

96.36 lifted cautiously] cautiously lifted E1,I

97.18 to basely] basely to E1,I

97.35 said I] I said E1,I

98.13 ladies] lady MS

98.14 woman] lady MS(u),E1,I

98.24 only seen] seen only E1,I

99.3 at] of E1,I

99.10 blackguard] blaguard MS

99.15 knew] know MS

99.20–107.3 and travel . . . barren country."] *omit* I

99.21–22 a later] another E1,I

99.25–101.1 End . . .| PART II] *omit* E1

103.7 Skibbereen] Skibereen MS

103.22 that] *omit* E1

104.6 That was] That's E1

104.7 years'] year's MS

104.22 that he] he E1

104.31 quiet] quite E1

104.34 blaguards] blackguards E1

104.40 be likely not] not be likely E1

105.1 Mass] Masses MS(u), E1

105.3 cried] said E1

106.4–5 I am . . . confidently.] *omit* E1

106.10 then] *omit* E1

106.32 give] gave E1

106.38 be] *omit* MS

107.2 potatoes] the potatoes E1

107.4 At nightfall] and at nightfall I

108.0 CHAPTER XVI] XV I

108.8 back] at the back I

108.15 younger] young E1,I

108.17 engaged] been engaged E1,I

109.13   till] til MS
109.13   stop] stops E1,I
109.19   a   hoarse   muttering]
    hoarse mutterings E1,I
110.8   please] pleases E1,I
110.15   and] *omit* E1,I
110.22   ¹of] *omit* MS
111.29   devil] deuce I
112.9   It . . . -light] In the red
    firelight it was E1,I
112.12–30   I could . . . stair-
    case.] *omit* I
112.14   -knows-] -know- MS
112.20   here] there E1
112.22   kick] knock E1
112.36   Bottles] Jem Bottles E1,I
113.3,10   *him*] him E1,I
113.15   saying] saying that E1,I
114.0   CHAPTER XVII] XVI I
114.5;   119.27; 127.13; 149.18;
    152.24;   166.2   Afterward]
    Afterwards MS
114.13   blow] boast I
114.14   this] the E1,I
114.25   was] there was I
115.2   of] *omit* E1,I
115.7   was] were E1,I
115.8   and] and the E1,I
115.9–10   To . . . all.] *omit* I
115.14–31   Once . . . cudgel.]
    omit I
115.22   ought] aught E1
115.24   sound] sounding E1
116.2   that] *omit* E1,I
116.17   of] *omit* E1,I
116.18   an] *omit* E1,I
116.29   horse's] horses' MS
116.32   forehead] head E1,I
117.5–6   in leaving] having E1,I
117.6   out of my] out my MS
117.17   o'] of E1,I
117.23   a] *omit* E1,I
117.26   intend] intended E1,I
117.29   gentlemen]   gentleman
    MS
118.1–3   Mr. Bobbs . . . Fullbil
    and] *omit* E1,I
119.0   CHAPTER XVIII] XVIII
    MS; XVII I

119.19   assent   and   thanks]
    thanks and assent E1,I
119.24   the long] *omit* E1,I
120.3   ¹at] to E1,I
120.18   indeed is] is indeed E1,I
120.24   corpse] image I
120.25   don't] doesn't I
120.29   fit] *omit* MS (*end of
    line*)
120.34   nor] or E1,I
120.39   Immediately]   and   im-
    mediately MS(u), E1,I
120.40   glass] tankard I
121.11   really] *omit* E1,I
121.19–21   —by . . . explana-
    tion] *omit* E1,I
121.21–23   Pontius . . . explana-
    tion] *omit* I
121.30–32   You . . . bah!] *omit* I
121.32   minutes of] minutes' E1
121.33–34   minutes of] minutes'
    E1,I
121.34   doesn't] does not E1,I
122.4   faint] *omit* E1,I
122.31–32   have   . . .   theory]
    omit E1,I
123.11   dramatical]   dramatic
    E1,I
123.14   cries.] cries of E1,I
123.25   mopped]   moped   MS;
    mopping E1,I
123.37   not had] not E1,I
124.16   dared] dared to E1,I
124.35   philosophy] philosophers
    I
125.17   pretend] pretended E1,I
125.21   the pigs] pigs E1,I
125.22–25   "Sir . . . father."]
    omit I
125.28   these] their E1,I
125.35   and . . . Fancher] *omit* I
126.9   chatted] chattered E1,I
126.11   old Fullbil] the old man
    E1,I
126.14   old Fullbil;] who E1,I
126.18   that] *omit* E1,I
126.33   for] of E1,I
126.33   gad's] God's E1,I
126.34   Knowledge]   knowledge
    MS(u), E1,I

126.34–35   nimble] *omit* E1,I
127.14   King] the King E1,I
128.1–132.18   On . . . least.]
   omit I
128.1   and I] and E1
128.2   said he] said that he E1
128.23   bid] bade E1
128.26   streets] street E1
129.11   upon]   down   upon
   MS(u), E1
129.33   to us] *omit* E1
129.35   mood] manner E1
130.3   or wine] and wine E1
130.6   I had] had I MS
130.34   Snowdon] Snowden E1
130.35   amidst] amid E1
131.16   but] and E1
131.24   would] *omit* MS(u), E1
131.24   speak] spoke E1
131.26   thought] thoughts E1
131.36   raspatory] caspatory E1
132.11   a] an E1
133.0   CHAPTER XX] XVIII I
133.3   hope] hopes E1,I
133.4   in] *omit* E1,I
133.6   feared] feared that E1,I
133.8   chose] choose MS
133.10   Gardens] gardens MS
133.13   had had] had E1,I
133.18   Gardens]   garden   MS;
   Garden E1
133.26   folk] flock E1,I
134.3–135.9   I saw . . . wiser.]
   omit I
134.7   aristocrat's]   aristocratic
   E1
135.36–136.17   "There goes . . .
   view."] *omit* E1,I
136.13   affected] effected MS
136.18   Stubbington] Stubbling-
   ton E1,I
136.24   devil] fellow I
136.24   lends Gram] lends him I
136.31   eldest] elder E1,I
136.33   There is] *omit* E1,I
136.33   talking] is talking E1,I
136.36–137.32   I see . . . Chord.]
   omit I
137.1   kicked] was kicked E1
137.7   in] *omit* E1

137.33–34   virtuous . . . gentle-
   man] honest lady or gentleman I
137.35; 138.13   Stap] Strap E1,I
137.36   thick] as thick E1,I
138.2   They . . . bibles.] *omit* I
138.10   and eat them] *omit* I
139.0   CHAPTER XXI] *omit* I
139.12–141.17   But then . . .
   her.] *omit* I
139.12   poor old] poor E1
139.13   arc] arc often E1
139.26   ear] ears E1
139.29   nor] or E1
140.1   the   blackguards]   you
   blackguards E1 (MS: blagards)
140.4   refused] refusing MS
141.7   who] that E1
141.11   twenty-five] fifty MS(u)
141.20   please] pleases E1,I
141.28   Catharine]   Catherine
   E1,I
142.2   the making]   he making
   E1,I
142.4   these] those E1,I
142.7   of] *omit* MS
142.13   of the] of the | of the MS
142.33   at any rate] *omit* E1,I
142.37   middle-age] middle-aged
   E1,I
143.5–19   If you . . . signals.]
   omit I
143.8   them in] the main E1
143.10   success] successes E1
143.12   unfair] *omit* E1
143.13   girl was] girl be E1
143.16   man nor maid] maid nor
   man E1
143.24–25   cutting   . . .   still]
   omit E1,I
143.28   innamorata] *innamorata*
   E1,I
143.30   Countess']   Countess's
   E1,I
143.31   animatedly]   animately
   E1,I
144.3   virgin] *omit* I
144.6   dreams] and dreams E1,I
144.8   saw] can see E1,I

144.11 the very] that very E1,I
144.13 rise] to rise E1,I
144.22–24 Indeed . . . back.] *omit* E1,I
144.28 to me] *omit* I
144.33 a circus] the circus E1,I
144.37 afraid] afraid that E1,I
145.1 very] the very E1,I
145.4 the best] best E1,I
145.10 them] *omit* MS
145.15 came] come E1,I
145.23 suddenly] *omit* I
146.0 CHAPTER XXII] XIX I
146.8 said he] he said E1,I
147.3 now] *omit* E1,I
147.5–6 friends and] *omit* I
147.18 Stap] Strap I
147.30 nor] or MS
148.23 had] *omit* E1,I
148.25–26 now was] was now E1,I
148.29 wished] wanted E1,I
148.32 situate] situated E1,I
148.35 Jem Bottles and Paddy] Paddy and Jem Bottles E1,I
148.36 coachmen] coachman MS
149.3–4 At sight . . . docilely.] *omit* E1,I
149.21 seems] seemed E1,I
149.27–28 This . . . careers.] *omit* I
149.37 ever] even E1,I
150.3 amid] among E1,I
150.10 golden] a golden E1,I
150.26 And in] In E1,I
150.38 ask] asked E1,I
151.5 have] *omit* MS
151.11 enlighten] enlightened MS
151.21–153.10 "With . . . matters."] *omit* I
151.24 Not] Now E1
152.7 sourly] slowly E1
152.18 at] for E1
152.20 great] street E1
152.25 offering] offering me E1
152.32–153.10 This matter . . . matters."] *omit* E1
154.0 CHAPTER XXIII] *omit* I

154.2 staunch] stanch MS
154.8 new] *omit* E1,I
154.16 definite] define E1,I
154.20 about] *omit* E1,I
155.3,4 Stap] Strap E1,I
155.9,12 was] is E1,I
155.15 That is] That's E1,I
155.15 word] world E1,I
155.36–38 And . . . But, tell] "Tell I
156.1 thing. I] thing," said I. "I I
156.4 that] *omit* E1,I
156.6 not] not yet E1,I
156.10 said I] I said E1,I
156.13 hard] a hard MS(u), E1,I
157.8 it weren't for] I were to lose I
157.9 praise] please E1,I
157.24 nor . . . any] and . . . no E1,I
157.28 ye] you E1,I
157.32 which] whom E1,I
157.34 this] his I
158.10 engage] engaged E1,I
158.37 served] serve E1,I
158.38–39 Thus . . . turban] *omit* I
158.38 no] no great E1
159.3 immediately] at once E1,I
159.4 we] he I
159.11 by a] by the E1,I
159.15 that] *omit* E1,I
159.23 left] *omit* MS
159.34 hour's] hours MS
160.23–29 Ships . . . world."] *omit* I
160.24 for] *omit* MS
160.25 little] but little E1
160.27 ships] the ships E1
160.32 and] or E1,I
161.5 bacon] a bacon E1,I
161.10 meditations] meditation E1,I
161.11 from] *omit* E1,I
161.12–13 his hair flying] *omit* I
162.0 CHAPTER XXIV] XX I
162.11 behind] with I

162.17 ground] the ground
TMs,E1,I
163.1 basket] baskets TMs
163.6 all my] all E1,I
163.12 expressed] express TMs
163.27 noted] noticed E1,I
164.18 huntress] mistress E1,I
164.24 had] *omit* E1,I
164.25 I am] I'm E1,I
164.32 him] to him E1,I
165.2 can't] cannot I
165.8 moment] moments E1,I
165.18 leaving] letting TMs
165.22 could come] come come
TMs
165.23 Lady] Lady's MS
165.34 from] *omit* TMs
165.34 ²little] *omit* TMs
166.4 to him] *omit* E1,I
166.11 climatic] *omit* I
166.17–29 Then . . . rescue."]
omit I
166.21 that] the E1
166.26 terrible] horrible E1
166.35 dove] ducked I
167.9 a] an I
168.0 CHAPTER XXV] *omit* I
168.5 tree] -bed MS
168.14–19 "No . . . you.] *omit* I
168.19 to fully . . . you] to instruct you fully E1
168.20 murdered. His] murdered," said I. "His I
168.23–31 "I confess . . . you."]
omit I
169.4 that] *omit* I
169.5 was] were E1,I
169.10 own] *omit* E1,I
169.13–14 and devil . . . her]
omit I
169.20 is] be E1,I
169.23 being of a] being a E1,I
169.26 which . . . existed] *omit*
I
169.26 really] *omit* E1
169.29,32 Corrigan] Donovan
MS
169.34 o'] of I
169.35 o'] of MS(u),E1,I
169.39 I am] I'm E1,I

170.1 'Twill] 'Twould E1,I
170.20 ye] you E1,I

[171.30 small talker." | *end of*
MS]

173.0 CHAPTER XXVI] XX I
173.1 the lads] my lads E1(p)
173.4 trapesing] trapezing I
173.9 done] done this night
E1(p)
173.11 ever] even I
173.13 frequented by] endeared
to E1(p)
174.1 in a] at a I
174.17 great] good E1(p)
174.31 round] around E1(p)
174.37 is] *omit* E1(p)
175.33 not] *omit* E1(p[c]),I
176.25 Doctor] *omit* E1,I
177.12 *et seq.* someone] some
one E1
180.0 CHAPTER XXVII] *omit* I
180.16 documents] two documents I
181.1 *et seq.* anyhow] any how
E1
181.5 *et seq.* anyone] any one E1
(*except at* 264.15)
181.9 *et seq.* everyone] every
one E1 (193.16; 256.37 I:
every one)
181.24.1 *omit*] XXII I
182.8 top] the top I
183.30 all] *omit* I
185.24 much short] far short I
188.10–11 he will] he'll I
188.25 other, come . . . not.]
other, whether kicked or not,
come there. E1(p)
190.8 are] is E1(p)
191.1 of] to I
191.29 I ever] I ever I I
192.15 that] it I
192.30 Ballymoyle] Ballymole I
192.32 answer,] answer it, I
192.37 ¹in] into I
193.9 misty] *omit* I
193.11 you're] you are I
193.16 before] against E1(p)

195.0 CHAPTER XXVIII] XXIII I

195.1 any] *omit* I
195.2 ever] *omit* E1(p)
197.8 Donovan] O'Donovan I
197.29 O'Ruddys] O'Ruddy's I
197.35 bidding] bidding him I
198.3 it's] its E1
198.5 with] *omit* I
198.36 ₂Watch me eye,₂] '~ ~ ~ ,' I
199.5 again] *omit* I
200.8 in] into I
203.15 of] on I
204.0 CHAPTER XXIX] XXIV I
206.17 ¹was] were I
206.28 in his] in the I
211.16 all together] altogether I
211.37 and] or I
212.31 the weapon] weapon E1(p[u])
213.23 a difficult] difficult E1(p[u])
214.20 have] has E1(p)
215.34 said] sad E1(p[u])
216.27 mouths] mouth I
216.32 know] *omit* E1(p[u])
216.36 upon] on I
218.0 CHAPTER XXX] XXV I
218.8 seemed] always seemed I
218.9 indeed] *omit* I
219.27–29 In . . . wig.] *omit* I
219.38 very] *omit* I
221.3 meantime] mean time E1
221.12 drawer] draw E1(p)
223.13–16 The good . . . more.] *omit* I
226.35 honest] early honest E1(p)
226.35 getting] going E1(p)
227.0 CHAPTER XXXI] XXVI I
227.8–12 There . . . happy.] *omit* I
228.36 all] *omit* I
230.20 around] round I
231.37 action] act I
233.22–26 He . . . nature.] *omit* I
234.7 and his wine] *omit* I

235.0 CHAPTER XXXII] XXVII I

235.1 I] *omit* E1(p[u])
235.1 town] place E1(p)
237.30 them] then I
238.4 Brede] Brede's E1
238.29 ordered] had I
239.5 and talking] *omit* I
241.19 while . . . money] *omit* E1(p)
243.3 in our] our I
243.9 Sullivan] O'Gorman E1(p)
243.10 the land] our land E1(p)
245.17 that] *omit* I
246.10 is the] is in the I
246.37–38 everybody] every body E1
247.15 Father] As Father E1(p)
247.23 were] was E1(p)
247.30 seemed] looked E1(p)
248.21 then] and E1(p)
248.24–25 -furnished] -finished E1(p)
250.2 more] most E1(p[u])
251.1 to it] near to it I
251.17 legal] civil E1(p)
251.27 means] means that I
254.17 was afraid] afraid E1(p[u])
254.20 when] and E1(p)
255.15 The] That E1(p)
256.10 a slight] some slight E1(p)
256.26 unlucky] poor E1(p)
256.33 yeomen] women E1(p)
256.36 mob, asking] men and asked E1(p)
256.37 up] *omit* E1(p)
258.0 CHAPTER XXXIII] XXVIII I
258.13 says] said I
259.3 afterward] afterwards I
260.12 lad] *omit* E1(p)
260.20 then] them I
260.21 of . . . done] would do E1(p)
261.5 O'Ruddy] O'Ruddys I
262.27 were] was E1(p)
263.27 if] *omit* E1
264.12 staring] staying E1(p[u])

264.16   the proof] a proof I

265.25   Sullivan] O'Gorman
    E1(p)

266.5   resemble] resembles
    E1(p)

266.6   upon] about E1(p)

267.28   little] *omit* I

267.29   Donovan] O'Donovan
    E1(p)

267.31   is] are I

ALTERATIONS IN THE MANUSCRIPT

3.7 churches] *preceded by deleted* 'dissenter chapels'

3.7 end] *preceded by deleted* 'a'

3.12 -abiding] *following period in black ink deleted in blue ink and text continues in blue*

3.16 there] *final* 's' *deleted*

3.22 plain] *preceded by deleted* 'bl' *and the start of an* 'a'

3.24 which] *followed by deleted* 'relate'

4.17 him] *followed by deleted period*

4.17 Donovan] *preceded by deleted* 'O' '

4.19 Bristol] *followed by deleted* 'after a'

4.27 was] *followed by deleted* 'a'

4.28 people] *followed by deleted* 'all of'

5.4 ¹to] *followed by deleted* 'g'

5.15 trade] *followed by deleted* 'from the' *and the start of a capital*

5.19 had] *interlined with a caret*

5.21 that] *followed by deleted* 'h'

5.23,29 a] *interlined with a caret*

5.27 Opposite] *preceded by deleted* 'Oppos'

5.28 forty] 'u' *deleted from* 'fourty'

5.37 Tisn't] *preceding* 'It' *deleted and* 'T' *written over* 't' *inserted before* 'i'

6.6 he] *preceded by deleted* 'as'

6.7 after] *preceded by deleted* 'to'

6.12 me] *preceded by deleted* 'hi'

6.17 ¹the] *interlined with a caret*

6.23 bare] *preceded by the deleted start of a* 'b'

6.23 there's] *preceded by deleted* 'tis'; *final* 's' *of* 'there's' *added*

6.23 truth] *period added and following* 'lies. It does' *deleted*

6.26 Colonel] 'C' *altered from* 'c'

6.33 were] *followed by deleted* 'all'

6.38–39 yourselves] 'ves' *written over* 'f' *before next word inscribed*

7.3 wished] *preceded by deleted* 'would'

7.7 and] *preceded by deleted* 'a' *and start of a* 't'

7.13 O'Ruddy?] *question mark written over exclamation point*

7.17 I] *followed by deleted* 'al' *and start of a* 't'

7.28 going in order] *interlined with a caret above deleted* 'returning'

7.36 overwhelmed] 'w' *written over a hyphen and next* 'e' *over start of* 'l'

7.37 that,] *followed by deleted* 'he'

7.40 be] *interlined with a caret*

8.12 also] *followed by* 'he' *deleted in black ink*

8.13 fair."] *quote marks added in black ink and following* 'Me,' *outlined in black for clarity*

8.31 termed] *preceded by deleted* 'turne'

8.35 him] *interlined with a caret*

9.4 gentleman] *preceded by deleted* 'man'

9.8 accommodation] MS 'accomadation' *has final* 's' *deleted before the period inscribed*

9.21 the] *interlined with a caret*

9.21 I] *written over* 'a'

9.24 I] *preceded by deleted* 'It'

9.30 His] 'H' *over* 'h'

9.35 Only] *followed by deleted comma*

9.37 from] *followed by deleted* 'Cl'

9.39 gentlemen] *third* 'e' *written over* 'a'

10.7 a] *interlined with a caret*

10.8 heaved] *preceded by deleted* 'lifted' *and the start of a* 'y'

10.13 soil] *followed by deleted period*

10.15 note] *followed by deleted* 'the arc'

10.15 or arcs] *interlined with a caret*

10.16 but] *followed by deleted* 'he'

10.19 both arms] *preceded by deleted* 'an armful'

10.19 and] *interlined with a caret*

10.20 I suppose] *not indented but preceded by a paragraph sign*

10.21 from] *preceded by deleted* 'for'

10.21 a] *interlined above deleted* 'one'

10.24 Some] *preceded by deleted* 'In'

10.25 here] *altered from* 'hear'

10.28 tall] *followed by deleted* 'elderly'

10.34 The] *preceded by deleted* 'the'

10.39 he] *preceded by deleted* 'I wa'

11.10 what] *followed by deleted start of a doubtful* 'h'

11.15 the] *interlined*

11.18 play] *interlined above deleted* 'cards'

11.20 nose] *interlined in pencil with a caret*

11.22 don't] 'd' *written over* 't'

11.25 if] *preceded by deleted* 'when the'

12.5 friend] *followed by deleted period*

12.10 carve] *interlined above deleted* 'achieve'

12.11 notice?] *question mark altered from a period*

12.12 the] *interlined with a caret*

12.17 me] *interlined with a caret*

12.22 out] *followed by deleted* 'to'

12.25 the day] *interlined with a caret*

12.25 leaving] *followed by deleted* 'my'

12.31 monologue] *preceded by deleted* 'k'

12.31 ceased;] *followed by deleted* 'an'

13.3 much] *followed by deleted* 'oul' *or* 'out'

13.6 him] *interlined with a caret*

13.7 expected,] *comma follows deleted period*

13.8 hair] *preceded by deleted* 'red'

13.9 knew] *interlined above deleted* 'known'

13.13 have] *interlined in black ink, not in Crane's hand*

13.18 conduct,] 'con' *interlined above deleted* 'co'

13.18 The sight] *preceded by deleted* 'this red—'

13.19 a] *interlined*

13.22 answered,] *comma inserted before deleted period*

13.26 it] 't' *written over* 'n'

13.27 an] *preceded by deleted* 'The'

13.39 time] *followed by deleted comma*

13.39 ditch] *interlined above deleted* 'hitch'

14.14 me] *followed by deleted period*

14.16 radiated] *followed by deleted* 'out'

14.17 an] *interlined with a caret*

14.19 thatch] *preceded by deleted* 'p'

14.21 represented] *preceded by deleted* 'was'

14.21 clothes] *followed by deleted* 'or nearly so'

14.32 kept] *followed by deleted* 'mu'

14.33 moved] *preceded by deleted* 'was'

14.34 me] *interlined with a caret*

14.38 you!] *exclamation altered from a period*

14.39 him] *interlined with a caret*

15.7 cloaks] *preceded by deleted* 'clothe'

15.11 swiftly] *interlined above deleted* 'quickly'

15.13 I] *written over* 's'

15.15 What] *preceded by deleted* 'Was I'

15.20 there] 'r' *written over deleted* 's'

15.20 is] *interlined with a caret*

15.39 possessed of] *interlined with a caret*

16.3 preceded] 'c' *over deleted* 't'

16.3 Colonel] 'e' *altered from deleted start of* 'l'

16.4 clear] *interlined above deleted* 'open'

16.6 gate] *preceded by deleted* 'gait'

16.24,26 'lashings'] *double quotes before and after are altered to single*

16.26 speaks] *interlined with a caret above* 'can speaks' *in which* 'can' *is an insertion*

16.26 lashings.' "] *period and single and double quotes added after deletion of following* 'of meat and drink." '

16.36 impudent] *final* 'ly' *deleted*

17.4 manners] *final* 's' *added*

17.11 and] *followed by deleted* 'then'

17.13 French] *preceded by deleted* 'rest'

17.13 Italian] *final* 's' *deleted*

17.16 as a] 'a' *interlined with a caret*

17.22 no] *interlined with a caret*

17.23 at] *interlined with a caret*

17.24 chose] *altered from* 'choose' *by deletion of second* 'o' *in pencil*

17.33 ¹and] *followed by deleted* 'as'

17.36 such] *interlined above deleted* 'so'

17.38 pricked] *preceded by deleted* 't'

17.39 on] *preceded by deleted start of* 'h'

18.8 reach] *preceded by deleted* 'g'

18.11 have] *inserted in pencil*

18.18 way] *followed by deleted* 'to do'

18.25 not] *interlined with a caret*

18.33 been] *interlined with a caret in brown ink*

18.35 And] *preceded by deleted* 'The'

18.35 been] *interlined with a caret*

19.2 Where] *preceded by deleted* 'Wear'

19.3 from?] *question mark altered from the start of a period*

19.7 judged] *preceded by deleted* 'de'

19.12 in London] *interlined with a caret*

19.23 ²be] *added in pencil*

19.24 heed] *altered from* 'head'

19.25 Lord] *interlined with a caret*

19.27 the loss] 'the' *written over* 'a'

19.27 too weak] *interlined above* 'to' *altered to* 'too'

19.29 Lord] *preceded by deleted* 'm'

19.32 staunching] 'u' *interlined with a caret in black ink*

19.33 none] *altered in pencil from* 'not'

19.35 him,] *comma inserted before deleted period*

19.37 stopped] 's' *over* 'n'

20.26 on our] *interlined above deleted* 'part'

20.27 ran] *interlined above deleted* 'made'

20.31 walking] *preceding quote marks deleted*

21.3 blaguard] 'u' *over* 'a'

21.10 wave] *interlined above deleted* 'weigh'

21.12 exultantly,] *comma inserted before deleted period*

21.18 grasping] 'ing' *follows deleted* 'ed'

21.18 at] *interlined above deleted* 'by'

21.25 boots,] *comma inserted before deleted period*

21.29 a] *interlined with a caret*

21.29 turf] *interlined above independently deleted* 'b peat'

22.4–5 now had] 'had' *interlined with a caret*

22.8–9 sureness] *preceded by deleted* 'certainty'

22.15 I grasped my pistols.] *interlined in blue ink*

22.28 my] *interlined with a caret*

22.36 angry] *interlined above deleted* 'sullen'

22.36 across] *followed by deleted* 'the'

22.39 I passed] *interlined with a caret*

22.39 with] *followed by deleted* 'fl'

23.6 Stand] *interlined above deleted* 'Halt'

23.7 said,] *comma follows deleted period*

23.9 is] *interlined above deleted* 'has'

23.10 the] *interlined*

23.13 tails] *interlined above deleted* 'tales'

23.20 grandly,] *comma inserted before deleted period*

23.25 me] *final* 'n' *deleted*

23.27 day] *interlined above deleted* 'night'

24.7 in my] *interlined with a caret*

24.13 mother] *preceded by deleted* 'fa'

24.14 ¹I] *preceded by deleted quote marks*

24.15 long since] *interlined above deleted* 'now'

24.25 a] *interlined with a caret*

24.25 horse,] *comma follows deleted period*

24.37–8 Bottles?] *question mark altered from period*

25.5 mother?] *question mark altered from a period*

25.6 speak] *followed by deleted* 'm'

25.15 ground] *followed by deleted period*

25.16 me] *interlined with a caret*

25.16 We] *altered from* 'He'

25.18–19 Bottles] *followed by deleted* 'at last'

25.28 resolved] *preceded by deleted* 'now'

25.33 illegitimate] 'ti' *interlined with a caret*

26.4 you] *interlined with a caret*

26.10 marched] *interlined above deleted* 'past'

26.22 me] *interlined with a caret*

27.6 himself?] *question mark altered from period*

27.10 head?] *question mark altered from period*

27.12 Bottles] *preceded by deleted* 'Jem'

27.12 it] *interlined with a caret*

27.15 Dame Bottles] *interlined with a caret above deleted* 'the mother', *of which* 'm' *may have been written over* 'o'

27.28 strange] *preceded by deleted* 'strage'

27.29 a] *interlined with a caret*

27.29 such] *interlined with a caret*

27.30 that he] *interlined above deleted* 'who'

28.15 at] *interlined with a caret*

28.20 metals?] *question mark altered from period*

28.29 the] *over* 'a'

28.30 Know] *preceded by deleted* 'Now'

28.30 a] *interlined with a caret*

28.34 if] 'i' *altered from* 'o'

28.35 make] *interlined with a caret*

29.9 Less] *prefixed by deleted quote marks*

29.9 and I] *interlined with a caret*

30.4 recalled] *followed by deleted* 'a pair of'

30.8 beauty] *interlined with a caret*

30.10 me] *interlined with a caret*

30.14 it] *interlined with a caret*

30.27 sole] *preceded by deleted* 'soli'

30.28 Forister?] *question mark altered from comma*

31.2 sense] *preceded by deleted* 'b'

31.5 the landlord] 'the' *interlined with a caret in a different hand*

31.15 Lights] *preceded by deleted* 'T'

31.17 Bottles] *preceded by deleted* 'Jem'

31.17 hugely] *interlined above deleted* 'greatly'

31.28 inn] 'i' *written over a doubtful* 'I'

32.3 inn] *preceded by deleted* 'Inn'

32.8 of the] *preceded by deleted* 'into the'

32.9 moved] *interlined with a caret above deleted* 'made'

32.10 upon] *interlined with a caret above deleted* 'for'

32.12 But] *followed by deleted* 'if'

32.12 an] *interlined with a caret*

32.14 you] *interlined above deleted* 'who'

32.16 the] *final* 'y' *deleted*

32.17 stairs] *followed by deleted* 'again'

32.22 with] *interlined with a caret*

32.32 after] *preceded by deleted* 'to'

32.34 At] 'A' *over* 'I'

32.36 you] *interlined with a caret*

33.4 finely] *interlined above deleted* 'well'

33.4 enough] *interlined with a caret*

33.5 mere] *interlined above deleted* 'just'

33.20 is] *preceded by deleted* 'has'

33.23 the] *written over* 'ru'

33.23 it] *preceded by deleted* 'tis poss'

33.38 slice] *followed by deleted* 'up'

34.5 still] *interlined*

34.6 the maids] *interlined with a caret*

34.9 and] *interlined with a caret*

34.10 nose] *interlined above deleted* 'ears'

34.12 ears] 'hearing' *was interlined above deleted* 'cars' *but then deleted and* 'ears' *inserted*

34.12 not] *interlined with a caret*

34.14 Paddy] *preceded by deleted* 'both'

34.17 sneer,] *comma follows deleted period*

34.17 Irishman!] *exclamation point possibly altered from double quotes*

34.23 else] *followed by deleted* 'your'

34.25 not] *preceded by deleted* 'bc'

34.34 Otherwise] 'O' *over* 'I'

35.1 negligently] *interlined with a caret*

35.2 but] *preceded by deleted* 'and'

35.4 precipitous] *preceded by deleted* 'sud'

36.3 of] *interlined*

36.21 how] *preceded by deleted* 'to'

36.24 scoundrel] 'r' *over* 'e'; *preceded by deleted* 'rogue.'

37.4 even] *preceded by deleted* 'if'

37.8 that] *followed by deleted* 'unless'

37.9 witch's] *apostrophe above deleted* 'e'

37.13 were] *interlined with a caret*

37.14 palms] *interlined above deleted* 'trees'

37.14 with] *interlined with a caret*

37.17 reflection] *followed by deleted* 'of Paddy'

37.28 My] *preceded by deleted* 'But m'

37.32 we] *preceded by deleted single letter possibly the start of a* 't', *but definitely not* 'I'

38.1 to] *interlined with a caret*

38.5 had] *interlined with a caret*

38.8 our] *interlined above deleted* 'her'

38.9 ²them] *interlined above deleted* 'lea'

38.10 perceived] *followed by deleted* 'when leaving'

38.11 when . . . Bristol] *interlined with a caret*

38.11–12 be able] *interlined with a caret*

38.17 you] *interlined with a caret*

38.21 "There] *preceded by deleted* 'Y'

38.22 done] *preceded by deleted* 'down'

38.25 tiller] *preceded by deleted* 'rudder'

39.5 At] *over* 'In'

39.7 Earl] 'E' *over* 'e'

39.18 lordship,] *comma follows deleted period*

39.20 when] *interlined above deleted* 'cam'

39.25 him?] *question mark written over period*

39.26 be-fuddled?] *question mark over period*

39.34 a door] 'a' *interlined with a caret above deleted* 'the'

39.35 parlour] 'ur' *over* 'r' *in different ink*

40.15 We] 'W' *written over* 'H'

40.20 Afterward] *followed by deleted* 'to mak'

40.30 Is] *preceded by deleted doubtful* 'It'

40.34 satirical] *preceded by deleted* 'st'

41.21–22 rascal. . . . me. . . . it.] *periods altered from exclamation points*

41.23 was] *interlined with a caret*

41.36 I] *preceded by deleted* 'O'

41.38 strong] *final* 'e' *deleted*

42.2 lady] *preceded by deleted* 'lit'

42.8 before] *preceded by deleted* 'bl'

42.9 an] *interlined with a caret*

42.18 the old] 'the' *interlined in pencil with a caret*

42.27 stands.] *period altered from exclamation point*

42.34   hands] *interlined above deleted* 'fingers'

42.38   the son of] *interlined with a caret*

43.1   chuckled] *followed by deleted* 'out'

43.3   upon me] *interlined with a caret*

43.6   adores.] *preceded by deleted* 'loves.'

43.8   Earl] 'E' *over* 'e' *and final* 's' *deleted*

44.7   not] *interlined with a caret*

44.7   fearing to dare anything."] *interlined with a caret above deleted* 'daring'

44.8   not] *preceded by deleted* 'so.'

44.11   You] 'Yo' *over* 'I'

44.13   you] *interlined with a caret*

44.23   a] *interlined with a caret above deleted* 'some'

45.1,7   gentlemen] *third* 'e' *over* 'a'

45.16   I] *preceded by deleted* 'he'

46.5   out] 'ou' *over* 'no'

46.15   lowering] *followed by deleted* 'po'

46.16   from] *followed by deleted* 'my'

46.18   as] *preceded by deleted* 'I'

46.21   clamour] *followed by deleted* 'b'

46.22   open] *interlined with a caret*

46.33   ¹I] *interlined with a caret*

46.36   peace] *deleted period follows*

47.2   there] *altered from* 'their'

47.7   he] *preceded by deleted* 'th'

47.9   sword] *followed by deleted* 'wil'

47.10   talk] *followed by deleted* 'be'

47.13   had] *interlined with a caret*

47.30,35   him] *interlined with a caret*

48.3   hampered] *interlined above deleted* 'disturbed'

48.6   at] *interlined with a caret*

48.15   feeling.] *preceded by deleted* 'business.'

48.18   wrong] *followed by deleted period*

48.23   ²Forister] *interlined*

48.25   intimately] *preceded by deleted* 'main'

48.26   each blade] 'each' *interlined above deleted* 'both'; *final* 's' *to* 'blade' *deleted*

49.5   enthusiasm and] *interlined with a caret*

49.11   killed] *interlined with a caret*

49.12   ²me] *interlined with a caret*

49.20   him] *preceded by deleted* 'me'

49.32   of mind] *interlined with a caret*

49.36   case] *interlined above deleted* 'we'

49.39   In the] 'the' *interlined with a caret*

50.4   make you] 'you' *interlined with a caret*

50.4   peer.] *followed by deleted quote marks*

50.9   -pole] *added in pencil after deleted* '-pool'

50.10   of] *inserted in pencil*

50.10   it] *interlined*

50.10   teaches] *interlined with a caret*

50.19   ¹a] *interlined with a caret*

50.20   means,] *followed by deleted quote marks*

50.22   desire] *preceded by deleted* 'to'

50.22   I] *interlined with a caret*

50.23   detected] *followed by deleted* 'in you'

50.24   you] *interlined with a caret*

50.25 me] *interlined above deleted* 'him'

51.1 reached] *interlined above deleted* 'arran'

51.4 The] 'T' *over* 't'

51.8 my] *interlined with a caret*

51.15 Donovan] *preceded by* 'O' ' *interlined*

51.16 real] *preceded by deleted* 'ow'

51.29 me] *interlined with a caret*

51.31 in] *followed by deleted* 'as'

52.2 estate] *preceded by deleted* 'worthless'

52.9 matter] *interlined with a caret above deleted* 'thing'

52.10 ¹an] *interlined with a caret*

52.12 his own] 'his' *interlined with a caret*

52.18 There] *preceded by deleted* 'A servant'

52.18 at] *over* 'on'

52.24 I] *preceded by deleted* 'the'

52.27–28 highwaymen] 'e' *over* 'a'

52.35 parts,] *comma added and following* 'or' *deleted*

53.2 morning] *followed by deleted period and quote mark*

53.11 acts for me] *interlined with a caret*

53.22 ²a] *interlined with a caret*

53.26 say] *preceded by deleted* 'hear'

53.27 my] *interlined above deleted* 'your'

53.31 poltroon!] *exclamation point inserted before deleted period*

53.34 is] *followed by deleted* 'in'

53.35 not] *interlined with a caret*

53.37 pig] *preceded by deleted* 'wrong'

54.5 Nell!] *exclamation altered from question mark*

54.7 told] *altered from* 'tell'

54.9 lose] *altered from* 'loose'

54.9 everlasting] *altered from* 'ever lasting'

54.9 hell] *interlined with a caret*

54.17 joke] *interlined above deleted* 'tale'

54.21 His] *preceded by deleted quote marks*

54.29 would] *interlined with a caret*

54.34 of] *interlined with a caret*

54.38 what] *interlined with a caret*

55.3 infant?] *followed by deleted typing instruction* 'typing stopped'

55.6 turned] *followed by deleted* 'j'

55.8 our] *followed by deleted* 'a' *and start of* 'f'

55.24 he] *interlined with a caret*

55.30 ruffles] *followed by deleted* 'although I'

56.1 Bath] *interlined above deleted* 'Bristol'

57.2 he] *preceded by deleted* 'if'

57.13 is] *preceded by deleted* 'to'

57.17 have] *preceded by deleted* 'had'

57.18 will] 'i' *over* 'o'

57.25 discouragements] *preceded by deleted* 'arrangements'

57.28 the] *interlined with a caret*

57.30 not] *interlined with a caret*

58.1 had] *interlined with a caret*

58.6 day] *interlined above deleted* 'time'

58.10 stiffened] *preceded by deleted* 'decided'

58.15 said] *preceded by deleted* 'o'

58.17 arrangements] *first* 'n' *interlined with a caret*

58.26 Each] *preceded by deleted* 'Neither'

58.31 ¹Colonel] 'C' *over* 'c' *in MS phrase* 'the Colonel'

58.39 at] *interlined with a caret*
59.5 intricacies] *second 'c' over 's'*
59.6 think of] *interlined with a caret*
59.10 my] *preceded by deleted 'ki'*
59.12 ¹liking] *preceded by deleted 'killing'*
59.13 position] *interlined with a caret above deleted 'note'*
59.14 a] *interlined above deleted 'my'*
59.15 However] *preceded by deleted 'Perha'*
59.18 go] *interlined with a caret*
59.20 much] *interlined with a caret above deleted 'great'*
59.21 inn] *preceded by deleted start of an 'I'*
59.24 garden] *followed by deleted period*
60.8 held] *followed by deleted 'th'*
60.15 talk] *interlined with a caret above deleted 'take'*
60.17 Westport] *preceded by deleted 'Wesp'*
60.17 Mary] *preceded by deleted 'Strep'*
60.19 indignant] *interlined above deleted 'angry'*
60.27 angry] *followed by deleted possible double quotes*
60.35 ¹harridan] *second 'a' over 'e'*
60.35 ²harridan] *'h' over 'H'*
60.35 ³harridan] *preceded by deleted 'Ha'*
60.36 to me] *preceded by deleted 'to be'*
60.38 kept] *'pt' over 'ep'*
61.11 lovely] *preceded by deleted 'fair'*
61.15 ability] *preceded by deleted 'desire'*
61.15 a] *inserted on the line after deletion of interlined 'my' with a caret*

61.16 adding] *'add-' interlined above deleted 'say' of 'saying'*
61.17 would] *interlined with a caret*
61.20 hat;] *semicolon follows deleted period*
61.37 cool] *preceded by deleted 'calm'*
62.10 for] *over 'in'*
62.16 worse.] *followed by deleted quote marks*
62.19 that,] *comma added after deletion of following 'I could'*
62.35 coldly:] *colon follows deleted period*
62.35 did] *'i' written over 'o' and 'd' added*
62.38 was] *interlined with a caret*
63.7 can be] *interlined with a caret*
63.13 be] *interlined with a caret*
63.14 physician] *final 's' deleted*
63.22 said] *followed by deleted 'the'*
63.23 gentlemen] *third 'e' over 'a'*
63.27 it] *'t' written over 's'*
63.28 ¹you] *preceded by deleted 'I'*
63.30 with] *interlined with a caret*
64.7 ¹I] *interlined with a caret*
64.14 no] *interlined with a caret above deleted 'to'*
64.15 potato] *final 'e' deleted, preceded by deleted 'bean.'*
64.16 did] *following comma deleted*
64.18 did] *followed by deleted 'more'*
64.20 be] *followed by deleted 'prop'*
64.28 low,] *comma inserted before deleted question and quote marks*
64.38 either] *followed by deleted 'yo'*
65.3 meanly,] *comma inserted*

after deleted period but before quote marks inscribed

65.6 what] *preceded by deleted* 'I have'

65.17 I.] *period inserted after a deleted period*

65.22 Colonel,] *followed by deleted* 'I'm' *and the start of another letter, possibly* 'I'

65.23 a] *interlined with a caret after a deleted illegible start of some letter*

65.24 you?] *question mark altered from period*

65.34 him,] *comma inserted before deleted dash*

66.4 me] *interlined above deleted* 'it'

66.6 lady] MS 'Lady' *has* 'L' *altered from* 'l'

66.18 he was] 'h' *over* 'w'

66.26 Royale's] *followed by deleted start of a letter, perhaps an* 'h'

66.32 can] *final* 't' *deleted*

66.35 and Forister] *interlined with a caret*

66.37 Strepp] *followed by deleted* 'and'

67.2 other.] *period altered from question mark*

67.3 his] *interlined with a caret*

67.9 to] *interlined with a caret*

67.9 had] *interlined with a caret*

67.11 one] *interlined with a caret*

67.18 but] *interlined above deleted* 'although'

67.18 I was] 'I' *interlined with a caret above deleted* 'it'; 'was' *followed by deleted* 'still'

67.22 natures.] *period over comma, and following* 'it' *deleted*

67.22 Their] *preceded by deleted* 'It'

67.30 the] *interlined with a caret*

67.32 moment] *followed by deleted* 'our'

68.4–5 The feeling] *preceded by deleted* 'An wo'

68.7 lowered] *followed by deleted* 'dizzily thinking'

68.10 bones] *preceded by deleted* 'lo'

68.15 Lord] 'L' *altered from* 'S'

68.21 our] *interlined*

68.25 renowned!] *interlined above deleted* 'famous.'

68.25 illustrious!] *followed by deleted quotes*

68.25 give] *interlined with a caret*

69.8 leaped] *preceded by deleted* 'fled' *and the start of some letter*

69.9 aside.] *interlined above deleted* 'away.'

69.13 I] *followed by deleted* 'was'

69.17 a] *interlined with a caret*

69.23 chairs] *interlined above deleted* 'fish'

69.25 for] 'r' *over* 'o'

69.30 us] *preceded by deleted* 'her'

70.5 not] *interlined above deleted* 'wish'

70.6 at] *interlined*

70.7 Plague] *interlined above deleted* 'Drat'

70.15 I say] 'I' *interlined above deleted* 'you'

70.25 charged] *followed by deleted* 'down'

70.34 position] *preceded by deleted possible* 'p'

[*strange hand begins here* 70.39 'Afterwards' *and continues to* 72.31 'horsemen.']

70.39 another] *interlined with a caret above deleted* 'a'

70.40 manoeuvres] 're' *in pencil over* 'er'

71.5,6 misapprehension] *first* 'p' *inserted in pencil*

71.9   that I] 'I' *interlined in pencil with a caret*

71.12 My] 'M' *in pencil over* 'Th'

71.18 the great] 'the' *interlined with a caret*

71.22 fashion] *followed by deleted comma and deleted* 'these g'

71.29 scandal] 'al' *added in pencil in space provided*

71.30 men] 'e' *written over* 'a'

71.35 fighting man] *interlined above deleted* 'swordsman'

71.36 ²a] *interlined with a caret*

72.12 a] *altered from* 'an'

72.13 duelling] *second* 'l' *deleted in pencil*

72.19 striving] *preceded by deleted* 'by'

72.26 approaching] *interlined with a caret*

72.28 door.] *followed by deleted interlined* ' "I saw Strepp and Royale among the horses." '

73.5   I] *preceded by deleted* 'A'

73.8   one] *interlined with a caret*

73.9   my horse] *preceded by deleted* 'the h'

73.11 mirth] *preceded by deleted* 'worth'

73.11 for] *followed by deleted doubtful* 'l'

73.12 women] 'e' *over* 'a'

73.15 rocky shore] *final* 'y' *over* 's'; 'shore' *interlined with a caret*

73.18 travel] *followed by deleted* 'Jem'

73.21 placed them] *preceding* 'placed' *is deleted* 'hav'; 'them' *interlined with a caret*

73.21 certain] *followed by deleted* 'in a'

73.22 hand.] *period inserted and* 'I had had' *interlined with a caret above deleted* 'with'

73.27 back] *followed by deleted* 'of'

73.29 at the] *followed by deleted* 'inn'

73.29 under] 'u' *written over* 'a'

73.29–30 Not puzzled] 'Not' *interlined with a caret;* 'p' *over* 'P'

73.30 saw] *interlined above deleted* 'knew'

73.30 not] *followed by deleted* 'the'

73.32 a duel] 'a' *interlined with a caret; final* 's' *in* 'duels' *deleted*

73.34 the] *interlined with a caret*

73.35 hostler] *followed by deleted period*

73.36 Small] *preceded by deleted* 'Sh'

73.38 was] *inserted in margin*

74.1   said] *preceded by deleted* 'I'

74.4   today.] *followed by deleted quote marks*

74.8   door. There . . . And] *period after* 'door' *deleted, then added at start of next line;* 'There be lanes.' *interlined with a caret misplaced before the added period;* 'A' *over* 'a' *in* 'And'

74.10 I flung] *preceded by deleted* 'I flung'

74.10 Now,"] *followed by deleted* 'he'

74.10 red] *interlined*

74.12 gentlemen] *third* 'e' *over* 'a'

74.13 fine] *interlined above deleted* 'good'

74.17 some] *preceded by deleted* 'long'

74.19 gotten] *preceded by deleted* 'recieve'

74.20 said] *preceded by deleted* 'vo'

74.21 would] 'w' *altered from* 's'; *preceded by deleted* 'too'

74.21 be] *interlined above deleted* 'are'

74.21   in] *interlined with a caret*

74.23   halt] *preceded by* 'would' *interlined with a caret; followed by* 'them' *interlined with a caret*

74.25   Lord] *preceded by deleted* 'Royal'

74.26   inn] *followed by deleted period*

74.28   Bath] 'B' *written over possible* 'b'

74.32   had] *interlined with a caret*

74.34   rampaging] *followed by deleted* 'together'

74.38   give] *preceded by deleted* 'lend a'

75.5   Bath.] *period added before deleted* 'to carrying his'

75.12   out] *preceded by deleted* 'onto'

75.16   puddle] *period inserted before deleted* 'and when'

75.19   platter] *preceded by deleted* 'plutte' *in which* 'p' *over doubtful* 'f'

75.20   been] *interlined with a caret*

75.20   gazing] *preceded by deleted* 'star-'

75.21   of] *followed by deleted* 'the'

75.22   bier] *followed by deleted* 'was'

75.23   candle-] *final* 's' *deleted*

75.23   swaying] *preceded by deleted* 'drifting'

75.27   best] *interlined with a caret*

75.29   people] *preceded by deleted* 'nearest'

75.33   beast] *preceded by deleted* 'best'

75.33   and I] 'I' *interlined above deleted* 'we'

75.34   my] *interlined above deleted* 'our'

75.38   close] *final* 'r' *deleted in pencil*

75.38   halted] *followed by a deleted letter, doubtfully a* 't'

76.3   them] *interlined above deleted* 'it'

76.8   I] *interlined with a caret*

76.9   be] *followed by interlined deleted* 'not'

76.13   the stones] *final* 'm' *in* 'them' *deleted and* 'stones' *interlined*

76.13   mix] *final* 'ed' *deleted*

76.13   people?] *question mark altered from a period*

76.14,15   Ballygowagglycuddi] *second* 'y' *over* 'e'

76.16   father's] *preceded by deleted* 'moth'

76.20   the] 'e' *written over possible* 'i'

76.20   and] *followed by deleted* 'thi'

76.22   reading] *preceded by deleted* 'red'

76.26   clatter] *interlined above deleted* 'clamour'

76.35   at] *interlined with a caret*

76.36   learning] *preceded by deleted* 'know'

76.38   see that] *first* 't' *of* 'that' *over* 'I'

76.38   in this country] *interlined with a caret*

76.39   for] *followed by deleted* 'drinking'

77.8   replied] *preceded by deleted* 'said'

77.9   Then] *followed by deleted comma*

77.13   milking] *preceded by deleted* 'the'

77.15   like] *preceded by deleted* 'ho'

77.18   voice] *interlined with a caret*

77.19   of the great earl!] *interlined above deleted* 'he said held a fortune in them!'

77.22   Earl's papers—] *dash over comma*

77.24 shouted] *preceded by deleted* 'crie'

77.26 little] *preceded by deleted* 'lit'

77.27 when] *interlined with a caret*

77.27 us] *interlined with a caret*

77.37 I] *preceded by deleted quote marks*

78.2 gentleman] *interlined above deleted* 'patron'

78.10 -opinionatcd] *interlined with a caret above deleted* '-opiniated'

78.10 consider] *followed by deleted* 'tha'

78.12 was] 'as' *over* 'ou'

78.13 bottle] *followed by deleted comma*

78.13 been holding] *interlined above deleted* 'had'

78.18 leisure.'] *single altered from double quotes*

78.19 those] *altered with a caret from* 'the'

78.22 said] *preceded by deleted* 'says'

78.23 driver] *interlined above deleted* 'coachman'

78.28 until] *interlined above deleted* 'when'

78.29 prettier] *interlined above deleted* 'lovelier'

78.35 angry] *interlined with a caret*

78.36 the] *preceded by deleted* 'she'

78.37 angry] *preceded by deleted* 'ag'

78.39 papers] *preceded by deleted* 'papers were absolutely important'

78.39 were] *preceded by deleted* 'were my destiny'

79.2 It had] *interlined with a caret above deleted* 'Now had it'

79.2 no] *interlined with a caret*

79.10 her] *preceded by deleted* 'my'

79.13 Irishmen] 'e' *over* 'a'

79.16,17 staked] *interlined above deleted* 'gave away'

79.19 give] 'i' *over* 'a'

79.23 spread] *interlined with a caret*

79.24 heap] *preceded by deleted* 'little'

79.25,26 five] *preceded by deleted* 'ten'

79.25 times] *interlined with a caret*

79.25 over."] *the quote mark is added and the period seems to be written over the start of an* 'a'

79.27 my] *interlined with a caret*

79.27–28 And two more yet.] *interlined with a caret after* 'again.'

79.30 My] *preceded by deleted* 'This'

79.37 papers.] *period inserted and following* 'for' *deleted*

80.8 around] *preceded by deleted* 'tow'

80.11 shall pocket] *interlined with a caret above deleted* 'will take'

80.13 appear] *interlined with a caret above deleted* 'show himself'

80.18 cloths] 'e' *of* 'clothes' *deleted*

80.23 and] *followed by deleted* ''tis good'

80.24 throw] *interlined above deleted* 'send'

80.27 took] *preceded by deleted* 'mounte'

80.29 a] *preceded by deleted* 'I'

81.1 named] *preceded by deleted* 'with'

81.5 Here] *preceded by deleted quote marks*

81.7 worship] *interlined above deleted* 'honour'

81.13 be] *interlined with a caret*

81.18 principal] 'le' *written over* 'al'

81.21 same,"] *followed by deleted period and* 'I'

81.23 slow] *interlined above deleted* 'mour'

81.23 tones] *followed by deleted* 'at once'

81.23 mournful] *followed by deleted* 'and'

81.31–32 sinful] *interlined above deleted* 'evil'

81.35 to hear you] *interlined with a caret*

81.37 happen] *followed by deleted* 'without'

81.37–38 afterward.] *final* 's' *deleted*

82.6 airy] *interlined above deleted* 'high'

82.7 Afterward] *final* 's' *deleted*

82.8 became] *followed by deleted illegible letter*

82.16 this] *preceded by deleted* 'even my father ever heard'

82.17 on] *followed by deleted period*

82.18 where] 'W' *marked with a slant and preceding* 'At' *inserted*

82.18 highway,] *followed by deleted* 'Jem Bottles'

82.22 It] *followed by deleted* 'so' *with* 'w' *over* 's'

82.23 after] *preceded by deleted* 'for'

82.27 And] *preceded by deleted* ' "Catch'

82.27 whom] 'm' *added above line after the typescript made up*

82.27 catching,] *followed by deleted quote marks*

82.28 "But] *preceded by deleted* ' "For he'

82.28 'tis] *followed by deleted start of possible* 'Ti'

82.36 while] *interlined*

82.36 staggered] 'ed' *interlined above deleted* 'ing'

83.7 swollen] *interlined with a caret*

83.11 But] *followed by deleted interlined possible* 'a'

83.13 Up-stairs] *followed by deleted letter, perhaps* 'l'

83.20 miscreant,] *followed by deleted quote marks*

83.31 him] *interlined above deleted* 'them'

83.32 sung] *interlined with a caret above deleted* 'called'

83.32 O'Rubby."] *period written over possible exclamation mark*

83.33 calling] *followed by deleted* 'out'

83.33 a] *interlined above deleted* 'his'

83.34 enter.] *quote marks before period deleted*

84.3 papers?] *question mark altered from period*

84.8 great] *interlined with a caret*

84.20 away] *interlined above deleted* 'back'

84.22 you] *preceded by deleted* 'him'

84.23 who] 'w' *written over* 'y'

84.37 seat.] *interlined above deleted* 'chair.'

85.4 man] *interlined above deleted* 'gentleman'

85.7 Bath] *interlined above deleted* 'Bristol'

85.9 yonder] *interlined with a caret*

85.25 The] *preceded by deleted* 'His'

85.28 Mary] *interlined above deleted* 'Strepp'

85.34 many] *final* 's' *deleted*

85.36 memory] *interlined above deleted* 'mind'

86.1 me] *followed by deleted* 'that'

86.5 O'Ruddy?] *question mark written over a period*

86.6 possession] *preceded by deleted* 'the'

86.7 everybody.] *followed by deleted quote marks*

86.11 head.] *period altered from a comma*

86.16 to] *added to margin*

86.18 voices,] *comma added after period deleted*

86.24 wished] *preceded by deleted* 'offered them.'

86.30 And] *followed by deleted* 'now'

86.30 me] *preceded by deleted* 'him'

86.33 me] *interlined with a caret*

86.33–34 flattery.] *preceded by deleted* 'talk.'

88.1 Earl] *interlined*

88.2 it] *interlined with a caret*

88.4 A] *over* 'I'

88.4 a] *interlined*

88.6 he] 'h' *formed over deleted period*

88.10 knew] 'e' *over* 'o'

88.18 the same] *interlined with a caret above deleted* 'it'

88.28 Strepp] *followed by deleted* 'in ironic musing.'

89.5 your] 'y' *written over illegible letter*

89.8 table] *followed by deleted* 'here.'

89.9 again] 'a' *over period*

89.26 ¹you] *interlined with a caret*

89.16 be] *interlined with a caret*

89.16 at present"] *interlined with a caret*

89.21 Ireland.] *followed by deleted quote marks*

89.22 moment] *interlined above deleted* 'time'

89.25 any] *interlined above deleted* 'again'

89.26 ¹you] *interlined with a caret*

89.28 he] *followed by deleted period*

89.29 can] *followed by deleted* 'stil'

89.30 plot. You] *period added and following* 'because' *deleted;* 'Y' *altered from* 'y'

89.33 must have] *interlined with a caret*

89.35 the] *interlined with a caret*

90.2 love,] *comma follows deleted period*

90.3 it,] *comma follows deleted period*

90.7 pure] *interlined with a caret above deleted* 'black'

90.16 snarled] *followed by deleted period*

90.17 swiftly] *interlined above deleted* 'suddenly'

90.19 ¹from] *preceded by deleted* 'of'

90.20 burn] *followed by deleted* 'brightly'

90.24 as I passed] *interlined above deleted* 'and'

90.26 I] *preceded by deleted* 'As'

90.34 nobleman] *interlined above deleted* 'Earl'

90.35 I would] 'I' *preceded by deleted* 'he'

90.36 Well] *preceded by deleted* 'Eh, well'

90.37 company] 'a' *over* 'o'; *not certain whether* 'p' *over another letter*

91.1 parts,] *comma inserted before deleted period*

91.2 know] 'o' *over* 'e'

91.5 meditated] *preceded by deleted* 'mediated'

91.9 out] *interlined with a caret*

91.11 thrust forth] *interlined above deleted* 'poked'

91.15 ¹Keep] *interlined above deleted* 'Kape'

91.15 ye] *interlined with a caret*

91.16 familiar voice] *preceded by deleted* 'voice answer'

91.16   fine high] *interlined above deleted* 'high shrill'

91.18   coming,] *comma inserted after deletion of following* 'for them' *with* 'you' *interlined above* 'them' *and then deleted*

91.19   how] *interlined with a caret*

91.21   been] *interlined with a caret*

91.24   Hoity-] *preceded by deleted* 'Hoity-old'

91.27   ¹you] 'o' *over* 'e' *and* 'u' *added*

91.30   for many reasons] *interlined with a caret above deleted* 'time to interfer'

91.31   recognized] 'd' *written over final* 's'

91.35   did] *interlined with a caret*

91.36   sure] *interlined with a caret and comma added in line*

91.37   would] *interlined above deleted* 'was'

91.37   be] 'she' (*perhaps altered from some other word*) *interlined above deleted* 'for' *and then deleted in pencil and* 'be' *in pencil added*

91.38   of] *inserted*

91.39   all] *preceded by deleted* 'with'

92.3   ends] 'n' *written over possible* 'd'

92.8   in] 'i' *written over* 'o'

92.8   spit] *preceded by deleted* 'then'

92.9   saw] *interlined preceding deleted* 'that'

92.10   heard] 'he' *over* 'sa'

92.10   It would] *interlined with a caret above deleted* 'Twas'

92.10   be] *interlined with a caret*

92.11   after,] *comma inserted before deleted period*

92.11   It] *preceded by deleted* 'Twas, she.'

92.12   am for] *interlined above deleted* 'would be'

92.13   stool] *followed by deleted quote marks and dash*

92.17   noble] *preceded by deleted* 'ancient'

92.21   thing] *final* 's' *deleted*

92.21–22   'Your . . . ladyship—"] *interlined above deleted* 'My Lady! Oh, my Lady"——; *the second in each case with* 'L' *over* 'l'

92.23   obeying] *interlined above deleted* 'under'

92.23   Earl] 'E' *over* 'e'

92.24   by a] 'a' *interlined with a caret above deleted* 'the'

92.25   beldame] *preceded by deleted* 'old'

92.27   ask] *final* 'ed' *deleted*

92.33–34   meanwhile . . . arms.] *originally placed after* 'her', *with* 'meanwhile' *interlined; then a line transposes the phrase to follow* 'belonged'; *a period after* 'belonged' *deleted and a comma inserted, the comma after* 'her' *deleted, and a period after* 'arms' *inserted and followed, within the line, by the original comma not deleted*

92.36   had] *interlined with a caret*

93.3   I.] *crowded in before deleted* 'Paddy' *in which following period is deleted in error*

93.4   this?] *question mark over exclamation*

93.5   ²like] *followed by deleted* 'I'

93.5   a] *preceded by deleted* 'the'

93.9   would] *preceded by deleted* 'was for seeing'

93.13   moments] *interlined with a caret above deleted* 'time'

93.18   had] *followed by deleted* 'I'

93.18   higher] *interlined with a caret*

93.19 and] *interlined with a caret*

93.20 food] 'f' *over* 'm'

93.28 ways] *interlined* (*as* 'way') *above deleted* 'quality'

93.32 known to be] *interlined with a caret above deleted* 'held'

93.34 me.] *followed by deleted quote marks*

93.36 sight] *interlined above deleted* 'manner'

93.38 turf."] *followed by, with new papagraph, deleted* 'The British had the weight in all way but they also ha'

95.5 learned] *preceded by deleted* 'great'

95.5 a] *inserted before deleted* 'a' *of* 'along'

95.9 by] *interlined with a caret*

95.11 strongly] 'tr' *over* 'ee'

95.14 be] *interlined with a caret*

95.18 that busy] *interlined with a caret*

95.21 protests] *followed by deleted* 'fro'

95.23 retired] *interlined above deleted* 'gone'

95.24 had] *interlined with a caret*

96.1 fiery] *preceded by deleted* 'deadly ra'

96.3 chanted] *interlined above deleted* 'sang'

96.5 caught] *preceded by deleted* 'again'

96.8 me] *followed by deleted* 'that'

96.12 out] *preceded by deleted* 'fo'

96.14 changed] *preceded by deleted* 'cha' *interrupted by a grease spot*

96.25 this] *preceded by deleted* 'as if'

96.29 points] 's' *deleted then returned*

96.31 Paddy,] *comma inserted after deleted period*

96.35 near . . . bed] *interlined with a caret*

96.36 gain] *interlined above deleted* 'have'

96.39 the wall] 'the' *interlined with a caret*

97.6 coat, waistcoat] *each preceded by deleted* 'my'

97.7 a] *preceded by deleted* 'f'

97.7 my] 'y' *over* 'e'

97.21 When] 'W' *over* 'w'; *preceded by deleted* 'Even' *and followed by deleted* 'the'

97.26 way] *preceded by deleted* 'cause'

97.29 so] *interlined above deleted* 'all'

97.30 are] *preceded by deleted* 'come down to be'

97.31 I] *preceded by deleted* 'A'

97.34 cease?] *question mark altered from period*

97.39 inn,] *comma inserted after deleted period*

98.2 The] *preceded by deleted* 'He p'

98.7 remember] *preceded by deleted* 'remb'; *followed by* 'old' *interlined with a caret*

98.11 lady] *followed by deleted period*

98.14 woman] *interlined above deleted* 'lady'

98.23 when] *preceded by deleted* 'and you'

98.36 cried] *followed by deleted period*

98.37 he] *preceded by deleted* 'his h'

98.38 her] *interlined with a caret*

99.4 We] 'W' *over* 'w'

99.4 it?] *question mark altered from period*

99.5 warily] 'w' *over period*

99.5–6 are many] *interlined with a caret*

99.9 mention] *preceded by deleted* 'ever'

99.12 leaving] 'v' *in pencil over* 'd'
99.16 Bath] 'B' *over* 'b'
99.23 a great] *preceded by deleted* 'g'
99.23 in] *preceded by deleted* 'w'
103.1 ambled] *interlined above deleted* 'jogged'
103.3 horseman] *preceded by deleted* 'swordsman'
103.6 Englishman?] *question mark altered from period*
103.7 cities] *preceded by* 'grand' *which has been deleted and above it* 'great' *interlined and deleted*
103.11 proud] *interlined with a caret above deleted* 'fine'
103.19 him] *followed by deleted* 'that'
103.20 him?] *question mark altered from comma*
103.20 poor] *followed by deleted period*
103.21 ¹am] *interlined with a caret above deleted* 'mean. would be'
103.24 ditches] *preceded by deleted* 'diches'
103.25 over] *interlined above deleted* 'into pools'
104.1 saying] *followed by interlined* 'that'
104.5 to] *preceded by deleted* 'do'
104.7 burned] *followed by deleted* 'an' *and the start of another letter*
104.10 I] *preceded by deleted* 'we'
104.10 burnt-] *preceded by deleted* 'burnt'
104.15–16 confidentially,] *comma inserted before deleted period*
104.17 their toes.] 'ir' *added to* 'the'; 'toes.' *interlined above deleted* 'ground.'
104.23 underlings] *preceded by deleted* 'servant'

104.25 to] *preceded by deleted* 'got'
104.28 said] *followed by deleted* 'what'
104.31 quiet] *interlined with a caret above deleted* 'fine'
104.31 people] *interlined with a caret*
104.33 Paddy] *followed by deleted period*
104.36 somewhere.] *squeezed in at end of line*
105.1 Mass] *final* 'es' *deleted*
105.1 ²said] *preceded by deleted* 'said'
105.6 we] *preceded by deleted* 'they'
105.23 the] *interlined with a caret*
105.25 am seeing] 'am' *interlined with a caret;* 'ing' *added*
105.27 less] *preceded by deleted* 'mo'
105.28 For] *followed by deleted* ',sure,'
105.32 talking] *preceded by* 'be' *interlined with a caret;* 'ing' *added*
105.33 ¹London.] *following quotation marks deleted*
105.34 town,] *comma inserted before deleted period*
105.35 ¹it] *preceded by deleted* 'th'
106.1 tower] *interlined with a caret above deleted* 'steeple'
106.2 been] *interlined with a caret*
106.6 up-bringing,] *comma inserted before deleted period and start of* 'A'
106.8 away] *interlined with a caret*
106.12 they] *preceded by deleted doubtful* 'T'
106.14 natural] *preceded by deleted letter, possibly* 'v'
106.14 I,] *comma inserted before deleted period*

106.16 a] *interlined with a caret above deleted* 'I'

106.16 take the purse of] *interlined with a caret above deleted* 'rob'

106.27 them.] *interlined with a caret before interlined and deleted* 'them.' *above deleted* 'it.'

106.28 fifteen] *interlined above deleted* 'ten'

107.1 am seeing] *interlined with a caret above deleted* 'see'

107.2 turf] *followed by deleted comma*

107.8 excitement.] *followed by deleted quote marks*

108.3 nature] *followed by deleted* 'that'

108.5 our] 'o' *over* 'y'

108.5 leisure?"] *question mark written over a period*

108.6 be] *over* 'is'

108.13 worthy] *interlined above deleted* 'good'

108.15 younger] *interlined with a caret*

108.22 Each] *preceded by deleted* 'Pint'

108.29 in] *preceded by deleted* 'ric'

109.1 said] 's' *over* 'o'

109.3 him against] 'him' *interlined with a caret*

109.3 wall,] *comma added after deleted period*

109.4 pot] *interlined with a caret*

109.13 bide] *interlined with a caret*

109.25 get] 'e' *over* 'o'

109.27 now] 'n' *written over* 's'

109.28 of] *followed by deleted* 'fence?" '

109.29 despair] *followed by deleted* 'but'

109.32 Jem] 'J' *over* 'B'

109.37 slew] *interlined above deleted* 'killed'

110.6–7 with sudden resolution] *interlined with a caret*

110.19 at] *interlined with a caret*

110.22 in] *interlined with a caret*

110.23 his] *altered from* 'he' *and following* 'would' *deleted*

110.24 would] *interlined with a caret*

110.28 sudden] 'u' *over one or two illegible letters*

110.28 look] *interlined with a caret*

110.29 further] *interlined with a caret and preceded by deleted* 'als' *above deleted* 'too'

110.35 to be] *preceded by deleted* 'to be'

110.36 in Bath] *interlined with a caret*

111.3 duties] 'ies' *over* 'y'

111.6 now] *prefixed* 'k' *deleted*

111.13 Now] *preceded by deleted* 'N' *possibly over some other letter*

111.15 you] *followed by deleted* 'nee'

111.16 enough] *interlined*

111.19 dejectedly] *interlined*

111.20 is] *preceded by deleted* 'aint'

111.21 for your honour] *interlined (as* 'honor'*) with a caret*

111.22 an] *over* 'is'

111.23 scoundrel!] *followed by deleted quotation marks*

111.24 added] *interlined above deleted* 'continued'

111.25 There's] *preceded by deleted* 'Al'

111.31 away] *interlined with a caret*

111.34 I] *preceded by deleted* 'In the'

111.36 position.] *period inserted and following* 'to window' *deleted*

111.39 they] 'y' *over* 'ir'

112.10 happiness] *preceded by deleted* 'half-savage'
112.11 numskulls] *altered from* 'numb-skulls'
112.12 could] *interlined with a caret*
112.14 dignity] 'g' *written over* 'd'
112.22 great] *interlined with a caret above deleted* 'grand'
112.24 returned] *interlined above deleted* 'gone back'
112.25 probably] *interlined with a caret*
112.27 on a] 'a' *interlined with a caret*
112.27 night] *interlined with a caret above deleted* 'day'
112.32 without] 'out' *added*
112.37 Jem,] *comma altered from exclamation point*
112.37 admiration,] *comma inserted before deleted period*
112.38 were] 'w' *written over* 'a'
113.1 looking] *preceded by* 'be' *interlined with a caret;* 'ing' *added*
113.1 habit] *interlined above deleted* 'way'
113.3 ¹looking] *preceded by* 'are' *interlined with a caret;* 'ing' *added*
113.6 there] *interlined*
113.7 wench] *interlined above deleted* 'girl'
113.7 many] *interlined with a caret above deleted* 'more than'
113.10 would be] *interlined above deleted* 'are'
114.1 the] *interlined with a caret*
114.3 ²man] *interlined*
114.6 ¹us] *interlined with a caret*
114.7 in] *followed by deleted* 'it'
114.9 servants] *interlined with a caret*
114.11 London,] *followed by deleted* 't' *and start of an* 'h'

114.11 strange] *interlined above deleted* 'black'
114.12 so] *preceded by deleted* 't' *and start of an* 'h'
114.12 called] *preceded by deleted* 'even'
114.14 fascinating] *interlined above deleted* 'interesting'
114.17 ²the] *interlined with a caret*
114.21 and] *interlined with a caret*
114.22 fear] *followed by deleted* 'that'
114.23 ²we] *interlined with a caret*
114.24 it] *preceded by deleted* 'h'
114.26 fog the] *interlined with a caret*
114.28 We] *preceded by deleted* 'I'
115.1 we] *interlined with a caret*
115.5 heavy] *interlined with a caret*
115.7 this,] *followed by deleted* 'was off'
115.9 the sky] *preceded by deleted* 'heaven'
115.9 an] *interlined above deleted* 'a most'
115.11 with] *followed by deleted* 'such'
115.15 travel] *interlined above deleted* 'way'
115.21 journey.] *preceded by deleted* 'way.'
115.23 fists] 'firsts' *with deleted* 'r'
115.30 ²for] *followed by deleted* 'my'
115.32 wish . . . prefer] *final* 'ed' *deleted in each*
115.32 the] 'th' *over* 'a'
115.33 to] *inserted before deleted* 'of'
115.38 him,] *comma follows deleted period*
115.38 you] *interlined with a caret*

116.2   he] *preceded by deleted* 'was'

116.4   my] *interlined above deleted* 'go'

116.4   face] 'e' *over deleted* 'ing'

116.8   -cut] *follows deleted* 'jowl'

116.10   with] *followed by start of an* 'L'

116.13   roared] *preceded by deleted* 'thund'

116.15   last,] *comma follows deleted period*

116.19   into] 'i' *written over* 'o'

116.20   see] *interlined with a caret*

116.21   accommodation] MS 'accomadation', 'da' *interlined in pencil with a caret*

116.26   Pig] 'P' *over* 'p'

116.31   landlord] *followed by deleted* 'touchin'

116.37   I] *interlined with a caret*

117.1   This] *altered from* 'The'

117.1   do] *follows deleted* 'due'

117.2   big] *a final letter deleted, perhaps an* 's'

117.3   should] *interlined with a caret*

117.7   not] *interlined with a caret*

117.12   or] *preceded by deleted* 'and'

117.13   gentleman] *followed by deleted* 'by a strange' *and the start of* 'r'

117.19   they] *interlined with a caret*

117.20   streets] 'st' *over* 'w'

117.20   be as safe] *interlined with a caret*

117.23   and staff] *interlined with a caret*

117.23   follow] *preceded by deleted* 'go'

117.26   stroll.] *followed by deleted quote marks*

117.32   myself] *interlined with a caret*

117.34   mirth] *followed by deleted* 'that'

117.35   Fullbil] *final* 'l' *deleted*

117.36   had] *preceded by* 'never' *interlined with a caret; followed by deleted* 'never'

117.37   illustrious] *interlined with a caret*

118.4   gentlemen] *third* 'e' *over* 'a'

118.11   whose] 's' *over* 'l'

118.13   the gentlemen] *interlined with a caret*

118.13   you] *interlined above deleted* 'me'

118.15   presence.] *followed by deleted quote marks*

118.15   himself] *preceded by deleted* 'is'; *followed by* 'is' *interlined with a caret*

118.18   in] *preceded by deleted* 'is'

119.1   led] *preceded by deleted* 'down'

119.5   little] *interlined above deleted* 'nothing'

119.6   soon] *preceded by deleted* 'at last I'

119.6   enough] 'o' *over* 'e'

119.6   bordered] *interlined above deleted* 'lined'

119.8   some words] *interlined with a caret*

119.18   another] *preceded by deleted* 'anth'

119.19   to his plan.] *preceded by deleted period*

119.21   my] *preceded by deleted* 'the'

119.27   I saw] *preceded by deleted* 'At first'

120.3   I] *over* 'l'

120.5   with] *inserted in margin*

120.6   His] 'H' *over* 'h'; *followed by deleted* 'present'

120.9   with] *preceded by deleted* 'in'

120.11   a] *interlined with a caret*

120.11   crowd] *followed by deleted* 'the'

120.14   intellectual] *preceded by deleted* 'support in'

120.16   During] *preceded by deleted* 'They passed'

120.17   gentlemen] *third* 'e' *over* 'a'; 'g' *written over* 't' *and start of an* 'h'

120.19   talk] *preceded by deleted* 'spe'

120.19   wittily?] *question mark altered from period*

120.20   even] *inserted in margin*

120.23   opportune] *interlined above deleted* 'time'

120.25   it?] *question mark altered from period*

120.27   literary] *interlined with a caret*

120.28   from] *followed by deleted* 'his g'

120.37   Fullbil] *followed by deleted* 'which'

120.38   hour] *followed by deleted period*

120.39   Immediately] 'I' *over* 'i'; *preceded by deleted* 'and' *and a period before it*

120.40   glass] *altered from* 'glance'

121.9   occur] *second* 'r' *deleted*

121.10   explanation] *interlined above deleted* 'conversation'; *followed by deleted* 'would'

121.11   before] *preceded by deleted* 'before the'

121.12   you] *interlined with a caret*

121.15   strength] *followed by deleted period*

121.15   all] *altered from* 'a m'

121.18   in] *preceded by deleted* 'by'

121.20   in the] *interlined with a caret over deleted* 'of'

121.20   of the world] *preceded by* ', sir it'

121.22   his blunder] *interlined with a caret*

121.23   of] *interlined with a caret*

121.28   these] *first* 'e' *written over* 'o'

121.28   could] *interlined with a caret*

121.32   explanation;] *semicolon added after deleted period*

121.33   There] *preceded by deleted quote marks*

121.37   anticipation] *preceded by deleted* 'gigan'

121.37   a] *interlined with a caret*

121.37   answering.] *interlined above deleted* 'reply.'

121.38   friend] *final* 's' *deleted*

121.39   he] *followed by deleted* 'slowly'

121.39   see] *followed by deleted* 'that'

122.1   a] *interlined above deleted* 'the'

122.2   invulnerable] 'a' *over* 'n'; *preceded by deleted* 'ut'

122.4   cracked] *interlined with a caret above deleted* 'old'

122.5   My] *preceded by deleted* 'By' *and the start of some letter*

122.12   delivered] *preceded by deleted* 'delivered'

122.31   interested] *preceded by deleted* 'me'

122.31   deeply] *preceded by deleted* 'greatly'

122.32   by the] 'the' *interlined with a caret*

122.33–34   adoption of the] *interlined with a caret*

123.4   sir,] *followed by deleted* 'then'

123.6   Chinese] *preceded by deleted* 'fl' *and the start of some letter*

123.6   to] *interlined with a caret above deleted* 'of'

123.8   answered] *interlined above deleted* 'h'

123.16   neighbors] *followed by deleted period*

123.19   pleased] *preceded by deleted* 'as'

123.21–22   gentlemen] *third* 'e' *over start of* 'a'

123.22 more] *interlined above deleted* 'my'

123.25 much] *interlined above deleted* 'great'

123.26 for the moment] *interlined with a caret*

123.29 bashfulness] 'ness' *interlined below deleted* 'ly'; *preceded by* 'in his' *interlined with a caret*

123.30 related] *preceded by deleted* 'has'

123.32 say] *interlined above deleted* 'contend'

123.37 replied] *interlined with a caret*

124.1 little] *interlined with a caret above deleted doubtful* 'th'

124.2 spirits] *interlined above deleted* 'demons'

124.4 the aid] 'the' *preceded by deleted* 'th'|

124.11 ¹ his] *preceded by deleted* 'Fulbil'

124.13 likely] *preceded by deleted* 'little'

124.19 Sirs] *preceded by deleted* 'Ge' *and start of an* 'n'

124.23 went] *interlined above deleted* 'was'

124.26 do] *interlined with a caret*

125.12 he] *followed by deleted* 'added'

125.23 great] *followed by deleted* 'without a'

125.26 people] *followed by deleted* 'in Ireland people'

126.16 saw] *preceded by deleted* 'f'

126.23 kill you] 'you' *interlined with a caret*

126.28 he] *interlined with a caret*

126.34 Knowledge] 'K' *over* 'k'

127.5 fellow] *followed by deleted* 'u' *and the start of some letter, perhaps* 'l'

127.7–8 ' 'Tis . . . -eaters,'] *single quotes altered from double*

127.9 for] *interlined above deleted* 'to say of'

127.10 old] *preceded by deleted* 'ma'

127.11 table] *followed by deleted period*

127.14 King] *preceded by deleted* 'a'

127.15 sickly] *preceded by deleted* 'burst'

127.16 bowed] *preceded by deleted* 'lo'

128.1 On] *preceded by deleted* 'o'

128.4 me] *interlined with a caret*

128.5 sleeping] *preceded by deleted* 'stayi' *and start of a* 'n'

128.14 do] *interlined with a caret*

128.15 "Oh] *preceded by deleted* 'He shook his head sadly.'

128.28 we] 'w' *over* 'W'; *preceded by interlined* 'In fact'

128.28 man] *interlined above deleted* 'lad'

129.1 later,] MS 'latter' *followed by deleted* 'I heard'

129.3 ¹ I] *written over illegible letter*

129.3 could] *interlined with a caret*

129.7 with] *interlined above deleted* 'amid'

129.11 water] *followed by deleted* 'down'

129.11–12 also sent down] *interlined above deleted* 'all se'

129.12 phrases of] *interlined with a caret*

129.12 clattered] *first* 't' *deleted*

129.14 ear] *preceded by deleted* 'fea' *and start of some other letter*

129.15 person;] *semicolon follows deleted period*

129.15 one] *interlined above deleted* 'a man'

129.19 My] *preceded by deleted* 'But'

129.24 skirmishes] 'es' *interlined above deleted* 'ers'

129.27 had started] *interlined*

129.30 that] *followed by deleted* 'mig'

129.30 might] *preceded by* 're- ally' *interlined with a caret; followed by deleted* 'really'

129.34 marched] *interlined above deleted* 'passed'

129.37 heed] *followed by deleted* 'to us'

130.1–2 frequently] *interlined above deleted* 'sometimes'

130.11 many] *preceded by de- leted* 'much'

130.21 some tale] *interlined with a caret*

130.25 which] *preceded by de- leted* 'th'; *followed by deleted* 'had'

130.26 Duke] 'D' *over* 'd'

130.28 of what] *interlined above deleted* 'about'

130.29 my happy] 'my' *inter- lined above deleted* 'the'

130.31 loud] *preceded by deleted* 'thundering'

130.38 could serve] 'c' *over* 'w'

131.9 "Paddy,"] *followed by de- leted* 'said I,'

131.10–11 gentlemen] *interlined above deleted* 'men'

131.12 answered.] *period over comma*

131.24 somebody] *followed by* 'would' *interlined in pencil with a caret after the type- script made up*

131.24 clear] *followed by deleted* 'a pilfe'

131.30 quiet] *interlined above deleted* 'silence'

131.35 weed] *followed by de- leted period*

132.2 all would] 'would' *inter- lined with a caret*

132.8 bird] *altered by deletion*

from 'bird's' *and following* 'beak' *deleted*

132.9 strenuous-] *first* 'u' *inter- lined with a caret*

132.11 the true] 'the' *interlined with a caret*

132.11 qualities] 'q' *over* 't'

132.13 I'll] 'll' *over* 'd'

133.1 ²the] *interlined with a caret*

133.1 Westport] *followed by de- leted* 'had'

133.10 Gardens] 'gardens' *inter- lined above deleted* 'place'; *preceding* 'these' *altered from* 'the'

133.17 forecast] *altered from* 'fore-cast'

133.22 Priceless] *interlined with a caret; followed by* 'silks' *with* 's' *over* 'S'

133.30 ladder] *final* 's' *deleted*

134.4 greatly] *preceded by de- leted* 'was'; *followed by* 'wished' *interlined above* 'in- clined'

134.5 fixed] *interlined with a caret*

134.11 amusing] *interlined*

134.12 her] *followed by deleted* 'people'

134.12 pairs] *interlined above deleted* 'ey'

134.16 faces] *preceded by de- leted* 'exterios'

134.17 women] 'e' *over* 'a'

134.23 Afterward] *preceded by deleted* 'This was attention'

134.25 eyes] *interlined with a caret*

134.27 out] *interlined*

134.29 their] 'ir' *over* 're'

134.37 own] *preceded by deleted* 'own'

135.5 however] *interlined*

135.15 ¹he] *preceded by deleted* 'it'

135.25 be] *interlined with a caret*

135.29 me] *interlined above deleted* 'you'

135.31 ¹it,] *followed by deleted quote marks*

135.33 only] *interlined with a caret*

135.37 said] *preceded by deleted* 'she'

135.37 had] *interlined with a caret*

136.14 she] *interlined with a caret above deleted* 'a woman'

136.15 "they] *preceded by deleted* 'think'

136.17 some] *interlined with a caret*

136.35 boot-] 't' *over* 'k'

136.35 almost] 'al' *over* 'in'; *following* 'inclined to be' *interlined with a caret*

137.5 you] *preceded by deleted* 'she'

137.17 examine] *preceded by deleted* 'handle'

137.28 able] *preceded by deleted* 'telling'; *followed by deleted* 'up'

137.29 fierce] *preceded by deleted* 'regular'

137.30 scandal] *preceded by deleted* 'calumny'

138.5 evil] *followed by deleted comma*

138.8 if] *interlined*

138.9 names] *preceded by deleted* 'even'

138.15 did.] *period inserted before deleted period*

138.15 mad!"] *period deleted and exclamation point inserted*

138.17 light] *preceded by deleted* 'blo' *and start of a letter*

138.17 a] *interlined with a caret*

138.18 he] 'h' *over* 'I'

139.7 know] *interlined with a caret*

139.11 Yes] *preceded by deleted* 'And'

139.20 hullaballoo] *final* 'o' *inserted*

139.23 lads] *followed by deleted* 'who'

139.29 mouth] *inserted in the margin*

140.8 were] *interlined with a caret above deleted* 'did'

140.8 getting] 'ting' *inserted*

140.9 thought] *interlined above deleted* 'said'

140.15 moved] *interlined with a caret*

140.17 seen] *preceded by deleted* 'heard'

140.24 distinctly.] *interlined above deleted* 'well.'

140.27 Nobody] *preceded by deleted* 'She'

140.32 as] *preceded by deleted* 'like a'

141.2 father,] *preceded by deleted* 'old'; *following comma inserted before deleted comma*

141.5 why] *interlined with a caret*

141.6 tatters] *followed by deleted* 'that'

141.9 devil] *interlined with a caret*

141.10–11 of twenty-five shillings a year] *interlined with a caret; original* 'fifty' *is deleted and* '25' *inserted in pencil*

141.13 would] 'w' *over start of a letter, perhaps* 'h'

141.14 but] *inserted in margin before deleted* 'only that'

141.20 swordsmen] 'e' *over start of* 'a'

141.22 Nothing] *preceded by deleted* 'It'

141.23 there] 'h' *over* 'i'

141.33 swordsmen] *interlined above deleted* 'fencing'

141.39 ²husks,] *comma altered from a period*

142.3 grow] *preceded by deleted* 'whi'

142.4   duchess!] *exclamation inserted after deleted period*

142.5   flatterers] *second 'er' over 'in'*

142.25   trembling] *preceded by deleted 'excitement'*

142.25   frequently] *followed by deleted 'I felt'*

142.32   -children] *'re' over 'er'*

142.33   advantage] *followed by deleted 'to h'*

142.34   enshrine] *final 's' deleted; preceded by 'is able to' interlined with a caret*

142.35–36   believing her] *originally 'believeing' but third 'e' deleted*

142.36   to be] *interlined with a caret*

143.1–2   and foot] *interlined with a caret*

143.3   mistaken] *'n' inserted*

143.3   idea.] *interlined with a caret above deleted period*

143.3–4   feelings.] *interlined above deleted 'dreams.'*

143.9   children] *'c' over a downstroke, probably the start of 'p'*

143.12–13   intrigue] *preceded by deleted illegible letter*

143.15   in] *interlined with a caret*

143.19   aid] *preceded by 'the' interlined with a caret; followed by deleted 'the' interlined with a deleted caret*

143.27   ²the] *'t' over 'p'*

143.31   as] *preceded by deleted 'as'*

143.31   over] *preceded by deleted 'to the docter'*

143.35   a] *interlined with a caret*

143.36   hear] *'ar' over 're'*

144.1   prudent] *interlined above deleted 'safe'*

144.9   to] *interlined with a caret*

144.20   was] *preceded by deleted 'seeme'*

144.22   irrevocable] *preceded by*

deleted 'feminine'; *followed by* 'feminine' *interlined with a caret*

144.25   gazed] *preceded by deleted 'glan'*

144.28   me] *followed by deleted comma*

144.29   bravely] *'ly' inserted*

144.31   she] *preceded by deleted 'I'*

144.32   it] *preceded by start of an illegible letter*

145.6   had] *interlined with a caret*

145.6   cause] *preceded by deleted 'reason'*

145.17   there] *followed by deleted 'like'*

146.4   him] *preceded by deleted 'me'*

146.10   spoke] *followed by deleted 'with an air'*

146.10   illness] *interlined above deleted 'anxiety'*

146.13   he] *preceded by deleted 'it'*

147.3   much] *interlined with a caret*

147.9   have you] *'you' interlined with a caret*

147.10   friend] *preceded by deleted 'Earl'*

147.16   fair] *'ir' over 're'*

147.18   to] *interlined with a caret*

147.26   he] *'h' written over illegible letters*

147.37   come] *final 's' deleted*

148.3   That] *preceded by deleted 'After'*

148.6   bowing] *'ing' added*

148.8   could] *'c' over 's'*

148.26   it,] *comma inserted after deleted period*

148.29   he] *interlined with a caret*

148.33   we] *interlined with a caret*

148.33   on] *'o' over 'i'*

148.34   we] *preceded by deleted doubtful 't'*

149.5   pretty] *interlined with a caret*

149.5   his] *interlined with a caret*

149.7   balance] *followed by deleted period and* 'If a'

149.13   Sunday?] *question mark altered from period*

149.14   "there] 'r' *written over* 's'

149.19   them only I feared] *interlined above deleted* 'some distance." '

149.30   home] *altered from* 'house'

150.3   home] *interlined above deleted* 'house'

150.5   We] 'W' *over* 'H'

150.5   reconnoitred] 'c' *over* 'n'

150.9   iron] *interlined with a caret*

150.9   way] *interlined with a caret*

150.10   after] 'ft' *over* 'nd'

150.16   infrequently] *preceded by deleted* 'very'

150.16   hum-] *preceded by deleted* 'c'

150.34   again] *interlined with a caret*

150.34   ²the] *interlined with a caret above deleted* 'again'

150.37   with] *interlined with a caret*

151.23–24   murmurings.] *followed by deleted quote marks*

151.27   ye.] *period altered from exclamation*

151.28   thinking] *interlined with a caret*

152.9   do] *preceded by deleted* 'would' *interlined with a caret*

152.12–13   respect] 'c' *written over illegible letter*

152.14   answered.] *period altered from comma*

152.19   bleed] *second* 'e' *interlined with a caret*

152.26   friends.] *followed by deleted quote marks*

152.31   although] *followed by deleted* 'I think'

152.37   your] *written over deleted* 'her'

153.9   said] 'i' *written over illegible letter*

154.6   would] *interlined with a caret*

154.20   on] *preceded by deleted* 'at'

154.26   modestly,] *comma added after deleted period*

155.5   as] 'a' *over* 'i'

155.6   trees] *preceded by deleted* 'regrets'

155.9   my] *preceded by deleted* 'a' *and some illegible letter, possibly* 'n'

155.17   we] *preceded by deleted* 'I'

155.24   Lady] *followed by deleted* 'Strep'

155.28   climb it] 'climb' *interlined above deleted* 'do'

155.28   say,] *followed by deleted* 'Pa'

155.30   anyone] *interlined above deleted* 'air'

155.32   plan] *interlined above deleted* 'suppose'

155.37   a tree] 'a' *interlined with a caret; final* 's' *in* 'trees' *deleted*

156.2   mind] *interlined with a caret above deleted* 'time'

156.4,10   the] *interlined with a caret*

156.5   have] *interlined with a caret*

156.13   is] *interlined above deleted* 'was'

156.13   eve of] *followed by deleted* 'a'

156.14   often] *preceded by deleted* 'said'

156.15   before] *first* 'e' *over start of* 'f'

156.16   killed] *followed by deleted comma*

156.17   in front of] *interlined*

with a caret above deleted 'before'

156.19 give] *followed by deleted* 'suc'

156.24 lady] *preceded by deleted* 'same'

156.25 the] *interlined with a caret*

156.26 all] *interlined with a caret*

156.34 is] *interlined above deleted* 'means'

156.34 that] *interlined with a caret*

157.4 foreseeing] 'ing' *added; preceded by* 'am' *interlined with a caret*

157.6 in anger] *interlined above deleted* 'angrily'

157.8 betters] *followed by deleted period; the rest of the sentence crowded in later*

157.21 idea] *preceded by deleted* 'impression'

157.26 am] *interlined with a caret*

157.27 serve] *followed by deleted comma*

158.5 man?] *question mark altered from period*

158.15 evil] *interlined with a caret*

158.18 our] *preceded by deleted* 'y'

158.26 danger?] *question mark inserted before deleted period*

158.28 sally] 's' *over* 'o'

158.29 father] *preceded by deleted* 'party'

158.34–35 paraphernalia] *second* 'r' *interlined with a caret*

158.39 Chord] 'C' *over* 'c'

159.1 put much] *interlined with a caret above deleted* 'laid great'

159.10 hum-drum] MS 'humdrum', *first* 'm' *altered from* 'n'

159.12 that] 'a' *over* 'e'

159.12 need] *preceded by deleted* 'ne'

159.12 you] *preceded by deleted* 'wo'

160.1 already] *preceded by deleted* 'have'

160.2 additional] *interlined with a caret*

160.26 form] *final* 's' *deleted*

160.26 is] *followed by deleted* 'an'

160.28 ourselves] *altered from* 'ourself'

160.38 have] *interlined with a caret*

160.38 by] *interlined with a caret above deleted* 'but'

161.5 to] *interlined above deleted* 'on'

161.6 not] *interlined with a caret*

161.6 reach the] *interlined with a caret*

161.9 I do] *preceded by deleted* 'O' *and another letter, perhaps an* 'n' *or* 'r'

161.10 meditations.] *altered by deleted* 'a' *from* 'mediatations'; *period inserted before deleted* 'wh'

161.12 madman] *second* 'a' *over* 'e'

161.13 behind] *preceded by deleted* 'bh'

161.17 speed.] *preceded by deleted* 'speech.'

161.20 bewildered] *interlined with a caret*

161.21 mouth] *preceded by deleted* 'mound'

162.2 once more] *interlined with a caret above deleted* 'again'

162.12 evidently] *preceded by deleted* 'so'

162.15 weapon.] *followed by deleted quote marks*

162.16 whom] *preceded by deleted* 'h'

162.19 ye] *final* 'r' *deleted*

162.24 me] *interlined with a caret*

162.25 -thief] *followed by deleted* 'h'

163.4 rim] *preceded by deleted* 'on-coming'

163.4 on-coming] *interlined with a caret*

163.7 a man] *preceded by deleted start of* 'T'

163.8 shoulder-] *interlined with a caret*

163.9 flushed] *preceded by deleted* 'lo'

163.17 Strammers] *first* 'r' *interlined with a caret*

163.21 grounds?"] 's' *added; question mark altered from a period*

163.22 floundering] *altered from* 'blundering'

163.24 plainly] *followed by deleted illegible letter*

163.26 did] *preceded by deleted* 'no'

163.27 Madam] *final* 'e' *deleted*

163.29 that] *followed by deleted* 't' *and start of* 'h'

163.30–31 privacy,] *comma inserted before deleted period*

163.32 Strammers] *first* 'r' *interlined with a caret*

163.34 out a] *interlined with a caret*

164.13 withdraw."] 'a' *written over* 'e'

164.14 a] *interlined with a caret*

164.16 width] *preceded by deleted* 'size'

164.18 huntress] 'h' *over probable* 'm'

164.23 had] *interlined with a caret*

164.28 mortgages] *preceded by deleted* 'trouble and'

164.30 than] *altered from* 'tham'

164.33 thick-] *interlined above deleted* 'wooden'

165.2 far] *some final letter deleted, perhaps an* 'a' *or* 'e'

165.4 moments] *altered from* 'minutes' *by* 'o' *over* 'i' *and,*

starting next line, 'ents' *after deleted* 'utes'

165.10 love] *preceded by deleted* 'onl'

165.18 ²be] *interlined with a caret*

165.22 remained stupidly] 'ai' *over* 'ia'

165.24 door] *preceded by deleted* 'ga'

165.25 the door] *interlined with a caret above deleted* 'it'

165.32 song] *followed by deleted period, a possible dash, and quote marks, and* 'Pa'

165.34 inn] *preceded by deleted* 'In'

165.35 at] *interlined above deleted* 'on'

165.37 And,] *preceded by* 'commence here', *typing direction by* Cora

166.2 I can] *preceded by deleted* 'as a man of honour'

166.3 saw] *interlined above deleted* 'say'

166.19 he] *interlined above deleted* 'said'

166.22 Imagine] *preceded by deleted* 'Imigan'

166.28 arose] *interlined with a caret*

166.28 me,] *comma inserted before deleted period*

167.1 the] *interlined with a caret*

167.5 the] *interlined above deleted* 'that'

167.7 even] *preceded by deleted* 'the'

167.10 an] *preceded by deleted* 'Iris'

168.2 as I] 'I' *over* 'a'

168.16 the ways of] *interlined with a caret; followed by* 'my' *with* 'm' *over doubtful* 'na'

168.18 research] *preceded by deleted* 'reseach' *with* 'c' *over* 'r'

169.1 had] *interlined with a caret*

169.2 occupied our] *interlined with a caret above deleted* 'took'

169.3 Strammers] 'S' *written over possible* 'B'

169.4 the] *interlined with a caret*

169.6 victim,] *followed by deleted* 'P'

169.7 affectionately] *preceded by deleted* 'lovingly'

169.17 draught.] *followed by deleted quote marks*

169.19 Aye] MS 'Ay', *final* 'e' *deleted*

169.20 old] *preceded by deleted* 'a'

169.23 good] *interlined above deleted* 'most fine'

169.24 good] *interlined above deleted* 'fine'

169.26 believed] *preceded by deleted* 'always'

169.26 always] *interlined with a caret*

169.26 have existed] 'have' *interlined with a caret; final* 'ed' *of* 'existed' *added*

169.27 well."] *period and quote marks inserted before deleted comma and* 'then." '

169.30 would be] *interlined with a caret above deleted* 'is'

169.32 could] 'c' *over* 'w'

169.35 o'] *apostrophe inserted to replace deleted* 'f'

170.5 London] *preceded by deleted* 'all'

170.6 park] *preceded by deleted* 'grounds, all'

170.14 Paddy] *preceded by deleted* 'Pa'

170.19 the wall] *preceded by deleted doubtful* 'n'; 'wall' *interlined above deleted* 'park'

170.20 'Have] *single quote mark changed from double*

170.21 be] *inserted in the margin*

170.28 doing] *preceded by deleted doubtful* 'g'

170.30 on] 'o' *altered from an* 'a'

170.31 him.] *interlined above deleted* 'it.'

170.33 been] *interlined above deleted* 'told me'

170.39 scenes] *interlined above deleted* 'events'

171.3 neighborhood] *interlined with a caret above deleted* 'vicinity'

171.4 you] *interlined with a caret*

171.4 had] *interlined above deleted* 'lacked'

171.5 the] *interlined above deleted* 'your'

171.9 with] *interlined above deleted* 'my'

171.10 knew] 'e' *altered from an* 'o'

171.11 great] *followed by deleted* 'big'

171.18 place] *preceded by deleted* 'part'

171.21 I come] *preceded by deleted* 'My'; 'come' *interlined above deleted* 'am'

171.23 And] 'd' *over* 'y'

171.27 pleased] 'p' *over period*

171.27 am] *interlined with a caret*

171.30 talker."] *end of MS*

COLLATION OF MANUSCRIPT VS. TYPESCRIPT

CHAPTER XXIV

162.0 to 165.37 (thirsty."|)

162.5 no artillery] no artellery
TMs
162.8 everything] every thing
TMs
162.9 discussions] discussion
TMs
162.17 ground] the ground TMs
162.24–25 garden-thief] ~ ∧ ~
TMs
163.1 basket] baskets TMs
163.4 on-coming] oncoming
TMS
163.7 woman I] woman that I
TMs
163.8 between] betwen TMs
163.12 expressed] express TMs
163.15 Tis] 'Tis TMs
163.15 the man] tha man TMs
163.30 disturb] disturbe TMs
163.35 Mary∧] ~ , TMs
163.37 Mary] Ma y TMs
164.1 rose-garden] ~ ∧ ~ TMs
164.12 leave,] ~ ∧ TMs
164.16 water-jug] ~ ∧ ~ TMs

164.20 grass∧] ~ , TMs
164.20 and,] ~ ∧ TMs
164.21 I'm] Im TMs
164.29 suitor] suiter TMs
164.31 "Here] ∧Here TMs
164.31–32 blunderbuss," she]
blunderbuss, | "she TMs
164.32 "Perhaps] ∧ ~ TMs
164.34 Dont ye] Don'tye TMs
164.35 caught] cought TMs
165.4 wasteing] wasting TMs
165.5,6 Mary"——] ~ ——" TMs
165.12 losing] loseing TMs
165.15 any rate] anyrate TMs
165.18 leaving] letting TMs
165.22 could come] come come
TMs
165.23 Lady's] Lady TMs
165.23 hand∧] ~ , TMs
165.27 determinedly] deter-
mindly TMs
165.34 from] omit TMs
165.34 little] omit TMs
165.35 Docter] Doctor TMs

ALTERATIONS IN THE TYPESCRIPT

[*The only alterations noted are those that might conceivably form different words if left in the unaltered state.*]

162.26   man] 'm' *over* 'a'
163.8   fire-arm] *preceded by deleted* 'blunderbus'
163.28   persuasions] 'ons' *over* 'ven'
164.14   of] *preceded by deleted* 'fo'
164.23   had] *preceded by deleted* 'to'
164.26   Irish] TMs 'Irishma' *with* 'ma' *deleted*
164.30   them] 'm' *over possible* 'i'
164.38   doubts] *preceded by deleted* 'threats'

CRANE'S NOTES DICTATED AT
BADENWEILER FOR THE COMPLETION
OF *THE O'RUDDY*

CRANE's dictation at Badenweiler in 1900 was written by Cora in a virtually unrecognizable hand. This is partly to be explained, no doubt, by emotional stress, but partly also by her postscript to a letter written to H. G. Wells on May 15, the day she and Crane had arrived at Dover: "I've a sore hand so can't write properly" (*Letters,* p. 284). The dictated notes, from the manuscript in Columbia University Libraries, follow in full:

DICTATED BY STEPHEN MAY 30TH
Upon our arrival at the little wayside inn, I left the devoted Doctor Chord and my long sword. Paddy, Jem and I then proceeded to find Strammers— [*A line across the sheet then separates this fragment from p. 4 written from the other end of the sheet down till it meets this first sentence.*]

[*On the same gray stationery, watermarked* "Sirrian | Mottled Grey | Wove || J S & Co Ltd.]

1

O'Ruddy goes in garden with Strammers & Paddy and Jem Bottles & as they pass along O'Ruddy keeps at tail of procession & happens to look throug green leafy arch & see Lady Mary & he dodges in there like the mischief & to his great surprise he finds her crying. There is a tender scene during which L. M. explains that Forrister & the Earl are in Drawing room [having a horrible time *deleted*] quarreling furiously over no less a matter than the papers. It is an easy matter for the O'Ruddy to whip paper from pocket & hand them to L. M. & with a look of gratitude she sped accross the lawn[.]

2

The O'R. waited in the little special rose garden. It was no time at all before she came back to him & this time she was in stronger sobs than ever[.] she had gone into the room where her father & Forrister were making such a stir over the papers[.] "Father" she had cried here are the papers" as she thrust them at the Earl, the Earl's infeebled fingers stiffened unaccountably & the contact ended simply in a collision that made the papers fall to the floor. F. pounced upon them savagely [& it was *deleted*] & as he went toward the door he waved them & cried "now at last I have them in my possession if I lose them I will lose my life at the same time. A moment later he was heard galloping swiftly down the drive. L. M. ran to me again. She was so breathy that she could hardly tell me anything but at last I judged the truth[.] F. had the papers & was off to his place somewheres in the S. of England "My brother Strep" she said "to me has already taken horse & is after him". I "will take Jem & will also ride for you" "Good" said she. ["I will see you well off" said she. *deleted*]

[*Back to other half of folded stationery on which p. 1 appears, with numeral at the fold in center.*]

3

["and I walk down the avenue" *deleted*] "Ill see you well off" said she.

[*The following notes begin on the same sheet, immediately following those of May 30. The first sentence begins a new tack. It is followed by a parenthetical question mark. After the marginal note that remarks on the need to bring Strepp and The O'Ruddy together again on the road, the narrative picks up again from the last sentence of May 30. The marginal note, connected by a hand-drawn line to the last sentence of May 30, is connected by another line to the space after "with a gentle smile." and immediately preceding "and three of us rode out of the inn yard." At that point the direction of the narrative seems to have been found again.*]

NOTES JUNE 3RD

"Look under it & you'll find him". (?) [*Marginal note*] Connect the meeting of S. with O.R. he catches him up on road. [*Regular hand*] with a gentle smile. [*Indicator line*] and three of us rode out of the inn yard. They scamper thru the sts of London accross one bridge & away to the South. Strp led the way. He countenance was sinister, dark resolute. He sky was suitably black yet sometimes this formiadiable body of avenger were obliged to pull up mainly through L. M.'s horse, which had gone lame.

Strep was in a passion he didn't [like *conjectured omission*] leaving

[*Continued on same sheet as first fragment of the May 30 dictation, now turned upside down so that this writing begins at what had been the bottom edge.*]

4

L. M. there alone didn't dare stay by herself— Nothing to do but to sit there & wait until the horse recovered this was anything but nice. The three of them spent little time and on a third day we galloped out of Tunbridge. (Forristers house Brede Place.) Early of that morning it began to rain first innocently then with the quiet pennetration of a Sussex rain while over the tops of the hedges swept the wind. It was very nearly dark before we reached our destination & we rode with care. Strep who seemed in a brown study has nothing to say. [The twisting & turning from the great gates *deleted*]

[*Continued on the opened-out inside leaf of stationery of the Lord Warden Hotel, Dover.*]

5

[into the Park. *deleted*] After passing the great gates & twisting & turn-ing in the Park was something fabulous every where were monstrous [pines *deleted*] oaks. The lightning shonn like silver on the road & on the pools of rain that we could see beyond. Suddenly we came to a inner & stronger gate as we passed through [we passed throu *deleted*] a road down toward a group of lights. For my part I had not expected to see a light. We here dismounted & Jem hid the horses in a [well *deleted*] good hollow. When he returned to us we walked down [before *deleted*] to the front door. Turning our [house *deleted*] heads to the right we could see the whole house. Most of it seemed alight. [The] devil seems to live here.

[*Continued on recto of Lord Warden Hotel stationery, beginning on the clear bottom half of the unfolded sheet and then going to the top half with its expansive letterhead.*]

6

Strep said: "I am puzzled." "No," said I "tis clear as anything" & without more ado I walked forward to the most solemn oaken iron crossed hinged front door of any cathedral. Now one remembers the little talk about these things. An ample faced jovial old serving man opened it for us & as we followed him into the corridor we cought a glimp into the enormous Kitchen where 7 or 8 servants led a genial life around the fire. I would like to see yor

7

Master said I." "One moment sir if you please sir" He led me [into *deleted*] along a corridor into a room [w *deleted*] bright with rugs, on floor Silver candel sticks burning brightly & finally we came out the four of us to confront the

[*new sheet*]

8

[him *deleted* the *deleted*] Forrister. [He *deleted*] "Well" he said. Here is the company of players! Come F—" said I "no playing on your part. We want those papers".

"Those papers" said F. "I haven't those papers."

"Where are they said I—for I knew the kind [*Marginal note:* (Whole thing to play up)]

"I gave them to Paddy. [*Closing quotes deleted by following* I] I myself do not care for the collection of papers, but I like riding in the open air on a good horse & to come down & spend a few quiet weeks in the old [?—*half illegible*] place & when I rode away with the papers I did [*illegible, possibly* ind, *and these letters possibly a slip for* "didn't ride"] very far out of London. I soon saw Paddy some place etc. & I gave him the papers". He said this very innocently. Strep was very doubtful. This is too frivolous. You must know that after he has killed me Strep will [not *deleted*] kill him. This is no nice thing

DATE DUE